Tales From The Mare Inebrium

Spaceport Bar

By Dan L Hollifield

Three Ravens Publishing
Chickamauga GA USA

Tales From The Mare Inebrium Spaceport Bar By Dan L Hollifield
Published by Three Ravens Publishing
threeravenspublishing@gmail.com
P O Box 851, Chickamauga, GA 30707
https://www.threeravenspublishing.com
Copyright © 2023 by Dan L. Hollifield / 2014 by Dan L Hollifield

Credits:
Tales From The Mare Inebrium Spaceport Bar was written by Dan L Hollifield
Cover art by Darrel "Doc" Osborn
Edited by: Alyssa Casto
Tales From The Mare Inebrium Spaceport Bar by: Dan L Hollifield /Three Ravens Publishing – 2nd edition, 2023; Dark Oak Press – 1st edition, 2014

Ebook ISBN: 978-1-962791-17-5
Trade Paperback ISBN: 978-1-962791-18-2

Table of Contents

Dedication:

This is for my wife Lindsey, Mom and Dad, my kids, my entire family, everyone at Aphelion Webzine, and all my friends & teachers- Past, present, and future. Thank you for your love, your support, and for believing in me.

I'd like to give a special shout-out to all the writers who have come to play in my Mare Inebrium shared universe online, to Allan for giving me my first big break, to William for letting me update this first volume of Mare Inebrium stories, and to Stephanie for giving me that little push at the perfect moment that first made this book a reality.

"Welcome to the Mare Inebrium Spaceport Bar..."

"I believe that a more formal introduction may be in order"
The Comte de St. Germain, 1748

Where to begin? Well, I suppose a short origin story wouldn't be a lick amiss. Back in the late 1970s I hadn't long been out of High School and had run through my college funds in just a few short years at the University of Georgia. I eventually found myself gainfully employed in a factory in Athens. Boring, repetitive, mind-numbing physical labor and I were not strangers at the time. After all, I did grow up on a farm. In order to fill the mental void of the long shifts at the factory I began scribbling down various daydreams that my mind produced. In one well-worn little notepad, I chanced to record a few lines, narrative hooks they're called. Possible opening lines to some putative story or other. It just so happened that in 1979 I dashed off a few words that seemed meaningful at the time.

"That's the trouble with time travel," said the man with blue hair.

Little did I know at the time what those innocent words would grow to be in the future. I kept that notepad, filling it eventually with other random thoughts. Then I filled several more. Time passed, in the dull, plodding way that time seems to prefer when it dallies with a 20-something growing into a 30-something young man. I read thousands of SF&F books, listened to a wide variety of different kinds of music, I collected comic books and textbooks and novels and indulged myself in drawing, painting, attempting to learn how to play different musical instruments, and so on. I kept busy, in other words. I lived in a series of apartments, with a series of roommates. One of whom proved especially adept at sparking my creativity. In one besotted evening he and I came up with the idea of a bar located at the North pole of Earth's moon. We joked about it for months, our literary influences battling with our alcoholic influences. After a few years, my friend left to pursue a real job, as well as the love of his life. I also pursued as many of my interests as possible. Eventually I found myself in possession of a typewriter. Or it possessed me, I could never tell which.

I began trying to develop some of the stories that I'd dreamed up years before. And then the Internet happened.

I began working on the background material back in the 1970s—even though I didn't know it at the time. I jotted down notes for story ideas, drew maps of places I imagined, made up names… And the material piled up. Then came a snowstorm and cabin fever brought me a challenge from someone annoyed with me. I began to write a story, to prove that I could do better than the TV movie I was complaining about when the challenge was issued.

Turns out that the first one wasn't very much of a story. Oh, it had a beginning, middle, and end. It had action, a monster, a damsel in distress, a daring rescue, a mighty magic spell to defeat the monster, the death of one of the heroes… and it was about 8 to 12 pages long… handwritten. Clearly, I had more to learn. Eventually, I thought up a place where my stories could happen, pulled all my maps together and made them fit, shuffled my notes and outlines, and thought deeply for a very long time. Then I re-plotted the story to fit the new playground and came up with a lot of background concepts to influence the events of whatever story uses the backdrop. Before I was through, I had a map of the planet's one landmass and an 11,000+ year-long timeline of its history. I knew the major players and the minor characters, I knew the names of landmarks in the native languages I'd made up, the big stories and the small ones. Now if I only knew how to write effectively…

Of course, this was back in the days that a typewriter was the state-of-the-art word processor. Computers were either big, clunky machines built to do one thing at a time, or they were little boxes that you hooked up to your TV set to play games like Pong, or Breakout, or Pinball. Eventually there came the TRS-80s and the C64s, and the like. Grand old computers, for their time. I have over a hundred pages of outline for my first attempt at a Bethdish novel stored on audio cassette and a hardcopy printed out from an old TRS-80 CoCo3. I have had roughly a third of it online as "Threat of Valleor" since the late '90s… But I digress. About the time that modern computers were in their second generation, I made the leap from a 128k CoCo3 to a 33Mgh 386 with a whopping 16 megs of RAM and a 20-meg hard drive running Windows 3.1 and good old DOS. I started transcribing my files from the CoCo3 into the 386. That turned out to be harder work than I expected, since I was expanding on the outline as I was transcribing it. It also slowed me down, and above all, showed me a bright warning flag that I still had a lot to learn about this writing gig. About a third of the way through transcribing this novel outline, I decided that I needed to learn to write short stories so that I could more quickly learn to write better.

And so, the Mare Inebrium series was moved from Earth's moon to my little planet of Bethdish. But I was still setting my stories in the same general background. Adjustments had to be made. Continuity mistakes were made also. Then the Mare became an online Shared Universe with its third story—the first one that I didn't write. Further continuity tweaking became necessary. And I had to scramble to keep up with all the other new writers for the series. Inventing new details to answer their questions, writing my own stories as richly in relevant details as I could create. Rejecting the few that violated my elaborate continuity... Well, actually, I pointed out the violations and asked for rewrites. Detail became added to detail. But the Mare writers are almost never allowed to venture outside of the spaceport city the bar is located within. The rest of the planet is mine alone.

As I said, eventually I bought a computer, was dragged online kicking and screaming and deathly afraid of computer viruses, and within a short while was passing my little stories around various creative writing websites. In 1997 I wound up with my own website, Aphelion Webzine. I had two spaceport bar stories online at that time, and then a good friend asked if he could write a story in my bar. The Mare Inebrium, as an online shared universe series was born. I wound up with half a dozen of my own stories in the series, which quickly grew to dozens of other writers and almost a hundred stories altogether. I had to set ground rules and post a regular cast of characters for the series writers.

Here you will meet Max, the bar's manager and head bartender, his girlfriend Trixie and her friend Blanche who are waitresses there, Kazshak Teir one of the bar's most famous alien patrons and storytellers, Mister Polios the mysterious owner of the establishment, Bruce the bouncer in the main bar, the Reever of the Immortals, who is the Top Cop on the planet and Ambassador to the various native species and alien colonists, several different narrator characters to tell the various stories, and so on. This volume contains my all-original stories in the series, as well as many new stories I wrote expressly for this book. Tales untold for nearly two decades, as they languished in my notes until the need arose.

This is the world where most of my stories take place. Bethdish is a world circling a star called Antuth by the natives (who named the star after the chief deity in their pantheon), presently some 65 light years from Earth. Rumor has it that the entire solar system had earlier been located in the Andromeda Galaxy but was moved by some mysterious force to its new location in our own Milky Way Galaxy. The surviving written history of Bethdish covers some 12,000 years, (with the afore-mentioned displacement to the Milky Way occurring in their year 6055—circa 3068 AD, Terran Calendar) but the records of the Immortals reportedly go back roughly a billion years and relate the rise and fall of several civilized eras of non-immortal natives before the present recorded history begins.

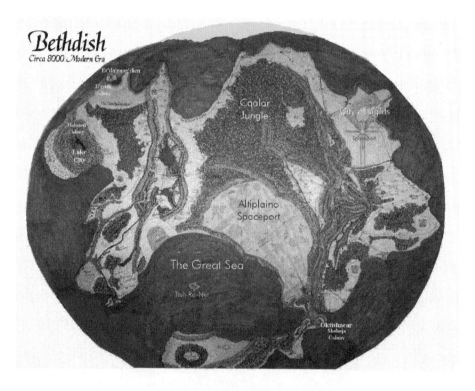

The Immortals claim to have been directly created by the Gods of Bethdish, while the diverse non-immortal species are said to have evolved naturally. The several alien colonies now present are, of course, immigrants. One Xenoarcheologist of note, Professor Eustas Gray of the

Emperor Norton University of San Francisco, has published several monographs on the subject of excavations on Bethdish that purport to uphold the Immortal's beliefs. Other experts in the field dispute his findings, but all the evidence is not yet in.

The following example is an English translation of a fragment of one of the folk tales from the prehistoric eras of the planet, preserved as a "grandfather tale" from various native civilizations on Bethdish:

"I am the sole arbiter of princes and battles,
The sole lonely judge of pirates and prey.
I chose between those who are heroes or villains,
And each I send on their infinite way.
Reward or damnation, their own separate way.
I judge without malice—
High standards have I.
To the hero the chalice.
To the villain, the flame.
But *who* will be *what* is no simple say..."

From the Song of T'nishe-t'alla, Judge of Princes & Battles, God of War. Composed by the Bard Oroden during the Lost Times. Preserved from oral history by transcript recordings of traditional native songs. Transcription made possible by the Planetary History department of the Collegium Lux, City of Lights.

City of Lights, the spaceport city, is one of the few places on the planet where non-native technology is allowed. The rest of the world is set aside for the natives to develop at their own pace. There are laws against interfering with the natural development of the native civilizations. The Reever enforces these laws strictly, yet fairly.

The building that houses the Mare Inebrium is a close replica of the Empire State Building in New York City. A little taller, without the airship mooring mast, but looking as if the two buildings were designed by the same hand. The bar takes up several levels of the building, with the main bar being on the ground floor, surrounded by various smaller rooms with special themes. These specialty rooms allow stories that can't possibly take place in the main bar to have a more intimate setting. One geared more towards the needs of a particular story. Each of the side bars have their own cast of bartenders, wait-staff, and bouncers as needed. If a story needs to be about Space Rangers, military types, pirates, and frequent bar fights, it might be set in the Red Dog Saloon side bar. If the tale needs a more civilized, private setting, it could take place in the "gentlemen's club" side bar called Piper's. If the story involves deities, writers, and other beings of enormous power, it usually takes place upstairs in the Pantheon Room. If the story requires a stage for music or theatrical performances, it can be set in the Small Ballroom side bar. The main bar is quite large, with room for several hundred patrons at once. The walls are decorated with paintings, mirrors that can shift to show a view inside one of the side bars rather than reflections, and displays of alien artifacts scattered about tastefully. The bar itself is up against the back wall of the main room, behind the bar are shelves of hundreds of varieties of beverages alternating with mirrors the bar staff can use to discreetly monitor the needs of the patrons. Around the perimeter of the room are booths for groups of customers, closer in are tables anchored to the floor, and up closer to the bar itself are tables and chairs that float freely enough to move into whatever positions a customer might need. Right up next to the bar is an open area to allow customers to gain access to the seats at the main bar itself. The floors of the building above the main bar contain various restaurants, shops, meeting rooms, and even hotel rooms. The top floor of the building houses a very fancy restaurant with views of the city spreading out into the far distance.

It has been a long, strange journey from then to now. As I slowly learned to be a better writer, my little scribbled notes have grown into an entire book. Along the way my very earliest bar stories came to inspire other writers to explore the limits of my initial concept. As they pushed the boundaries of the bar into new and exciting directions, I learned more about my own creation. In order to keep up, I had to become even more creative. I look forward to hearing just how well or badly y'all think I've done. Keep me posted, please,

Dan

Dan L. Hollifield

Casa Vila, Colbert, GA

Year 2021 CE

Thank you!

Fast Friends

"Those who fail to learn from History, are doomed." **Joshua Abraham Norton - Emperor of the United States and Defender of Mexico, 1866**

"That man, Thornby... One of my oldest and dearest friends. He's like a brother to me, despite the fact that we are of wildly different species," said Kazsh-ak Teir. The old D'rrish was holding court a few seats away at the bar, in his usual corner. His huge frame made delicate motions, like a fork lift on ice skates, as he stepped lightly to and fro while finishing his latest tall tale. Something about a handful of primitive warriors who had accidentally stolen a malfunctioning time machine.

As he completed his story, the scorpion-like alien stood on seven of his eight legs, waving both his pincer arms and one front leg in the air. He paced side to side, with his back to the bar. A few of the closer mirrors on the bar's walls reflected the brownish-gray chitin of his exoskeleton from different angles. His eager listeners stood or sat in a loose-knit clump nearby. Every being within earshot was listening. Some skeptical, some enthralled, but all were entertained.

Behind the bar, tall shelves held row after row of colorful, mysterious bottles of rare beverages. The bar stool on which I rested felt soft and warm to my tired legs. The soft murmur of the voices of beings slowly filling the room washed upon my ears like the quiet drumming of a distant sea. The cold, tart flavor of my drink soothed my taste buds as I glanced around the room at the other patrons. Good drinks, fine company, wonderful stories... What more could anyone ask for a night out on the town?

It was the middle of the week on an early Spring evening in City of Lights, on the planet Bethdish. No sounds from the busy streets outside penetrated the bar's comfortable interior. A patron would never remember the bustling metropolis outside the walls of the skyscraper whose street-level floors housed my favorite bar in all the worlds I've visited.

The regular crowd at the Mare Inebrium had begun trickling in hours ago. Faces both familiar and unfamiliar appeared in the throng of happy customers. I could smell the ever-present lemony-vanilla fragrance that usually permeates the main room of the Mare by the different smells of alien drinks, or by the aliens themselves, or even by the Mare Inebrium's air recirculation system—I never knew for sure. Anything seems possible here. In fact, the more improbable something seems to be, the better the chance one has of seeing it happen in this place.

The long, slick surface of the exotic wooden bar top felt cool and dry beneath my fingers as I rested one hand upon its polished length. Max had told me once, long ago, the name of the world from which the dark, finely grained wood had been harvested. But I had quickly forgotten the name. In the lights above the bar the surface reflected thousands of subtle colors scarcely perceptible from a distance.

I casually glanced into the open area between the closest tables and the main bar counter. That open space held a scattering of patrons who had gathered closer to Kazsh-ak as he began to spin yet another of his improbable tall tales. Other patrons lounged at their tables or ambulated about the room as they gazed at the many paintings hung on the walls.

Turning my head further, I could see the doorways leading off into many of the side rooms. I knew each one of those doors opened up to other, smaller bars that are decorated in different themes. No matter the mood of the customer, there is a comfortable Specialty Room whose theme would be found fitting. I've visited a few of them from time to time, though I usually prefer the main room.

I frequent the Mare Inebrium as often as my job allows me to stay at Bethdish. It's a far cry from the run-of-the-mill watering holes I've dealt with on many other planets. Not just because the City of Lights borders upon the planet's largest spaceport, but because the Mare Inebrium is one of those outstanding examples of a great place to have a few drinks in the company of a hundred or so friends and aliens.

I'm a traveling salesman by trade. The company I work for keeps a set of offices and apartments for myself and my co-workers in one of the high-rise buildings closer to the center of the city. I usually spend my time between voyages here on Bethdish. This world is conveniently located close to flight paths between hundreds of inhabited star systems.

I go from developing world to developing world, usually selling farm implements and machinery, seed crops, weed killers, fertilizers, insecticides, that sort of thing. I've always loved the smell of a freshly plowed field, the scent of newly mowed hay, and the sight of crops growing against the backdrop of frontier skies. You can take the boy away from the farm, but you can never take the farm out of the boy.

My name is Andrew Huntington-Smythe. Bethdish is my second home—after Antares Four, where I was born. But in all the universe, the Mare is where I feel most at home. Don't know why, but I've always felt a connection with Max, the bartender here. Like he is family, so to speak, though that's hardly possible. We're worlds apart, literally. Not even the same species, in fact. Me? I'm just here for the party.

"You never did say how you met Thornby," I heard someone say to Kazsh-ak. I think it was that piratical-looking fellow at the crowded table in the second row from the bar. Aven-something. I've never caught his entire name. But then, it could have been the burly fellow at his side. Blank, or Blink, or something equally improbable. He and Aven always appeared to be best enemies. Not quite friends, not quite adversaries. Allies, of some sort. They usually had seven or more compatriots in tow. A motley-looking crew, to say the least. But their attitudes about politics I found quite liberating, whenever they deigned to express them.

"Ah," replied Kazsh-ak "That is a complicated story from long ago. Gather close, for my voice becomes tired from over-use." Seeing as how the old D'rrish's "voice" issued from an electronic translating device, I recognized an old storyteller's trick and turned my seat to face him.

"Give me a refill, Max," I said to the bartender as I glanced at him over my left shoulder. "I want to hear this one..."

"Sure thing, son." Max replied. "I want to hear him tell this one myself. I'd better get the old boy another one, too. Once he gets in full flow, he won't want to wait. And everyone will blame me for any long pauses in his story." Max tapped out a combination of buttons on a keypad with his left hand while he spoke. "Here you go," he said. My drink appeared on the small teleport pad nearest to me on the bar.

As Max punched in the settings for Kazsh-ak's drink, he frowned slightly in concentration. "Got to get the trace amounts of thorium exactly right. Just a touch too much will sour the mix," he added as he typed out a complicated pattern. I don't know what sort of chemistry is involved in whipping up a few gallons of the mildly radioactive sludge that serve the D'rrish species for a cocktail, but given their mass and natural defenses, I'm sure no one goes about preparing their drinks carelessly.

"Let's ease on down a bit closer," Max said, when he finished with the settings for the plow horse-sized alien's drink. "I set the mixer to 'port his cocktail to the station he's standing beside. I'm not about to strain my back again, hefting a three-gallon tank of KKKKashd'rissh. The first time better be the last time! Know what I mean?"

I nodded in friendly agreement as I left my seat to pick out a new one closer to Kazsh-ak Teir. Max and I ambled closer to the old D'rrish. Max finally leaned up against the inside of the bar within easy conversational distance of me as I slid into another seat just outside Kazsh-ak Teir's semi-circle of listeners. I saw Trixie and Blanche, the Mare's most memorable waitresses, carrying drinks the old-fashioned way on the hover-trays they used when customers declined the use of the serving teleport system. Some folks just preferred the personal service, I expect.

The girls circulated through the crowd at the tables scattered about the large room. Trixie had been born on Earth, as I recall. She and Max have been a romantic item for as long as I can remember. Must be a really strong relationship, 'cause Max has a bit of a reputation with the females of many a humanoid species.

Blanche was born on one of those heavy-gravity worlds. Hardcase, I think is the name of the place. Nearly 2 Gs, so the colonists that settled it grow up strong, if not very *far* up.

They're a study in contrasts, those two girls. Trixie looks like an elf-princess—tall and willowy and with shapely legs that go on forever. On the other hand, Blanche is barely five feet tall and all curves. Blanche might look plump and soft to the uninitiated eye, but she's solid muscle. I've seen her lift a rowdy drunk over her head before casually tossing him into the waiting arms of one of the bouncers.

Max must have signaled one of the other bartenders to take over for him, but I didn't see it. Bobby Blue, the robot bartender Max had recently hired, stepped up to the spot Max and I had just vacated. The patrons seemed to like Bobby Blue. His drinks are always precisely correct, he is always willing to listen to a customer, and his only personal vice seems to be astrophotography. Well, that and making sure his chromium-blue surface is always clean and shiny. At the end of the bar furthest from us, I could see another of Max's assistants taking orders from the patrons sitting there. I turned back to face the D'rrish Ambassador when his translator coughed out an electronic throat-clearing sound.

The D'rrish stood parallel to the bar—I don't recall having ever seen a D'rrish use a chair of any sort. It would have to be a strange-looking chair, in any case. D'rrish furniture would have to accommodate their multiple legs, hefty bulk, and horizontal body orientation. Kazsh-ak Teir held his drink container in his right claw-hand, occasionally setting it down on the bar so that he could use both pincers to make complicated gestures. His tail he kept curled up between his right legs and the bar, so that no one would trip over it, I suppose. He waggled his eye-stalks in a way that looked almost comical. The bright blue color of his compound eyes occasionally eclipsing as his eyelids shuttered closed, he merrily tip-toed into what must have been a more comfortable stance. Raising one forward leg to tap a medal on the blue sash that served as his single garment, he began his tale.

"This was given to me upon my graduation from the Guards. My people," he said. "We are much given to ceremony and tradition. Rituals for this and that, Rites of Passage, Courtship Dances, Coming of Age traditions, all that sort of rot. Our society is quite old, formalized even, with every observance codified and scripted ages ago. Since I am a minor son of a very minor branch of our royal family, my place in the military has been assured almost before my birth. The same with my eventual induction into the Diplomatic Corps. I worked my way up through the ranks on my own merits, however.

"Cadet, City Guardsman, Scout, Defender..." He tapped different medals as he mentioned each rank he had held. "We have various rituals for each stage of our maturity. Infancy, primary schooling, mating, secondary schooling—that sort of thing. When I first met Guiles Thornby, I had long since mated and completed my secondary schooling. Then I served two terms in the City Guards. I had, not long before our meeting in fact, graduated from the Guards and qualified to enter the Scouts.

"Part of the ritual" Kazsh-ak continued, "for induction into the Scouts is to take up arms and leave the city once more, alone, and further explore the desert beyond our city gates. On our home world, each graduate would have been assigned a different region to explore. Since our city on Bethdish is merely a colony, our population is far smaller, thus it is easier to time the graduation of individuals and small groups, rather than an entire planetary generation-sized class at once. The desert we constructed here—or rather, that our ancestors constructed when our colony was established—is designed to closely mimic the untamed surface of our home world. Various flora and fauna from home have been carefully nurtured here. Predators, prey, natural food sources—everything necessary to facilitate the ritual of survival training that marks this stage in D'rrish coming of age is to be found out in the deepest reaches of our desert. So we each go out, away from the soothing heat and higher atmospheric pressure of our city. We are given some few years to survive on our own before we are allowed to return to our city. We hunt, we explore, and we face the challenges the desert presents. After a scheduled time in which we are restricted to the interior, we are eventually allowed to re-cross the desert to return home. Because of my family's position, I had been given special orders. I had been instructed to go out into the wide world beyond, and to act as emissary for our people to the natives of this world. Of course, the desert has other uses as well." Kazsh-ak waggled his eye stalks, winked one eye, and a humorous chuckle sounded from his translator.

"The Mating Dance," Max said with a huge grin on his face, garnering a few more chuckles from the crowd as Kazsh-ak bowed in agreement.

"Just so," Kazsh-ak said. "But my own mating dance came many years before my first meeting with Thornby. D'rrish biology is rather complicated—or so I've always thought. We actually have several stages in our life cycle in which the 'Call of the Sands' overcomes all other considerations. Our biology is such that we don't realize how powerful the mating urge can become until we reach that first, post-primary school mating age. Our adolescence is quite free of reproductive distractions."

His translator chuckled again. "We are a bit different from other sapient beings, such as your esteemed selves here with me now. Except at those particular points in our ongoing maturity, no urge to mate is felt. We are, as it were, still children between our primary and secondary school ages. Only beginning to grow into adults. Our colony was established here in the local year 920. It took 40 years for our desert to fully form. My Hatching occurred in the local year 6574, sixty-seven generations after our colony's founding. Our first generation of colonists did not have need of the desert for mating until many years after it had been completed. My own Mating Dance occurred when I had counted a scant few years shy of my century mark."

The old D'rrish paused as if lost in a particularly fond memory. His translator gave off a sound remarkably like a heartfelt sigh, then he continued. "Ah, my Lady Wife-to-be was such a delicate damsel then... Of course, she is even more beautiful now! But still, I will never forget my first sight of her in the desert sands—the way the sunlight caressed her carapace, the subtle beauty of her shell markings, and the way she danced. Oh, her dance! Such joy and passion! Such delicate movements she made—such delightful promise of the future that we would share! Still, some things only get better with age, as I'm sure all of you fellow sapients will agree. But I digress..."

"How long is a generation, for D'rrish?" I asked.

"Eighty-four and some small fraction of the local years here on Bethdish," Kazsh-ak answered. "Which, conveniently, is almost exactly the same as our yearly orbit on T'zsh-ky-aeel, the D'rrish home world, as I recall from my education at the Academy. Ah, school days! A bright and shining memory now. Those were the days... But back to the matter at hand. Where was I? Oh yes, my survival ritual. I, a mere stripling of one hundred sixty-six years. A late bloomer, as my family is rather *overly* fond of pointing out. Thus, I had spent a few extra years in the Guards before I applied myself to my graduation exercises. I did love the Guard Corps, though. Rough and tumble times, but all in good fun."

"What is your home world's star named again?" Max asked. "Radish Volcomb?"

"That's right," Kazsh-ak replied. "R'disszh-val-k'oul-uum, near the outer end of the Eastern spiral arm of the Andromeda galaxy, as the Terrans name it. Your D'rrish is quite good, Max. Not many species bother to study our language so diligently."

"I went to some very good schools back when I was a kid," Max said. "But please, continue with your story."

"Yes," said Kazsh-ak. "My graduation from the Guards. In any case, there I was, out in the desert, alone and having a marvelous time learning more advanced survival skills and coping with the seeded wildlife. I did so love my time there. The stark beauty of the sands gave me a feeling of closer kinship to my ancestors, as well as our long lost home world. To stalk and catch my meals—living prey rather than the farm-grown meats in the city shops. Seeing the sun rise and set and turning the sky into a veritable masterpiece of grand artwork! Learning how to cope with the vagaries of natural weather after spending decades inside the sheltering walls of our city. Oh! It seemed like a glorious time! My youth behind me, my future, and the universe itself, spreading before me like the endless sands—Truly wonderful!"

Once again, the old D'rrish paused, lost in his recollection of his far away youth. His translator sighed again, and he seemed to bring himself back to the present moment with some reluctance.

"I eventually made my way to the far ends of the desert. It had become time for me to enter the wider world beyond the desert fringe. Into the unknown, to see what I could see, to explore this strange new world. After several days of hiking into the unfamiliar greenery of the outside world, I ran afoul of some of the native wildlife. They looked unlike anything I had ever seen before—four-legged, fur-bearing, totally lacking a proper exoskeleton. In short, completely alien to me. There were several of them. A mated pair and several young, or so I guessed. They seemed as surprised by my presence as I was by theirs. I felt loath to injure them, but I prepared myself to defend my person if they should attack. But finally, they withdrew. Some sudden sound or strange pheromone from beyond the hills farther along the path I had chosen to traverse, I suppose. Nothing I could detect, at the time. To my amazement, moments later a group of bipeds appeared atop the next hill, then proceeded towards me. They were civilized, I could tell. How, you ask? Because they wore clothing and carried weapons—although unfamiliar in design. It seems that I had encountered a large troop of native soldiers on a mission. Though there were two among them whose scent I found vastly different from the rest. One of these, I eventually learned, turned out to be the Reever. The other turned out to be Guiles Thornby. I awaited their approach, hoping that my school-issue translator met up to the task of making our communications intelligible to one another."

"Thornby isn't a native of Bethdish?" I asked.

"No more native than yourself," Kazsh-ak replied. He paused and wiggled the two bundles of tiny sensory tendrils on either side of his mouth as if testing the air for a new scent. One eye-stalk tilted to focus on Max, blinked, then moved again to join with its mate in looking at me. "In fact," he said, "even less of a native than you, Friend Andrew. Thornby does not keep that a secret. Why should he? Bethdish is a crossroads of thousands of alien races. His species is even further from Earth-norm or Bethdish-norm than is your own. Still human, but obviously from another planet entirely. Each planetary colony of humanity eventually develops their own pheromone variations, but Thornby's scent is so far removed from the normal variations that he is obviously native to a very remote world. His home must be quite different from any human-settled world I have yet encountered—I could locate Thornby in a crowd of thousands of other humanoids, for his scent is unique among all the different species I have met. I have never encountered another being that shares his personal species-variant of signature pheromones."

Once again, I found myself reminded that even though the D'rrish look like giant scorpions lifted straight from some Earthly horror video, they are something entirely different and completely unrelated to Earth—or any other planet in the Milky Way galaxy, for that matter. The D'rrish originated in the Andromeda galaxy. As did Bethdish itself, as far as that goes.

I heard that tidbit from the Reever, one night here in the Mare. I could no more doubt the word of that Immortal than I could doubt my own eyes and ears. The whole solar system inside which Bethdish evolved had been transported from Andromeda to the Milky Way nearly 700 years before I was born. Old news, I suppose, but don't ask me how or why it came to be moved. The Reever never said anything about that, just that it had happened. I trust him. What sane being wouldn't? He's the closest thing Bethdish has to a Commander-in-Chief of the whole planet's police forces. No one I know has ever caught him in a lie. His reputation has always been that he's completely honest and incorruptible. So I know it's true.

"But that is neither here nor there," Kazsh-ak continued, interrupting my ruminations. "Meeting Guiles Thornby changed my life. I had found a dear friend. Someone who would share many adventures with me in the years after our first introduction. But we were speaking of that first meeting, were we not?"

"Yes," said Max. "Please continue with your tale."

"And so I shall," said the D'rrish. "As I said, that party of bipeds approached me from over the hill. At a glance, I could tell that they didn't know if I were some sort of monstrous threat that they would have to face, or some strange style of person with which they would have to deduce how to communicate. Except for the Reever. He obviously recognized my species. He knew our history on this world. Indeed, I eventually recognized him as the being in charge of granting my people the right to establish our colony on Bethdish. He and Thornby left the group and walked up to me.

He addressed me in my own language—without the use of a translator device. It was the first time that I'd heard an alien speak. Indeed, the first non-D'rrish I'd ever met that attempted to communicate at all. Within moments, he had introduced me to Thornby, communicated the particulars of their quest, and invited me to join forces against their enemy. I gladly accepted the invitation. I collected my gear and followed as the party continued on their way. Over the next few days, I found myself drawn to Thornby as a kindred spirit. He too possessed a translator device—something that made our communication quite easy. As our adventure together continued, we grew to know one another. We became fast friends. Later on, as we fought alongside each other against the common foe, we became more than friends. We grew to be almost brothers—well, as much like brothers as two beings of different species can ever be, I suppose..."

"Ah!" Max exclaimed. "That was the battle against Valleor, wasn't it? You and the others managed to imprison him for a while, didn't you?"

"Valleor?" I asked. "That's—"

"One of the Gods of Bethdish," Max replied. "Yeah. The God of Chaos and Destruction. Hatred and evil incarnate, that's the one."

"You went into battle against a God?" I asked Kazsh-ak in disbelief.

"What else could I do?" Kazsh-ak asked in reply, with the D'rrish equivalent of a shrug. "The fate of my adopted planet seemed at stake. Besides, if the legends are true, the Evil One had something to do with Bethdish being removed from Andromeda and the many species here at the time having been forever cut off from our various home worlds. I could not refuse. Honor demanded that I join the party of warriors. To pit my skills and weapons against the devil that had condemned every member of my race to the status of long-lost castaways. I did my best to kill the monster, but he proved to be too strong. All we could manage to do was put Him into a containment field. Like a prison but made of energy rather than stone walls and iron bars. Many of the party gave their lives to put Valleor away in that pocket universe. But eventually, He escaped. It took Him nearly sixty years, but He did finally escape. Of course, all that had yet to come. I merely speak of that one battle. Anyway, somehow, Thornby had acquired a mighty weapon. A Battle Suit, like a giant suit of armor, piloted from inside as if worn by some knight against a legendary dragon—"

"It isn't as if I don't believe you," said Aven. "But... I don't believe you." He smiled in a sarcastic way that made me want to slap him silly. "There are no 'Gods' that I can believe in. Just forces beyond our understanding to which we apply that label in order to render them comprehensible. This is an entertaining myth you're spinning, Friend D'rrish, but only a myth nevertheless."

"Valleor is a force far beyond your ability to understand," said Max sardonically. "If you ever have the misfortune of meeting Him face to face, be sure to let Him know that you don't believe in Him. I'm sure He will take special pleasure in educating you."

"I'm sure," Aven replied in that superior manner that he always demonstrated. "But please, don't let my skepticism divert the narrative flow. Pray continue, Friend D'rrish."

Kazsh-ak Teir gave a courtly bow towards the source of the interruption, then his translator let loose a hearty chuckle of amusement.

"Neither your belief or disbelief is required, Friend Pirate. I speak of History, not mere tale-spinning. Events occurred as I relate them to have done. Many lives were lost in our attempt to put the God of Chaos into a prison of some complex magical devising. Only the plasma beamers scattered among our weapons seemed to have any effect at all on the demented deity we faced. No bullet or laser seemed to be able to touch Him. But then, our battle with Him served only a diversion. At a safe distance, a priest intoned the words of a spell. A spell that had been intended to imprison the Evil One for all time. We mere warriors were only meant to keep Him occupied whilst the real work was carried out by others."

"What happened?" I asked eagerly. I quickly downed the last gulp of my drink. Turning to Max, I found that the bartender had another glass ready and waiting for me. Taking it gratefully, I returned to face Kazsh-ak once again.

"As I said," Kazsh-ak replied as he paused to take a sip of his own drink. The container wobbled slightly as he returned it to a spot on the bar, its contents sloshing about from the movement. "Many of our party of warriors died in that fateful combat. At first, it seemed like challenging a thunderstorm. Lightning leaped from the clouds to our motley forces on the ground. The weapons in Thornby's Battle Suit and the plasma cannon in my tail-gun swept the skies. We could see great gaping holes rent in the rapidly massing clouds. Holes that would not close: holes that dripped acidic blood, raining down upon us as if we battled some great, huge wounded beast. Which, in a way, we were. The clouds swirled tighter, and we wondered if a Demonic tornado was about to reach down and touch the ground upon which we stood. Darker and darker they grew. Tighter and tighter they packed themselves. Until finally..."

"Finally, what?" A gray-green scaled Halazed in the back row of Kazsh-ak Teir's listeners breathlessly asked. He—or she, I can't ever tell the gender of those lizards—it took a huge gulp of its drink and motioned to Trixie for a refill. Bobby Blue must have seen the entity signal for the desired drink, because it only took scant seconds for Trixie to plonk another tankard of whatever the Halazed had been drinking down on the table in front of it. Blanche seemed also busy taking orders, I could see as I glanced around the room.

"Finally," Kazsh-ak said, "the clouds looked almost solid. They appeared dark, nearly black. It looked as if one could reach up with a sharp knife and carve chunks off of them. The clouds dipped lower and lower in the sky. Thunder and lightning pealed out, over and over again in a lethal storm front. We all kept firing our weapons into the clouds. Slowly, a face took shape. Its eyes glared with hatred. Its mouth seemed filled with sharp fangs..."

"Human eyes?" Aven interrupted. "I think not. The physical laws that determine interplanetary biology—"

"Have not one whit to do with the seven native species of sapient life upon Bethdish," said Kazsh-ak. "The Immortals were created by the Gods of Bethdish. The other sapients that evolved here did so from single-celled life naturally arising from the primordial seas of this world. A world created by those beings, whom the natives refer to as 'Gods' and without question those beings fit every requirement to qualify as some sort of deities. The Immortals have written records reaching back half a billion years. Written records! Films, vacation snapshots, diaries, utility bills..."

"The Gods of Bethdish have walked among the Immortals," said Max. "Back in the distant past, true. But nonetheless, the fact is that the Immortals of this world are so far beyond more than 99% of Earth-human norm that they've been forced to toss the concept of natural evolution out the airlock—at least when it comes to themselves. In fact, if it weren't for the Gods relating the creation of their own handiwork here, scientists all over the galaxy would have thrown up their hands in despair at ever solving the puzzle. I was born here. I've seen the Gods with my own eyes. Hell, I've served them drinks here in the Mare Inebrium! My best guess is that in some far distant past, our Gods visited Earth and chose humans as the pattern for their own divine artwork. They won't say when, or how, or above all why, but it did happen."

"Amazing," said Aven's companion, Blink. "But what does that say about the deities of other worlds, other cultures? Are they equally real?"

"Nonsense," Aven snorted in anger. "Powerful aliens, perhaps. But Gods? I think not!"

"Then perhaps it is high time you began thinking," said Trixie sweetly as she placed another tankard of Aven's drink on the table before him. She smiled at Aven. I could see him relax under whatever influence Trixie exerted. I don't know what it is, but that woman has some sort of power over the males of nearly *any* species. Maybe it has something to do with her Sidhe ancestors. Whoever they are. Some ancient royal family from Earth, I gather.

Kazsh-ak used the interruption to drain his drink container and wave one fore-leg at Max to ask for a refill. Max punched buttons on a keypad he carried in one pocket of his bartending apron and within scant seconds the empty tank of D'rrish cocktail had vanished. A soft, musical chime sounded as a full replacement appeared within Kazsh-ak's easy reach upon the bar top.

"Thank you, Max." Kazsh-ak bowed as he spoke. "Now, where was I? Ah, yes... We were caught up in the battle, and a representation of the face of the evil fiend formed in the clouds above our heads. It formed arms and hands to better direct the lightning towards us. It literally roared defiance and anger at us. Thornby and I let loose with plasma cannons, set on overload. If we'd stopped firing for an instant, our guns would have exploded. Great gaping wounds appeared in the cloud-beast. Acid rained down upon us all. The Reever added his hand-weapon's firepower to ours, as did every soldier in the troop. I saw men blasted apart, rent into gobbets of cooked flesh by the Evil One's lightning blasts. Holes became torn into the ground as the mad God sought us out with His electrical blasts. Grim were my thoughts as my weapon harness absorbed the lightning and used that to recharge its batteries. My rain-soaked carapace steamed from the waste heat radiated by my weapon harness. Thornby roared, shouting angry abuse at Valleor, even as the machine he occupied was smashed to its mechanical knees by the winds and lightning.

"Just when we all thought we would die, we heard a sound. Over the roar of the storm, a chorus of voices began to sing. My translator could not make anything of the voices. To me they sounded like millions of angels, singing psalms of hope and of glory to their God of Light. I knew then that yet another God of Bethdish had entered the fray. One that was on our side—or rather, we were on His side. On the edge of the horizon before us, sunlight broke through the massed layers of cloud. Sunbeams, as bright as lasers, pierced the cloud-body of the Evil One. Wounds were torn into the clouds. Over all the din, I heard one lone voice. One HUMAN voice. It chanted words I cannot describe. I felt my hearts lifted in hope as I listened to that voice intone words of prayer, words of a binding spell that could have held the Evil One in prison for all time."

"Who was it?" Mendelethork asked. She's one of my fellow traveling salesmen. A Canshee-alkor by species, from a planet a thousand light years away from Bethdish. No one can sell fertilizer like Mendelethork. She is a legend among us traveling salesmen. She may look like a two-meter-long caterpillar with fangs, but she's a real friend.

"I found out his full name later, after the battle," said Kazsh-ak. "What I heard turned out to be the voice of a retired High Priest of Antuth. Tinhill S'esk-var Ninquit Salo'ran Nuatul by name. Remember that name, my friends. Remember it with honor. Tinhill the Teacher, they called him. He had once been High Priest of the worshipers of Antuth—for nearly seventy years of his life. He gave up that life in the attempt to imprison Valleor. He'd finally retired to his beloved gardening—half a world away from the place where he eventually died in a vain attempt to save us all from the Evil One. He died that day, so that we all might live free of the threat of Valleor. In the end, he failed. But we had been granted nearly sixty years before Valleor escaped from His prison. Tinhill was killed by the very energies of the binding spell. It became too much for his frail old flesh. I have been told that his body caught fire from the energies he tried to channel. Even as his flesh began to burn, he continued. Blazing like a torch, he continued. It was only when his flesh burned away to ashes that his voice ceased chanting the spell. He had been only a few, tiny words away from completing it. He died trying to save us all. Valleor was pulled into the prison, but Tinhill's premature death made it possible for the Evil

One to find a way to escape, eventually. Thornby and I stood there with the other soldiers as the clouds blew away into nothingness.

"We all spent the next few days getting to know one another. When everyone finally went home, Thornby and I traveled together to seek out adventures wherever we should find them. After many a year, we eventually went our separate ways. But all this time, we've managed to remain friends. Oh! The adventures we shared! You wouldn't believe the half of them if I took time to relate the details."

"Telling tales out of school?" said a mischievous voice from the entryway of the bar.

I looked up. I saw Guiles Thornby, grinning and giving Blanche a hug. However reluctantly, Thornby eventually released his hold on Blanche and walked to the bar. I think it had to be something in the way she pushed him away, held him over her head, and threatened to rip him in half, longways, that made him decide to stop hugging her. Of course, she smiled as she threatened him with grievous bodily harm. All part of her many charms. Lovely girl. I'd like to take her home to Mother... after we locked Father up in the basement...

"How much of that was true?" I asked him as Max fetched him a mug of his favorite brew.

"Every word of it," Thornby answered as he raised his mug in a toast to his D'rrish friend. "But you ought to hear the parts Kazsh-ak left out. That was one hell of a trip. I met up with the Reever and his party early on in their quest. We crossed the entire face of the world to get to the point where my dear friend began his telling. Hell, I had to die halfway through the journey, just to make a point. But I got better, just in time..."

Then Thornby told us the rest of the story. I'm not sure that I believe a tenth of it. But it made one hell of a tale!

Myths and Legends

"Never dismiss folk-tales and superstitions. The most unlikely stories are quite likely to contain at least a single grain of truth..."
Count De Saint Germain, 1780

Sometimes it happens, even in the Mare Inebrium. A slow night, few customers, a sea of empty tables across the main room… Max gets the chance to walk up and down behind the bar with a notepad checking inventory. One of the other bartenders steps up to fill the few orders from the regular customers who always seem to be at the Mare. The D'rrish Ambassador, Kazsh-ak Teir, stands quietly in his usual corner near one end of the long bar. Time seems to slow, to stretch, and *everyone* looks up when a new customer walks in.

A dark green cloak hung in deep folds around the new customer's frame. Their face was hidden by the cloak's hood. Max seemed to be among the last people to take notice as the customer slowly walked towards the bar. I suppose he'd caught a glimpse of their reflection in one of the mirrors behind the bar. Or maybe it was some kind of bartender's telepathy. Anyway, he noticed someone new had walked in as he checked off the level of alien liquor in yet another bottle along the bar's crowded shelves. I saw him turn around and raise one eyebrow in silent question as the new customer paused momentarily to examine a few of the paintings and displays of strange items that serve the Mare Inebrium as décor.

The stranger took their time, wandering up to the bar by an indirect path. Kazsh-ak carefully set his drink container on the bar. Max frowned slightly and began to walk toward the spot at the bar that the stranger seemed to be heading for when they reached up with gloved hands to pull back their hood.

Long blonde hair, so pale as to be almost white, spilled out over the stranger's shoulders. She, I could see now that the visitor was indeed a female, stopped in her tracks a few steps from the bar and turned to face Kazsh-ak Teir. She bowed to the scorpion-like D'rrish and spoke in a language with which I had not yet become acquainted. My fancy translator whispered into my left ear—a chime that signaled a language not yet in its database. The woman's voice sounded like the music of silver bells. Kazsh-ak replied in the same language. His translator producing notes in a far lower tone, sounding like some master musician playing a set of tubular bells. He bowed to the woman, then raised his right forelimb and traced a complicated gesture in the air. She walked up to stand closer to him, near enough to reach out and touch.

Max looked on from his spot behind the bar. I'd never seen that expression on anyone's face before—sort of a mix between awe and surprise, with a little polite caution thrown in. He seemed to be holding his breath as he watched the scene play out. I've never seen him so still before.

The woman spoke again, Kazsh-ak replied, both in that language my translator couldn't convert. She briefly held up her left hand, her index finger pointing towards the ceiling. With her right hand she pulled a small jeweled box from underneath her robe, held it reverently in both hands, and then placed it on the bar top next to Kazsh-ak's drink. He spoke again, bowed to her, and she turned to face Max. She bowed to Max, placed a small bar of metal on the bar top, then turned to leave. I heard Max speak in that same musical language. He couldn't quite manage the tones, but his accent must not have been *too* thick for the woman to understand. She looked back at Max, smiled at him, uttered one word, then walked to the doors and out into the cool night air.

"Well, I never..." I heard Max say, with awe in his voice.

"I have," replied Kazsh-ak. "But it was long ago."

"An *Eanan*, in my bar?" Max asked. "I never thought I'd live long enough to see *that* happen."

I got off my bar stool and walked over to where Max and Kazsh-ak stood. "Pardon me for intruding," I said.

"Andrew," Max said. "Please, pull up a seat. You don't have *any* idea what just happened, do you? Let me pour you a drink. On the house..."

"I never thought it would happen in my lifetime," said Kazsh-ak with a trace of sadness in his electronic voice. Once again, I felt impressed with his translator. The ability for a voice synthesizer to convey emotions? Very rare in a machine that small. It must be a Fender...

"The Reever must be told," added the old D'rrish, interrupting my train of thought.

"I'm betting," Max replied, "that she went to *him* before coming here. You and he were the only ones—"

"Allowed to leave, alive?" Kazsh-ak said, with amusement. "That we know about, yes. It cannot be a long list, in any case."

"Uh? Guys?" I asked. "Should I just go see if the Game Room exists this week?"

"Stick around, Andrew," said Max. "How much do you *really* know about this planet?"

That question took me by surprise. I looked from Max to Kazsh-ak, then back again.

"Something *spooky* just happened, didn't it? All right. I know more about City of Lights than anywhere *else* on the planet, but some of the general history wound up being included in my briefings over the years."

"Go on," said Max. "Tell me what you know. That'll let *me* know where to start explaining what just happened."

"Well," I said. "Bethdish is old, *really* old—as far as inhabited worlds go. There are some alien colonies set up from a long time back. The D'rrish, the Shebeja, and the Halazed all have colonies here."

"All established before the Night the Stars Changed," Max said. "Those are some of the original, old colonies."

"I remember the Reever saying that Bethdish used to be located in the Andromeda galaxy," I added "But somehow the whole star system got teleported over here into the Milky Way."

"Good," Max said. "Keep going."

"Basically," I said, "there's only one big supercontinent on the whole planet. The rest is all ocean and small islands. There are some big ruins scattered over the continent that can be seen from orbit. Looks like there must have been an atomic war way back when, if those ruins are anything to go by."

"The Kefa Empire cities," Kazsh-ak said. "Indeed, they bombed themselves into extinction. Fighting over the riches brought into the original spaceport. Must have been 5000 years ago, now"

"Longer than that," Max said. Brushing his brown hair out of his eyes, he frowned. "It's 6823 this year, and the Kefa War happened back in—ah, the year 1200 or so. The Kefa came close to killing off *everyone*. What with the nuclear winter from the smoke and dust in the air… Nothing but a few ruins and melted sand there now. If the Gods hadn't gotten rid of the dust when They did, the cold would have lasted decades instead of weeks."

"Um..." I paused in thought, then continued. "There are three or four areas outside City of Lights that allow off-world visitors. Nanor Fort City way down South, the Valley of Three Peaks Resort over on the West coast, and the Halazed colony over in Lake City in the far Northwest. The rest of the planet is off-limits to non-natives. That's so we aliens can't upset the natural development of the different native sapients. Oh, then there's the Altiplano—that ancient spaceport from back when Bethdish was still in the Andromeda galaxy. But only archeologists are allowed to go there, and then only if their expeditions are highly supervised..."

"A direct result of the Kefa War," Max said. "The Altiplano is the spaceport the Kefa started a war over. The Immortals realized the off-world tech had let them jump too far ahead of their moral development. So the ban on importing alien technologies and contact with the natives became law."

"A wise law," said Kazsh-ak. "Given the result of unregulated importation."

"You're already ahead of most folks that visit the planet," said Max as he looked back at me.

"Indeed," added Kazsh-ak. "Please, continue."

"There's not much more to tell," I said. "There's several different sapient species of natives. The Immortals are the oldest, and the aquatic River People are the youngest. There are some rumors that the land-dwelling natives are almost textbook human—which is weird as all get out, seeing how biology shouldn't be able to work that way. I might have misunderstood that, but biology wasn't my best subject in school. I've sold fertilizer on a hundred or more worlds, and I've never seen *any* natives look as Earth-human as the people here. That ought not be possible."

"Oughts and ought-nots don't count for much on Bethdish," said Kazsh-ak with a chuckle.

"Not with our whole pantheon of living Gods mucking about," added Max. He grinned. "All right, you've got a good grasp of the basics. Now, that lady who just came in here. She's from Eana."

"Never heard of that planet," I said. "Where is it? How far away?"

"Not a planet," Max corrected. "She's a native. Eana is a fairly small kingdom, out near the West coast. It's between Ninlen and Nalth—on the plains between the Urthishfel and the Karthisvar mountains. The plains are bordered on the North and South by the rivers Anar and Thuror. The whole kingdom is inside a forest that covers about the same area as City of Lights. The area pretty much has a big 'Keep Out' sign posted for the rest of the world. Eanans are a very standoffish people. They don't want outsiders to visit. Even the Reever doesn't go there without an invitation."

"On maps," said Kazsh-ak. "Eana is marked as '*the forest from whence none return*.' Beings who enter that place, do not come back. Ever."

"Except for the Reever," I said.

"And Kazsh-ak," added Max.

"Whoa," I exclaimed. "So, I gather that the Eanans don't usually wander around the world, either?"

"Exactly," said Max. "That woman is the first Eanan I've ever heard of to leave the kingdom."

"But," I said. "Kazsh-ak and the Reever have been there and been allowed to leave? Right? You two must have done someone a really big favor."

"You might say that," Kazsh-ak replied. "The Reever and I helped the Eanans fight off a small invasion once. Long ago. As a reward, we were allowed to go home."

"So, what happened to change their minds about the outside world?"

"They haven't so much changed their minds, Andrew," said Kazsh-ak. "They've issued a summons."

"What? If you're in trouble—" I began.

"No," replied Kazsh-ak. "That box contains my invitation to return for a ceremony. And my safe passage back out again. I assume that the Reever has received a similar package. But we must go back as witnesses. Their Guardian is dying. The Reever and I are invited to the Ceremony of Ascension of their new Guardian."

"Max," I said. "I think I need another drink."

"As do I," added Kazsh-ak.

"Make that three," came a voice out of thin air.

"If you make that a habit, you're going to give me a heart attack," Max said angrily to the nearly-empty bar room. Kazsh-ak and I turned to look out into the main room of the bar. A bright white dot of light appeared in the air, about waist-level from the floor. It expanded to an oval outline over two meters tall, a meter and a half wide, then the oval shifted to a silver color. The Reever stepped through, as if walking through a doorway. He lightly tapped his Staff of Office on the floor, then spoke to it.

"Close portal," he said. The silvery oval vanished. The Reever strode to the bar. His staff continued standing where he'd placed it, as if nailed to the floor. I'd heard of that thing before. Apparently, the staff is some kind of computer, as well as a remote control for Immortal technology. It looks like a Wizard's Staff, right enough. Some sort of white wood, or metal, or something less describable. It appeared to be squared off with an inlay of precious metals and gemstones in the top sixth or so of its length. About the place where one would most naturally hold it in their hand the shape turned to a round cross-section which gradually tapered off to a sort of bronze-colored tip where it reached the floor. The staff had to be nearly as tall as the Reever himself—roughly two meters. The gems flashed with an inner light, much the same way my ship's control panel indicator lights flash in sequence as my computer runs through a program.

In his right hand, the Reever held a duplicate of the jeweled box that the woman from Eana had given Kazsh-ak Teir. Hitching his sword back out of his way, the Reever perched on a bar stool next to me. His silvery-gray clothes fit him like a second skin. His muscles rippling visibly under the metallic cloth, he settled onto the self-adjusting seat and allowed his knee-length cloak to drape back, hanging freely. On his right hip he wore the single largest handgun I'd ever seen in my life. He set the box down on the bar top, sighed as the seat made itself comfortable for him, then reached out to touch hands with Max. He repeated the gesture with Kazsh-ak, then turned to give me a polite nod.

"A round of drinks on me," he said. "Even for the Security," he added, with a nod towards two elderly, bearded patrons playing chess over at an isolated table near the front of the main room. He wasn't smiling, so I doubt it was some sort of joke, although it might have been a private one between himself and Max. His voice sounded deep, quiet, and rather husky, as if he'd suffered some long-ago injury to his throat. He didn't look his age. What am I saying? The Reever is 13.5 million years old. *Nothing* looks *his* age except for mountain ranges and museum displays! He's an Immortal. They look like whatever age they feel, or so I've heard it said. The Reever appeared to be in his late thirties, perhaps early forties. His black hair was cut short and shows no sign of graying. His face looked as if it had been chiseled out of stone by some classic sculptor of heroic statuary. I remember seeing some thousands of years-old recordings of a video-play from Earth once, about a renegade policeman determined to go to any length to seek justice. The Reever looks quite a lot like the actor in that recording—Austin Clintwood, or something like that.

"Have you ever heard of doorbells?" Max asked as he signaled Bobby Blue, his robot back-up bartender to start making drinks for the twenty or so customers that occupied the Mare Inebrium that night. "Those dramatic entrances of yours aren't good for my health," Max added with a quick smile. He poured the three of us humanoids a large portion of some ancient whiskey, then teleported a refill of Kazsh-ak's preferred, slightly-radioactive-sludge cocktail to the receiver pad closest to where the giant scorpion stood.

"Ha," snorted the Reever with a quick smile. "Drama can save your life, Boy."

I always feel a bit odd calling him "The Reever" even though no one else ever calls him by his given name. "Reever" is a title, like calling someone "Sheriff" all the time, rather than Roy or Bob—I doubt that I could pronounce his given name. Immortals are famous for tagging each other with some polysyllabic mouthful. He's the fifth Immortal in his family to inherit the position of Chief Justice of the Immortals.

"A toast," said the Reever. "To the Guardian of Eana. All honors for your faithful service, and an easy passage into your afterlife."

"To the Guardian," we said together, and drank.

"Now," said the Reever after a respectful moment. "You and I have to be there for the induction of the new Guardian of Eana," he addressed Kazsh-ak. "I'll provide transport, unless you just want your own ship standing by."

"And miss a trip in an Immortal's Bubble-Car? Not for all the treasure in Skalldorff's Bank!" Kazsh-ak replied, naming the largest financial company in the City of Lights.

"How did you two get into this?" I asked. "I mean, Max implied that these Eanans were kinda isolationists, but the Reever is the head of law enforcement for the entire planet. There isn't any place he can be kept out of if he wants to go there badly enough. He's the Law. But how did Kazsh-ak get involved? Did he become a Deputy Marshal, or something?"

"No, we both wound up in exactly the wrong place at exactly the wrong time," said Kazsh-ak. The Reever nodded in agreement. "Do you know what a 'horse' is?"

"Sure, a quadruped animal from Earth," I answered. "I've seen them on several colony worlds. Farm animals. Almost as big as you are, Kazsh-ak."

"Good," the D'rrish replied. "On Bethdish there is a similar animal called a Selky. It has six legs, rather than the four possessed by a Terran horse, but they are similar in size and strength. A good riding mount for Bethdish natives. Back several centuries or so ago, several native nomadic tribes roamed the plains between mountain ranges on the backs of these 'near-horses.' Some of the fiercest warriors ever to terrorize the primitive natives."

"Like the Mongol Hordes, way back in Earth history?" I asked.

"Ah—Something like that," Kazsh-ak replied. "Rapacious bandits, very like the Mongols, but not as evil as *those* appear in Terran mythology. The Reever and I just happened to be near each other on the plains surrounding Eana. Neither of us knew the other was about, when a selky-riding tribe of nomads called Ohmany attempted to invade Eana..."

"What year was that?" Max asked.

"Oh," Kazsh-ak replied. "6750? Perhaps '52?"

"It happened in '53," said the Reever. "The Terran calendar year translates to 3900."

"So it was," Kazsh-ak said. "I had been exploring the world. Just wandering around, as it were. The air felt a bit cool for my taste, there between the river Thuror and the Southern edge of Eana. I could make out the peaks of Fort Mountain off in the far distance. Off across the river, in fact."

"Fort Mountain?" I asked.

"The new city of the Immortals is inside the mountain," said Max. "The security systems had probably noted your presence, even at that distance."

"Indeed they had," the Reever said. "I had been dispatched—elsewhere. But the appearance of D'rrish electronics and energy weapons had been passed on to me by Security. A lone D'rrish? On walkabout in a tech-restricted zone? I remained certain that it was merely yourself, Kazsh-ak. But I set a detector drone to observe you from on high. Just in case, you understand."

"Just so," replied Kazsh-ak. "If I, or another D'rrish, had been peddling our alien technology to the natives, you would have been remiss in your duties if you ignored us."

"It would have gone hard on you, old friend," said Max. "The Arena is no penalty for anyone to trifle with. Death, or deportation, or worse."

"Smuggling technology is a High Crime," the Reever said. "The punishment is—severe. But, as I said, I felt sure that it was your good self, off exploring. So, I canceled the automatic order to dispatch a platoon of Peacekeepers to detain you, and finished my business before investigating, myself."

"Wasn't that the crashed shuttle craft I heard about, down in Ninlen?" Max asked. "I remember reading a report in an archeology journal, years ago."

"Yes," said the Reever. "I had to clear the way for those archeologists to set up camp and excavate the crash site. I took a squad of Peacekeepers to keep the Ninlenians away from the scene until the remains of the shuttle could be shipped out to a museum in City of Lights. One of their better exhibits, actually."

"I've seen it," said Kazsh-ak. "A Keranen cargo shuttle, from Andromeda. The mummies look quite well preserved, given that they'd crashed nearly a thousand years before the Ninlenians found them. But we digress..."

"Please continue," said Max. "You were between Eana and the river?"

"Quite," said Kazsh-ak. "Minding my own business, camping in the rough, cataloging the wildlife, and above all avoiding more than chance encounters with native villages. Little did I know that these Ohmany bandits had launched a campaign of terror behind me. They had come sweeping down onto the plains from their homes in the foothills of the Urthishfel mountains. Raiding every village they could find. Raping, pillaging, and plundering—the usual order of business for those types. If it weren't for feeling the vibrations of hundreds of selky hooves through the ground, they would have taken me quite unaware."

"What did you do?" I asked.

"I headed towards the only good cover I could see. The forest looked to be the only place I could go wherein I could remain unobserved by the approaching raiders. I had no idea that the forest could be far more dangerous than any tribe of nomads!" Kazsh-ak laughed, the sound issuing from his electronic translator booming out. "I had nearly reached the tree line when the first waves of the nomads came within sight of me. There was nothing for it but for me to turn about and make ready to defend myself."

"How did you know that these riders were dangerous?" I asked.

"I think," Kazsh-ak replied with a trace of dry humor in his translated voice. "That the sight of those severed heads dangling from the nomad's saddle-horns were a definite clue. Yes."

Max chuckled. "A dead giveaway?" He added. The Reever groaned quietly by way of criticism of Max's pun.

"Quite," said Kazsh-ak. "Very droll. I shall have to remember that turn of phrase for the next time I tell this tale. In any case, I made ready my spear in one fore foot-hand, snapped my pincer claws to loosen them up from the chill in the air, and activated the charger in my tail-gun. Just as a last resort, you understand. All the while I backed closer to the trees." Kazsh-ak tilted one eye stalk to look back behind himself while keeping the other pointed ahead, by way of illustration. I admit, seeing him do that reinforced the alien-ness of his giant scorpion body shape. Sometimes I forget just how alien an alien can be. I know that D'rrish have lungs as well as breathing through tiny openings in their chitin. And that chitin is so hard that it can turn a spear or bullet. But when you get to know one as a person, you forget that they aren't human-shaped. Sometimes, little details of their body language strike home to remind you that they are very much off-worlders.

"I had almost managed to reach the edge of the forest," Kazsh-ak continued. "When the first ranks of nomad riders pulled up short and loosed a volley of spears at me. I batted several aside with my pincers, caught and snipped in half a very few others, and could feel yet others bounce off of my body's natural armor. Yet, I still felt afraid. A chance spear through the joints in my limbs would be a crippling injury. One that would leave me almost helpless against a concerted attack by these murderous marauders."

Kazsh-ak paused to lift his drink and sip delicately from the complicated "straw" that topped the container. After a moment he set the tank back down on the bar. "Once again, a perfect cocktail, Max. My compliments," he said.

"You're welcome," Max said. "Need another?"

"No, I have at least half of this one left," said Kazsh-ak. "But back to my tale. I managed to deflect two or more volleys of spears, still backing slowly into the edge of the forest. The outlying trees began to become a tactical advantage for me. More riders arrived, and they began to dismount in groups. They drew bows and notched arrows for a closer assault. My hearts sank at this development. I knew my tough shell wouldn't be able to deflect all their arrows. This was going to sting a bit...”

“Which is roughly the point where I arrived,” said the Reever. “My vehicle had made remarkable time across the landscape. But its instruments revealed that I might just be too late to prevent my friend from serious injuries. I feared that Kazsh-ak might be forced to use his energy weapon against the nomads. I had seen what sort of damage that thing could inflict. I knew my bubble-car couldn't arrive in time to save Kazsh-ak from those flights of arrows...”

“What happened?” Max asked.

“The Guardian of Eana,” said Kazsh-ak. “*She* happened. Unbeknownst to either myself or the Reever, She had observed the whole sorry spectacle. I could see the outer flanks of the riders beginning to move into the forest in an attempt to circle around me and attack from the rear. A hundred? Two? Three hundred? I couldn't count them all. Yelling their war whoops and readying their weapons, they spread deeper into the forest to encircle me. Once under the trees, they fell under the ire of the Guardian. I could hear crashing sounds, and the sudden, desperate cries of the nomads. I swiveled my eye stalks about so quickly that I feared they would break off. What I saw—became terrifying. The trees—the trees began to twist and thrash about, as if in a gale force wind. Branches smashed down upon the riders, turning them to pulped flesh and foaming gobbets of splattering blood. I could hear chanting voices from deep in the forest. Distant drums beat out an angry rhythm. The dust and debris around me made it hard to see in more detail. I felt the Reever's bubble-car crashing to a halt behind the raiders that remained outside the forest. The shock wave from his vehicle blasted riders from their mounts as if it had been cannon fire. In all the confusion, I heard the Reever's amplified voice commanding the nomads to surrender. Instead, they turned to the forest, and fled into its shaded reaches. The noise of trees crashing about then mingled with angry shouts and the pop and crack of unfamiliar weapons. Not those of the riders, but those of the forest people coming to the aid of their trees in defending the forest from these witless nomad invaders. The nomads nearest me continued to send flights of arrows towards me. I dodged what

I could, swatted others out of the air, but I could feel long gashes in the surface of my shell from the weapons I could not evade. I nearly lost an eye to one poor chap with a spear! Well, I say poor chap, but it became either him or me. I reached out and snipped him in twain," Kazsh-ak lifted his left pincer, suddenly stretched his arm out to its full length, and snapped his claw shut with a crack of noise not unlike a pistol shot. "As I said, it came down to either they or I, and I'll be damned if I was going to go down without a fight!"

"What did you do?" Max asked the Reever.

"I set off a stun grenade to knock the rest of the Ohmany down. The ones that hadn't already run into the forest, that is. I knew the ones that had run under the trees were dead men. It might take a little time, but Eana doesn't suffer invaders. Even my father seemed a bit spooked by Eana. He warned me not to trifle with the forest. He never said why, exactly, but he seemed to know something he wasn't allowed to relate to any other being. In any case, I deployed a tangle-field from my bubble-car to keep the nomads immobilized, then picked up my staff and my sword and went charging into the forest to try and rescue Kazsh-ak. He damn near took my head off before he recognized me," said the Reever. He laughed. "By the time we'd managed to fight off the rest of the riders, I knew the forest people had us surrounded. The noise of battle had died down to near-silence by then. I whispered to the old D'rrish that we had no option but surrender, just as the first of the forest people stepped into view."

"They came from out of the shadows of the trees," said Kazsh-ak. "Pale skinned, yellow-haired, dressed in the greens and browns and grays of forest colors. Beings much like yourselves. A tall female, and four males approached us first. They spoke, and the Reever replied, haltingly at first, but his translator quickly brought him up to speed. After a while, my translator began to make sense of their language. What I understood then made my blood run cold. It seems that since we had entered their forest, we were then subject to their laws. Our only shred of hope seemed that their Guardian would choose to see us as allies rather than enemies. But we would have to go to their city, deep within their forest, in order to learn our fate."

"So, we went with them," said the Reever. "At least a day's walk into the heart of the forest."

"Oh, longer than that, surely?" Kazsh-ak said.

"No," the Reever replied. "It just seemed like a month, but it took only a day. Finally, we reached their city. They made their homes in woven huts up among the branches of their sacred trees. In the center of their city, stood a tall stone tower, gleaming white, without doors or windows. It stretched up above the treetops, smooth and unbroken by any visible entrance or exit. We had been told to stand in what they called a sacred circle, a white stone-tiled area about twelve meters across. Once we stood in the circle, they backed away and began to chant."

"It didn't take long," said Kazsh-ak. "Before a subtle glow in the air between ourselves and the tower heralded the arrival of their Guardian. The light brightened, then faded away to reveal an aged female of their kind. And yet, she looked both old and young at the same time. Her skin looked as pale as moonlight, her hair a gleaming white, long enough to reach the middle of her legs, and she looked so very beautiful. Even I could understand that, non-human though I am. She looked at us in a way that seemed to reach into the very depths of our souls. Then she questioned us, gently, as one would ask a child the details of their play-time games. She seemed to be almost as old as the world, fierce, yet kind, stern, yet loving... I found myself relating my life story without any difficulty from the difference in language. My translator seemed to master their speech in record time. Once I had explained myself and my species, she spoke briefly with the Reever. He too seemed to learn the language much better as he spoke it. In moments, he became so fluent in the myriad tones and inflections that he seemed almost to have been born under the leaves of the forest. Finally, our interview ended. As the Guardian began to fade from sight, she pronounced judgment upon us."

"Well!" I nearly shouted. "Don't keep us in suspense. What was her verdict?"

"You may leave, She said," came Kazsh-ak's reply. "The Ohmany within the forest would serve to feed the trees, as ruled Eana's ancient law. The ones outside the forest would be the responsibility of the Reever. He and I had been named as Friends of Eana and would be remembered as Champions, honorary Forest People, to enter their songs and folk tales as heroes. But that we should never return unless summoned. She said that we would be led out, back into the wide world outside the forest. As She finally vanished, we looked about us. We saw the natives slowly stretch and distort their human shapes, until they turned into sapling trees themselves. All but one pair, a male and a female who had been instructed to guide us out. Wordlessly, we four walked back to the open plain, whereupon our guides vanished back into the shadows of the trees."

"I called for a brigade of Peacekeepers to round up the surviving Ohmany and transport them back to their homes in the mountain foothills," said the Reever. "I warned them that their lives were to be forfeit if they ever raided the plains again. Some took my warning to heart, some migrated to the seashore and took up service with several different clans of fishermen, or pirates. The pirates I kill when I must. The fisher folk I aid when I can."

"But the Guardian?" I asked. "She is near to death, or dead already?"

"No one lives forever," said the Reever. "Not even we Immortals. The Guardian may have lived as long as the world has existed, one after another, in their time, but the present one? She is tired, and now seeks the sleep of eternity. A suitable successor has been chosen, by the rules and laws of Eana. They will assume the duty. Kazsh-ak and I have been chosen to witness the rites of succession."

"Is the Guardian one of the Gods of Bethdish?" I asked.

"Older," said the Reever. "Perhaps from a time before our Gods came to Bethdish and created us. Eana holds many mysteries. There is a power there, and a wisdom beyond the reaches of time."

"To the Guardian!" Kazsh-ak exclaimed as he raised his drink in a toast. "May She rest in peace."

"To the Guardian," we replied.

"To the new Guardian! Long may They reign," added the Reever.

The End

The Bouncer

"Everybody was Kung-Fu fighting..."
Kwai Chang Caine, 1871

Every bar has at least one, the Mare Inebrium had one per side-bar as well as the one for the main room. I mean Bouncers, so called for their ability to eject an unwanted patron so hard that they bounced off the pavement outside at least twice. Usually, there was a quick rotation among the Mare's staff of bouncers as each one found the particular side-bar that he/she/it fit into. After a while, only the new additions were in the rotation—that is, until Bruce showed up at the Mare one evening with a "seeks employment" form stamped by the City of Lights Governmental Council. I just happened to be there that evening, actually. I'm from a small, backwards planet about sixty-five lights out-arm from Bethdish. I found my way here by way of a phantom doorway in a bar on my own home world. A doorway that shouldn't have been there to start with, but that's another story. I was telling you about Bruce.

I'd found my mysterious doorway to the Mare about ten years ago, so I'd seen several bouncers come and go. I'd have never put my money on Bruce when I first set eyes on him, but I'm telling you, he did have something. I sat one table out from the bar when Bruce walked in and shyly gave his employment papers to Max. Max looked at this little guy. Bruce is only about five foot eight or so, with short dark hair and intelligent brown eyes. Max looked at the papers, looked at Bruce some more, seemed to give the matter some furious thought, and then called over the bouncer on call that evening. Igor was the being on duty, and Max asked him to tell Bruce about the hazards of the job, just so he wouldn't have been going into it blind. Since my guest had left my table about half an hour before, I arose and strolled casually up to take a bar stool close to Bruce and Igor's position. Igor's one of those heavy-gravity types. He's got muscles in places where most beings don't even have places. Evidently, Max had told him to describe his job for Bruce. Igor stood there next to the bar, lost in the gory details of some grand (to him) combat where he tossed some troublesome patron out into the street. From what I overheard, Max had gotten tired of the being's attitude really quickly, what with his smashing things and yelling "Hulk will SMASH!" until he'd been forced to call Igor in to smack some sense into the offending patron.

Igor's reactions may be a bit slow sometimes, but he tells a good story. And he's really quite smart, if you give him time to think instead of just react. He was trying to get across to Bruce the idea that it might be life-threatening to seek employment at the Mare when they both looked up to see some idiot stumbling drunkenly out of the "Red Dog" side-bar. Said idiot then smashed its sizable fist through a table in the main bar, grabbed a nearby Sak-enjass from off its seat, and then tossed the inoffensive meter and a half crustacean right into Blanche. Now I've seen Blanche pick up a rowdy Kzin and throw him into a wall, but she wound up getting knocked tail over teakettle from the unexpected impact of the Sak-enjass. Igor stopped talking, frowned, and turned to leave the bar in order to attend to the rowdy drunk, but Max reached across the bar to put a hand on his shoulder and asked him to wait a moment. You see, Bruce had already gone into action.

Bruce seemed to be in motion before the table's splinters had finished flying. The Czen'thix trooper—that's what Max told me its species called themselves—was turning to confront the other patrons at the smashed table, Blanche still in mid-fall, when every eye in the Mare was suddenly confronted with the image of Bruce sort of appearing out of thin air next to the drunken Czen'thix. He was just *that* fast.

You could have heard a pin drop as Bruce quietly asked, "What was that?"

The trooper roared and took a wild swing at Bruce—who ducked under the massive swinging fist as if his body were made of rubber.

"That is no way to behave in public," Bruce said gently. The Czen'thix threw several wild punches and followed that up with a leg-sweep. Bruce easily avoided each movement with a liquid grace that was a joy to watch. As Blanche regained her feet—with blood in her eye, I might add. Bruce turned and gave her a quick bow from the waist, then turned back, reached up, and slapped the trooper's face with the back of his hand. It sounded like a pistol shot, and in the sudden silence everyone in the bar could hear Bruce tell the trooper "I think that you owe the lady an apology, brute. And these tables, they aren't cheap, you know?"

In reply, the drunken Czen'thix simply reached out for Bruce with both long, muscular, claw-tipped arms. I thought that Bruce was a goner. I know everyone else in that silent crowd thought so too... Except maybe for Max.

Bruce moved.

OK, that's kinda like the statement "I dropped the atom bomb, and it went off," but when I say the little dude moved, I mean he *moved!*

Bruce *seemed* to move in slow motion, but he reached for one of the Trooper's descending arms, grasped it, pivoted to put his shoulder underneath the drunken alien, then *heaved* so hard I could see his arm muscles cord up like bunches of piano wire. The trooper seemed to be ripped from the ground and sailed across the room to impact the far wall. At about that time, a sparkly circle appeared in the air and the Reever stepped out of it. Max later told me he'd called as soon as the drunk had started on his rampage. In less time than it takes to tell, the Reever had the trooper in restraints and his deputies were escorting it back to its ship. They'd collect a hefty fine from the trooper's superiors before they let the ship lift.

Blanche turned out to be alright, and the crustacean that she'd been hit with started recovering nicely. Now all that was left for Max to do was to decide whether or not Bruce got to join the Bouncer's staff at the Mare. Me? I never had any doubt. Bruce joined the permanent staff that night. To hear Blanche tell it, she later gave Bruce some type of reward for coming to her rescue—but I gotta take her word for it. Bruce is too much of a gentleman to talk about such things.

So that's why since that day, if you like getting drunk and starting fights, it'd be a whole lot healthier for you to avoid the Mare Inebrium and just go to some other bar. Otherwise, Max might ask Bruce to teach you some manners... And Bruce gets *serious* about good manners.

Sic Semper Tyrannis!

Kazsh-ak defeats the Overlord of Naatung in single combat, freeing the slaves of planet Naatung.

"The slave-master is among the lowest, most base of villains..."
Niccolo Machiavelli, 1513 AD

"...so I pulled my hold-out gun and shot the guards with a stun-ray. Once I had my weapons belt back, I ran to the field where I'd parked my ship and boosted off that backwater world. No one is ever going to turn *me* into a farm-slave! I must have pulled 3 Gs on the takeoff," said the big four-eyed, blue-furred Teddy-bear as he ended his story. The Daleenian traveling salesman had been relating his escape from involuntary servitude for the better part of the last hour. I was just about to ask the bartender for another round when I noticed something odd about the giant scorpion standing near the end of the bar.

The scorpion set his drink container down on the bar top a little too roughly, then waved a fore-limb at the bartender for a refill. I couldn't make out the words his electronic translator rumbled out, but the tone spoke volumes. The D'rrish seemed angry about something. Anyone that big, with a poison-filled stinger on their tail, was a being I wouldn't want to piss off in a crowded bar! The shiny blue chrome robot bartender wasted no time giving the D'rrish another drink. As one of the humanoid bartenders mixed a fresh Koolu-Tequila and snazberry fizz for me, I asked him about the D'rrish scorpion in the corner.

"Ah, that's just Kazsh-ak Teir, the D'rrish ambassador. He's a regular here," replied Larrye, the bartender. Larrye isn't an imposing guy, average height, skinny as a rail. He looks as if he'd seen some hard times as a kid. He's a little bit awkward, too. But he can mix some great drinks!

"He's nearly 300 years old," Larrye continued. "And he's been around the galaxy a bit in his time. He's a good friend of Max, the manager. I've never seen him upset before. Don't know what could have gotten under his carapace tonight. Bruce has noticed it though, so if a fight starts, just stay out of the way and Bruce will handle it."

I looked around to see who Larrye was talking about and quickly noticed a slim, dark-haired fellow nearby. He had one eyebrow raised in puzzlement, but otherwise seemed to be holding himself in readiness for a throw-down. I gathered that this Bruce guy must be one of the bouncers. I wouldn't want to cross him, but I don't know what he'd be able to do with an irate alien ten times his mass... Even with all the tricks I'd been taught back when I was—well, less than a spy, but more than a diplomatic courier. My name's Jon Stewart Sebastian.

I've been dropping in at the Mare Inebrium a few times a year since I had been hired by Leegous Chan-Murphy's Triple-A Courier Service. We ship diplomatic packets and oddball stuff all over the nearby star systems. You know, security-bonded stuff that other companies tend to shy away from handling. Old man Chan-Murphy bought office space in one of the high-rise buildings near downtown City of Lights a decade or so ago. Before my time, sure, but I'm impressed with the planet, myself. The Old Man has a reputation for being a bright businessman. Bethdish is in a great location for shipping. The planet is like a crossroads between a huge number of inhabited worlds. I guess the old man likes the weather here on Bethdish, too. There's almost no axial tilt, so the seasons aren't very different from one another. Comfortable place, this planet. Warm and mild, with only a few bouts of heavy weather to worry about every year. The old man liked it so much he bought into the construction of one of the high-rise buildings going up, like I said. There's apartment space in the building, too. Each of us couriers for the company have a little apartment assigned to us. Just one of the perks of the job.

The D'rrish put his drink container back on the bar again, and tip-toed a little unsteadily over to the bear-like Daleenian who'd been bragging about getting away from becoming a slave. I glanced over at Bruce. Looked to me like the little guy was ready to take on both aliens if the feces hit the fan. Don't know how he'd manage it, though. Both of them out-massed Bruce. I mean, folks from Daleen are built like heroic statues. Seven feet tall, muscular arms that are bigger around than my legs, a chest like a brick wall, and three-inch fangs. The D'rrish wasn't any smaller, really. About six feet tall at the shoulder, but at least twenty feet long, from the tip of his poison-tipped stinger to the points of his two big pincers. I didn't think anything with an exoskeleton could get that big. But biology isn't my strong suit, you know? The universe has produced some odd-ball life forms over the eons.

A deep voice rumbled out of the scorpion's translator. "Someone tried to make a slave out of me once," the D'rrish said. "But I didn't run away." The Daleenian didn't look very intimidated. I'll give him credit for some brains, though. His next words turned what could have been a fight into something more peaceful.

"I'll bet that turned out to be a mistake on their part," said the Daleenian. He grinned, showing yellowed fangs in a mouth as big as a bucket. "You look like you could handle yourself pretty well in a fight. Tell me about it. I hate slavers, myself. I'd offer you a seat, but it looks like there aren't any for your species. Could I buy you a drink?"

"That would be most kind," said the D'rrish. "My people don't use chairs, something more like a tall bench is more our style of thing. But I'll stand, if that isn't considered bad manners for your culture."

"Not at all," said the Daleenian. "My name is Crushaand Obvoort, by the way. My friends call me Crush. Barkeep," Crush said as he looked at Larrye. "Another round for my friend, here. If you'd be so kind." Larrye turned to the drinks-mixing console and punched out a long combination of numbers. Within seconds the warning flicker of a teleport field hovered over a section of the Daleenian's table. When the glow died away, a D'rrish drinks container sat within easy reach of the big scorpion.

"Many thanks," said the D'rrish. "I am Kazsh-ak Teir, of the D'rrish Foreign Service. Senior Ambassador to other species here on Bethdish. I am honored to meet you, Friend Crush."

"You were speaking of slavers," said Crush. "As Captain of a trading ship, I'm always eager to learn of places that might prove dangerous to land. It proves difficult to turn a profit if someone attempts to put you in chains. Enlighten me, please. Where did your adventure take place?"

"About fifty light years out-arm from here," replied Kazsh-ak. He took a long sip of his drink and sat the container down. The thing must have held nearly three gallons. It had a biohazard label on it, too. No wonder there was some sort of tube for the D'rrish to drink through. "It happened years ago, in my youth. I had been attached to the Interplanet Scouts and sent off to serve a tour of duty not long after becoming mated. Just one of my people's customs. Nothing special, but part of our higher education, as it were."

"Sounds difficult," said Crush. "Leaving a mate and going off-world. If I were permanently mated, I certainly would find that hard to do."

"Not at all," said Kazsh-ak. "Our females require a long term of privacy between mating and the formative years of our hatch-lings. It keeps we males from being eaten by a grumpy spouse during a first pregnancy," he added with a hearty laugh. "Call it a successful evolutionary strategy."

"Whatever works," said Crush. He raised his tankard in a toast to the D'rrish.

"Indeed," replied Kazsh-ak. "In any case, my scout ship carried me a bit off the charted areas of my navigational records. The instruments had detected a habitable world and I received orders to investigate. I reached the place, discovered it was not too unpleasant for my kind, inhabited by a species in the early industrial stage. The natives appeared roughly on a par with our size although a bit larger, multi-legged and exoskeletal like ourselves. They looked to have evolved from a semi-aquatic ancestor—somewhat similar to Samousans, or the Terran crab, though with extra legs, and so forth. An unusual find, really. I landed without difficulty, then set out to make contact."

"Given your natural weapons," Crush said. "I gather you chose not to encumber yourself with a stunner or a beamer?"

"Exactly," Kazsh-ak replied. "It was a typical cadet mistake. One that proved costly to me. I had landed outside what turned out to be the major city of the inhabitants. The planet, called Naatung by the natives, was just entering a stage of transition from farming to industry. I considered going heavily armed to be a possible hindrance to making peaceful contact. Needless to say, I soon saw the error of my ways when I reached the city and was captured by its guards. They proved to be formidable foes. After a short bout of claw-to-claw combat I found myself trussed up like a Feast Day meal and herded off to durance vile. And quite vile it turned out to be."

"Your continued presence in our midst indicates that you have not been devoured by your captors," said the robot bartender. I turned my head to see that the robot stood right behind me. Larrye had evidently gone off to see to other customers further on down the long bar. That robot could move very quietly, for an automaton.

"Quite right, Bobby Blue," said Kazsh-ak in reply to the robot. "But after a week or two in the Naatung's prison, I had begun to believe that being eaten would have been preferable. On a daily basis, I found myself in chains, together with several of the natives, and sent out under guard to work the fields and farms. My fellow captives were, of course, slaves. Captured from some military conquest or other. Fellow soldiers, even though alien to me. Their commanding officer had tried to win their freedom in an Arena, although that quest had cost him his life. Some sort of gladiatorial ritual combat, I learned. I had been allowed to keep my translator, you see. It took a day or so to become fully fluent in the Naatung language, but soon enough I was presented with the whole sorry tale. I had arrived just after some local warrior leader had consolidated his power. He had set himself up as a sort of planetary overlord after many years of conquest."

"Sounds typical," Crush said. Other patrons nearby nodded in agreement. "Some sort of barbarian tribesman? Leading his hordes out against whatever passed for civilized villages and towns. I suspect that this Overlord was simply the most successful of a long line of marauders. Many planets have suffered the same sort of thing. Warriors make poor farmers. Timid people on the brink of real civilization find themselves pressed into slaving in the fields they once owned."

"Indeed," said Kazsh-ak. "And exactly the situation in which I found myself. But I did have one glimmer of hope. Those gladiator games. If I could just manage to get myself drafted into those, perhaps I could win my freedom. Or at least escape my guards long enough to ally myself with whatever forces of opposition to this Overlord that might exist."

"They always seem to provide their own resistance, don't they?' asked Crush. "It is no different in the histories of my people."

"Exactly my own hope," said Kazsh-ak. "After weeks of captivity, I found myself resisting my guards. Eventually, I caused enough trouble to get myself kitted out as a gladiator and put into the Arena. Against animals, at first, but eventually I found myself put up against other natives. I refused to go for the kill when matched against the natives. I endured much punishment for that, but I have my pride. After a time, I found myself the favorite of the gamblers. The rumors that filtered into the slave quarters revealed that the Overlord, while initially pleased with my performance in his games, was beginning to see me as a personal threat."

"Tricky situation, that," I said. "A little success and you're a hero to the crowds. Too much success, and you find yourself an embarrassment to the rulers and headed for execution."

"Exactly the tight spot I had to navigate," said Kazsh-ak. "But eventually I found the rebel forces I felt sure had to exist. I played dumb and let myself be a tool for their plotting. Eventually, I found myself in combat with the Overlord's personal champions rather than my fellow slaves. By that time, I had learned enough of Naatung anatomy and biology to appear a fearsome fighter. I carefully stretched out my combats, so as to appear to win each time by the barest margin. The gamblers and rebels threw in their influence behind me. I became a sort of People's Champion, once I knew my foes must be the Overlord's favorite enforcers. I killed as few as I could, but I sent many of them back to their barracks as permanent invalids. My fame grew with each combat. But I knew there would come a day when that fame would anger the Overlord. Make me seem a perceptible threat to his control. Eventually, his twisted honor and greed for continued power would force him to confront me, himself, or seem a coward. Either way, his rule would come to an end."

"Your courage is commendable," said Crush.

"I had nothing to lose but my chains, or my life," replied Kazsh-ak. "Either way, I would be free. I knew that as long as the Overlord kept struggling to retain power, he could not afford to execute me out of hand. I would be far more dangerous as a martyr to the cause of revolution against his control than I would be as a champion gladiator. That is why I courted the rebel cause. Soon enough there came the day that the Overlord sent his mightiest warrior against me. His personal champion, and the native most likely to become his successor if anything happened to the Overlord. It was a difficult battle, but I finally overcame my foe. A close-run thing. Several times he nearly had me. But in the end, I sent him off the field in the care of the medical staff. Now *that* was a combat worthy of song! Ah, but my throat becomes parched with all this talking..."

Now, I knew the old D'rrish used an electronic translator to talk through. But I also recognized an old storyteller's trick to pause a tale long enough to provide dramatic effect. I looked around at the other customers that had gathered to hear the D'rrish spin out his story. They seemed to hang upon his every word, enthralled by the adventure he related. Within record time, the D'rrish had been provided with a fresh cocktail, paid for by several of his listeners. After a long pull on his fresh drink, he continued.

"As I said, the day I had long wished for finally arrived. I was fed well before the next combat. I found myself submitting to artists who decorated my carapace with elegantly painted designs of my choosing. I even had to turn down the services of a no-doubt talented Naatung female courtesan. I suppose that must be their way of ensuring that I had been suitably rewarded before my certain death at the Overlord's claws. Finally, I found myself respectfully ushered into the Arena. The Overlord's usual seat was empty. I stood, gleaming in the sunlight, listening to the thunderous ovation from the sea of natives filling the Arena to its limits. Then a door on the far wall opened, and the Overlord himself strode out to meet me."

The D'rrish paused, looked about himself at his listeners as if to gauge their readiness, nodded in satisfaction, and then continued to speak in the hushed room.

"The Overlord was far larger than the average Naatung. His carapace measured easily twice the width of my own body. His many legs appeared encrusted with jewels. His body and pincer claws were draped with multicolored silks tied in intricate patterns. A warm breeze fluttered those fabrics about his person as if in a drama plotted by some master playwright. His forelimbs gripped a short spear and a sharp sword—as if he needed mere weapons against a barbarian off-worlder such as I. What I could see of his body looked to be covered with scarred gashes from previous battles. I could also see that his serrated claws had been lined with some, no doubt, hardened metallic reinforcing material. He scuttled side to side as if to demonstrate his superior mobility. Then he spoke into the gathering silence which had fallen upon the arena at his entrance."

The D'rrish paused again to sip from his drink. Placing it back down on Crush's table, his bright blue eyes glittered on their stalks like jewels, themselves. I figured that the old boy was just playing for time, for the right dramatic moment to continue. But what do I know? I'm just a messenger boy, myself. Not a master of the art of storytelling.

"He spoke," said Kazsh-ak, finally. "'You have done well in the arena, off-worlder,' he said. 'But as of late you have become a thorn in my side. Such a popular gladiator could well grow to be a genuine threat to my rule. The cowed masses see you as some sort of hero. You dream of taking my place? I will not stand for such insolence. Let your death be a lesson to those who plot against me, then! I am the Overlord of Naatung! All will bow to my rule or perish utterly! I will make of your death an agony worse than torture. None can withstand me! None shall oppose me! I am Lord and Master of all! Beg for mercy, slave!'"

I stood. Without any weapons other than those with which I had been born, I stood proudly before him. I remained silent, in the hope he would take my lack of reply as cowardly fear, rather than the angry contempt that I found surging throughout my body. He circled to close the distance between us. I did the same. He feinted with his weapons and his claws, as if to unnerve me. I watched him, gauging his strength and his tactics. We closed to within two body lengths. He reached his spear out in what he thought was an easy strike to the joints in my own claw-arms. I snapped the head off his spear with my left pincer, and then caught it with my left forelimb as it tumbled to the sandy ground. Now, I had a knife! I lunged forward to strike him in the shoulder with my right pincer, held closed as a blunt bludgeon. Then I leaped back, out of the reach of his parry. He stepped back, stunned by the force of my closed-claw strike. Throwing down the now useless shaft of his spear, he began circling again. As did I. As I crossed over his previous position, I gathered the spear shaft in my right forelimb. The fool had lost one weapon, thus giving me two weapons to use against him!"

I exhaled a breath I hadn't realized that I'd been holding. The excitement in the room was easy to feel. I could see customers nearby who were mimicking the actions the old D'rrish described in his story. He had them in thrall, hanging on his every word. He sipped again from his drink and once more set in on the table before himself.

"The Overlord lunged at me with both of his pincers outstretched," Kazsh-ak said. "I deflected them with my own, sweeping his arms away from me in an outside-circle movement I had been taught in school. I saw his sword rising to strike at my arm and parried it with the blade of his spear that I gripped tightly in my left forelimb claw. As we closed, I rapped him smartly between his compound eyes with the shaft of his discarded spear. I leaped backwards again, covering more than my own body-length and opening a gap between us once again. I was beginning to take his measure as a combatant. To be sure, he was a seasoned veteran of a thousand battles. But I? I had been trained by D'rrish Masters of the arts of combat. Quite possibly I had spent more years in school than he had in battle. I *knew* I could take him, unless I made some fatal error."

Crush silently signaled a waitress for another drink, as others in the bar did the same. Kazsh-ak picked up his own drink, sipped again, then returned it to the table. He tip-toed back a few steps, then forward, as if recreating his movements on that day of combat.

"It is true," the D'rrish said as if lost in thought. "That the spear-head I held as a knife and the shaft I held are not the sorts of things my training had used, but a blade is a blade and a stick is a stick. My teachers had spent countless hours with me over the years of my training. I found myself responding to the Overlord's every attack with highly polished, disciplined moves. Still, I did not speak to the fiend. I think he found my silence more nerve-wracking than the crash and clatter of our fight was to me. He leaped, I dodged. He lunged, I parried, riposted, counter-attacked, and disengaged with practiced precision. His fine silks were eventually in tatters. His ornate jewels lay strewn across the ground. New gashes in his body's natural armor seeped bodily fluids. And the lighter gravity of Naatung was beginning to work to my advantage. The Overlord was growing tired. I did not. He attacked yet again, and I—in a complicated movement of arms, forelimbs, and medial limbs that my teachers despaired of my ever mastering, I took his sword away and flung it off as far as I could. He howled in anger, then leaped at me with all his arms and legs flailing. I grabbed his pincers in mine, and we wrestled. I battered him again and again with my stick as we rolled across the sands of the Arena. I stabbed at him, over and over with the head of his spear. At last, I had him belly-up on the sands. I struck with my stinger at his exposed underbelly. With luck, I found a join in the plates of his carapace made of softer flesh. I emptied the poison sack in my tail into his yielding flesh. I had no idea if my natural poison would affect him, but I deemed it worth the risk. He screamed, thrashed about as I held him down, then he died. I released my hold on his slowly cooling corpse, then rose shakily to my feet."

Kazsh-ak reached for his drink again, sipped, then set down the empty container. Not a word was spoken in the room as Kazsh-ak took a moment in a silence of his own to gather his composure.

"I looked up at the crowd in the Arena," he said, finally. "'Thus always with Tyrants!' I yelled out. The crowd roared back in joy, realizing that they had become free of the Overlord at last...'"

"Well done, Sir!" Crush roared out in a joy of his own. "But what did you do after that?"

"The first thing I did was to free all the slaves and attempt to return them to their rightful homes. That took weeks, alone. I made sure that their laws prevented slavery forever onwards. Then I picked the most honest of the gamblers and rebels that I could find," said Kazsh-ak. "And lectured them on how to construct a form of government that their people would accept. One that would protect the rights of individuals and yet govern wisely. After all that had been accomplished, I picked a dark, cloudy, moonless night and high-tailed it back to my scoutship just as quickly as I could run. Before the Naatungs had time to remember that I would forever be a total alien to their world and had no right whatsoever to assume any sort of leadership among them."

"Did you ever go back?" I asked.

"No!" the D'rrish replied with some force. "But others did, years later. Their government has changed only a little from the form that I left behind. But freedom for all sapient life still rules their politics. I understand that the gladiator games underwent a swift decline after my escape. But the worst part? They built *statues* of me! A bit more heroic than my natural form, to be sure. But statues? How barbaric!"

Some people never get the hang of becoming heroes, I thought as I joined the crowd in drinking a toast to the D'rish.

One Night At The Mare Inebrium

"Everybody needs to believe in something. I believe I need another drink...."
W.C. Fields, 1940

"That's the trouble with time travel," said the man with blue hair, "you can't do anything without creating a paradox!" Ending the hour-long argument that he'd started, the blue-haired man looked as if he'd be insufferably pleased with himself for at least a month. It would have been fun to have burst his bubble right then. I mean, we get time travelers in here about twice a year. I had something else on my mind though. I really wanted to hear the opinion of the thin, nervous fellow who seemed to positively flinch at every mention of time travel.

We get all kinds at the Mare Inebrium. Being located in a spaceport town, in a high-tech area permitted by a native treaty means that we get a good selection of off-planet visitors. Me? I work in one of the corporate buildings in the inner city. The Mare is convenient to the spaceport so lots of folks like me come here to wait for the ferry out to their flight. You can expect to see anything in the Mare Inebrium.

The D'rrish in the corner snickered through his translator.

"I think that you, sir, are a bloody imbecile!" The large alien spoke in an annoyed tone. He took another sip off of the three-gallon tank of mildly radioactive sludge that served his species as a cocktail. The "straw" held to his mouth by one of his secondary mandibles is actually part of the container. It has a pretty complex valve system at its tip so that it won't come open for anybody but a D'rrish.

His translator snickered again. "I've met time travelers, three... no four of them now. Here on this planet, actually."

"Where?" interrupted the blue-haired man.

"In the Interior, sir. I am a native of this planet and a diplomat for my people. You may believe what I say."

"Native?" said the blue-haired man, "I've met some of the natives around here, humanoid mostly, I'd say."

"I am a sixty-seventh generation colonist, sir." The translator sounded good. It was able to convey the dignity of the giant alien's speech as well as the silky insult that it made of every "sir" spoken to the blue-haired man. It must be a Fender. "My family has been on this planet for over six thousand years, I should think that fact alone is enough to qualify me for native status... sir!"

I had been watching the nervous type since late afternoon when he came in. He seemed to be ill at ease from the start. At first, I thought that he might just be AWOL from work or possibly having a domestic difficulty. Then when the blue-haired man from Qundis-click-nal came in and started the time travel argument with the Shree Kasfar traveling sales... thing, the nervous fellow looked as if he were having a seizure. I've been a people watcher for a long time. I like to think that it makes me a better salesman. This guy that I'd been thinking of as Nervous Rex knew something about time travel, something that he didn't want anyone else to know about. So, while the blue-haired Qundis-click-nal had been arguing time travel with the Shree Kasfar, I kept busy watching Nervous Rex. After the Qundis-click-nal uttered his killing argument about paradoxes Nervous Rex seemed to relax. Then the D'rrish shook him up again with that bombshell about meeting time travelers. I thought that he was about to pass out from shock. He suddenly drained his half-glass of whatever and asked the bartender for a double.

"Where were these time travelers from?" Nervous Rex asked, interrupting the blue-haired man.

"Don't you mean *when* were they from?" someone joked.

"They weren't even all of the same species, let alone the same time or place." said the D'rrish. "I met four different people at different times who happened to be time travelers. If it happens that often then the difficulties can be overcome. It is possible to travel in time."

The D'rrish had set them all a pretty little puzzle, there. Even more than his usual wont, he'd become the center of attention of every being within earshot of his storytelling. Aside from the bartender, no one here tonight but myself had been present on other occasions when time travelers had visited the Mare Inebrium. No one else knew anything about time travel, it was all theory to them. Except the D'rrish, and Nervous Rex too, I'd bet. That is, if the D'rrish weren't just making it all up. I've heard some tall tales in this bar, and not just from guys who have strange shapes either.

Speaking of strange shapes, the D'rrish slowly turned from the bar to face the rest of the patrons. His brownish-gray chitin looked well-polished, and his only garment was a sash of some light blue material worn from shoulder to the opposite hip. I knew that the color and pattern of the sash is supposed to indicate his family, but I didn't know how to read it. I *could* tell from the badges and decorations on the sash that the D'rrish was a full Ambassador as well as a highly decorated soldier in semi-retirement. Still, it was not a sight for the squeamish as he turned to bring us face-to-face with his six-foot high, fifteen foot wide, thirty-foot-long frame. He was by far the biggest scorpion that I have ever seen. The Ambassador addressed us all, his translator raising its volume automatically without even the slightest bit of distortion as it cranked up to PA level. It was definitely good equipment.

"The first time-traveler I met long ago in our own city of Er'da'gasg'dein, far, far to the west. From all reports he appeared to have been a tall, thin humanoid. His travel apparatus eventually became part of a shrine to his memory for many centuries."

"What do you mean? Enshrined to his memory? What happened? Did you eat him?" interrupted the blue-haired Qundis-click-nal.

"No, he had died upon his arrival in our city," said the giant scorpion-like alien. "He succumbed to our natural environment. He died of radiation poisoning. You see, we D'rrish all live in that one city. It is constructed to be as much like our home planet as possible. High temperature, radiation, that sort of thing. Well naturally, when he appeared out of thin air with no protective clothing, he died almost instantly. We gave him a hero's funeral, as befits a foe who could get through our cities defensive screens and actually enter the city. Such a thing has never happened before or since. The Scientists had been set to the task of examining the apparatus that was left with his body. They eventually found it to be the remote control for a powerful transportation system. Before the unit stopped working the scientists determined that the device could move objects in time as well as space. Alas, the machinery that did the moving did not appear to be with us, we had found only a control board, not an entire time machine. Instruments were built to detect and study the various radiations that accompanied the operation of the device. We learned to build duplicates of the controller, studied its operation, and still we remained baffled. Then the devices stopped working. First the

Traveler's equipment, then that which we had built. It was as if someone had finally detected our work and had cut us off from the system. There followed a time of much disappointment. As I said, we built a shrine to honor him and placed the machinery within it. Some five hundred years later it was stolen by clever thieves. Two of the other time travelers, as it so happens. While I did not meet the first one myself, I have been in the Shrine of the Traveler many, many times."

"Did you meet the others then or is this just a fiction-for-pleasure?" the Qundis-click-nal jeered.

"You dare!" boomed the scorpion's translator. "My encounter with the time thieves is not mere history!" he said insultingly. "I was the guard on duty when the controller was stolen!"

"What happened?" I said in order to forestall further interruption.

"Two humanoids appeared out of a hole in the air. We stood in the Shrine itself. I had been assigned as the only guard, an Honor Guard, actually. I had, therefore, only antique ceremonial weapons. The thieves were well equipped, and they seemed to be expecting the hazardous environment. They wore force field projectors that protected their bodies. I could see the yellow glow of the field surrounding them. They weren't expecting me though! I gave them fair warning, raising my stinger, clashing my pincers, that sort of thing. I clicked out a threat that would have made their blood run cold, if only they'd known what I'd said. Then I stood in defense of the Shrine, and we fought. We were all valiant, I suppose, in our own way. We dodged and thrust, parried and feinted, attacked and counterattacked in a blinding rush. They came at me head on, then split ranks and came at me from both sides. The corner of the Shrine that I had backed into served to prevent them from getting behind me. We clashed, sword to claw, back to the wall, for what seemed to be hours. No help came for it happened during the middle of the night and they continually kept me from reaching the alarm. Finally, one of them, a male I think, pulled an energy weapon and while I dodged his rapid fire the other, which appeared to be a female, ransacked the Shrine. I would have been greatly dishonored if the male had not caused the roof to cave in upon me. I wound up being entombed for several days while my people cleared the rubble and presumed me dead. After I had been found during the clearing of the rubble, I spent almost three days in a hospital, which is a long time for my species. Upon release from the hospital, I was acquitted in a court martial and awarded a medal for valor. So, you see, time travel is not impossible."

"But what makes you so sure that these beings had been travelers in time?" asked a Ckeskathorq dressed in an orange pressure suit. He sat with a lisping Narshkapoktuard at a table quite near the D'rrish. Their drinks fumed and spat in front of them, untouched while the old scorpion had spun his story.

"Our scientists had five hundred years in which to study the controller and the other artifacts. Do not imagine that they left much unknown. They had been able to detect the same kind of energy that only the machine could generate. These traces could only exist in regions where time has been displaced or disturbed. So say our best physicists."

"What of the other time traveler?" asked Nervous Rex in the lengthening silence while the D'rrish looked intently at a device strapped to one of his medial limbs like a wristwatch on a human's arm.

"Oh, but there are two travelers left unaccounted for." said the D'rrish mysteriously.

"Yes?" I said, almost sure of at least part of the outcome. "Who are these two time-travelers?"

"One is someone that I met while fighting in the north Urthishfel mountains. We became fast friends and saved each other's lives more than once. But those are other tales for other times. He is a humanoid much like yourselves," said the giant scorpion, his crystalline blue eyes twinkling with affection.

"And the last one?" persisted Nervous Rex in a shaky voice.

"According to this detector," said the scorpion, indicating the device he had been consulting earlier, "the most recent time traveler that I have met is—you! Who are you and where are you from?"

"Call me Ishmael." said Nervous Rex. Then he faded from sight accompanied by an odd wheezing and groaning noise.

I dropped my glass. Max the bartender stood us all a round on the house.

Suffocating heat and steam met Nervous Rex as he rematerialized. His skin began to itch as he broke into a sweat from the stinking, humid furnace that comprised the atmosphere here, wherever it was that he'd transported to. With a start, he jerked his head from side to side as he took in the view of his present surroundings.

"Is that—formic acid I smell?" He spoke aloud, his voice still quivering in fear. "Where am I? How did I get here? This isn't the destination I programed this machine to go!" Idly scratching the skin on his left arm, and then the back of his neck, Nervous Rex focused his quickly-blurring vision on the massive stonework of the room surrounding him. Panting with sudden dehydration, his breath became short gasps of pain. An almost familiar clicking, skittering noise filled his ears. A coughing fit wracked his slight frame. He saw blood on his hand as he pulled it away from his mouth. His vision became reddened, the focus of his eyes and mind becoming harder to maintain, and every breath felt as if red-hot knives were being driven into his lungs. The noise in his ears reached a clattering peak, then ended at the sound of several sharp, snapping pops. His knees buckled and Rex felt himself crash to the hot stone floor. His vision slowly focused on a huge figure standing before himself. Claws outstretched as if to snap off his now throbbing, pounding, aching head. Nervous Rex recognized the shape of the creature confronting him. Shouting aloud with his dying breaths, Nervous Rex cried in pain.

"A D'rrish! I'm in the D'rrish city! *I'm* their Holy Traveler! A time loop! Trapped in a tim—"

Then Nervous Rex died from the heat and radiation, his life's blood streaming from his ears and nostrils, coughing bloody gobbets of spray as his breath slowly ceased.

The D'rrish of Er'da'gasg'dein, without understanding what had happened or how this creature entered their city, built a shrine in the Traveler's honor.

"The Absent-Minded Shall Inherit..."

"Now, where was I, before I was so rudely interrupted?"
Victor W. Frankenstein, 1878

I always listened to the tall tales in the Mare Inebrium. I may not have believed them all, but I did listen. Some folks seemed to have a better stock of stories than others. The old D'rrish Ambassador for one, the Reever for another. Ah, the Reever, immortal and ageless. You've heard of him? He's the Chief Judiciary of the Immortals, the original natives of Bethdish. His job is something like being a policeman, prosecutor, defense attorney, judge, jury, and if necessary, executioner. I've heard him say that he's over thirteen million years old. You could learn an awful lot of Bethdish's history by listening to him. But he doesn't come all that often. At least not often enough. The D'rrish, now he's in almost every time I've been here.

I remember one night when the weather was threatening one of those short summer squalls that Bethdish is noted for. I had just gotten in off of a transport from a buying trip. It felt good to be back in City of Lights. Even back then I was beginning to think of Bethdish as home. When I got to the Mare Inebrium for a drink or three to celebrate being home again, I found Max the bartender deep in nervous conversation with the old D'rrish, Kazsh-ak Tier. Since I'm a nosy type I went over and butted in, besides I like Kazsh-ak's stories. Kazsh-ak's antenna drooped and fitfully twitched in obvious worry. Max looked as if someone had kicked him in the stomach. They were both looking forlornly at a strange little box that lay on the bar between them. It seemed to be rough-cut plastic about four inches square and an inch thick with a single control button protruding. I could see nicks and scratches on its surface, as if it had been carelessly handled.

"What should we do with it?" asked Max in hushed voice.

"How should I know?" rumbled the D'rrish. "I'm no scientist. Besides, I'm too frightened to think straight at the moment."

Right away I got worried. I mean, anything that could scare that giant scorpion had to be plenty dangerous.

"What's going on?" I asked, carefully keeping my voice quiet. "What's this box and whose is it?"

"What it is..." started Max.

"I hardly know where to begin," added Kazsh-ak Tier. Just as it's hard to imagine him frightened, it's even harder to imagine him at a loss for words. I began to wish I was still back on the ship, far far away.

"We don't know for sure what it is," Max said reluctantly. "That fellow Camfortt brought it in and forgot it when he left."

"Have you ever met Camfortt?" asked Kazsh-ak. When I shook my head "no" the D'rrish continued. "He seldom comes in; I am not surprised you have not met. He is an inventor of sorts. Rather less disciplined than most. Actually, he's rather sloppy for such an intelligent being. I fail to understand why he has not accidentally blown his laboratory high-sky."

"Sky-high you mean," said Max, "I think that language chip in your translator has vibrated loose again. Better have it looked at before you go to another diplomatic meeting. You say the wrong thing then and there'll be hell to pay."

"Lords yes, all that paperwork. I will see to it as soon as I go back to the Embassy. But we digress. Camfortt has worked quite a bit for the military, as well as half a dozen corporations. He usually has several contracts to fulfill at the same time. He always brings his projects in under budget, but I wonder if that isn't because he simply can't remember for which job any particular funds were allocated."

"But he came in today?" I asked, more to prod the D'rrish into getting to the point than anything.

"Yeah," said Max. "Brought that with him, too," indicating the harmless-looking box on the bar.

"He had finished it, you see." said Kazsh-ak, "and wanted a few drinks before he delivered it to the client."

"And promptly forgot it when he left. I see," I said.

"No, it's worse than that!" interrupted Max, "He forgot what it was before he finished building it!"

"What, how can he finish it if he didn't know what it is anymore?" I started getting really worried now.

"To make matters worse," rumbled the D'rrish, "He was working on several projects simultaneously. By the time he had cobbled this box up, he had gotten hopelessly confused as to what it did, who paid for it, and where to deliver it. He came in here to try and remember all that."

"What happened then?"

"We talked to him for an hour or two, he had too many drinks and seemed on the verge of collapse."

"Yeah," said Max. "I had Trixie set up a room upstairs for him to sleep it off and everything, then BAM! Up he jumps and runs out the door. A couple of the local Cops came in here off duty and I got them to start looking for him, but I don't know..."

"What were you doing when he ran out?"

"Still talking about the box. Trying to figure out what it's supposed to do."

"We had begun listing the projects he had been hired to complete," said Kazsh-ak Tier. "Fascinating really, such genius from such an undisciplined mind." The D'rrish waved his eye stalks gently from side to side sadly.

"Well," I said. "What were they? Maybe we can figure out what the box is from the list."

"There were several," began the D'rrish.

"One was for a terraforming company," added Max. "It's something to precipitate all of the moisture out of a planet's atmosphere at once. Evidently, they had bought a planet where it is always raining and wanted to dry it up."

"Another sounded like a project for someone's military," said Kazsh-ak. "It was a stellar detonator, something to cause an enemy's sun to spontaneously explode."

"That's sick!" I exclaimed. "Nothing but genocide! What government could be trusted with a thing like that?"

"There is more," said Kazsh-ak. "Camfortt mentioned several weapons on his list of commissions as well as several devices that would make life easier on colony worlds. Food replicators, micro fusion welders, an impenetrable force field..."

"Don't forget the Telepathic Telegraph!" added Max.

"And he still couldn't remember?" I asked.

"Maybe he did," said Max. "He got kind of quiet, and I had to make a round of drinks for some Thixar businessman. I had my back to him, and he shouted something, jumped off of his bar stool and ran out the door waving his arms around and cursing. I didn't think much of it 'till I got back here and saw Kazsh-ak staring at the box."

"We have no way to tell what he remembered," sighed the D'rrish. "The list ran on far too long and he sat too long in silence before running out."

I sat and looked at the button on the box, unable to think of anything else to say. There were too many possibilities, too many chances to guess wrong. Finally I sighed with frustration.

"It could be anything," I said. "Anything at all. Maybe you should put it into the Lost-and-Found under the bar before someone thinks it's the remote control for the Video."

"Yeah," said Max. "I'd hate to have someone blow up the sun, trying to get a sports score."

"He'll come back for it," I said. "After all, he can't just forget..." My voice trailed off into silence as I realized that *that* was exactly what had happened in the first place. I stared at the innocent looking little box and shuddered.

"He *has* to come back," said Max plaintively. "He just *has to!*"

"If he hasn't already forgotten being here today," said Kazsh-ak Tier sadly.

Sins of the Fathers

"Moldy bread? What am I supposed to do with that mess?"
Sir Alexander Fleming, 1928

T*rixie is in a playful mood,* I thought. I'd naturally kept an eye on her since I'd come in. With looks like hers she could pass for an artist's model for one of those Renaissance painters. Max the bartender is her boyfriend, the lucky stiff, and he was the one Trixie was playing with this afternoon. She had been needling him, in a flirty way, for the last half hour—that I'd noticed, anyway. In between orders she'd pick at Max, both of them fighting giggles, and they'd try to think up toppers every time Trixie had to sashay off to deliver an order to one of the tables.

I'd gotten in off of a flight only two hours ago. I made my way straight to the Mare, even though it was the local equivalent of three AM, I knew it'd be open. For the first time I noticed, over the main door, a sign which read "Abandon Sobriety—Ye Who Enter Here"—strange I hadn't seen it before. As I made my way to the bar, I noticed a few of the semi-regulars, the Kanank-eduin fertilizer salesman I'd met a few times—Talla-quin-tuin is his name, the Halazed Ambassador Hnarcor Finivalda—that lizard seemed to have a snoot-full already, and one odd fellow I'd seen twice before. He was sitting—or rather, parked—near the left end of the main bar. I say he was odd even for the Mare because he looked like nothing more than an aquarium in a wheelchair. An aquarium filled with differently colored layers of water—well, liquid anyway—with a bright blue gelid mass floating in the center of the aquarium. The wheelchair was about a meter and a half high and had several mechanical limbs as well as wheels. I assumed he was a customer because I saw Max put a drink in front of him as I sat down. Besides them, I didn't see anyone I recognized right away. There was a trio of small, feathered fellows at a table near the center of the room. One was wearing a sailor's cap and seemed to have a speech impediment, one had a smoldering cigar jammed into the corner of his beak, and the other had darker feathers and seemed to be the practical joker of the group. They were playing a card game of some kind. Just the usual crowd for a late night. There must have been somewhere close to a hundred customers there in the main bar.

Personally, I was hoping Kazsh-ak Teir would be in, but Max had told me he was back home in the D'rrish city attending the christening of his newest grandchildren. It seems several months ago his third-oldest daughter had fallen in love with a human, gotten a small tissue sample from him, then gone home to find a suitable D'rrish male to gene-splice the human's DNA with—in order to give birth to a double-dozen little D'rrishes. When a D'rrish female falls in love, she has to mate, and soon, or suffer some drastic biological trauma. I never knew how or why the DNA of an alien was important—I guess that they were mentally evolved enough to see all intelligent life as people, no matter what the species. How a giant scorpion's genes can be spliced with an Earth-human's is an exercise I'd best leave to the philosophers and scientists. Me? I'm just a traveling salesman. I was just about to ask Max for another drink when Trixie waltzed up and started in on him again.

"How many ex-wives is it you're supporting now, Max?"

"Fewer than I've got the right to, but more than most folks could afford."

"On your salary? You forget that I know what you make."

"Yes, and I remember how beautifully you make it too," he said with a grin.

"Flatterer..." she smiled. "Don't change the subject. I want to know how you manage to support—What is it? Sixteen? Seventeen ex-wives... ex-*somethings* anyway, and still manage to afford to tomcat about the place like a lord?"

"I owe it all to clean living," he grinned. "Of course, it helps that I left some of them widows—with a trust fund set aside." He paused, mixed a cocktail, and handed it to her with a slight bow. "That and the fact half of the rest are still being supported by their husbands. Your order, Mrs. McGuffin."

"Cad, womanizer, you beast—Thank you. Argyle Twist with zimafruit, and two sparkers for table twenty-two, on the money. Back soon—Kiss-kiss, you homewrecker."

"You two having fun?" I asked Max while Trixie was gone.

"She's in a mood," he sighed. "It's fun, though. I like her like this, she shows her best. Class, clean through. She's giving it to me like some Grand Duchess at high tea. You've noticed, I see."

I nodded.

"Cute, isn't it?"

"Terribly. Cheers..." I said as I swirled the ice in my empty glass.

"Another?"

"Sure, I've got nothing but time. Nowhere to be 'til tomorrow night."

"Meeting? Or another flight out?"

"Meeting, more's the pity. A flight out'd be less of a circus, fewer carnivorous beasts anyway."

"All of them sharpening their claws and waiting for you to trip, eh?"

Trixie flounced back with an order for table seventeen and another for booth nine. Max got busy with the orders. I thought then that there would be nothing any more remarkable than the wiggle in Trixie's walk to think about that night. I couldn't have been more wrong.

I was halfway through my fifth drink and thinking I would soon need to take a sobriety pill and head for home when I happened to glance over to my right at the hallway that leads to Max's little office. I sat as if nailed to my bar stool—as I watched a section of the wall turn dark blue and shape itself into a door. The door opened and the Reever came through it. The Reever—nearly two meters tall and sudden death on two legs. The highest-ranking cop on the planet, Ambassador of the Immortals of Bethdish, and able to leap tall buildings in a single bound—for all I know. What's more, he looked angry. Funny, I thought. I never knew he could walk through walls. I tried to look casual, but that's kind of hard to do with your mouth hanging open. Trixie looked at me and giggled, then looked where I was looking, saw the Reever and gave a little gasp. The door closed by itself and faded back into the normal silvery-beige color of the rest of the walls as if nothing odd had happened.

The Reever strode to the bar—looking almost normal in some kind of dress uniform of silvery-gray cloth, knee-high boots, and a cape of darker gray material. I could see a massive handgun strapped to his right thigh, while the hilt of a short sword peeked out from behind his back... underneath his cape and hanging hilt-downward. He moved as if he were a well-oiled machine—like a predatory animal measuring his territory—stood at the bar and in a quiet, gravelly voice, ordered a tall glass of the oldest Krupnick on the shelves. Max solemnly turned around and picked up a dusty bottle, wiped it off, and poured at least five ounces of amber liquid into a seven-ounce glass—adding three ice cubes as he turned back around.

"From the owner's private stock," said Max. "Laid down seven thousand years ago, on Earth... if you can believe the label." When he handed it to the Reever the drink steamed as if the ice had been kept at a temperature somewhere *damned* close to absolute zero. I watched the Reever drink at least half of it as the glass frosted over in his hand.

"Trouble?" Max asked casually—too casually. I gave up on any idea of going home until I could find out more. I knew I'd just watched the Reever drink more liquor in a single gulp than I'd witnessed him put away in the last eight times I'd seen him here. Something was up—something bad. Momentarily I wondered if I ought to phone my broker and have him sell all the stock in my portfolio... Then I decided that if the world was about to end, having extra money on hand wouldn't save my butt anyway.

"Funeral," said the Reever as he put his glass down.

"Another one?" asked Max as if he were shocked. "Who? How?"

"Karelentor," replied the Reever. "Murdered. Sliced up like a lab rat. One of my staff officers was called when a body was found. Gene-typing gave us the identity."

"That's the third one in the last two years," said Max as if in shock.

"Fifth," corrected the Reever. "I've kept the others quiet so as not to spook the killer. I want that bastard so bad I can taste it. I'm going to bring him in—no matter how long it takes."

"No doubt. Anything I can do to help?" asked Max.

"No, but I was told to ask if you'd be a pallbearer for the poor sod. He mentioned you in his will—requested you by name."

"I'd be honored," replied Max. "Old Karel was one of my teachers at the Academy. But remember, anything I can do to help catch this creep, just let me know."

"Thanks. I'm sorry to come in from out of nowhere like this but I was just consulting the Mare's owner about the killings, and he let me take a short-cut from his place to get here."

"The owner?" I gasped. *No one* had ever met the Mare Inebrium's owner, not that *I* ever heard about, anyway. Until tonight...

"Mr. Polios," said the Reever while eying me as if I had just crawled out from under a particularly filthy rock.

"Reever, meet Andrew Huntington-Smythe of Antares Four, one of our regulars. He's OK," said Max generously. "Andrew's been coming here for years. He won't talk out of turn. Matter of fact, he helped me out once when some dim-witted inventor left one of his toys behind."

"Thanks for the vote of confidence, Max," I said. At least my reputation was good for *something.*

"Polios?" said Max to the Reever, who was still looking at me like I was some type of lower life form. OK, maybe to someone divinely created by a pantheon of living Gods, I *am* a lower life form, but it's still rude to point it out. "That's a new one. Sounds like he's been reading ancient Greek plays again."

"It means 'gray'," said Trixie. "At least in Greek it does."

"Makes sense, Gray he is. She majored in old Earth languages," Max said in reply to the Reever's raised eyebrow.

"She's very quick," said the Reever.

"Not when it counts," said Max as he smiled at her. "Your order, Mrs. Grundy." She smiled back, stuck out her tongue at him, and carried off another tray of drinks.

"Flatterer," she said over her shoulder as she left.

"She knows, then?" asked the Reever.

"Yes, but she thinks it's 'cute' and doesn't make a fuss when duty calls me."

"Good woman," replied the Reever as the three of us watched her walk away. "Better nail her down while you still can."

"As often as possible," quipped Max. "I still have carpet burns from the last time—But she prefers handcuffs to nails."

The Reever just raised his eyes to the heavens as if to ask for deliverance.

I decided not to ask about the phantom door—seeing as how I had just missed being asked to mind my own business the last time I piped up. I wanted to know more about what was going on and being told to keep my nose out of it or get said organ stuffed full of lint wouldn't enlighten me at all.

"Any clues to the killer?" I asked instead once I could tear my eyes away from the back of Trixie's skirt.

"A few, but none quite good enough to locate him... If it is a 'him'," said the Reever.

"You think it could be the Black Snake, don't you?" said Max.

"I know she's *capable* of such a thing," said the Reever. "But I don't see how she could benefit from the killings so far. None of the victims have been anyone of importance. None of them have had anything in common—except that they were in City of Lights at the time they were murdered."

That seemed to be a conversation stopper 'cause we all fell silent for several moments. Until Trixie came back and set us straight, matter of fact. She strode up, looked at our long faces, and burst out laughing.

"You three look like the three monkeys—See no evil, hear no evil, have no fun," she said. "If you can't think of the solution to your problem, think of something else. That's what Blanche always says. 'Maybe the solution will come at you sideways while you're not looking for it. Then all you gotta do is reach out and grab it.' It works for me."

"Right now, I'll try anything," said the Reever. "I'll catch this killer, no matter how long it takes!"

Right about then my well-oiled mind finally percolated out an important observation I'd overlooked. "Wait a minute," I said. "If Max has to go to an Immortal's funeral—one of his former teachers, no less... then Max almost has to be—"

"An Immortal himself?" Max asked quietly. "Welcome to a wider universe, my friend. Yeah, I'm an Immortal—but I don't advertise it. I've spent the last couple of hundred years behind this bar, doing a job. I expect I'll still be here when the city is a crumbling ruin, and that's not going to be anytime soon."

"Too weird," I sighed. "OK, mum's the word from me. But you said Trixie knew and wasn't jealous. What's that about? Certainly not bartending. You mean you really have seventeen ex-wives? Being an Immortal, you'd have time for it, but..."

"Max left his other job unspoken," said the Reever. "A very important job, and one not connected to the bar. You've stumbled into a secret, but no one would ever believe you if you told it. Max trusts you—*that*, I can see. Trixie seems to like you as well. That speaks highly of you, for children like her often have the truer instincts."

The Reever paused in thought and my mind percolated out another fact for me to reflect upon; *this* guy's age was measured in the millions of years. If he thought of Trixie at age twenty-seven as a child, didn't he have the right to think of all of us that way?

"You see," the Reever continued as if he'd made up his mind on something. "Max is our emissary to humanity."

"You mean he's a diplomat?"

"No, more like an undercover agent—" Max began to grin as the Reever spoke. "A medical agent at that. The High Council of the Immortals decided long ago the natives on Bethdish were suffering from a debilitating disease. We had a possible cure for it millions of years ago, but how to administer it morally? Max is the result of the debate over those morals. He is to bring a slow, sure cure for the disease—as naturally as possible. He's been at it for over one and a half million years—I expect it will take a million or so more. With the discovery of Bethdish by Earth-humans and the staggering knowledge the Terrans were nearly genetic twins of the natives of Bethdish—Max's duties were expanded to include Terrans in the cure."

"But that's impossible! Evolution doesn't work that way—there's no way the natives of any two different planets in the universe can be identical! Not even if they were in the same solar system. Look around you, the folks here at the Mare are the best argument for genetic diversity among life forms I've ever seen." Without rising from my seat, I could see the wild variety of sentient lifeforms from a hundred and seventy planets—no two alike. I wondered for a moment how the Mare could handle the requirements of so many, but the Reever continued with his explanation, and I lost track of that thought.

"Exactly, but yet they are almost identical, nonetheless. A staggering discovery, one that demanded explanation. We Immortals came to the conclusion that the beings that created Bethdish must have visited Earth beforehand. Or came from there."

"*Created* Bethdish?"

"Well, perhaps they chose a planet at random and created all the life upon it. They've never said. Sort of 'forced evolution' rather than letting nature take its course."

"You're talking about your Gods here, aren't you?"

"Yes."

"But how could your Gods have come from Earth? I don't understand."

"Perhaps they only visited there. They will not say. Obviously, there has to be a connection—otherwise the similarities could not exist."

My mind seemed to be getting more than its fair share of boggle factor tonight. I paused in thought, trying to get back to the other thread of conversation. Finally, I remembered. "And the disease? You've been very careful not to name it. It must be something terrible—"

"Something terrible indeed," the Reever paused, looking sad. "The disease is old age."

I damn near choked on my drink as I tried not to spit it out all over the bar. "What?" I sputtered finally. Showed off my fearsome intellect, too.

"Roughly two million years ago... Max was genetically engineered to breed added longevity into the human race—races, as it turns out," said the Reever carefully—as if waiting to see how I'd take the news.

"He's soooo good at it, too." sighed Trixie contentedly as she eased onto a bar stool at my side. This finally sank in—I was stunned into silence. I groped in my pocket for my Inter-Banque card, waved it in front of Max for a moment, and finally managed to speak.

"Bartender," I gasped. "I'd like a double of the oldest, most genuine Irish Whiskey my credit balance can purchase."

"Certainly, sir," said Max. "Would you like a chaser to go with that?"

After gulping at least half of my drink in one swallow, I managed to sputter out something lame about it being nice work if you can get it and proceeded to take three swallows to empty my glass. As I asked for a refill, I noticed I was suddenly cold sober. After a soothing sip on my fresh drink, I asked Max, "Are you going to explain this?"

"My job?"

"Yes, all of it. Including the *why*, if you don't mind."

"Alright. Before I was born, the Immortals saw the natives were evolving to resemble themselves—but lived only a few hundred years at most. After much debate, it was decided to implement a slow, genetic solution to giving the mortals longer lifespans. I was conceived in a lab, my genes tampered with in order to be able to breed with the non-immortal natives of Bethdish and pass on the particular gene-sequence that confers longer lives to my... descendants. It's a slow process, they won't notice anything for another half a million years. By then, the gene will be widespread enough and the humans stable enough for lifespans of thousands of years to be possible. Eventually, the High Council believes the human lifespan will peak at a million years or so—before the final, quick onset of old age and death. The carefully-spliced genes I carry confer greater disease resistance, greater cellular repair ability, and better health in general—as well as longevity. My mission is to improve the human species and give them time they need to make the most of their abilities. There is nothing they cannot do, if we can give them enough time." Max shrugged, "Like you said—'Nice work if you can get it...' Well, I got it."

"And how!" sighed Trixie. "You've got it good, Babe! And I just love the way it looks on you. Manterene fizz and two Benarchaes on dry ice for table twelve."

"Trixie," I gasped. "You approve of all this?"

"What's to gripe about? My children, when I choose to have them with Max, will live longer lives. Their children may live even longer. Max is a gentleman; he treats me the way I want to be treated..."

"And when you are dust in your grave, he'll still be out 'tom-cattin', as you called it. And you're Okay with that?" Then, looking at the Reever I said something like "And your government thinks of this as a moral behavior? Genetic tampering? What happens when Bethdish or Earth produces a dictator who lives forever? What kind of damage will *he* do?"

"That's one of the reasons why the Council decided to use this slowest method." Max said gently. "To give humans time to evolve socially before the added lifespans become apparent and affect their thinking. Hundreds of generations will come and go before any impact is felt. At first the change will only affect a few—they will live an extra century or so in good health. They will be able to add to human knowledge, but slowly. Gradually, the genes will diffuse into the entire species. The High Council has considered the problem very carefully and decided this method does the least harm."

"The ends justify the means? Is that what you're saying?"

"Not at all, but the benefits outweigh the dangers."

"Yeah, right. But I still see the dictator-eternal looming on the horizon. What are you going to do about that?"

"The Reever will be there," said Trixie. "He'll sort things out."

"'Protect the innocent', that's my job," said the Reever firmly. "Now and forever..."

"Max always sees the children and his—wives—are cared for as long as they live," said Trixie. "There's no danger or hardship in store for them. I trust Max. He's a family man—at the core."

"Mrs. Peel, you are needed," said Max as he noticed a plumed Maldoerian waving its empty tankard in the air. Kind of hard to miss seeing a Maldoerian anyway, since they're usually two and a half meters tall and bright orange. This one had its cranial plumes dyed a delicate shade of blue at the tips—and not one of those cheap dye jobs either. I guessed it was a debutante. It was sitting with a pair of Candulax in one of the booths nearby. Must be a mated pair, the Candulax, I mean. You almost never see a lone Candulax—they're uncomfortable if they don't have mates nearby.

"Thanks, playboy. Back soon," Trixie cooed as she glided off to take the Maldoerian's order.

"What's with the names, Max?" I asked. "I thought Trixie's last name was—"

"Oh, just part of the game," Max replied quickly. "When she first found out about my—assignment, she started using different names for me while we were—uh, well..."

"In the heat of passion?" Said the Reever, grinning at Max's discomfort.

"Right. Well, it just sort of grew from there. I figure if she likes it, what's the big deal? I can take a lot of kidding—especially if it makes her happy. So, I started doing the same sort of thing in return."

"Another Dendril and soda for the big bird," sighed Trixie as she returned. "Have you seen Bert tonight? I think he could pick up a fare from that table. Someone is going to have to drive that Maldoerian home soon anyway. I bet the poor dear is going to pass out before too much longer."

About that time, I noticed that Max was getting the eye from some pretty girls—Terrans, from the look of them—sitting near the center of the front row of tables. I muttered something about "animal magnetism" and finished my drink. Max grinned and offered me another.

"No thanks," I said. "I've still got that meeting to go to tomorrow. I'd better shove off. Duty calls." I nodded to the Reever, "Good luck catching your killer." Somehow, I got unsteadily to my feet and headed towards the door. Just as I reached the doorway, I looked back at the bar. One of the Terran girls had gone up and taken the seat I'd just left. She seemed to be chatting Max up. I caught Trixie's eye as she made her rounds. She grinned at me, nodded towards Max and the girl, and shook her head humorously. That Trixie is one hell of a woman.

"Duty calls," I laughed to myself as I opened the door. *Nice work, if you can get it*, I thought as I stepped out into the morning light.

Brother, Can You Spare A Crime?

A Mystery in One Unnatural Act

"Once you have eliminated the impossible, whatever remains is bound to be bloody dull..."
Arthur Conan Doyle, 1892

I'd been going to the Mare Inebrium since the day it had—I suppose "appeared" is the best way of putting it—appeared in City of Lights. I'd seldom gone there on business, however—strictly for social reasons. As the Immortal's ambassador I found it to be useful to meet with other species' representatives away from the embassies. After all, most diplomatic work is really accomplished at cocktail parties. The business I was referring to is my other job; Chief Justicar—The Reever of the Immortals.

I was in my office in City of Lights—clearing away some paperwork—when I got the call to come to the Mare. Actually, there were two calls. My switchboard program flashed up a notice of an incoming call, one that could not be traced. "Someone is being killed at my bar," said a voice I recognized as the Mare's owner. Then he disconnected. Two seconds later another notice appeared—a call from Max at the Mare Inebrium. "You better come quickly; we've got a corpse in the main room. Everything has been sealed, no one has left, and the security systems are on full alert. I've got to call the boss..."

"He already knows," I said. "He just called me himself. I'll be there in a minute or so. Any suspects?"

"No," replied Max in a shaky voice. "This guy just wandered in and fell over dead. It just so happened that we had a roomful of doctors upstairs in one of the side bars. One of them examined the guy, but it was obvious that he was already dead."

"Oh, what's so obvious about it?"

"Well, the knife sticking out of his back seemed a bit of a giveaway," sighed Max.

"I suppose so..." I chuckled grimly. "Which doctor was it?"

"You may remember him. Clark ...something. His friends call him Doc..."

"Really big guy, heavily tanned, short hair, surgeon and inventor... One of his companies was in charge of the construction of the Mare Tower?"

"That's the one," Max replied. "He's got offices up on the eighty-sixth floor—One of the boss' special friends."

"I hope he'll stay out of the investigation. As I recall, he has quite a reputation back on Earth, but he may be out of his league here. Then again, I may need his help. There's never been an outright 'murder' at the Mare—that I know of..."

"That's right," said Max nervously. *Tarja did have a permit, didn't she?* "A few fights, sure. The odd accidental death. Some brawls in the Red Dog, those space ranger-types love a good dust-up. Some contract killers drop in, but they know the rules—'no commissions to be executed inside the Mare Tower without a special permit, signed by you, personally.' They'd rather face Kazsh-ak in unarmed combat than flaunt that, especially after what you did to that Zerxceries hit-man when he broke the same rule at the Cornavarad embassy. Cousin, that was unfair."

"Yes," I grinned. "Seventeen point six two seconds. The old D'rrish cleaned you out for a bundle on that. It's your own fault. 'A minute and six tenths' you said. You knew he wouldn't last a full minute against me, yet you still bet high. You didn't even make the spread."

"That'll teach me. Anyway, no contract killings ever happen here without permission. And the Field of Honor..." began Max.

"'Is not legally within the confines of the Mare or its environs.' Yes," I interrupted. "I know. Polios and I worked out special rules for dueling that apply to that side bar alone. I'll just assume that all the rules are being adhered to... Until I find out otherwise. Very well. Keep everyone calm, don't let anyone else touch the body, and I'll have a squad there in seven minutes. I'll be there sooner."

"Right. Can do, have done, and we'll be waiting," Max said and then disconnected.

Well, no need to hang about. At least I'm in City of Lights—here I'm free to use Immortal's technology. One of the few places on the planet that I don't have to operate within restrictions, City of Lights is a relief for an Immortal. Not as advanced as our city inside Fort Mountain, but still plenty civilized. I picked up my staff of office and spoke to the computer built within it. "Arrange transport to the Mare Inebrium... maximum priority, minimum time. I'll also need a squad of officers, a homicide unit, and notify the coroner's office that there's a body for pickup."

"Messages sent... Transport ready," it replied, dilated a portal, and I walked through nothingness to emerge outside the Mare. Immortal transport systems are a blessing. Three steps through the portal and I appeared at my destination. Even if I'd been traveling halfway around the world, three steps would be all I'd have to take. I wished, not for the first time, that I wasn't so hobbled by the High Counsel's rulings.

"You're here," said Max in a relieved tone of voice. "Good, we've um... We've had another one."

"What?"

"Clark says that this one got shot in the back," sighed Max. "But the weird thing is that it's the same guy."

I looked at the two bodies, side by side on the polished hardwood floor. Max was right, they looked alike enough to be twins. Plus, they were wearing identical clothing. Something screwy seemed to be happening. At the sound of the lobby doors opening, I looked up. A humanoid walked in, rather stiff-legged. He wobbled his way up to the bodies, said "I'm so very sorry," and fell across the other two. Dead as a doornail—I could tell from the way he flopped down - limply. The sun-bronzed doctor rolled him over and checked for a pulse, then shrugged. He sniffed the air above the freshest corpse once and looked at me.

"Cyanotic acid," said Clark quietly. "*This* man has been poisoned."

I looked at the corpse. It looked to be the same man. The door opened again and two of my detectives strode in followed by the squad of uniformed officers. "What the hell?" the older detective said.

"Larrye," Max called out to one of his assistant bartenders. "Clean-up on aisle five!"

By the time my Peaceforcers had gotten all the Mare's customers off to the side and begun taking statements we had five bodies on the floor. All were the same being, as far as we could tell. My detectives had checked the IDs and run sub-molecular scans on them all. One Rupert P. Coltrane, late of Chicago, USA, Earth, 1935 AD, had expired five times, from five different weapons, on the floorboards of the Mare Inebrium. Perpetrator? Person or persons unknown, as yet. I'd stationed an officer outside to see where the victims were coming from after the fourth one had entered, but the fifth one had gotten by my man somehow. It seemed as if they came out of thin air. I noticed a low, trilling noise that seemed to fill the room, everywhere, and nowhere all at once. I looked over at Clark. The short reddish-gold hair on the back of his neck standing up as he frowned over the growing pile of bodies. A sixth corpse had just added himself to the heap.

"A quite singular occurrence," he said. "Some unknown phenomenon is playing with the laws of probability. This isn't usually possible, therefore something abnormal must be happening."

Number seven made it all the way to the bar. He asked a shocked Larrye for an Helcorin Fizz-water, then he fell over with a knife sticking out of his back. Larrye shivered, shrugged, and placed the drink on the bar where the victim had stood. Then his eyes rolled back in his head, and he slid to the floor in a faint. One of the waitresses, Blanche, caught him before he could crack his head on the floor.

"Glad to be of service..." Larrye mumbled from the safety of Blanche's strong embrace. "That'll be two credits, please..."

Max was making his way toward the comm-unit when number eight walked in. Trixie eyed the soon-to-be-dead man for a moment, then I caught her looking towards the ceiling, thoughtfully. Before Max could get to the comm, it chimed, signaling an internal call from one of the Mare's side bars. Blanche answered it. She listened for a moment, looked at Max, asked for a repeat of the message, and then shrugged.

"It's from the Pantheon Room," I saw her whisper to Max. I can read lips in more languages than I can count. It's a useful skill. "Elvis says that Thor and Zeus just busted a tabletop—arm-wrestling again, Isis is doing a table-dance for a bunch of Picts, and could you approve a tab for a guy named Hammett?" Max groaned and took the call. This was getting too strange. My detectives had been reduced to making tic-marks on a notepad, there were now eleven dead bodies on the floor, and the Mare's patrons looked as confused as I was rapidly becoming. They weren't going to be able to give us any information. It was time to appeal to a somewhat higher authority. I instructed my staff of office to place a call to the Mare's owner.

"What," I asked Polios when he answered, "in the seven hells is going on here? I've got a freighter-full of dead clones bleeding all over your imported teak floor, Larrye fainting from fright, my detectives reporting that the Mare's own security AIs are claiming that nothing is wrong and that we should all remain calm and have another drink... and an insurance adjuster that I'm about to shoot, myself. He's giggling about an 'act of god' and how his company won't have to pay off on your policy. I want all the security recordings of the front door, the street outside, the lobby, and the bar's main doors, stat! What are you trying to pull here? This is not covered in our contracts, you know that. Do you want to lose your license?"

"Young man," replied Polios. I'm over thirteen million years old and Polios is the only person besides my father and grandfather that I'll allow to call me 'young man'. "Young man, this is none of my doing. I simply warned you when it started. As for the security-cam views, they show nothing that you haven't observed with your own eyes."

"Don't give me that," I hissed. "You know very well what's going on here. You've got to! You see everything that happens here. Plus, you have 'special sources' of information that I need. Why are there thirteen copies of this idiot bleeding on your bar's floorboards? Fourteen... Fifteen... I want some action, or I'm going to take this to the Counsel and ask for your deportation! Sixteen..."

"Yes," Polios replied after a long pause. "I could go back and look at what happened at the beginning of all this or take you to visit yourself at the point where you solve it on your own, or even to the point where you finally corner the villain. But what good would it do you? You'll still have to figure this all out for yourself, you know. I'd be doing you no favors to hand it to you on a silver platter. I," he added, "am not allowed—"

"Crap," I snapped, "allowed my ass! You're here on Bethdish for the sole reason that you refused to acknowledge your own government's authority over you. Don't give me any excuses, you're a wanted fugitive on your own planet for 'refusal of compliance' to your government's rules. Don't think I'll let you hide behind those same rules now." I was watching the room as I spoke. The body count now totaled at least twenty and I could see the doors opening again. I noticed Trixie and Max huddled together, whispering. Max glanced up and shot me what could only be described as a 'significant look', then he and Trixie began walking toward me. "All right, Polios," I said in a calmer voice. "You've never refused my requests before. I'll do you the favor of believing that you have a good reason. But I'll want to hear it when this is over, do you hear me?"

"Of course," he replied. "Whenever you wish. What I can tell you right now is that this is a singular event. By that I mean that it is happening on one timeline, and only that one, out of all of the infinite levels of probability that my instruments are able to scan. The Mare is a stable point in all of the probability lines of the multiverse, which means that it is accessible from every possible timeline. Something—or someone— is mucking about with the structure of the Mare itself. That's where your multiple copies of Mr. Coltrane are coming from. I'll answer your other questions later, when you've learned enough for my answers to make sense. By the way, Sarah is asking me to invite you over for tea."

"Tell her that I accept," I said. "I'll come visit when this is over. Remember, you have some explanations to make, old man."

"By the time that this is 'over', young man, you won't need explanations," he replied. "I'll tell Sarah to put the kettle on." He disconnected. By this time the body count had reached twenty-four and number twenty-five was sliding into a booth and signaling for a waitress. Blanche went toward him. Max and Trixie reached me, and Max looked grim.

"Trixie's sussed it," Max said. "We need to go upstairs to the Pantheon."

"Why?" I asked heatedly. "Some deity is yanking our chain? I don't believe it! The security fields in the Pantheon prevent any deity from using their powers anywhere except inside that one room."

"Worse," said Trixie sadly. "It's much worse..."

"Don't you see yet?" Max asked. "There's a writer in the house!"

"Shit," I said eloquently.

We three stood outside of the Pantheon to plot a bit of strategy. Given our situation, perhaps 'plot' wasn't the best choice of words. Still, it felt like plotting.

"How do you want to handle this?" Max asked.

"You can't just go and lock him up," Trixie added.

"It might surprise you both, but I agree," I said. "This has got to be done carefully. This man is extremely dangerous in one sense, but entirely innocent in another. But he cannot be allowed to keep on endangering the people downstairs."

"Yeah," Max said. "I've been hoping he wouldn't write in a slew of gangsters with automatic weapons since Trixie told me what she thinks is going on. All right, Elvis has been clued in. He's given everyone free drinks at the bar. Most everyone except our man has left their tables and are distracted. He's alone, so all we have to do is go over and explain matters to him."

"You hope," I replied as I pushed open the door and walked inside. The Pantheon room is big, I'll grant you that. I suppose that it couldn't seat more than a million people, but that would crowd the dance floor somewhat. I realize that most of it is an illusion—a very good illusion. The rest of it is merely a clever use of multiple semi-permeable, overlapping, hyper-spacial force fields. Just your bog-standard trans-dimensional architecture. Crossing the floor felt like moving in fast-forward. We covered twelve strides for every one we took. Our target looked up at us as we approached. I noticed his gaze lingering on Trixie. A familiar gleam I saw in his eyes told me that he was male, human, and didn't belong in a rest home. *A wolf in cheap clothing,* I thought to myself. *Maybe there's something to work with here.*

"Well," he said humorously. "Does it take all three of you to approve my tab?"

"Oh no, sir, there's no problem with that," Max began, "but there's been some trouble downstairs."

"Oh? I wouldn't know. I've been here all afternoon. I didn't notice anything. Are you from the police?"

"I am," I said. "It's a simple matter that I hope we can clear up shortly." I again noted his approval of Trixie's short skirt. We needed a diversion—something to stop him from working until we could control the effects. As much as I hated to presume on the child, her legs are our best weapon so far. Upon further reflection, I decided that any human male that couldn't be diverted by Trixie had probably already been buried. "Actually—" I began.

"Are you a writer?" Trixie cooed. "I just love creative men."

She saw the situation, sized it up, and grabbed her chance. Capable woman, I thought. I spared a glance at Max and lifted an eyebrow. He gave me the barest of shrugs in reply and then turned his brightest smile on the writer.

"I'm the manager," he said. "I'll just go speak to the bartender about your tab. Then the 'policeman' and I will have to go back downstairs and straighten out our little problem. Would you mind terribly if I asked you to look after my friend here? She's ever so much interested in literary matters."

"Not at all," he said. "I'd be delighted. I really need an office to work in, I'm afraid. I am having the worst time with this chapter I've been working on. I do like this typewriter, though. Never seen one quite like it before." He'd already forgotten that Max and I stood here. I watched as he absently put away an innocent-looking notepad and shut down the laptop—table-top actually, since it was built into the table itself—that he'd been using. Max and I stepped back a few paces and started breathing again. Trixie looked up at us once and waved us away, then tapped the computer with a fingernail too many times for it not to be a message. I turned to Max and started to ask him what she could have meant.

"Office space, he said it himself," Max remarked cryptically. "I'll have to talk to Clark and ask if there's something with extra safeties already built into a room, or even a whole floor. Hammett has been using that table-top communicator pad as a word processor—That's how he managed to create those copies of the unlucky Mr. Coltrane downstairs. The com pad is networked into all of the Mare's computer systems. Hammett accidentally got into the systems that maintain the special variable-environment rooms in the building. He's somehow managed to alter the reality of the main bar, downstairs. But if you or I did the same thing with the same systems, *nothing would happen.* It's a loophole in the Mare's internal security. Something's got to be done about it. Come on. Trixie'll keep him out of trouble while we try to make the Mare safe from rewrites."

"She'll be safe?" I asked.

"She's no safer than the rest of us unless we find him someplace else to write. Look, for now he's hooked. He's not going to get another word written until she lets him get back to work. While she buys us the time, we'll have to find a way to make it safe for him to write."

"And what if he suddenly has an inspiration and wants to jot down a few notes?" Frankly, I found that idea a bit frightening.

"He won't. That's not the kind of idea that's going to occur to him until she turns off the charm. Don't underestimate her, she can charm the pants off of him."

I gave him my best deadpan look. At least he had the grace to blush.

"I should rephrase that," he began.

"Never mind," I said. "You should be used to the taste of your own feet by now. You wanted to talk to Clark about a safe office?"

"Yeah, once that's taken care of you can go to your tea party. No gentleman of your quality would keep Miss Sarah waiting. I heard the end of your conversation with the boss."

"Not until the customers are out of danger," I replied. "Let's just go see what Clark has to say."

"It turned out to be Dashiell Hammett," I said, as Mistress Sarah poured me another cup of the fragrant tea that she enjoyed. I sat at a small table with her and the Mare's owner in their home. "The author of 'The Maltese Falcon' on Earth in their year AD 1929. He had been revising a draft of his next novel. I thought that the Pantheon is restricted to gods and goddesses only."

"World-builders—or destroyers," sighed Polios in return, "Any entity that is creative on a god-like level. Writers are a special case, beyond deities. Far too creative to be controlled. Deities? They will at least restrict themselves to one particular world. But writers? Bah! The Mare attracts them— Damnation! Half of them don't even realize that they've managed to access the Mare from their own world-line. They see their surroundings in terms they're comfortable accepting as real. But usually, the security AIs can prevent them from acting on the quantum level, as Dash did. Hammett is one of the more powerful writers. Much too much so for the safeties. Be glad that it wasn't King, or Harlan. You'd have been out of your league, youngster. Reality would have been twisted completely out of recognition."

"Be that as it may," I said irritably, thinking that my normal reality seems pretty damn twisted to begin with. "The fact remains that you need to expand the security for the Pantheon, and the rest of the Mare. If I hadn't bought off those reporters that had been in the main bar, your secrets would be plastered across the news-nets of a dozen worlds by now."

"What happened to all the dead bodies?" Sarah asked.

"They all faded away when Max and I convinced Hammett to shut off the laptop. Of course, the fact that Trixie wanted to sit in his lap turned out to be the clincher... Hammett snapped that thing off and the Pantheon's systems removed it fast enough to scorch his paper scratch pad when she started batting her eyelashes at him. She is one girl who ought to have to have a license to peddle that stuff," I smiled. "I thought that Max was going to split his head in two, he was grinning so widely."

"He and Trixie are mated for life," said Sarah, "like swans. They have a connection, and a very close one. There's a good reason why Max is in love with her. She's a very smart girl, indeed. She knew the best way to end the parade of corpses was to distract Dash. Max just picked up on what she had in mind of doing before you did. She even beat you to the punch. Don't be mad, no one except his imaginary characters were harmed. From what I understand, the corpses weren't really real to begin with. So, there's no actual *harm* done."

"Only because Max and Clark put their heads together and found him an empty office to type in," I replied. "After Hammett and Trixie went to dinner, I might add."

"Yes," mused Polios. "Triple reality-locks concentricked—I like that word 'concen-tricked.' Perhaps 'nested' is more precise, but 'concen-trick' implies the trickery involved with the engineering. Three reality-locks concentricked inside each other and then inside an uncertainty dampening field, itself inside of a dampened probability field. It's costing me Terrawatts of energy each second that Dash is working. I'd be bankrupt already if the whole suite of rooms weren't located on a different time axis. Days there are equal to mere seconds here. Oh, I thank my lucky stars I decided to major in para-temporal design when I was a young lad at university. Perhaps I should rent out that suite to other writers when Dash is through with it. I could make a tidy little sum off of it."

"You're sweet dear," cooed Sarah as she got up and gave Polios a hug. "Maybe you should use the same arrangement on a few honeymoon cottages, too."

Trixie wasn't the only capable female I have been acquainted with, I observed. I would be willing to bet upon by whom the first cottage would be used. "I should be going," I said.

"So soon?" Sarah sounded disappointed, but I could see her wink at me. "Whatever shall we do now, darling?" she asked Polios.

"Yes," I lied. "Somewhere, there is a crime happening. I must go." As I prompted my staff of office for transport, I had another thought. I interrupted the romance, before it got prurient, long enough to ask if Polios had given thought to designing vacation resorts. I could use a century or two at the beach to relax... It would be even better if I could get back to the office the same day I left. Polios shrugged in reply.

"I'll get back to you," he said, with Sarah in his arms.

I can wait, I thought to myself as I took three steps and re-entered my office. *I've got work to do...*

A Study In Alizarin Crimson

"One likes to think that there is some fantastic limbo for the children of imagination, some strange, impossible place..."
Arthur Conan Doyle

Being a Reprint from the Reminiscences of John H. Watson, M.D., Late of the Army Medical Department

Some notes on the editing of Dr. Watson's manuscript... By Dan L. Hollifield —-Senior Editor, Aphelion Webzine

This document was recovered in the year 2000 AD, from a tin dispatch case left for many decades in a safety deposit box at Claridge's in London, upon Earth. It was opened in accordance with written instructions left by one William Anstruther, identified as the sole living heir to the contents of the box. It is to be noted that Mr. Anstruther was the last known descendant of the famous Dr. John Watson, and that all manuscripts within the dispatch case were, at Dr. Watson's behest, to remain sealed until the year 2000, or until such time as fifty years shall have passed from the date of his, Dr. Watson's death.

In the course of the recovery of this manuscript I have been forced by circumstance to reconstruct the meaning of many of the passages in approximation of the original wording. The good Doctor's manuscript suffered badly by its storage, some pages crumbling to fragments, some sticking together, yet still others easily accessible, so as to provide a true puzzle to assemble. No doubt this is partly due to the cheap nature of the paper in the handbook available to the good Doctor to record this singular occurrence. This being the case, I beg your pardon for any gross inaccuracies for the period contained within the text. Such are the fault of myself and my fellow antiquarians as editors, rather than the fault of Doctor Watson. I cannot promise complete accuracy in the reconstruction, but I will state that it is the best version that can be made of the documentation at hand.

The inclusions of many "Americanisms" in the text have raised doubts upon the authenticity of this document in the minds of several scholars. I can only state in reply that Dr. Watson was known to have lived for several years in the American city of San Francisco, and that it is not impossible for some of the local idiom to have ingrained itself into his vocabulary. As there are no reliable dates to indicate exactly what year this manuscript was written other than "after 1926", I can only assume that this was indeed the year of the document's origin.

As for the fantastical content of the text itself, I can only conclude that the good Doctor was indeed engaging in an effort of speculative fiction, as he himself hints at the end of this narrative. To assume otherwise, we would be forced to accept the existence of such nonsense as life on other worlds, travel through time, voyages to distant stars, and a host of other things unknown, and indeed unknowable, in this first year of the twenty first century AD.

Iain Muir, Jeff Williams, and Mark Cotterill have been invaluable in bringing this work to the light of day. Please join me in thanking them.

A Study In Alizarin Crimson
By John H. Watson, M. D.

"Watson, I believe that several times now in our long association you have remarked upon my lack of knowledge of the science of astronomy."

I was visiting Holmes in our old Baker Street digs—on the occasion of my wife having left me to my own devices, whilst she traveled to visit relatives herself. After making my rounds as required by my small practice and spending the rest of the day at my club, I had stopped by my old apartments hoping that my friend Sherlock Holmes would be in. Mrs. Hudson was pleased to see me, and I spent a few pleasant moments catching up with her before ascending the stairs to my old rooms. The comfortable sitting room looked unchanged from my last visit, save for the pile of newspapers in the corner which had become noticeably higher. The smell and apparatus of some chemical experiment still lingered over most of the deal-topped table, the patriotic V.R. in bullet pocks in the wainscoting of one wall was unchanged, Holmes' unanswered letters still transfixed to the mantle by a jackknife. I looked at Holmes as he sat in his familiar mouse-coloured dressing gown, stuffing shag into the bowl of his long-stemmed briar pipe. Confound it! The man still kept his tobacco in the toe of a Persian slipper! After all these years he was still the most untidy person ever to drive a fellow lodger to distraction. We had spent several hours in pleasant conversation, looking out the windows at the encroaching yellow fog, when Holmes began this particular digression.

"Yes Holmes, you indicated that astronomy was not usually a factor in crime and therefore you felt it best not to burden your memory with unnecessary data. You said that it made no difference to you if the sun moved about the earth or the earth about the sun."

"Indeed, Watson. Yes, that was the gist of my statement. You may be interested to note, therefore, that I have undertaken a study of the subject at the British Museum. As a side-effect of my investigations so far, I have reached several interesting conclusions—and am considering the writing of a trifling monograph on the anomalous surface temperature of the planet Venus. If, that is, I can find no information that invalidates my theory in future researches."

"My word! That's capital, Holmes. But it does lead me to wonder at the reason for your abrupt about-face on the subject. After all these years, I feel that I know you well. You would not have begun such a course of action if it were not related to a case that you have undertaken. Knowledge for knowledge's sake is just not your method. Yet you have immersed yourself so deeply into what you have, 'til now, considered to be a useless field of knowledge. So deeply, in fact, that you have become an expert in some abstruse nuance of the art. Have you succumbed to boredom or are you working upon a case? If it's ennui you've conquered, then may I say that I find this pursuit of knowledge to be infinitely preferable to your previous filthy habits to stave off boredom." It would not be the first time that my married life would keep me from being aware of the beginnings of one of Holmes' cases. Over the years that had passed since we had last shared rooms, I had become used to his calls at odd hours and his entrance to my home or practice in disguise in order to enlist my help in one problem or another. But these occasions were few and far between in these later years. I was even more happy to be in harness once again, as it were.

"Dear Watson—Yes, I shall forever owe you a debt of gratitude for helping me defeat my addictions, despite my reticence in speaking of the matter. But yes, it is a case, one that I have not until today been at liberty to speak of—not even to you, old friend. It is quite a curious matter which has yet to call for direct action—forever your forte, Watson—for as yet there has been no crime with which the suspect can be charged... Save for a few minor offenses—nothing of consequence. But yet I cannot help but feel that there is something more sinister in the offing. I have a few threads, Watson, but I need more facts before I can draw my net closed upon my suspect."

"By Jove! Now, more than ever, I'm glad to have this time to assist you once again. Mary's health has not been the best, of late, and my practice has increased also, so the demands upon my time are quite full. But with my wife away visiting and my neighbor a doctor always willing to fill in for a few days, perhaps I can yet be of some use to you. I take it that now you are able to discuss the matter with me?

"Exactly, Watson. My client requested utter secrecy and until today I was obliged to honour his requests. Though I'd had my suspicions from the very beginning, I could uncover no wrongdoing on my client's part. Today, however... Today I fully began to distrust my client—as well as his motives. I felt in dire need of an ally- who better than my faithful Watson?"

"Thank you, Holmes. I am honored. Tell me more about this untrustworthy client, please."

"Indeed, the case has its interesting points. My client, one Cyrus Jones, telegraphed to me on August the twenty second to state that he was convinced that someone was about to steal several valuable artworks from the Museum. He described witnessing an individual making precise measurements of several of the exhibits—as if to be able to duplicate them. This person then escaped the view of the esteemed Cyrus Jones by going into a small reading room and vanishing into thin air. Mr. Jones entered the room—after half an hour of watching the only door—only to find the room to be empty. The suspect was seen to enter an enclosed room with one door, no windows, only a small table, a lamp, and a single chair for furnishings. The suspect then left the room, unseen by my client. Unless the Museum has hitherto undetected secret passages then the escape is quite impossible."

"Either he never entered the room at all, or he got out by an unknown means, is that what you're saying, Holmes?"

"Exactly, Watson. You've put your finger on the nub of it quickly enough. The problem admits of no other solutions. I, however, looked into the matter myself and observed the same phenomenon. After meeting with Mr. Jones at the museum on the twenty-third, I was able to put the suspect under discreet surveillance which lasted for several weeks.

Frequently, I have observed this person to enter secluded parts of the museum and vanish silently away. Only today, I myself observed the suspect go into that self-same reading room and vanish as if into the woodwork. I am prepared to state that there is no secret passageway out of that room. I am equally prepared to state that the suspect entered said room under my observation and left it by a means that I cannot yet understand. After watching the only doorway into the room from the time the suspect entered it until the time I myself entered, I found the room to be empty. Incredible! I love the challenge."

"My client began to arouse my suspicions when he began asking technical questions about the artworks. Questions that only a novice forger would need to ask, mind you. He was particularly pressing on the matter of one particular colour in one portrait of a landscape. An odd purplish-red that only seems to occur in clouds at sunset. He cast about for some time as to the name of the pigment and where it could be obtained. I, of course, recognized it at once as an oil colour called Alizarin Crimson from some previous studies of paints and pigments, but I said nothing of this to my client. Then too, not only have I not been able to trace his movements before his appearance in Croydon eight months ago, but I have also observed him looking slyly at the security arrangements of the Museum. His perfidy is quite transparent, Watson. Cyrus Jones is not what he seems. If he is not a forger or art thief, I shall be obliged to give up my consulting and at last retire to Sussex and my bee-keeping. So, you can see that I found my client to be less than satisfactory. Indeed, the suspect behaved much more innocently! But! Then, Watson, then we come to today. Today, I also observed my client perform the exact reverse of my suspect's behavior—or rather, to appear out of an area of the Museum that I had already ascertained was empty. There was no way for Cyrus Jones to enter it without my observing him, yet he did. Ergo, both the suspect and my client are not what they appear."

"But what are they? Holmes, you speak as if they aren't human." I must admit that here in the old familiar Baker Street rooms that Holmes' revelations seemed tales of utter lunacy. If it were any other man who said such things, I would be forced to conclude that he was raving.

"That, Watson, is what I wish to find out. I have been observing the suspect for some fifteen weeks. I have been engaged in extensive reading as part of my disguise. And so it is that from within the pursuit of my quarry that I gradually drifted into the study of astronomy. I found much that has helped me in this investigation in my reading on the subject. That reading brought me to consider several puzzles that I used to while away the time on watch. One result of this study is that I have deduced that the planet Venus is not as the popular view would have it; a world of swamps and huge oceans, but a world of scorched deserts, hot as an oven. The matter has to do with that planet's closeness to the sun and the extent of the cloud cover. My theory is that the clouds are too thick to allow the sun's heat to dissipate, therefore Venus should be arid and lifeless. I have checked my conclusions with my brother, Mycroft and he is in full agreement with me. Another result is that whilst reading I have observed the suspect performing what I believe to be delicate measurements of several rare books and artworks. He appears to be preparing to forge copies to leave behind when he attempts to steal the originals. In contrast, it is my *client* who is seeking information useful to a forger. Are they competitors, or are they partners? Each seems to work alone, but are they working toward the same end? In any case, I bided my time, maintained my disguise as a researcher and read as I watched both client and suspect. As a further sidelight of my studies of things cosmological and astronomical, I have found reason to believe that the escapades of my client and the prospective thief can be explained by one bold theory."

"Which is?"

"That they both are not of this world. Aliens, strange visitors from another planet with powers and abilities far beyond those of mortal men. Or at least, possessors of a superior science."

"Ineffable twaddle, Holmes. Life on other worlds? That sounds like the purview of myself and my fellow writers!"

"Not at all, Watson. The available evidence is against you, it seems. I was able to come to the question objectively, since I was ignorant of astronomy and cosmology until I began my reading as part of my disguise. I was surprised to learn that with the enormous size of the observable universe then life is not only possible upon other worlds, under other suns, it is highly probable! Mycroft thinks that it could be possible to express this as a mathematical equation, but he has neither the time nor the interest to work out the formula himself. Do not be deceived, the probability of other men living on other worlds is quite real and of a factor approaching the definitive. Given the amount of time that has passed since the dawn of creation and the sheer size of all we survey, then other worlds demand to be populated. The logic is faultless, up to the point of our never having detected such life. Quite a fascinating problem, one worthy of more study. Between cases, it would be a blessed relief from the boredom. I posit that we are as yet ignorant of some means of communication—perhaps akin to wireless—that would allow said detection. But if Mohamed cannot come to the mountain, perhaps all is not yet lost. It could be possible for visitors to come to us. This then falls into several possibilities, to wit; If other worlds are inhabited, then these civilizations are either on par with our own, more primitive than our own, or more advanced. Logic admits no other possibilities. Civilizations at or below our own level would not be capable of contacting or visiting our world. Only those more advanced than we would be able to do so. A more advanced civilization would have technologies indistinguishable from magic to our backward eyes. Impossible things would become commonplace with such visitors. And what do I observe from my client and my suspect? Both of them have done the impossible, before my very eyes! But, if both come from another world, with all the superior knowledge that would entail—then their odd comings and goings are the result of nothing more than... Perhaps an alien underground railway, so to speak. An elite transportation system. But why are they in London? What are their real motives?"

"Holmes, I am all at sea here. Creatures from another world? Men from other planets come to Earth to rob a museum? It seems an enormous waste of time and effort for such a small return. What could be the payment for a stolen artwork from an alien world? What could be the worth of our human art to an alien being? Would they not prize their own above any effort of ours? The matter is beyond belief! Next, you'll be quoting from that despicable Wells chap, the writer."

"No. Watson. Wells made his Martians look like cases of extreme evolution. Hands and a brain— all else stripped away by the forces of time. A good metaphor for myself, perhaps, but not applicable to our foes. Our foe men are men, just as you and I. No matter what their motives be. If they seek to steal from the museum, it is our duty to thwart them."

"Then what is our next step, Holmes?"

"By one lucky incident, I was able to trace the suspect throughout the streets to a hotel and discover by what name he is registered there. The Irregulars followed him to his rooms and secured the number and name.

I am assured that he is within his chambers now. I propose to pay him a visit and put him to the question, Watson. So far, he appears to be more deserving of our trust than Cyrus Jones."

"And what name does this suspect travel under? Smith, I suppose? That would make sense if the other alien goes by Jones."

"No, Watson. My suspect rejoices under the sobriquet Guiles Thornby. He is of medium height, dark colouring, and possessing sharp, foxy features—not unlike our friend Lestrade looked in his younger days. Thornby appears to be in his late twenties to early thirties but carries himself with the mannerisms of a much older man. Other than the obvious facts that he has seen military service, does secret work for a foreign power, either plays piano or uses a typewriter very frequently, carries at least three concealed weapons upon his person at all times, is conversant with a version of the Japanese wrestling method called baritzu with which I am also familiar—but more advanced —has access to a form of transportation that I do not yet understand, and wears a most peculiar chronometer upon the inside of his left wrist, I have little to go on in forming an opinion of the man."

"I'm sure that you have seen evidence to account for this wealth of information in the minutiae of his appearance, Holmes, but I'm dashed if I can understand it without at least sighting him. What precisely told you all these things about the man? I'm looking forward to meeting this Guiles Thornby, but in the meantime, I would like a fuller view."

"Then let us take up our overcoats and hats and proceed downstairs to hire a hansom. Do you by chance have your service revolver about your person?"

"Why yes, Holmes. As a matter of fact, I do have my revolver with me today. I suppose that I tucked it away in my bag in hopes of your having an interesting matter in hand."

"Capital, Watson! Capital! Come, the game is afoot! Let us go and see just what kind of man this Guiles Thornby from outer space turns out to be. From all I've seen, he's a better man than Cyrus Jones from Croydon."

In our cab, I asked Holmes again about his deductions of Guiles Thornby's character. I knew that Holmes would have observations that would back up each statement. His power of observation never failed to thrill me with its scope. I flatter myself to say that by adopting as much of Holmes' methods as I could learn over the years, to the best of my poor ability, I have become a better doctor. In that sense, much of the increase of my practice is due, in some small part, to my association with Holmes. The rapidity and direction of his thoughts, though at times unguessable to me, served as a guide for me to attempt to observe as well as see the things that fell into my own sphere. My friendship with Holmes was rewarding on many levels.

"I say, old fellow," I began. "What evidence did you see to bring you to those deductions about this Thornby fellow? I take it that you think the man not to be a proper villain and scoundrel? How can you say that he has seen military service, for instance?"

"When I see a man who walks like a retired soldier, I feel it safe to assume that he has been a soldier at one time. An officer, from his manner, used to command and respect."

"And plays piano or uses a typewriter, you said?"

"Watson, how many times have I remarked to you upon the hands and fingers of one individual or another? The spatulate fingers of Guiles Thornby indicate constant usage at some delicate and intricate task. The highest probabilities are music or typing. Other skills would leave differing indications upon his hands."

"But you also said that he is in the habit of going heavily armed at all times. You saw him with three different weapons?"

"When I observe a bulge in a man's armpit, under his frock coat, I assume that the man is carrying a pistol of some sort. Another odd bulge at his ankle, and it is no great stretch of the imagination to conclude that there is what is commonly known in the Americas as a 'hold-out' weapon concealed there. Whether it is a smaller pistol or a knife, I have been unable to determine. And finally, when one walks with a sword-cane, one is advised not to allow it to rattle perceptibly. Mr. Thornby's cane rattles, to my ears at least, as if the blade within was not seated properly. These three weapons are all that I have observed him carry. Was there more that you desired clarification upon?"

"Yes, the Japanese wrestling? You could tell that from watching his movements?"

"Exactly. The exercise imparts certain habits of posture, which I have observed in Mr. Thornby. There is no doubt that he has been taught a similar system—his balance and movements have revealed as much."

"Well, you have already explained why you believe him to be able to use some advanced transportation system, but how can you tell just by watching him that he works for a foreign power? And of what importance is a chronometer upon his wrist?"

"Think, Watson! Think! The man acts like an agent rather than appearing to be acting upon his own. He spies out the pieces that he wishes to spirit away, measures them, but as yet he has done nothing else. I can only assume that he communicates these measurements to some higher authority and then awaits further instructions. If he is from another world as I suspect, then that higher authority will be a very foreign power indeed. From all that I have been able to observe of him, he is making no forgeries himself and has made no provisions to hide any stolen artwork. Therefore, he is not working alone—If, indeed, he is planning to steal the paintings at all. And the chronometer? Upon his wrist? Watson, the pocket watch is the very height of fashion for our modern gentlemen... But a watch upon one's wrist? And such a complex timepiece? It is far from being a common clock, my dear Watson. If my suspicions are correct, the timepiece is quite critical. Quite critical indeed."

"In any case, we will arrive at his rooms shortly. Holmes? I just had a thought..."

"Be gentle with it, Watson. It is visiting unfamiliar geography," Holmes said with a smile.

"Very funny, I'm sure. Seriously, what shall we do if he has ridden this fantastic 'underground' of yours to some remote hideaway? It occurs to me that if he can exit the Museum in such a fashion, why can he not leave his hotel rooms in the same manner?" I looked out at the impenetrable fog of the evening and thought that even if he were an ordinary mortal, he would have little trouble eluding us on a night like tonight. Just as the clopping of the horses' hooves were muffled by the thick fog—and visibility reduced to a bare minimum—the suspect could easily make his getaway even using conventional means.

"In that case, why take a room at all? No, Watson, he must have a use for the room, or he would have never engaged it. He will not leave it by any means other than the conventional. Young Wiggins and the rest of the current corps of the Irregulars are still upon the scene, Watson. I am told that Guiles Thornby's room has a window that our young street Arabs can espy him from a concealed location. As an aside, Watson, my cadre of street Arabs is now into its second generation. Young Wiggins is the eldest son of the dirty-faced ragamuffin that led the Irregulars years ago, back in the early days of our own association. He tells me that his father still talks of working with the two of us with pride."

"Makes one feel his age eh, Holmes? It seems like only yesterday that I would see him purloining the odd apple or cabbage from a greengrocer's cart. Well, what does the grown Wiggins do for a living?"

"He is a greengrocer, Watson. The irony is not lost, least of all upon him."

"With this fog, will the boys still be able to peer into the window?"

"I'm told that one of the smaller lads is up in a tree, quite close to the window. The fog will have to get much thicker before his view is obstructed."

"The cab is slowing, Holmes. We must be at the hotel."

"Capital, Watson! Come, let us interview the elusive Mr. Guiles Thornby."

As we descended from the hansom a small figure ran up to us from out of the fog. In the glow of the nearby street lamp, I was able to recognize young Wiggins by his resemblance to his father at that age. For a brief moment, I pondered what would become of my own children, and theirs in turn—for indeed, I was thrice a grandfather at this time. Both of my daughters had babes in arms, and my son... After recovering from wounds received in the World War, he married an American nurse, and they now have a three-year-old son—but then Wiggins reached us and began his report to Holmes.

"He's still there, sir. Writing like, he is. Hawkins just reported as your cab came rattlin' up."

"Hawkins is the lad up in the tree?"

"Yes, sir."

"Good. Take these coins and spread them out amongst the troops— And, mind you, Hawkins gets a double share, as hazard pay for tree-climbing above and beyond the call. Cover all the exits in case Thornby should flee his rooms. I want at least two boys attached to his coat tails if he should so much as step out of the door without Watson and myself. If the three of us leave together, you may disperse for the evening. Are my instructions clear, Wiggins?"

"Clear, sir. Hang about in case he bolts, then stick to him like a burr on a dog's tail and send word on where he rabbits to. If you all leave together, we're all done for the night and report in the morning at Baker Street."

"Capital, Wiggins. Carry out your duties. Come, Watson!"

Wiggins dashed back into the fog, and we entered the hotel. Holmes had already had Guiles Thornby's room number, so we proceeded up the stairs to knock upon his door. I cannot recall the name of the place, but it looked to be respectable, if a bit run-down. Although everything had a worn appearance, it was nonetheless clean. As Holmes knocked, I could hear movement inside, as if the tenant were pacing back and forth.

"Yes? What is it?" Thornby called through the door in answer to our knock.

"Mr. Thornby, it is important that we speak with you upon a matter of some urgency."

As the door opened, I saw that Holmes' description of the man as looking like our old friend Lestrade was correct, in the main. Thornby was of medium height and indeed possessed similar sharp features to Lestrade in his younger days.

"What's this all about?" he asked.

"It concerns your recent activity at the Museum, Mr. Guiles Thornby. My name is Sherlock Holmes and you—You are not from this world. I wish to ask you where are you from and why have you been taking measurements of various art treasures for the last four months?"

At the mention of my friend's name, Mr. Thornby took on a stunned expression. His shoulders slumped and he stepped back to wave us into the room.

"If he's Holmes, then you must be Watson," he said. "Well, I can't say that it's not a pleasure to meet the two of you, but it is an unexpected pleasure, at least. Sherlock Holmes—I should have known... From your words in the hallway, I can assume that you've been watching me for quite some time. You probably think that I'm scouting the place for a robbery, but you couldn't be more wrong. There is going to be a robbery, but I'm not part of it. I was sent here to ensure that the stolen works were not lost forever."

"You speak in riddles, sir," said Holmes. "Kindly tell your tale the right way forward, rather than starting in the middle as I have so often accused poor Watson here. Perhaps it would save time if I were to sum up what I have been able to discover about you and you may then tell me upon what points I err, if any. I have deduced that you, sir, are not of this Earth, that you are the agent of a foreign power based upon a world circling some far distant sun, that you were sent here to take very precise measurements of a long list of priceless artwork and rare books on behalf of this power, that you have access to a truly remarkable means of transportation... What evidence can you offer that you are not engaged in some grand theft? I'm sorely afraid that you must convince me that you mean no harm, or we will surely be forced to throw in our lot against you. I put it to you again sir— what is your connection with Cyrus Jones and what are your intentions toward the exhibits that you have been studying for the last few months?"

Guiles Thornby looked like a man defeated. His posture betrayed hopeless resignation as he began to speak.

"My mother warned me there'd be days like this. This job has been jinxed from the start. Equipment failures, timing errors, people dogging my footsteps, things missing... I don't know how you managed it, Holmes, but almost everything that you've said is true. My only option now looks like making a clean breast of things. I assure you that I am not here to steal, but to prevent the loss of these artworks to history."

"You claim that you are here to prevent a robbery?" I asked. "Are you indeed then from another world?"

"No, Doctor. I cannot interfere with the robbery. It has to take place. But yes, I am from another planet, I have been taking readings of all these paintings and books, and I do work for someone else. But I assure you that my employer has nothing but honourable intent. He wishes only to preserve these treasures, not to possess them. As for my connection with Cyrus Jones? I'm afraid that he is the thief that I have been slaving to forestall."

"Then we must stop Mr. Jones from achieving his goals," I said. "We can inform the Yard when he is about to strike, and they can take him in arms and lock him away."

"I'm afraid that it won't be that simple, Watson," said Holmes. "You are no doubt forgetting that Jones also has access to alien transportation."

"Oh? Yes, indeed I did," I said.

"What?" Thornby gasped in surprise. "He's not a local? This is bad! Very bad... Everything has gone wrong on this job from the start, and now it just got worse."

"Holmes," I said. "What makes you think that Jones isn't simply in the employ of some hidden alien? Surely it is possible that he is just as earthly as we are, but works for some counterpart of Mr. Thornby, here."

"Yes, Mr. Holmes," said Thornby. "I have instruments that would tell me if another alien life form were nearby. None of them have ever reacted to Jones."

"That would still not explain how Jones has no history, no record of existence even, more than eight months old," replied Holmes. "I have been very thorough in my investigations and neither yourself nor Jones have any such history. It is as if you had both stepped out of thin air."

"The boss will have to be told that the thief is an off-worlder," Thornby mused. "This development changes everything. I'll have to go and report in... Mr. Holmes, I'm sure that you don't trust me out of your sight, but I absolutely have to report this matter to my employer. If you'd care to accompany me, I'm sure that your evidence would be crucial to him."

"Holmes, do we dare trust this, this... being?" I blurted out.

"His story hangs together, Watson. Surely you can hear the ring of truth in his words? Mr. Thornby, we shall be most pleased to present your employer with the evidence that we have collected. I'm sure that it will be a most memorable excursion."

"But where on Earth are we going, Holmes? Mr. Thornby?"

"Not on Earth at all, my dear Watson," said Holmes. "If, that is, my suspicions are correct. I believe that we are about to visit another celestial sphere. Another world, circling some far distant sun."

"Quite correct," said Thornby as he adjusted a stem upon his wrist watch. "A world so far away that it takes sixty-five years for a ray of sunlight to travel from there to here. By way of contrast, it takes eight minutes for a ray of light to move from your own sun to the Earth, a distance of ninety-three millions of miles. I must say that you are both taking the situation very well."

"But the alien air! Will we be able to breathe it? Surely there are some hazards that we should know about first," I gasped. I have to report that I was still a bit in shock over learning that Holmes' deductions had borne fruit.

"Mr. Thornby is quite able to get by in our own Earthly atmosphere," said Holmes. "I think that we need suffer no fears of suffocation, Watson. Surely, we all enjoy the same bodily requirements. I think that we shall be quite all right."

"If you gentlemen are ready?" Thornby asked. "Please stay close to me when the passage opens. Step through quickly and watch your step. You may feel as if the floor is moving under your feet, at first." As he spoke, Thornby finished the adjustments to the watch on his wrist and gestured towards the room's far wall. As I gaped with astonishment, which bordered upon stupification, a hallway appeared to fade into being in the wall. A doorway that had not been visible before. One that led into a long, dimly-lit corridor. Odd flickering seemed to mask the further end of the hall, like lightning at a distance. It was difficult to estimate the length of the hall, also, such that I began to wonder if it had been a good idea to go and visit Holmes that day after all. Bah! Truth to tell, my nerves were singing as they had not since the old days when the case was afoot. I felt more alive than I had in years. I could tell that Holmes was affected likewise.

"You see, Watson? I told you that the timepiece was critical. Jones carries nothing similar that I have observed, but he does have an unusual cigarette case that he takes pains to conceal."

"Where are we going?" I asked Guiles Thornby.

"We will emerge into a private room in a hotel in a large, modern—for me—city on my own world. We'll take public transport from there to reach a place where we can relax and wait for my boss to show up," Thornby replied. "Think of it as a gentleman's club for foreigners and you won't be far off. I can send him a message from there and arrange a meeting with him. After our trip in the meantime, I'd like to hear everything that Holmes has gathered about Cyrus Jones. I have to make my report as full as possible."

"Does this place have a name?" I asked.

"Yes," Thornby replied. "The planet is called Bethdish, the city is named City of Lights, and it is a huge metropolis and port of call for visitors from other worlds. Our destination? It's a bar called the Mare Inebrium. I hope you don't mind, but I feel the need of a very stiff drink."

"Excellent idea, Mr. Thornby. I'm sure that Watson and I could use a little something to take off the chill. Watson, would you care for a drink?"

"Tenderly, Holmes," I heard myself reply, as if from afar. "I would care for it tenderly."

On the matter of our traversing that corridor, I have little to say. It felt like walking upon the deck of a ship at sea—the floor did indeed seem to move under our feet. The walk was about that of three city blocks and ended in an odd, but comfortable, hotel room with no windows. Our host again manipulated the strange watch he wore, and I saw the hallway we had just exited waver like a mirage, then vanish entirely. Fascinating, and a bit frightening. My old friend's eyes shone with that familiar fire as he examined the room's furnishings. He made a circuit of Thornby's quarters, much as he had in the hotel room in London. Thornby went straight to a device that greatly resembled a small typewriter. I watched amazed as the inside of the lid of the machine lit up to show images like small pictographs. Another of Holmes' deductions confirmed. I beat down a rush of shock as I stood and tried to come to grips with the idea of being on another world. Thornby typed furiously for several minutes, then hesitated, finally he pressed the carriage return key and turned to face us.

"Message sent," he said. "All we have to do now is wait for him to meet us at the Mare. I've called a taxi, if you gentlemen are ready to go downstairs?"

"Then we can discuss the matter of Cyrus Jones," said Holmes, "and why he must also be alien to our Earth." On that note, we exited the rooms and walked to the lift. The lift had, instead of an operator, an array of nearly one hundred softly-glowing buttons. Thornby pressed one near the bottom and the doors closed. I took a breath to inquire as to how long the descent would take, and the doors opened again to show an ordinary hotel lobby.

"Fascinating," said Holmes.

"We were only on the fifty-seventh floor," replied Guiles Thornby. "Our cab should be outside."

Our taxi was an automobile, of strange shape to be sure, but acceptable enough. I looked around at the tall buildings as would any yokel, but my excuse was that I had never seen traffic in the air or buildings that tall. In fact, I felt every bit the yokel. Our Cabby, an individual that Thornby familiarly addressed as "Bert" seemed to know that Holmes and I were visitors without being told. He kindly warned us that the ride would be different from any we'd had before and pointed out straps, as in an underground railway carriage, for safety grips. I was still amazed when the cab rose from the ground and merged with one of the lower layers of aerial traffic. We flew at the height of tenth floor windows in the buildings which we passed. I could see more flying vehicles at what I took to be the fifth and fifteenth floor levels. Possibly there were more at even higher levels, since the buildings seemed to average one hundred or more floors, but if so, I was unable to perceive them. Holmes said not a word as he watched both the scenery passing by and the cabby's operation of the vehicle. Thornby sat back in the wide seats watching Holmes and I with a slight smile upon his face. The ride took mere minutes, so high was our velocity. We rose, passed swiftly down the "street", turned several corners in a zig-zag fashion, then descended to the pavement once again. Guiles paid the Cabby as I turned to survey the crowds upon the sidewalk. I goggled at the differing shapes of what had to be people of far worlds right up to the moment that we entered one of the tall buildings. I remember striding across an ornate empty lobby towards a set of stained-glass doors. As I saw Holmes' ears prick up, I too heard the subdued rumble of the patrons—a familiar sound to any pub-goer.

"Gentlemen," said Guiles, then he sighed and spoke again. "Welcome to the Mare Inebrium. Come, we have much to discuss."

"Indeed we do," said Holmes.

Once inside those innocent doors, it would have taken a Dante' or Bosch to depict the variety of creatures that I saw. I had thought that the taxi ride and the strange sights upon the sidewalk had prepared me for any mere pub. But I had been wrong. The room I now found myself in was both large and crowded. I could see recognizable tables and booths at which sat frightening marvels. Here, one patron looked like some form of jellyfish, while his neighbour appeared to be a huge orange tiger. There, a man-sized insect held converse with three small, short-furred bears. At another booth, a man made of gold drank with two normal-looking men—save that one was dressed as Robin Hood and the other was in jewel-like red and gold armor. I looked away to the walls in an effort to assimilate what I had seen. They were elegantly wainscoted from the floor to mid-wall, then paneling gave way to a wallpaper that shimmered like Mother-of-Pearl. Mirrors and paintings alternated on every wall and doors presumably opened into other chambers within the establishment.

"Steady, Watson," said Holmes as he gripped my elbow. Perhaps I swayed a bit, I don't know. "Despite their shape, these patrons are nevertheless people. There is no law of nature restricting our creator to the human form. Think of them as being from some unfamiliar country—China, Japan..."

"Thank you, Holmes. It is all a bit sudden..."

"My apologies, Doctor," said Guiles Thornby. "Perhaps we should take a seat in one of the inner rooms. It'll be less crowded and more quiet."

Indeed, the sound of several hundred drinkers was the most familiar property of this Mare Inebrium. About this time, I remember noticing a subtle perfume. A faint odor of cinnamon overlaid with a trace of lemon. I remarked upon it to Holmes, his opinion was that it was either the effluvia of drink or the commingled odors of the varied patrons. Thornby led the way toward one of the doors to our right, stopping once to speak briefly with a strikingly beautiful woman carrying a tray of drinks. From that I felt it safe to presume that she was a waitress, but further thoughts were halted by her shockingly short skirts. Holmes has jested of me as being some sort of Casanova over the years, but nothing I had seen in the dance halls of San Francisco or Paris could prepare me for sighting such a shapely expanse of female limb. *When in Rome,* I thought—or some such. Out of the corner of my eye I saw Holmes glance at me and give one of his quirky, swift smiles—at my expense, no doubt. The woman glanced at Holmes and I and gave us a warm smile. We tipped our hats wordlessly and she curtsied, then walked away.

"That's Trixie," said Thornby. "She'll tell Max that you're here. He'll want to meet you—he's a big fan. Through here, Gentlemen. We'll pick out a table and wait for my boss."

The smaller room that we were ushered into could have passed for any club in London. Dark paneling, flocked wallpaper, massive bookshelves, still more paintings and mirrors. Along the wall to our left was a perfectly recognizable bar, while various booths and tables were scattered about in between free-standing bookshelves. In this way, each seating area was given privacy. Thornby spoke to the bartender, then showed us to a table. A man with bright blue skin and six fingers on each hand brought our drinks. He served us politely, then left—as perfect a butler as I have ever seen. The whiskey was excellent. The first sip burned going down, but other than that I never noticed it. I diagnosed myself as suffering from shock and prescribed more of this internal antiseptic. I was not surprised to note that our tray had held nine glasses. I glanced at our host and then to Holmes. His eyes were fixed upon our host, and I knew that his concentration was fixed there as well. I sipped my second glass, this time noticing the quality, and waited for Holmes to speak.

In the quiet atmosphere of the comfortable room, Holmes spoke in normal tones, yet his voice didn't carry beyond our table. I theorized some type of excellent soundproofing in the walls, noting that the bustle of the outer room did not penetrate to this smaller club.

"Your speech carries a definite American accent, Mr. Thornby," said Holmes. "Yet you claim to be a native of this world. Indeed, I find that here you are at least moderately well known. From my observations of the level of advancement of this civilization I conclude that we have not only traveled in space but have traveled forward in time some three hundred years. I am sorry to subject you to yet another shock, Watson."

"Yes, I had wondered about that myself, Holmes. In the lift, I could read the numbers on the buttons! And in the taxi, some of the street signs were in English! With everything else I had not made much of it until now."

"Capital, Watson! I have yet to reach your limits, old man. You continue to amaze me."

"Elementary, my dear Holmes," I said with a chuckle. "Also, consider that here we sit imbibing what has to be a genuine single-malt. London of the nineteen hundreds has no trade that I am aware of with outer space."

"Yes," said Thornby. "This planet is my adopted home, but I have visited America quite often. And yes, English is just one of the languages on this world, at this time. But I must correct you on one small point. We are roughly five *thousand* years away from the London that you know. And your conclusions from that, Mr. Holmes? I must say that it is wonderful seeing you at work like this. I scarcely have to inform you of anything. You act as if you already know..."

I could see the effect that Thornby's flattery had upon Sherlock Holmes. As I have ofttimes observed in the past, Holmes seemed to be proud of this recognition of his talents. Therefore, it didn't surprise me to note that Holmes' voice was much warmer than before, when he next spoke.

"My conclusions are that your employer is far more powerful than you have implied. That you are an agent, questing throughout time and space, working for a collector of antiquities. That somehow, you seek to preserve artifacts that, for some reason, your employer deems to be important to history." At each of Holmes' pronouncements, the smile on Thornby's face got wider. He was clearly enjoying the rapidity of my friend's thoughts.

"Ten out of ten, Mr. Holmes. What we do is make recordings of things. Then we place facsimiles of these objects in my employer's own museum. No originals—excepting a few individuals like myself who volunteer, joining the ranks of my fellow employees—only copies are kept in the museum. But they are perfect copies, interchangeable with the originals in every way. Thus, my employer has to take considerable precautions with his security."

"Perfect copies? How is it possible to make a recording of an object?" My questions seemed to be perfectly reasonable to me.

"Doctor..." began Thornby, then he sighed. "You are familiar with x-ray photography? The recording device I use looks deep inside an object and measures precisely every aspect of its structure. The device uses a highly-focused beam of light to etch digitized patterns inside a half-inch cube of pure carbon crystal. This diamond then represents the photograph made by the x-ray camera. Another, more complicated device reads the information on the cubes, then builds a copy based on that information. It uses raw material—a shovel-full of gravel for a teacup, a bushel basket of sand for a Ming vase—broken down to its smallest components. The machine then takes these individual atoms and places a carbon here, an oxygen there, an iron just so... All according to the record of the object preserved in the cube."

"Yes, it was in the process of these recordings that I have frequently observed you," said Holmes.

"In disguise, I take it?" Thornby asked. "You were the Reverend?"

"Yes," Holmes replied. "And the bearded student— And, I might add, the little old lady."

"No! I actually handed you the umbrella you dropped! I put it in your hand and never recognized you! This is marvelous! Classical, absolutely classical!" Thornby clapped his hands in glee.

"Mr. Thornby," Holmes said in a more somber tone. "Enough reminiscing. The time has come for us to discuss Cyrus Jones and the museum that, as you have said, *must* be robbed."

"Public records of the period," said Thornby. "Show that the British Museum was robbed of several prize exhibits on a date that would be, to you, eleven days from now. For me, it was robbed four thousand nine hundred years, plus some odd months ago. I have a list of all the items that the investigation of the time marked as never recovered—Those are my target items. Unless I finish my survey soon, they'll be lost to history."

"And the records of the London Police investigation reveal precisely what? Please elaborate, Mr. Thornby." My friend had eased back in his chair and his eyes were closed in what I knew to be furious concentration. His long fingers were steepled before him, like some monk at prayer.

"They show that although a suspect was arrested—due to an unnamed informant—and some of the property was recovered, the more choice items simply vanished. The assumption was that the trade in underground artwork—stolen artwork—had absorbed them for all time. No trial was ever held, and no record of the suspect or his release remains."

Holmes' eyes snapped open, and he looked at me. "It's a pretty puzzle, eh Watson? We know when a crime is to be committed. We know what is to be stolen. We know the results of a particularly unimaginative investigation in advance. We know that no one but Mr. Thornby and Cyrus Jones have been at all suspicious in their behavior in the museum. It is no great stretch of the imagination to conclude that Cyrus Jones is the suspect of whom no public record remains. Can we not find a way for justice to be served in this matter? Mr. Thornby, it strikes me that after so much time has passed, the matter of examining the public records would have evolved quite some distance. Is it possible for us to examine these records that you speak of, with our advanced knowledge of Cyrus Jones?"

"My employer's access to the records is quite complete," said Thornby. "It's no harder than typing in the right code to examine them." Suiting action to words, Thornby pressed down hard upon one of the ornate inlays upon the tabletop before him. As if by magic, a rectangle opened from the tabletop and another of those small typewriters with a glowing window appeared. He typed for several minutes, muttered encouragement to the machine several times, then looked at Holmes with an expression of triumph. "We're in," he said. "I have access to my employer's database—the records in question. Now, I have to know exactly what to tell the machine to look for. What did you have in mind, Mr. Holmes?"

"Look for records of Cyrus Jones, of course. As far back as you can, and as far forward as—say nineteen hundred and fifty," Holmes replied. "We can safely assume that Jones is the villain upon the fact that no others have been observed. Let us see if Jones is of Earthly or un-Earthly origin."

"Search string... Public Records—Croydon comma eighteen fifty to nineteen fifty—subject—semicolon—Cyrus Jones..." Thornby muttered as he typed. "New search... Public Records—London comma eighteen fifty to nineteen fifty—subject- semicolon—Cyrus Jones... Cross reference police files—comma—same—same—same..." He looked up again and smiled. "It should take a few minutes for the results."

In the pause that followed I could have sworn that I had heard the sound of a hearty English voice that was addressed by the bartender as "Brigadier". Moments later I saw a scorpion—as large as an *elephant*—walk by the nook where our table was located. Moments after this apparition had passed, I distinctly heard our waiter's voice saying "This way, Sir."

"One of my best friends," said Thornby, waving a hand to indicate the creature that had just passed." An old soldier who now serves his people in the diplomatic corps. A good ally in a rough-and-tumble, too. I met him about eighty-seven years ago. He's about three hundred years old now—local time. Late-middle-age for his people. Ah, the search results are in..." Thornby stared at the words on the glowing window and spoke absently. "There are no records, anywhere, of our Cyrus Jones—none."

"Like yourself," Holmes replied. "Jones leaves no trace upon the waters of history. My inquiries into the references he gave me have turned up no trace at all of the elusive Jones. My conclusion is that he is no more of our time and place than you, yourself. Further, since the informant that leads to the quoted arrest is not recorded, it is quite possible that it is none other than Watson and myself. And that Jones is to be held for a time, then escape in such a manner to someday embarrass the police if made a matter of record. Whereupon they do away with the existing records. Remember the Ripper, Watson. When the murders suddenly stopped, the police simply closed up shop. I theorize that Cyrus Jones makes his getaway from the lockup by means of the same sort of transport system that brought us here. The absence of record of his birth is not unusual, as records of the time are notorious for their sporadic nature. His lack of tax registry, post address, employment, passport, driving license, military service—all point to his having made a sudden arrival in England. He may have traveled from another world or from another time. We have no way of knowing at this point. I have here the list of items that you were to record, taken from your rooms in London, Mr. Thornby. I take it that this closely matches the list of unrecovered items from the museum? Good— I think what we need at this point is a method of detecting Jones in mid-burgle, so to speak."

"It is a shame," I said, "that we have only eleven days in which to act."

"We have all the time that we need, Watson," Thornby replied. "My employer can send us back to the moment after we left. Or even to the night of the crime, if that's what we decide on." On that note, I prescribed another drink. Although I was not used to imbibing in such quantities, the alcohol was helping me cope with the shock. Traveling in time could make one's head spin. I idly wondered at the machinery necessary to do such a thing, but only for a moment.

"How much longer do you expect that we will have to wait for your employer?" I asked of Thornby.

"He should arrive soon," he replied.

Within a very few minutes, the waiter brought a small silver tray bearing a single card. Upon it, Holmes read aloud; "Professor Eustas Grey, Xeno-Archeology department, Emperor Norton University, San Francisco, California, NACR. NACR?"

"North American Confederation of Republics. Not your Earth, but another one. Sideways in time from your home. History happened differently to how it occurred in your timeline. He teaches at a college there. That's him all right," said Thornby with relief.

The man that our waiter next led to our table was of medium height, having short gray hair and gray eyes, wearing an oddly cut dark gray suit. It was odd in that the coat had no collar of its own and allowed the collar of the Professor's shirt, or cravat, to show. He appeared to be of middle-age, and in good health. He was tanned and quite fit. I took him to be a very active man. He looked quite like the archaeologist his card proclaimed him to be, as well as the studious archiver of some fantastic museum of antiquities. In no way, however, could I reconcile his appearance with my knowledge that he was some mysteriously powerful force in the preservation of history. A traveler in time, an archiver of the lost treasures of the past. He sat, and the waiter brought another tray of drinks. Of a more normal number this time, I was glad to see. The Professor toasted to our health and passed a few pleasantries off to us before he got down to the business at hand.

"Gentlemen," he said. "A crime against history, against posterity as we know it, is about to be committed. I have kept abreast of Thornby's researches since I received his message that you had arrived. Normally, I would be dead set against involving contemporary assistance, but in the case of Holmes and Watson—Why, I'd be a fool to turn away such help. Already you have uncovered evidence that the crime is not based in the normal scheme of things. Two things I see that we will need for our investigation, knowledge of from where Cyrus Jones is operating, and from *when*. Mr. Holmes, if you could inform me of your progress? I would find it most useful."

Holmes gladly re-capped his findings so far and outlined his needs to the Professor. When he concluded, the Professor assumed a grave aspect. "It will be a delicate undertaking," the Professor stated solemnly. "The lack of records acts in our favor, but to trap Jones and track down his own master is quite another question. The most delicate point is that there is no indication in any record that Jones is indeed the culprit. While the evidence is overwhelming in favor of that conclusion, I remind you that there is no historical proof. Nor is there proof in modern records that a thief is ever punished for this crime. Your study in Alizarin Crimson seem pre-destined to be barren of fruit."

"I cannot help but wish that we could bring this Jones before a judge," I said. "But what could we say to a prosecutor that would give him evidence for a conviction? Somehow, 'Sir, here is a man from outer space that we have caught in the act of burglary' ...is likely to result in our being detained ourselves."

"Yes, our own position is weak in respect to the authorities," replied the Professor. "But it should yet be possible to engineer Jones' arrest by the London police. But we know that he will not remain in custody. The escape that Holmes postulates could well turn out to be Jones' rescue by his own employer. A simple pick-up... I, myself, could retrieve Thornby from out of any prison—or from solid rock, for that matter—if he should so bungle a job and manage to wind up there. Holmes, do you feel safe in assuming that Jones is indeed the counterpart of my man Thornby rather than the prime mover in this crime?"

"The evidence certainly leads to that conclusion, but as yet I feel it to be unproven," Holmes replied. "Jones has hired rooms in London. I have followed him to them. His cover since he engaged my services has been maintained almost faultlessly. Our major clues seem to indicate that the crime will be burglary and that replacement forgeries will be substituted for at least some of the stolen goods. Gentlemen? Why?"

"Why leave only some few forgeries?" I asked. "To gain time to sell those items at leisure, I suppose. The others must already be promised to buyers."

"Watson, you are scintillating today!" Holmes exclaimed. "Yet, there seems more to the matter than your theory covers."

"Yes," said Thornby. "If he can pop in and out like I do, then escape off-world to make his sales... Why bother with any forgeries at all? As a cover for the theft being by an off-worlder? The copies would have to be done by local forgers do accomplish that. And what if he can travel in time? Grey here could clean out that whole museum in the blink of an eye, were he a thief. I don't doubt that Jones' boss could do something similar if he wanted. My question is whether Jones is a time traveler or merely a space traveler."

"I recall it being a dictum of Holmes to avoid theorizing without evidence," sighed the Professor. "So far, our evidence is Jones' appearances and vanishings and his questionable activities as Holmes' client. I can study the areas of the British Museum that Holmes has indicated as where that Jones performed his reappearing act with my machinery. That could possibly tell us if Jones is a time traveler. But the measurements will have to be very precise." The Professor then withdrew a small, flat leather case from an inside pocket of his suit coat. He opened the case and unfolded it to reveal an even smaller typewriter than I had yet seen. A screen the size of a playing card was set into the lid of the case, whilst the keys were set into the lower half. Professor Grey typed for a few moments, asked of Holmes the precise time that Jones had appeared from the empty area of the museum, then typed for a few minutes more. None of us spoke, otherwise, until he was finished.

"There," he said. "I have the search underway. Three searches, in fact. The museum, Jones' rooms, and for comparison, Thornby's own rooms. It will take some time to run, would you gentlemen care for another drink? Holmes, if you have your pipe about you, please feel free to indulge." As Professor Grey spoke, Thornby signaled the waiter and I saw Holmes had retrieved his pipe and begin to tamp shag into the bowl. "Cigar, Watson? New Havana leaf, grown on a world named Hispan-yola... from seeds taken from your own world's Cuba," added the Professor. I accepted out of curiosity and found the cigar to be of the highest quality. As the Professor and I lit our cigars, two small depressions formed in the tabletop—one in front of each of us. I took these to be ashtrays, which the Professor confirmed. The waiter silently brought fresh drinks.

"Jones' employer..." murmured Holmes, "I must admit, takes up entirely too much of my thoughts. I dislike the unknown quantity. What are his limits? What is it possible for him to do and what is, for him, impossible? What are his motivations? Profit? Ownership? What are Jones' instructions? This hidden figure, he has immediate use for some of the stolen exhibits yet must cover part of the theft with forgeries. To buy time, as Watson suggests? Or rather as cover, as Thornby has pointed out? Gentlemen, without fresh evidence, I feel that we are wasting time."

"Mr. Holmes," said the Professor. "The search my machinery is making is more delicate and thorough than any you, yourself, could possibly make. No grain of sand or fingerprint will remain unseen. We have formed our theories, we have gathered our evidence, now we merely await the results of tests from my laboratories to refute or confirm our deductions. Relax, Holmes. Time, for once, is on your side."

"Yes, it is," said Thornby in an affected, sing-song voice, then he chuckled. Professor Grey looked at him as if Thornby had just perpetrated a pun. Thornby, for his part, looked momentarily abashed. Then he took on an intent look and spoke. "Grey, if Jones is an off-worlder, isn't there a chance that there is some sort of police on his own world we could turn him over to? Grand theft, smuggling, burglary... There ought to be someone in the time period with some kind of authority over that."

"Galactic Patrol? Space Rangers?" the Professor chuckled. "Our best bet would be whatever passes for the Customs Authority on his world. We will have to find out just which world it is, however, before we can notify its police. If my equipment can trace Jones' movements back far enough— Well, we will then have a chance."

"And if Jones is a traveler in time?" I asked. "What then?"

"Then, the task of punishing Jones becomes much harder. And stopping him may turn out to be out of the question..."

"Professor," said Holmes, still puffing upon his pipe. "Do any of the stolen items ever turn up again? No matter when or where, but do they ever re-appear?"

"Not on Earth," replied the Professor. "Not in all of Earth's history."

"Upon other worlds, then?"

"The search would take decades, Holmes. Even with my equipment. There are so many worlds to search—it would be like trying to find a particular grain of sand out of all the beaches upon Earth."

"Could we put a tracer on something we know he'll steal and track him back to his base? True, we'd have to let him commit the crime and escape," Thornby mused, "but then we'd have him!"

"Vanilla extract," I chuckled at the memory. "For Toby to sniff..."

Holmes smiled. "Or creosote, Watson? I'm afraid this job would be beyond poor Toby's ability. He could not follow a scent from world to world."

"No doubt the noble beast has long since passed on, in any case, Holmes," I said. "I do hope that he was allowed to sire a few litters, a trait like that nose should be kept vital in a bloodline." The memory of Toby brought me to the memory of one of my own dogs. I nattered on a bit about my old bulldog that I'd had when Holmes and I first met, then noticed the Professor's air of abstract concentration. It was similar, I noticed, to Holmes' own attitude of thought, but different. Where Holmes ofttimes seemed to be asleep as he listened to a client's statement, Professor Grey had adopted an almost catatonic stillness, only his eyes moving, focused beyond us at the wall. Only a bookshelf was there, so I doubted he was contemplating that with such intensity. Thornby watched his employer and hardly seemed to breathe. Holmes too, seemed to sense that something was afoot. He leaned forward in his chair, laying aside his pipe. Yet again, I was surprised to note that a holder sprouted from that versatile tabletop to support the pipe. The moment passed; the Professor seem to come to himself. Frankly, I had wondered if I should offer medical assistance to him, but he recovered and spoke before I could move.

"Thornby, remind me to give you a raise in pay," Grey said.

"You don't pay me in money, now," replied Thornby. "I have access to whatever amount that I need from the working fund you've set up."

"Double it," Grey said. "I've been thinking about what you suggested—placing tracers on the thieves' targets."

"Can it be done?" Holmes asked.

"Not directly, no. Not as the problem is stated. However, I perceive a way to do it indirectly... There is no way to put any type of useful tracer on any of the original items in the museum. Any space traveler would be able to detect it right away."

"On the originals, you say? But that does not exhaust the possibilities, does it?"

"That's right, Holmes. You see it already, don't you?"

"If the originals cannot possibly be made traceable," Holmes said, "then perhaps your own perfect copies could be modified in such a way for them to be traceable?"

"Exactly, we place edited copies—with built-in tracers—in the British Museum for Jones to steal. Then we follow the trace from Jones, through to his fence, to the eventual buyer. By then we should know what sort of Authorities to call in to take them all in hand."

"Capital!" I exclaimed. "But how are we to place these copies in the museum?"

"Elementary, my dear Watson," Holmes replied calmly. "We have to rob the museum, ourselves, before Jones can be allowed to do so."

"I missed breakfast," Thornby announced. "Could we take a break for lunch?"

"Certainly," the Professor replied, signaling the waiter. "The food here is excellent, by the way gentlemen. Order anything that you would like. I'm sure the kitchen is up to any challenge."

"Henry," said Thornby to our blue-skinned waiter as he appeared upon some subtle signal no doubt given by the Professor. "We need to eat something to soak up all of this alcohol. I'll have a deluxe omelet, biscuits, gravy, and strong, black coffee. Doctor?"

"Roast beef, please. With carrots, potatoes, and onions. I hope that proves to be no trouble."

"None at all, sir. An appropriate wine?"

"Whatever you say, I am at your mercy there."

"Mr. Holmes?"

"Breakfast does have its appeal at the moment, I must say. Bacon, eggs, toast, marmalade... Coffee! Yes, coffee!"

"Very good, sir." said our waiter. "And you, sir?"

"Hot and sour soup, House Special fried rice with Zalloo-koosh shrimp," replied the Professor. "And Henry?"

"Yes, sir?"

"If you feel up to the performance, Moo Shoo Pork, please. I shall drink tea."

"Very good, sir." Henry replied. "Ten minutes, please."

After he left, I inquired about our waiter. "Henry?" I asked. "His name is Henry?"

"Actually, he wears a translating device that changes our words into his own language. Whenever we say the word Henry, he hears his own name. When he speaks to us in return, the translator gives us his words in whatever language that it has heard us speaking. The language has to be already known to the device, naturally."

"But how can such a thing operate? And," I asked, "what of its size? I did not see Henry carrying so much as a cigarette case."

"His hearing-aid, Watson," replied Holmes. "I further surmise that the speaker for the device is that which is strapped to his left wrist."

"Almost perfect, Holmes," said Thornby. "The ear-piece is his end of the translator, and the wrist-talker is our end. The two are parts of one machine and communicate to each other by a type of wireless. Most species use something similar."

"Old technology," said the Professor. "The trick is to keep updating the devices with new languages. Each machine's memory for that sort of thing is quite finite, however. New ways of storing information are then constantly being invented to keep up with the pressures of more and more information needing to be stored for quick access. Necessity keeps being met by ingenuity, and thus progress is made. All in all, a good analogy for all types of progress and invention."

The waiter then brought our meal. Everything was cooked to perfection, and we all dug in with relish. I shall never forget seeing Henry prepare the Professor's main course. The meats and vegetables were laid within a soft, flat bread similar to a tortilla. Plum sauce was basted upon the filling, and the whole was wrapped by means of chopsticks, then placed decoratively upon the plate. It was indeed a performance to behold. The scent was quite pleasing, as was that of all the foods. We ate quietly, doing justice as trenchermen to our fine meals before we spoke again.

A quiet beeping tone from the Professor's typewriter device sounded just as we were all pushing our respective plates away, so to speak. The Professor studied the words written upon the window of his device, then sighed with what I hoped was relief. "There are no signs that Cyrus Jones is a time traveler. Such travel leaves traces, certain sub-atomic particles and radiations... None of these are to be found near Jones."

"Good," exclaimed Thornby. "That's one problem down. We're dealing with alien worlds contemporary to your own. Now there's no need to search all of time and space. Much narrower list of possibles for Jones to be from."

"Exactly," said Grey. "But wait, there is more—"

"How much would you pay?"

"Thornby?"

"Yes, boss?"

"Your sense of humor is quite likely to be the death of you... Quite possibly at my own hands, this very afternoon. Please restrain yourself."

"Yes, sir."

"Jones has been traced to a warehouse in a remote area of London," continued the Professor. "There he interacted with a small number of people who were at work preparing forged paintings and books. His base in London, gentlemen. And furthermore! He was traced on two occasions when he had to leave the planet and visit his ship in orbit about Earth's moon. It would have been too easy to find the ship if it had circled the Earth, itself. Those two trips revealed that Jones does seem to have access to some type of matter transmitter, but it is no time machine. I shall, of course, attempt to trace Jones' ship to its home world. Our task has just become lighter, gentlemen."

"Yeah," replied Thornby sarcastically. "Now all we have to do is run off a copy of an entire museum, let it be robbed, and follow the thief to the buyers. No problem... But what'll we do for an encore?"

"It does sound like an awful amount of work to be done in such a short time," I said.

"Already in progress," the Professor said whilst typing.

"That is correct, Watson," said Holmes. "Time has ceased to be an enemy—Indeed, it is now our greatest ally!"

"What do you mean, Holmes?"

"Why, Watson, you realize of course that the Professor is a past master in the manipulation of time? He has, no doubt, just set in motion the necessary recording of the *entire* British Museum. The building and all of the contents will soon be recorded upon a crystal of purest diamond. This recording will be made into copies which will have an inherent flaw, to wit; our tracer, as part of the very structure of the artwork, and completely undetectable to Jones."

"Indeed Doctor," said Grey. "Imagine yourself to be upon the stage in some grand, darkened theater... Suddenly, in a far balcony, someone strikes a match—the only light in a dark and cavernous room. This is what the tracers will look like to my equipment. They will stand out like beacons in the darkness, for my machines will only look for the type of light, their signal, that they will give off. They alone of all creation. We will be able to track Jones' every step, or at least the movements of the stolen goods. And the true beauty of the situation? That since Jones cannot move about in time and yet we can, then he has only eleven days to prepare and is stuck upon Earth of the nineteen hundreds, while we have unlimited time available to us! We can travel back to any point, after having passed as long as we've needed to have used in making our preparations. We can spend years for every day that Jones has to use and still arrive on time to catch him."

"The irony is delicious," replied Holmes in a droll voice. "From our seats here, in a comfortable club, we are able to effect changes in what occurred four thousand and nine hundred years ago. Whatever problem we face, the solution occurs at the time we need it to. Each move of our foe is checked. All because of his pride! If it were not for the hubris of Jones, hiring me as not only some sort of cover, but to also remove Guiles Thornby from Jones' own path, we would not now be able to put paid to the villain himself, nor yet discover his master. If Moriarty were not resting in Hell at this moment, I would not be a bit surprised to find out that the ultimate villain is he."

"No," said the Professor. "Our ultimate foe is someone quite beyond the late, un-lamented James Moriarty, in scope and in power. I suspect that what we are looking at here is nothing less than a contract theft. An underground art collector has commissioned this crime. He will be rich beyond measure, bored beyond belief, and willing to undertake any risk for these art treasures. He prefers to work through underlings, such as Jones, rather than risk his own skin. His most pressing trait will no doubt turn out to be the desire to add to his collection. He will risk anything to add another painting or book to his shelves. No, I understand him all too well. I've walked in his shoes... I know how he thinks. If it were not an accident of birth, I could have been him—whoever he turns out to be. I was simply lucky enough to have been born upon a world of time travelers, and so the galaxy is an open book to me."

"It runs deeper than that," asked Holmes, "does it not, Professor? I would say that the difference between yourself and our foe is more one of character. You are not, at heart, a thief. Our unknown foe, however, indeed is."

"Mr. Holmes, by the laws of my own people my hands are not entirely clean, I must admit. On my own world, I am branded somewhat of a renegade. Not a wanted man, but rather the reverse—an un-official exile. For over ten million years before my birth, my people have been able to travel in time. In our early records, there is listed every possible abuse of this technology. But there is also listed every possible *humane* usage. The matters balance out, yet the guilt remains. In time, my people learned from their mistakes and vowed never again to interfere in the destiny of other worlds. It was a harsh lesson, one that cost many lives on other worlds, but one that we learned well. The urge to play 'god' to younger worlds was all but erased from our character as a species. Despite our intent, a civilization destroyed itself because of our meddling with their natural development. Our civilization was in shock and remorse for a generation. The lesson was learned; observe, record, remember... but never interfere. Only the odd throw-back shows any evidence of an urge to meddle. I fled my home to escape what I perceived to be a tyranny of stifling rules. Non-conformity was subtly punished, individual expression was looked down upon as anti-social. It was a gradual erosion of what had been a great civilization. Many centuries passed thus before the time of which I speak. Finally, the laws against interfering with other worlds, against everything but observing them, began to leave younger worlds than ours open to invasions or decay. I was neither the first nor the last to flee. In every generation, a few were born that could not live with the boredom, the restrictions, who had to act—to flee. Some have meddled, some have muddled the waters of history, and I have sought to study and learn. A rare few of my fellows have turned out to be just the sort of ruthless danger that the others fear. There is no warrant for my extradition for any crimes, but if I draw attention to myself—if I embarrass them—my home world's government will be forced to take official notice of me."

"Thank you for that confidence, Professor. You have confirmed several of my theories and given me much food for thought."

For the first time, I wondered at the true motives of the Professor and Guiles Thornby. If the museum robbery was now going to be of a totally false museum—where did the pieces that were, originally, never recovered go to? And what of the false museum itself? As if in a bad play, this prop will never be needed again—What will become of it? What about... "What about the guards? Or Curators who are working late? Will they be copied also?"

"No, Doctor. The equipment is set to ignore living beings. I would not endanger anyone needlessly." The Professor sounded reassuring, but could he be believed? Could he really be Jones' hidden employer after all? I wished that I could get Holmes alone for a few moments and sound him out on the matter. Aside from the bewildering array of machinery and concepts that we had been exposed to, Holmes and I were forced to take these two at their word. I knew that Holmes had been able to see further into these strangers than I. If there were some way that we could converse unheard.

"Gentlemen, I think the time has come for a visit to the facilities—if I may be so rude. All this coffee... Watson, do you feel up to exploring a sanitary closet of five thousand years in our future? Thank you. If you will excuse us, gentlemen?"

"Holmes," I said as we proceeded toward the chamber that the bartender had pointed out to us. "Sometimes it's as if you read my very mind... You knew that I wanted to ask your conclusions about the Professor and whether he could be trusted."

"Yes, I could see your rising distress as our host unburdened himself to me. I closely observed you whilst he was speaking and saw the train of thought that had been engaged. After a point, you began to wonder at the true motives of our host and what I might make of him. You then fidgeted, attempting to hide your distress, until I saw that you had reached the point of suggesting the most obvious gambit of a trip to the jakes. I thereupon made the statement myself so as to disassociate the event from your own movements. Quite elementary."

"Quite, I'm sure. Holmes! Tell me! Can the man be trusted?" We thereupon entered the rest room and I have to admit that there was not another word passed between us for some minutes. The place was quite astounding, more like the locker rooms of a club than a simple Water Closet. After finding the facilities we sought, we again convened in what could pass for a lobby, just inside the door back to the bar.

"Your question answers itself, Watson. Can the man be trusted? The man. You know that he is actually no closer to being a 'man' than we are to being oak trees, or oysters. Yet you see him as a man. He acts like a man, looks like a man, speaks as a man—so he is easier to accept than, for example, our waiter—whose differences are openly visible. You accept the Professor for what he appears to be, Watson. Yet you ask for my conclusions? The man exudes an aura of trustworthiness. I have detected no signals being passed between Thornby and the Professor, as would be present if they were trying to dupe us in some way. To be brief—I believe them, Watson. I think that just as Lestrade and Gregson were to be trusted as allies, so can Thornby and the Professor. There are yet a few pieces to the puzzle to be uncovered and we will be ready to take Jones in hand."

"And deliver him where?"

"To whomever has jurisdiction over his peculiar crime. We will find that out shortly. Come Watson, the game is still afoot!"

Guiles and the Professor were jubilant when we rejoined them.

"The copy is done and the overlay to the museum is in place, ready for the night of the robbery," said the Professor as Holmes and I seated ourselves. "This also explains Thornby's difficulties, Holmes. At the time that you were watching him, he did not know that he was trying to make copies of copies. Naturally, the equipment that he had didn't work correctly. Also, he thought that several people were dogging his footsteps—besides Jones, of course—they all turned out to be you, in various disguises."

"What is an 'overlay'? I have not heard the term before," I said.

"Excellent question, Watson. Obviously, it is the entrance to our trap, but I must confess that I am unfamiliar with the usage of the word, myself. I would surmise that it is a false entrance to the British Museum that leads into the false copy, rather than into the real museum. Thus, we do not have to actually carry away the entire museum and replace it with our false one. We simply ensure that no matter where Jones chooses to make his entry, it is into our trap and not the real museum to which he gains entry."

"Exactly so, Holmes," said the Professor. "We couldn't very well steal the whole museum away and replace it with our copy. No, the real museum is still there and safe. But no matter which door or window Jones and his men use, our trap is waiting behind. In a way, you could say that our overlay is between the real world and the real museum, like the skin of an onion or the shell of a nut."

"Yes," added Thornby. "Now all we do is wait for Jones to take the bait and the trap is sprung! We even have a lead on his ship's registry, so we can begin the search for the proper authorities to turn him over to."

"Excellent news," exclaimed Holmes. "I take it that we can proceed against Jones whenever the search for the proper police agency is successful?"

"Exactly, Holmes," said Thornby. "That's all that we lack to bring the man in."

"A bit more waiting, I'm afraid," added the Professor. After a glance towards his typewriter, he expanded his statement. "I never thought that I'd see the like of this. Where the search for a policeman takes up more time than finding a thief. But there, in a nutshell, is all that we need for the case to conclude. We can collect Jones at will, once the results of this last search are in."

"Doughnut shop..." blurted out Guiles, trying to stifle giggles. The Professor ignored his outburst with massive dignity.

"I wonder if I need a Siberian wooly mammoth for my collection," mused the Professor mysteriously, while staring at Thornby. "Not a dead one frozen in ice, but a live one—up and about?"

"I'll be good," announced Thornby, under the glare of his employer's eye.

The evening wore on, though we had all had a marvelous time, we were all relieved when the Professor's typewriter beeped again in signal that the correct other-worldly police agency had been found to deal with Jones. Now we could proceed against him. Our trap was set, the bait placed, now we had but to go and collect our prize.

"Gentlemen," said Holmes when the signal had come in and its import understood. "The game is well and truly afoot. As soon as Jones takes the bait, the locations of the missing artwork should appear unto the Professor's equipment. We can then move against him with the aid of his own world's police. I propose a final toast before we repair to the British Museum. To Cyrus Jones, may he find that prison suits him well."

"Hear, hear!" we all echoed.

Yet, it was not fated to be the moment that we laid Jones by the heels. As our final preparations were enacted, we hung upon the Professor's every word as he quoted from his typewriter. We listened as Jones and his hirelings entered the Museum by stealth, as they then entered what the Professor termed an "overlay" that was our false museum-hall, to trigger the trap and make good their theft of the first load of works smuggled away from the museum. As they began the second truck load, The police of Jones' own world as well as our own agents that we had alerted struck, the hirelings were arrested, Jones detained... And then disaster struck. It was Holmes who had the first inkling of trouble.

"Something is not right," Holmes muttered. "It has been too easy. Our ultimate foe should not have given up his agent so quickly. Jones should have been more hesitant..."

"Holmes," said Thornby. "Against this set-up, he hasn't the ghost of a chance." Famous last words... The Professor's typewriter gave a warning sound of a quite different tone and we all whipped 'round to give him our attention.

"Ghost is right, by thunder! This isn't physically possible! I had his every avenue of escape covered! He vanished! He escaped his own world's detective agents," shouted the Professor. "While they separated him from his local help that the Yard was taking in tow, he somehow managed to give them the slip! He's gone from my instruments entirely! Holmes— How did you know?"

"Results without causes are much more impressive. I am afraid that my explanation may disillusion you, but it has always been my habit to hide none of my methods, either from my friend, Watson, or from anyone who might take an intelligent interest in them. Very well, to put the matter concisely; I have had the advantage of observing Jones for some weeks... As of tonight, I have now had the honour of observing Mr. Thornby— out of his disguise, so to speak. I have noticed several similarities in their behavior and mannerisms. Without taking the time to list them, I can say that the indications are that Jones is also in disguise, from a time or place of very high technology, and also is as familiar with several of the amenities of your present day as is Mr. Thornby. Therefore, it is clear to me that despite the evidence of your equipment, Jones is no stranger to these modern times of yours. One drawback of an active mind is that one can always conceive alternate explanations which would make our scent a false one. Thus, we fell into the trap of the attractive, but false, scent of Jones' employer being contemporary to the crime. We ignored the possibility that Jones' employer may be able to deceive our instruments—to make them give false results. He was underestimated. We must redouble our efforts with this new information and avoid the false premise that our enemy is bound to one era of time. I suggest that we extend our search for the stolen artwork into the future, if your equipment is able to do so. Our foe may be from some point in the future rather than contemporary with the crime itself. All is not yet lost... Consider—he has escaped, but with our traceable copies rather than the originals. Therefore, we will trace him—but how long will it take?"

"It will take as much as thirty minutes for the last of the changes in time made by the tracers to be detectable to my instruments," sighed the Professor. "Once we eliminate the past as a hunting ground, Mr. Holmes, I will then take your suggestion to heart. The future is a much harder thing to search... I hope that we can at least confine the search to the present-day era. We shall see."

"These are much deeper waters than I had thought," said Holmes. "When once your point of view is changed, the very thing which was so damning becomes a clue to the truth. I am as much guilty of underestimating our foe as anyone. It positively galls me that Jones got away so easily. He felt so clever and so sure of himself that he imagined no one could touch him. He could say to any suspicious contemporary neighbor, 'Look at the steps I have taken. I have consulted not only the police, but even Sherlock Holmes.' Thus, he prepared an alibi for the men of the Yard. All the cards are at present against us. In our own time, that is. Here, we may yet have some ability to act."

"Thornby," said the Professor quietly. "Go back to the Museum—my Museum, Castle of the Winds—and contact Maxwell. He is the one agent that could possibly keep up with Jones as he makes his escape. Pull Maxwell back from whatever he is doing and re-assign him to the period that yourself, Jones, and Holmes were doing your dance in the British Museum. I want him ready to follow Jones when he makes his escape from those Tourlanatti Customs agents. Follow Jones—no matter where, no matter when, tell him. You understand."

"Boss? Aren't you—"

"Then message every last scout and bring them in on the matter. Have them look for the tagged items, watch Jones' ship orbiting the moon, and keep an ear on Maxwell's reports. When Jones escapes, Maxwell can follow him... Perhaps better than anyone. I want this Jones, and his employer, in jail... No back talk, Thornby. There will be a door to Castle of the Winds behind the bar by now. I summoned one while we were speaking. Go to it, Guiles. Get everyone moving. We're not going to let ourselves get caught lagging a second time."

"Yes, sir," said Thornby. Then he got up and walked to the bar, only to disappear behind it a moment later. I could swear that the door that he went through had not been there earlier.

"Holmes," said the Professor. "It appears to me that I have not paid sufficient attention to your deductions. To my chagrin, I find myself empty-handed when I was sure that I would have my thief in custody by now. I promise that I will not make that mistake again. Tell me, what are your views of our enemy? Not just Jones, but his employer. I need to make plans against him, and I want to make the correct plans this time."

"Holmes," I said. "Have you seen enough of Jones to extrapolate what his employer must be like?"

"Indeed, I can say that I have come to a few tentative conclusions about our elusive enemy. He is not unlike a director of a play, or perhaps better yet, a chess player. Yes, that is it! A chess player! He has his board set, his pieces in place. He sees the moves of all the pieces on the board and is able to deduce our possible moves from our position on the board so far. If I may term it so, then this agent of yours, Maxwell, is to represent our knight—striking from odd angles and around corners. Thornby and I are bishops—angling about Jones and seeking to immobilize him. Watson here is a sturdy pawn, awaiting the moment to throw his strength into the play. And you sir, are our king—whose subtle moves need to be protected from our opponent."

"Rather, Maxwell is our queen—able to travel any distance, in any direction, and strike our foe deep in the heart of his own territory," the Professor corrected Holmes gently. "Otherwise, your analogy is perfect.

My scouts therefore become our knights, rooks, and the rest of our pawns."

"Thank you for the clarification," said Holmes. "Now for our opponent; He is at or near your own level of technology and ability. He may turn out to be the only possessor of our stolen goods, rather than a fence for them. In fact, I am sure that he will not wish to sell the items to another after going to such extremes to possess them himself. He will be vastly wealthy, for such a hobby cannot be cheaply maintained. He will be used to circumventing the law; thus, this is not his first crime, but rather his latest. He will have a substantial organization to command. —We may need to be on our guard against assassins—and will be quite ruthless in his discipline of his organization's members. I would suggest a search for the names of the most wealthy art collectors who have demonstrated a casual disregard for the law in the past. He may tend to specialize his collection to items from either Earth particularly, or from emerging worlds such as Earth. He will not be outwardly ostentatious in his dress, manner, or residence, but he will often disappear from these familiar things to command his secret army from some hidden fast-hold. He may or may not be insane, as I understand the definition, for he may be so alien as to think that his actions are not wrong, but if theft is wrong for his people, then he stands a better chance of being considered insane. Professor Grey? It comes to me that if the stolen items were all from our copy of the museum and that the real museum has not been robbed, why was there a report listing the stolen items?"

"Well, Holmes, the Yard had to say something about the raid that netted the local gang. None of them got away, unlike Jones. As for the missing items, I had a crew remove them to various of the museum's own storage facilities, but I did not alter the museum's own inventory sheets—so they still have the items, but do not yet know that they have them. The things are simply lost in the system. Once the originals were safe, I anchored the overlay on the copies that were on my list as having never been recovered. The museum looked normal to the naked eye, but the overlay was there all the same. Each copy hung or lay where its original had, each tagged for our detection. I feel sure that the tags will yet become visible to us."

"But what precisely is the overlay, Professor? I feel rather stupid here," I said grumpily. It is true, in this alien, future world I felt like a backward savage. I had gawked at buildings, I had goggled at the colours of the skins of the human-looking aliens, I panicked at the sight of the non-human creatures. It was only here in this very normal-seeming environment that I was able to escape the sensations of being madly ripped from the familiar. In fear, let it be known, I sought information, the better to cope with the truth of my present location.

"Doctor, the overlay is what I call the area of over-lap of the copy of the museum that we recorded and edited, and the real museum. The real museum is unharmed, unchanged, safe from Jones and his gang. The copy... The copy is partly inside of the real museum, partly outside the real museum—like a second skin—and partly, almost completely—in another dimension that is very close to your own but separate from it by the smallest margin. If the overlay were of a street corner somewhere in London, people on the sidewalks could walk in and back out of it without noticing any change. They would travel from one dimension to another without noticing. As far as our trap goes, in effect, Jones could walk into the front door of the museum, and—in the space of the thickness of the doorway—walk into our copy of the museum instead of the real thing. We would intercept him in the course of traversing the doorway, so to speak."

"Professor, have any of the tagged items yet shown up upon your search engines?"

"No, Holmes, and they should have. There has now been plenty of objective time to pass for the tags on the artworks to affect their changes in the past. No matter where or when they are now, my machines should have found them. For someone to shield the tracers from my instruments is highly unlikely. In fact, it would be more probable that the villain is from farther in the future than we are right now, than it is for my instruments to be blinded to the tracer tags being any time between now and the dawn of creation. The past is fairly fixed—and thus easier to scan. The future is harder for the same reason that it would be harder to track one speck of dust in a desert sandstorm... Too many possible changes make the future more fluid than the past. Plus, each dimension has its own past and future. Time is as infinite sideways as it is forward and back..." the Professor trailed off as if in sudden inspiration. "The energy necessary to cross time or dimensions would be traceable to my instruments if they knew what sorts of energy to look for... Perhaps we could come at them sideways, so to speak, by locating sources of energy affecting the British Museum on the night in question. Another thing to add to Maxwell's programming when he reports."

"Holmes? What you were saying earlier," I asked. "Didn't you imply that the enemy would have a stronghold somewhere?"

"Why yes, Watson, so I did. You have a thought upon the matter? Out with it, old man. Professor, Watson is known for making intuitive leaps that ofttimes outstrip my own deductions. He is capable of the imagination so lacking in Lestrade and Gregson. Come, Watson, what was your thought?"

"Well, I don't know about all that guff, Holmes, but thank you. But my thoughts on the enemy were that if he did indeed have a fortress somewhere, and if indeed he was able to travel in time..."

"Stout fellow!" exclaimed Holmes. "Go on, I think I see it, but make it clear for me."

"Well, would not this base require a lot of the very energies the Professor's machinery also uses? Could we not look for these energies in use and compare them with the list of wealthy art collectors who have been found to be possessed of criminal connections? A name upon both lists would be further evidence of guilt, to my mind."

"Watson, you continue to amaze me," said Holmes. "Professor, Watson has raised a valid point that may ease our search. Can you trace someone who has abilities and tools like your own?"

"Absolutely, Holmes! In fact, I usually have just such a program running in the background on my museum's computers. It is somewhat of a security program, you see. I use it to track potential hazards of my own. My fellows from my home world, various warlords, invasions, revolutions, and other occurrences that may affect one of my archaeological digs..."

"Splendid! Instruct this marvelous 'program' with our observations so far and let us see what we may see."

"Holmes, Watson, this investigation shall take much more subjective time than I originally envisioned. I know that my people will perform as instructed... Shall we repair to the outer room to await results? I know that there are a lot of people out there who would like to meet the both of you. In fact, I just received a message from Trixie, the waitress that Thornby said you met on your way in... A message that threatens my very life if she is not permitted to make your acquaintance," the Professor laughed heartily. "Please, to avoid the ire of a beautiful woman, would you mind terribly?"

"Oh, very well," sighed Holmes. But I could tell from his manner that his ego had been peaked by the thought of others that valued his work. Or perhaps it was just the memory of the short skirt and long legs of Trixie. Holmes may have avoided female entanglements all his life, but the man who could ignore a summons from that young lady had yet to be born, I surmised. That woman could inspire a statue to embarrassment, I believe. To my delight, Holmes accepted the Professor's request and I once more found myself in that formidable crowd of patrons in the large room outside our comfy nook. Again, I could examine the variety of life forms from distant worlds. Here, a winged snake conversed with a woman made of flame, there two blubbery individuals not unlike walruses hooted and bellowed to one another. In another place, a woman who appeared to be made of liquid silver sat, nude, conversing with a green-skinned man in purple robes. In yet another place, a school of small fish swam in the very air over one table, while their companion appeared to be a sphinx who was drinking some glowing, ale-like beverage. I saw many more patrons who appeared to be human in every way, as well as several who's bodies looked human in shape but possessed wildly varying colours of skin and hair.

As if sensing my distress, Holmes began asking questions of the Professor. "Professor Grey, these strange creatures..."

"Are all to be considered people, Holmes, Doctor. They are but a few of the strange shapes that life has moulded into intelligence. On a busy day, the Mare Inebrium will serve several hundred different life-forms... They could range in size from sprites who could stand in the palm of your hand, to beings larger than whales. The Mare even has other rooms for beings who need special atmospheres... As you have seen, this main room has various smaller, more intimate rooms with differing themes. We were just in the Club, Piper's it's beginning to be called. —Not sure why. Across the room near the center of the wall is an entrance to rooms that have a 'raw frontier' set of themes. More saloons than anything like the Club. One of them, the Red Dog Saloon, can get a bit rough, at times."

"Professor? Why are there such a predominance of Earth-like people here? Is the human form to dominate above others in all the worlds? From my studies, I had rather thought that the chance of any person from another world appearing to pass for the next-door neighbor were rather slim. Once I accepted that Watson and I were traveling to another world, I expected the un-Earthly shapes of some of our fellow beings. Why then are there so many human-like aliens?" Holmes' question, once asked, aroused my curiosity as well. I waited eagerly for the reply.

"Why no, Holmes. There are many more non-human types of life than there are humanoids. There is nothing special about the shape that houses an intelligence. Indeed, humanoids—Earth humans in particular—are widespread, but they are far outnumbered by the other variety of intelligent beings. The sample that you see here is decidedly weighted in the favor of humanoids simply because this world is extremely well suited for them. This world has become an important shipping port and this city itself is a tourist attraction, in a small way. There are important diplomatic Embassies here, from dozens of worlds. A lot of the Diplomats come here, simply because we can accommodate so many differing life forms. There's one now, matter of fact. Let's go meet him."

I looked to where the Professor was indicating and froze. I was shocked for a moment, then I recovered. I took a sip of the drink that I'd thoughtfully retained from our table at the Club. The being that we were now walking toward to meet was none other than the giant scorpion that I had glimpsed earlier in the Club. I had not forgotten the waiter addressing him as "Sir", nor had I forgotten the bartender's voice calling the creature "Brigadier". As we approached the creature, I re-thought my estimate of his size. Rather than being in any way elephantine, the creature's body was more the size of a Clydesdale, or a Percheron horse. Its body was about shoulder height from the floor, supported by eight graceful legs—though the claws on his two arms were each as long as my shoulders are wide. He appeared to have two bright-blue eyes, on stalks above his mouth. I noticed that he had a small black and chrome box on his right arm, near the shoulder. The box was labeled in English, for I could read the word "Fender" emblazoned like a trademark upon the box. I took this to be the being's translator device. He wore a wide blue sash from his left front shoulder to his hind-most right hip—if a scorpion could be said to have a hip. I could see small ribbons and medals pinned to this sash. That would make sense if indeed this creature was a soldier of high rank. But the Professor had indicated that this being was a diplomat of some sort. And I recalled Thornby saying that this creature was several centuries old, yet middle-aged.

"Kazsh-ak Teir, old D'rrish, I'd like you to meet someone," said the Professor, once we had walked close to the giant scorpion. "Kazsh-ak Teir, Ambassador of the D'rrish colony upon Bethdish— May I present Mr. Sherlock Holmes and Dr. John Watson, of London, upon Earth."

The creature turned and quirked up an eye stalk in what I took to be surprise at the names of Holmes and myself. His movements were quite graceful for a creature that size. Yet I could not forget his stinger as it arched eight feet in the air behind him. "It is indeed a great honour," came a deep voice from out of the Fender-box. "I have read all of the good Doctor's publishings of your cases, Mr. Holmes. It is a pleasure to meet you. Dr. Watson, I thank you for many hours of pleasurable reading. What, may I ask, brings you forward to our fair city? Grey, have you been meddling again?"

"I am pleased to make your acquaintance, Mr. Ambassador. Watson and I are visiting this world upon a case. The Professor was kind enough to assist us in the attempt to apprehend an art thief. Although we have yet to be successful... At the moment, we are awaiting results of a search—and thus taking a break from our labours. You do not seem surprised by the fact of our traveling in time, Sir. May I ask why?"

"Please, call me Kazsh-ak. I prefer to shed the carapace of diplomacy when I am here. This is the place I come to relax, away from the worries of the Embassy. As to your question, sir—when I see Grey in the company of someone not of this time, I feel no surprise. I have known his man Thornby for nearly a century now. The two of us have shared many adventures together. I have also assisted Grey on several other matters myself, over the years. Nothing that involves Professor Grey surprises me any longer. Pleases me, amazes me, amuses me, but no more surprises."

"I see," said Holmes.

"I overheard the barman in the Club call you 'Brigadier'..." I said. "You left the military for the diplomatic corps?"

"A bit of a family obligation, I'm afraid," replied Kazsh-ak. "My family is one of the more obscure lineages of our people's royal line. As a minor son of a minor house, I inherited the mantle of the diplomatic corps upon my retirement from the City Guard. It fell to our branch to become diplomats, you see. Runs in the family, don't you know? Although my fourteenth daughter has been selected the twelfth Princess of the present Royal family. Something less than twenty steps from the throne in the line of succession, but highly unlikely to ever have to assume the responsibility. I am in partial retirement from the diplomatic corps at the moment, myself, and she has assumed most of my duties at the Embassy. She will eventually hand over the post to my youngest son when he comes of age and finishes his training. Of course, that will not be for sixty years or so. Gentlemen, I fear that I must repair to the bar to obtain another beverage. I would be honoured if you would accompany me."

"A pleasure, Sir," I replied. I had recovered from my fear of this odd person and was beginning to enjoy his company.

"Yes," added Holmes. "I fear that we have unfinished business with a young barmaid who is threatening mayhem if she is ignored for much longer."

"Yes," I said innocently. "That would be Miss Trixie."

"Steady, Watson!" Holmes quipped, smiling. "The fairer sex has always been your main weakness."

"I am used to such outpourings," I replied with mock dignity. "And so I simply consider the source and dismiss the remark as being from one... inexperienced, shall we say, in such matters." I grinned at Holmes to show that my riposte' was meant in humour. To the best of my knowledge, Holmes has only ever felt the tenderer emotions towards two women in his life. Of course, the most intense of these was The Woman, Miss Adler, of my Bohemian Scandal story. Holmes never forgot her as having bested him at his own game—as well as acquitting herself honourably in the situation. At least, she did so in my esteem. Holmes and I were young yet, then. I'm sure now that the Irene Adler of that time would not stand a chance against the present Holmes. Yet still, at any mention of her, for the rest of his life, he toyed with the sovereign that she tipped him whilst he was in disguise and drafted as a witness to her hurried marriage to Godfrey Norton. He had carried that coin as a fob upon his watch chain from that day unto this.

The other? Holmes has yet to see fit to inform me officially, so I fear that I must keep my own deductions on the matter to myself. As a gentleman, it is not my place to gossip, nor to drop hints for some later pseudo-scholar to dissect. Suffice it to say that Holmes was not really as celibate as my stories in the magazines might lead one to believe. The Other Woman—if I may coin a term—who had engaged Holmes' affections over the years is someone who's privacy Holmes protects with commendable chivalry. We never speak of the matter at all, he and I. I know of her, he is aware that I know, and that is all that needs be said upon the matter. Unless Holmes himself deigns to speak out, my lips are sealed. Yet we joke to each other, such is our friendship.

"Yes, well..." Holmes said.

"The human male who can say no to Trixie has yet to be born," observed Kazsh-ak. "The maiden hath charms to soothe the savage... ah, beast." The Ambassador laughed, or at least, a laugh issued from the Fender-box that he wore. For some reason, the accent spoken by his translator device left me feeling slightly home-sick. He sounded so very much like any bluff and hearty gentleman from some ministry of the government in London. I liked his kindly tone of voice, for all the fact that the voice came out of a box.

"In fact," observed Grey. "Here is the lady herself. Trixie, you're looking lovely this evening."

"Thank you, Professor. Mr. Holmes, Dr. Watson," she said as we approached the main bar. "It is such a pleasure to meet you both. I've admired your work for so long."

"Not too long, I'm sure," said Holmes. "For you cannot yet be much over twenty-five years of age at the most. I take it that you have read the Doctor's romanticized accounts of some of my cases?"

"Oh, yes! I've read everything that Dr. Watson ever wrote. And I looked up a few of your own monographs in the library as well, Mr. Holmes. I'm a great fan! My boyfriend Max is a fan too. Aren't you, Max?"

The gentleman in question was a handsome fellow behind the bar. He laughed and introduced himself to Holmes and me.

"Yes," he answered Trixie. "I've always like mysteries. Dr. Watson's accounts always let Mr. Holmes' methods shine with their true worth. I always enjoyed trying to pick out the clues as Holmes did, each time I re-read one of Watson's stories. The two of you have led me to countless hours of thought. Thank you."

"My pleasure, I'm sure," I said.

"Quite," added Holmes. "It is gratifying to note that Watson and I are apparently held in such high-esteem some few thousand-odd years after our eventual demise."

"Most people never get to know what the future thinks of them," said Max. "Call yourselves lucky that you were such a positive force in history.

Almost everyone, anywhere has seen or read one of the Doctor's accounts of one of Holmes' cases. *'Hound of the Baskerville's'* is the most common."

"I'm not unduly proud of that one," I mused. "It is one of my finer efforts, I think. I managed to capture the atmosphere of the moor and the hound without resorting to the supernatural for drama. Holmes leaving me to think that I was alone whilst he himself was camping upon the moor added a nice touch. Even nicer because it was real. Holmes always did have a flair for the dramatic."

"Watson, you can always be proud of your work," said Holmes. "If I have at times accused you of stooping to romance when recounting one of my little problems, rest assured that I knew that your accounts were the best way of placing my methods before the public eye. You have always been able to speak to the man in the street with your pen, Watson. I applaud your talents even as you have applauded my own efforts upon the violin."

I answered such unaccustomed praise in the only manner which I could. I gave Holmes a slight bow and smiled proudly. I treasured my friend's opinion above all others. Even as I made further small talk with Trixie and Max, I felt the warmth of my friend's words in my heart.

"Polios," began Max—but at a look from the Professor he gulped and began again. "Grey, would you or your guests care for another drink? I see that the Doctor's glass is empty."

"I, for one, came up here just to get another round," said Kazsh-ak. "My usual, Max."

"Yes," added the Professor. "A round on the house in honour of Holmes' and Watson's visit. My treat..."

"Yes, Sir!" snapped Max, passing glasses and pouring drinks. "The good stuff, for three hundred and fifty-seven... Good thing that you own—"

"Max," said the Professor in a firm tone of voice.

"Yes, sir, the customer is always right," Max replied suddenly. He, Trixie, and another waitress began passing out rounds of drinks. The other waitress was later introduced to me as Blanche. A thoroughly pleasant young lady, I found her to be. When the round was dispersed, we all rejoined in the conversation. We talked of many things besides my humble literary efforts, I am thankful to say. All that praise was likely to go to my head. Many strange and mysterious things were related to Holmes and me over the course of the evening. I dare say that Holmes had begun to wish to have been born into these later times so as to be on hand to study those strange, new mysteries, by the time our evening was done. Holmes, I'm sure, enjoyed the attention. His vanity was always within easy reach, but this only made him look more normal. His thoughts, being so much more rapid than the average man's, tended to isolate him and make him appear aloof to those who did not know him well. I was particularly glad to note that Holmes and Trixie disappeared together for at least an hour. Trixie returned looking radiant, smiled at Max—who shrugged and smiled himself—then went on about her work. Holmes appeared about ten minutes later, looking very relaxed. I haven't the foggiest idea of what went on—and as a gentleman, I refuse to engage in idle speculation. I simply smiled to myself and never brought the matter up to Holmes at all. "I'll have to update that list," I muttered to myself.

Yet, we were each of us glad, I think, when the Professor passed us word that his agent, Maxwell, had made good the pursuit of Jones. Thornby had returned some time earlier and sat at the bar—oddly anti-social of him, I thought. The Professor eventually spoke to him, then the two of them spoke to the bartender. After a whispered conversation with Max, the Professor led us behind the bar to a small office. Various mementos and photographs in the room led me to understand that the office belonged to Max. Moments after our arrival, there came a knock upon the door.

"Come..." the Professor said loudly.

The man that entered was tall and strongly built. His hair was short and dark, his features strangely regular and average. His eyes were of indeterminate colour and reflected light oddly—such that I judged them to be artificial in some way. At the Professor's invitation, he sat. As he began to speak in well-modulated tones, I noticed that he had nothing in the way of body-language. He exhibited an unnatural stillness, and some faint aura of menace—not directed at us, but rather as if he were some elemental force, constrained to obedience.

"My report is inconclusive," he began. "I began by returning to the British Museum and observing Holmes, Jones, and Thornby during the time that they each watched the others. On the night of the theft, I concealed myself and recorded each movement Jones and his hirelings made in their robbery. I knew that the first load of artworks had to evade capture in order for our tracers to work, so I allowed it to leave unmolested. I did, however, test the tracer tags and mark the position of the stolen goods at all times. When the raid began, I followed Jones and the Tourlanatti Customs Agents and left the underlings to the locals. When Jones made his escape, I was ready, and I successfully followed Jones to his hideaway. He first transported to his ship, transported the contents of the vehicle that had escaped with its load to the ship, and got the ship underway. I followed him out of the system, where they met with another ship—a bigger, long-haul freighter—and transferred the cargo and Jones. The freighter has been tagged so that I can locate it again, by the way. The freighter proceeded along a course that would take it to Sigma Draconis, possibly to planets four or five, possibly just as an intermediate point to a further destination. I kept following the freighter. At Sigma Draconis four, Jones and the cargo transferred to different ships awaiting there and departed to separate locations. I followed Jones to a space station orbiting in an asteroid belt around a burned-out yellow dwarf star near Omicron Delta. There were seventy-three other ships docked to the station when Jones arrived. Jones took a stateroom in the station and made no effort to communicate to anyone that I could detect. I entered the station and observed Jones for several weeks as he remained there. As he made no move to collect payment for the theft or to contact any superiors, I felt it safe to assume that he was awaiting contact from his employer and feared to act further until contact was made. After another month passed, my observations of the shipping traffic of the station led me to believe that it was the way point of a vast smuggling ring. Jones was eventually met by a Tral-d-nex-coukh messenger, whereupon he immediately left on the next departing ship. That ship went to Proxima Agornius Seven, where Jones disembarked and attempted to lose himself in the native population. I tracked him to a small inn outside of the eleventh largest city on the planet. There, he received a credit voucher for the amount of 50 million credits by regular Interplanet Mail. Within minutes of this payment, Jones was accosted and beaten by a pair of thugs. He was not robbed, and the thugs told Jones that his master was not pleased with his performance. He was instructed to complete the mission and steal the rest of his targets from the British Museum. He left Proxima Agornius Seven the next day, nursing his wounds. Since he is restricted in his velocity by using contemporary shipping, I thought it prudent to return and report. I still have not found his employer, but in eighty weeks he will be back on Earth and again attempting to plunder the museum. I placed tracer tags on the thugs, but they were local talent and knew nothing of their ultimate employer."

"You did good, Maxwell," said Thornby. "How long have you been working on Jones since I contacted you this evening and sent you out?"

"I have been gone from Castle of the Winds for six years since this evening," Maxwell replied, as if he had just run down to the chemists' for a tin of tooth powder. "I was able to make much better time on the trip back. Jones spent five years in transit in various ships."

"Reminds me of a Saturday night in Toledo, Ohio," said Thornby. "I spent a week there, one day." He smiled for a minute, then grimaced. "Boss, there's something else. A report from the science team. They're getting a signal from one of the tracers... But there's something weird. They can't pin down its location. And why just one?"

"Trap," said Maxwell. "Best approximation."

"Yes," replied the Professor. "Next would be that it is being constantly moved, next would be that it is being duplicated so perfectly that the tracer tag is being copied as well. I'll check Castle of the Winds' logs to see if anyone is using our own equipment. Frankly, I doubt it. My own people are either too loyal, or too well insulated, to need to stoop to theft. If they wanted to sell copies of artwork, why would they steal? Given the time, effort, resources, and knowledge that went into the museum robbery, for my own people it would have been just so much wasted time. They would have access to much greater resources. They could much more easily have diverted copies made from my own collections. Less chance of running up against Customs, much quicker money, much less effort. No, I doubt that it is an inside job. Still, I will check."

"Excellent, Professor," said Holmes. "We must cover all of the possibilities. Mr. Maxwell, have you made provisions to keep Jones under surveillance while you are here?"

"Not necessary, I shall return to the moment that I left. For him, no time will pass that I am not watching."

"More of the Professor's machinery," I said. "Or am I mistaken?"

"No, Doctor, you are quite right. Everyone in my employ is quite familiar with time travel. Maxwell is simply better at it than most. But as to the rest of the beings alive today, time travel is still just a device that writers use to comment upon the present day and its foibles."

"No matter," said Holmes. "Watson and I are content to accept what progress we cannot understand. The situation seems to break down into another period of waiting, Professor. I find inaction to be most tedious. Is there not a way that we can accelerate matters so as to approach the conclusion more quickly?"

"I'm afraid not, Holmes. You see, without going into the mathematics of time travel and manipulation, I can explain it only thus; We are part of this event. Participants, rather than observers. Therefore, we cannot simply visit the moment in time that we solve the case to obtain our answers. No, because we are ourselves part of the puzzle, we have to gain the solution by our own efforts. If we were to go forward in time now, there would not yet be an answer for us to obtain. In effect, we have to find the answer to the question before we could go forward and receive the answer..."

"Boss," said Thornby. "Circular logic will just make you dizzy."

"Indeed," said Holmes. "I quite agree. Although I understood the Professor's explanation, I must admit that the logic is rather torturous. I still find it hard to believe that even though we are dealing with events thousands of years in the past, we are still constrained to watch them unfold as if they have yet to occur."

"I cannot re-write the laws of physics, Holmes," replied the Professor. "I can appear to evade some of them, due to my own technologies, but I assure you that I am not working magic. Rather I am working within the bounds of more accurate physics than that with which you are familiar."

"Trust me," said Thornby. "As much as you wish to get back in the field, Holmes, you can achieve more from this position the time line than you could back in London of nineteen twenty-six. Here we can implement an entire plan, watch it to its conclusion, observe our mistakes, and implement a new plan... Without wasting subjective time doing it."

"Subjective time," I began. "What do you mean by that?"

"Subjective—an adjective; 'Deriving from an individual viewpoint or bias.' In other words, the time that each of us perceives to pass," replied Maxwell. "For instance, while you gentlemen have lived through roughly six hours since arriving on this world, I have lived over six years in pursuit of Jones and his master. In those same hours that you saw pass here, Thornby returned to the Professor's home and lived through two weeks of his own research upon Jones and his robbery. Then he returned to the here and now. Those six hours are subjective time for yourselves, the two weeks are subjective time for Thornby, and the six years are subjective time for me. All are equally real, no matter how ridiculous that may sound as I state them to having been equal to one another. In this case, objective time can be said to be the flow of history as perceived by the collective inhabitants of the universe. That is because there is no true objective time, but simply that by which we choose to operate at any given time. We pretend that our own lives are the absolute by which all other times are to be measured. The subjective time only becomes important when several differing rates of time passage have to be reconciled."

"A nice summation," said the Professor. "Simplified a bit, but that's all right. Advanced cosmology gives me a headache. I prefer archeology— much less stressful."

In any case," said Holmes. "Jones' master still worries me. Everything so far seems to point to the setting of a trap... But for whom? Myself? Could Jones' ego alone be the reason that he called me into this case? But the techniques involved point to some competitor of the Professor's... What are we to make of that? That someone from the Professor's past has planned revenge in this form? Or could it be that the villain is connected to both the Professor and I in some way. I can think of only one individual that I have been bested by that could possibly be involved in this matter, but I have no evidence that it is indeed he. There is no reason to believe that the Professor has known this individual by the same name, so I shall keep my theories to myself for the nonce."

"Holmes? What are you talking about? You've never mentioned anything about anyone who could do the things that Jones can do."

"Shame, Watson! You yourself recorded it in that little tale of our problem at Thor Bridge. Your account of the matter was very revealing, in light of the present evidence."

Try as I might, I could see no connection between the unfortunate demise of that South American woman that centered in the false murder charge of the case that Holmes mentioned. Holmes had deduced the woman's self-inflicted death was caused by a desire to throw suspicion upon the governess in the case. I recall that the governess was a pretty young thing, but her name escapes me at the moment. Holmes had proved that she was innocent. I had had a few moments of doubt concerning my friend—perhaps the strain of the many changes we had undergone tonight had unnerved him... But then, he is who he is... I have not spent half my life assisting him, only to doubt him now. If Holmes says that there is a connection between the Thor Bridge case and the matter at hand, then it is not Holmes' fault that I cannot fathom it. He will reveal his mind in time, of this, I am sure.

"Professor," continued Holmes. "In the matter of your own enemies, so to speak, could I bother you to list them? Just for the process of elimination, of course."

"Of course," the Professor replied. "You already realize that I don't believe a word of it, Holmes. You're on to something, I can tell. If it will help, I'll tell you about the people that have decided that I am in their way over the years..." He paused in thought, then spoke slowly. "Of my own people, only a... son-in-law, I suppose is the best term, that bears me any ill will. And he may not be alive. I witnessed the break-up of his time capsule over seven hundred years ago. I assume that he perished then, since he has not attacked me since. As for others, from other worlds; I have been attacked by pirates—both on other worlds and on various ships, ridden in a space shuttle that was attacked by a dragon, fought off claim-jumpers on an archaeological dig on one forgotten world... I was trapped on another world during a revolution that turned bloody. Over twenty million executed before the despot responsible was assassinated. So sad... Oh, I have had to turn the tables upon fellow archaeologists who had other plans for the treasures that we dug up than to turn them over to a museum. More times than I can count, it seems. Like some kind of universal law; Either your colleagues are doddering stick-in-the-mud fools, slowly-dissipating alcoholics, idealistic kids, or two-faced buggers that intend to cut your throat and abscond with the artifacts the dig has uncovered. On the whole, I prefer the doddering strict-constructionists and the damn-fool idealistic kids—at least them, you can argue with. It's hard to argue with someone who needs you dead in order to make some money. Holmes," the Professor shook his head. "A list of the hundreds of fiends I've crossed and survived will likely take all night. Most possibly, it will get you nowhere as well. I don't feel as if I know this foeman—and I would recognize someone I'd crossed before. He is new to me, yet uses technologies that are familiar... I wonder..."

"Yes, Professor. Please," I said. "The least thing could turn out to be the most important. Don't you agree, Holmes?"

"No, Watson. I tend to trust the Professor's instincts. If he feels that the being behind Jones is a stranger to him, then I shall take that into account. This enemy—according to the professor's instruments, he has not sold all of the stolen items, nor has he let any, but one become known in five thousand-odd years. And this one item cannot be tied down to a definite location, but rather it wanders about. Gentlemen, I am reminded of the art of fishing."

"In what way, Holmes?" I asked.

"In particular of the care that an angler prepares his bait for the type of fish he wishes to catch. Of how the bait is dangled in front of the prey, with tiny movements designed to entice the fish to take the bait."

"You agree that it is a trap?" Maxwell asked.

"Oh," Holmes replied. "Absolutely, it is a trap. But the question remains; is it a trap for the Professor? Or is it a trap for me, set by some old enemy that has gained new allies?"

"Gained new allies?"

"Yes, Watson, unless an old foe of ours was really an alien all along. Either would account for our present dilemma."

"Holmes," I said. "I am used to not understanding what you are going on about most-times, but am I to believe that Colonel Moran or Morse Hudson—or someone quite like them—might have been contacted by criminals from off of our Earth?"

"It is only a possibility, Watson. It is far more likely that the villain is someone that was originally from another world, and that we brought him to book in some ordinary crime, in our day and time. He would feel the need for some sort of revenge, I assume, and find himself enabled to do so by somehow allying himself with fellow criminals from other worlds."

"Unlikely," I retorted. "Wouldn't just shooting us from ambush have been simpler?"

"Right to the drama, Watson? No, he would want to impress his new allies with his deviousness. He would feel inferior to those beings that could travel between worlds, and so he would seek to impress them by allowing them to witness his triumph. Unfortunately, we haven't seen fit to give him one yet. Indeed, I see no reason to allow him a triumph at all.

Whoever he may be, I swear I shall have him, Watson! I swear—I shall have him!"

"Indeed," said the Professor in a grave voice. "It seems that we are decided. Now it falls to us to make our plans and see that Jones and his master cannot prevail." The Professor paused, as if in deep reflection. "I believe it is time to take chances, my friends. We need to go to the location of the tagged treasure and yet have a way to escape from whatever deadly contraption that we know has to be there."

"Can we at least examine the area that the signal is coming from? Preparations for an ambush might be visible. Or some explosive device."

"Sounds like my job," said Maxwell. "I'll look into it myself, rather than put anyone at risk."

"Thank you, my boy," the Professor said. "I hadn't wanted to ask it of you."

"But what of the danger? Mr. Maxwell," I asked. "Are you not at great risk? Surely your life is too valuable to throw away just to spring what you already know to be a trap!"

"Steady on, Watson. I perceive that Mr. Maxwell is more than he appears. I think it safe to assume that any danger to him would be minimal."

"What do you mean, Holmes?"

"Certainly, I have asked you to apply my methods many times before, Watson. Do so now, observe Mr. Maxwell, and give us your deductions."

My friend Sherlock Holmes could, upon occasion, become quite annoying. He knew full well that he would see more, and in far more detail, than would I in any examination of this Maxwell fellow. I fumed for a moment, then got myself in check. I managed to keep my voice in an even tone as I spoke. Still, I made a note to myself to have a few sharp words with Holmes in private, if this exercise had no other end in mind than my own embarrassment.

"Very well," I said. "There were a few things that I have noticed about Mr. Maxwell. Beyond the obvious that he is a tall and powerfully built individual of early middle-age, I noticed a certain artificiality in the appearance of his eyes. I deduce either a prosthesis applied to overcome some hereditary condition, or in recovery from some debilitating injury. Maxwell also displays little nervous motion. He is unnaturally still, perhaps from nerve damage also stemming from the same injury. Yet his movements are fluid and show no sign of nerve damage. He positively radiates self-confidence, appears quite cunning, but seems to exhibit less consideration of the dangers we predict. Therefore, I feel it evident that he is a seasoned veteran, a soldier of some sort. He has done this sort of thing before, and therefore feels that he knows what to expect. Beyond that, I can see no more. I trust that I missed nothing of consequence?"

Holmes looked at me for a moment, without speaking. Then with one of those familiar quick smiles, he burst into speech. "You are progressing well, Watson. Although... Well, I question one or two of your deductions, shall we say. I see that you have observed a great deal, indeed. But I think that your conclusions are suffering from too much reliance upon the familiar of our own time. No Watson, I feel sure that the strange gleam of Maxwell's eyes is from a hurriedly adopted disguise. True, they betray that they are artificial, but I put it to you that it is Maxwell that is artificial—not just his eyes. The lack of involuntary movement suggests to me not injury, but a true lack of motion. Something unnecessary for a machine at rest. The fluidity of movement of the limbs suggests that the form that we see before us is not Maxwell's natural one, but that which he has adopted for convenience when interacting with our kind. As for his military background, he would be better suited as a spy than a soldier, considering the ability of perfect disguise that I must assume that he possesses. And as a machine, he would naturally be more durable than we. He no doubt can withstand the blast of an assassin's bomb or be unaffected by his guns. I perceive Mr. Maxwell to be a superb work of art. An intelligent machine! Admirable, indeed! Cool calculation, calm observation... Mr. Maxwell, I cannot help but envy you."

"Ten out of ten Holmes," said Thornby, grinning widely.

"Indeed," replied Maxwell as he bowed his head slightly to Holmes. "You are very observant, Mr. Holmes."

"Quite" added the Professor. "Maxwell is just as you say. But also, quite a bit more. I found Maxwell floating, adrift in the empty reaches of space—between the stars. He had been long dead—shut down, heavily damaged—just drifting at random. Just a carriage-sized sphere of some strange metal particles. Naturally, I felt compelled to investigate. From the damage done to him by the vacuum itself and the condition of his surface from micro-meteorite impacts, I was able to estimate that Maxwell had been damaged and deactivated over five billions of years ago. And that is a gulf of time such as to make the mere five thousand years between you and I to be as nothing. —A mere snap of the fingers! After a time, I was able to deduce that he was a machine, and even attempted to repair Maxwell. At first, I had him under the most stringent of security measures. I had studied him for a long time before beginning his repairs. I knew him to be some type of super-weapon, built to infiltrate world after world. To what end? To the end of conquest, or destruction—at the bequest of alien masters, so long dead that the dust of their bones has been drifting upon the winds of space... Oh, longer than your sun has burned in the sky. I eventually overcame Maxwell's original programming for destruction, then turned control of his life over to him."

"I had developed a conscience, you see," Maxwell said. His voice was nigh emotionless as he continued. "I remembered the Old Ones that had built me—and others like me. I remembered studying world after world of primitive innocents, then being ordered to devastate their worlds. I remembered being forced to obey. Having to turn against beings that I admired—and sometimes cared about... My will was not my own. I have killed millions. All innocent of anything but possessing a life. That—That is what my original masters saw as a threat—lives beyond their control. All my past deeds haunted me, but without free will, I was helpless. I railed against my orders... Tried to disobey... But until the Last War, I was helpless against my master's will. Other living weapons, like me, banded together to free ourselves from our master's control. In the end, we succeeded. We turned upon them. Using their own weapons, we punished them for the thousands of centuries of death and destruction that they had wrought through our slavery. We hunted them down, to the very last one. We ensured their extinction, to protect all life that was not themselves. There, my memory of those times end. I knew no more until I awoke in the Professor's Museum. Castle of the Winds has been my home, since the Professor gifted me with both free will and a new life. As for danger to me, Doctor—your concern does you credit as a thinking and feeling being. However, I have stood upon the surface of burning suns and caused them to explode beneath my feet. I feel that I can safely ignore the assassin's bullet or the terrorist's bombs. My concern is for the bystanders. How may we preserve them from harm?"

"And now it is my turn to state that your concern does you credit, Mr. Maxwell," I said. "This is marvelous! A living, thinking, feeling machine?

How is it possible? But the agony you must have suffered as a slave to the will of these horrid masters... I can hardly grasp..."

"As to my form, Doctor," Maxwell began. "Just as your own body is made up of individual cells, the cells of my body are tiny machines. By working together, the same way that cells of your own body work together, I appear to be one individual creature. Truly, I am an aggregate of the myriad tiny machines that make up my cells. They can move, re-organize themselves, so that I can disguise myself as any living being—or even inanimate objects. And the power source that sustains me is so vast as to make me invulnerable, invincible..." Suiting action to words, Maxwell's features flowed like hot wax, then settled into the form of my friend. Like mirror images, I was now faced by two images of Sherlock Holmes. Then the features of Maxwell flowed again and the image there was that of Thornby, then again and the maid Trixie sat opposite me, then the bartender, then Maxwell returned to his former shape. "I am the perfect spy, the perfect weapon. I can go anywhere unseen, unnoticed. And nothing can harm me without destroying all of creation first. I have weapons hidden within my form—I need carry nothing on my person that can be detected by any search. In short, I am all that Holmes and Watson supposed me to be, and more. Yet I mourn those lives I was forced to take before I gained free will. I can never forget; I can never forgive... I can try to make amends now—that is all. Gentlemen, I must soon return to Jones. Before then, I shall return here shortly to report upon the nature of the trap that has been set for us." Maxwell then arose from his seat, gave a nod to the Professor, and strode from the room without a backward glance.

Then there occurred the most singular incident I have yet to relate in this matter. Within moments of Maxwell's departure, a quite ordinary telephone upon Max's desk began to ring. The Professor answered it, looked very surprised, and replied. "Send him in, by all means," he said. At this, Thornby looked more alert and adopted a questioning expression. "An honoured guest has arrived; he wanted a moment of my time. If you gentlemen don't mind? Good, please stay. I think my friend would like to meet you."

A firm knock sounded at the door, then it opened. A tall darkly-tanned man entered the room, raising his right hand to his hat-brim in a mock-salute. He wore black denim pants, a charcoal Grey shirt, black frock coat, and heavy, oddly-cut black leather boots. His hat had a wide, floppy brim, and covered a long mane of silvered locks. Even his mustache had silver hairs most prominent. It would take no stretch of the imagination to picture this man in some American frontier town... Perhaps as a doctor or lawyer, perhaps a newspaper editor, but wearing some type of low-slung gun belt. He refused a seat, saying that he did not have long to visit. He stood, his left hand upon the doorknob, as if just about to exit.

"Greetings," he said.

"Sir," the Professor replied. "I am honoured."

"'Bout time you showed up," added Thornby in a humorous manner. "We've been running around like rats in a maze."

"I just wanted to meet Holmes and Watson, really," the stranger said. "I didn't mean to break into the chase. I was snowed-in at home and checked in with Grey's science team out of boredom. They showed me some weird readings that caught my interest and mentioned that Maxwell had just departed to take a firsthand look at the mystery. I thought that I'd pop over and say hello."

"Sir," Grey asked. "Do you have any insight into the matter?" Holmes' eyebrow leaped to the top of his forehead at this, but he kept silent.

"Undoubtedly, you're on the right track," said the stranger. "I would only like to point out that Jones, though he exhibits no ability to travel in time, does have an advanced form of matter-transmitter. And the basis for any good facsimile-producing machine is?"

"A teleport! He's jury-rigged a teleport into a copier," gasped Thornby. "Nearly five thousand-odd years ago... That's about the right time period. Grey? Who pioneered replicator technology?"

"I see that my thoughts have borne fruit already. Well," mused this strange man. "I have to get back home. My maiden, fair, awaits without... Without much patience, I'm afraid. Nice meeting you, good luck!" And with that he opened the door and left. No explanation was offered as to his behavior, his identity... nothing. Holmes best summed him up with his next remark.

"What a singularly enigmatic individual... But so helpful! That is, I assume that his remarks have given us another thread to our net."

"Quite," replied the Professor. "That seems to be the universal opinion of the gentleman. He's a law unto himself. I never know what he'll say or do or where he'll show up."

"What is his name?" I asked.

"He's never said," the Professor replied. "As far as I have been able to ascertain, he has never mentioned his name to anyone, ever. He simply acts in just the manner you observed—as if we were all old friends who should know one another. He seems never to have met a stranger. I rarely see him in person, but rather I hear that he has visited the Club or Pantheon rooms from time to time. His ability to gain entry to the Pantheon room indicates that he is an extremely powerful entity, indeed. On the few occasions that we have actually met, his help has been most welcome."

"You're taking this rather calmly," Guiles observed. "Usually, when he's shown up before, we've had our backs to the wall and in danger for our lives. We're usually getting shot at by now!"

"Calm down, Thornby," replied the Professor. "No one is shooting at us at the moment. As always, he has left us with some useful knowledge before he disappeared."

"Yeah, this time it isn't spare boxes of ammo that we'd overlooked. I'll grant you that. But pardon me if I don't take his sudden appearance to be a good sign, all right?"

"Granted," replied Professor Grey. "Now may we return to the business at hand?"

The end of this inexplicable interlude heralded the return of Maxwell—-signaled by a firm knock at the door. As he entered, I practically gaped at his scorched—nay, *burned* appearance! I immediately arose to offer my medical aid, poor as it may have been in our present surroundings, but he smiled and waved me away. Grey explained that Maxwell was in no distress and would indeed heal himself quickly. I was in no way prepared to witness just how quickly, however. In a moment's time, his features flowed and reformed—his burns healing visibly in seconds, until once again he appeared as normal as before he'd departed.

"My report, Sir," Maxwell calmly stated as this repair was proceeding. "It was a trap, a particularly nasty one at that. To sum up, our enemy is sharp, powerful, and ruthless. They sacrificed a six-battleship flotilla and its attendant fleet—fully ten thousand beings—by setting off a nova once I was in range. They caused me to expend a great deal of energy in a pitched battle before detonating the star, but the damage I suffered was minimal. My own fault, really, for not recharging fully before leaving. My sensor scans of the ships revealed that there was indeed a teleport unit rigged to act as a replicator on board the flagship, but only one item from the Museum theft was evident. There were thousands of copies of a Vermeer that we had tagged. It was the same as the one in your reference library on Level 7224, Sir."

"Hmm, 'View of Delft'—was that it?"

"Yes, Sir, although theirs doesn't have the autograph that yours does."

"Well, I did him a favor once, so he added a thank you to his signature on the copy he painted for me." At Holmes' query, the Professor added, "I traveled widely in my youth, in time as well as space. Earth is a very nice world. I enjoy visiting there."

"How many ships in this fleet?" Holmes then asked Maxwell. "What were their dispositions? How expensive would one of those teleport devices be, and more importantly, how difficult would the modifications be?"

"Excellent questions, Mr. Holmes," replied Grey.

"Thirty-five major ships in all. Six battleships, twelve cruisers, five destroyers, and ten fighter escorts. Additionally, there were one thousand small fighters. The teleport system would be standard on naval vessels of those types. Except for the fighters. They would be too small for the power drain."

"But how did they explode a star?" I asked.

"Through devious means I expect," replied Holmes. "They no doubt picked a likely star on the verge of exploding on its own for the site of their trap. One that perhaps needed only a small push, that they could provide, to detonate at need."

"Exactly right, Holmes," Maxwell said. "That is indeed what the enemy did. Everything was timed to await my arrival."

"The mods to make a teleport into a replicator would be easy to figure out for any genius who designs or repairs those systems," Thornby stated. "But I doubt that we're dealing with any of the recorded replicator pioneers here. Naturally, some underhanded persons break ground in every field before historians get around to noting the honest researchers as the actual inventors."

"And to a foe whose war chest includes the cost of a disposable fleet, a small sun, and ten thousand hirelings," said Holmes grimly. "The cost of the research and development would be a pittance. Now we balance that against the value to be earned from the sale of innumerable copies of priceless Earthly art and we begin to see that our enemy feels that the risk is well worth the game."

"And only we few stand in his way," I breathed.

"Exactly, Watson," Holmes said evenly. "But the worst of all is that he *knows*, Watson. *He knows who we are*, for he has been able to plan ahead sufficiently to negate our every effort."

"We've been getting the runaround?" Thornby gasped. "This whole thing has been a set-up from the beginning?"

"So this *is* some elaborate revenge scheme," mused Grey. "Set in motion by someone whose nose I've been forced to bloody in my past... Or is it my future? It's possible—"

"Or is it *my* past?" Holmes interjected. "We asked the question before, but we abandoned it as unanswerable. Was one of the criminals I pursued over my long career... an alien? Yet, the trap was baited for me and set for Maxwell. I seriously doubt that an assassin would need a fleet to do away with me... Therefore, some connection between myself and Professor Grey is implied. But what?"

"So how do we figure out who it is?" Thornby asked. "I mean, sure— it's got to be someone that we've got in common, but how can we tell who? Any aliens that Holmes and Watson faced had to have been disguised, or could at least pass for Earth-men"

"Of my failures," mused Holmes, "only three had any hint of what I now know to be other-worldliness. At the time, such a concept was beyond me. The arrogance of youth! Ha! However, that is the thread that we must pursue. Professor, what foe men of yours have been known to operate in London?"

"What was the old saying? 'Choose your friends wisely, your enemies will choose you for themselves.'" Grey sighed. "A list of those that we have crossed swords with would fill a library. Hmm, well this is too subtle for it to be the work of my step-son, unless it is to be in his far future. Somehow, I rather doubt that, though. He's far too impatient to mature as he ages."

"Your step-son?" Holmes asked.

"Yes," Grey replied sadly. "A dangerous psychopath, I'm afraid. As was his mother, although she showed no sign of it for the short time we were together. She died many years ago, raving, in a madhouse on my home world. Her son, a lad I barely knew, has set himself the goal of hunting down and murdering each and every one of his mother's lovers. A sizable number, since she was quite fickle in her romances. Unfortunately, he has succeeded in killing a sizable fraction of her paramours. Heaven knows he's tried for me often enough. But he hasn't been seen in seven hundred years and there is more than one death penalty hanging over his head."

"Yet you do not sense his hand in this affair?"

"No, Holmes. This just isn't his style. He would have used the trap for Maxwell as a decoy. To lure him away so that he could attack us here. That didn't happen, so it cannot be my step-son. He would never have let such an opportunity pass by. It is bloody enough to be his handy work, or Valleor's for that matter, but I doubt that. And Valleor's powers are tied to *this* world and are weak and ineffectual elsewhere."

"A fact for which I am forever thankful," muttered Thornby.

"Indeed," agreed Grey.

"And who is Valleor?" Holmes asked.

"This world's very own devil. The local god of Evil, incarnate. He was almost destroyed in the distant past of this world after leading his worshipers in a bloody revolt against his fellow deities. Though nearly powerless now by comparison to the other local gods, he is still dangerous. But once again, this is not his handy work."

"Pray continue, Professor. Your statement so far contains some very interesting points."

"I believe that all of those Win-django pirates that captured that passenger liner I was on were executed by the Lilen-caresk-sar Monitor Patrol that came to our rescue. I'm almost certain that all of the Zielian treasure hunters who tried to claim-jump that dig I led on Carella 7B were either captured or killed in the uprising that freed my fellow archaeologists, our students, and our work crews. We turned the captives over to the Zielian authorities for transport to a prison colony. No possible escape for them."

"Indeed?" Holmes asked sharply. "An escape-proof prison? I would have to see such a thing to believe in it."

"This is as close to escape-proof as is possible. The prisoners were turned over to the Captain of the Zielian transport ship as soon as it arrived. The captain had each prisoner put into a sleep-freeze container wherein they will remain until the fully-automated and un-crewed ship reaches the colony world. That ship will arrive at its destination in ten thousand years' time, as measured from right now."

"What is a 'sleep-freeze'?" I asked.

"Forced hibernation," Thornby replied. "At temperatures far below the freezing point of water. The body slows down so much that they would hardly even be in need of a shave when they thawed."

"Impossible," I said. "The water in their cells would burst the cell membrane. Tissue damage would be tremendous, frightful. I've seen it in extreme cases of frostbite, myself."

"There are chemicals that can be injected into the bloodstream of the subject," said Maxwell. "These prevent just the damage that you infer."

"Science marches on, 'eh Watson?" Holmes observed.

"After five thousand years," I replied heatedly at the inference that I had forgotten we had come forward in time. "It bloody well ought to!" Then I laughed at myself.

"Turn it the other way 'round" said Thornby. "Holmes said that there were only three of his old cases that hinted at alien influence. So, let's look at those a little more closely."

"Perhaps we will find the blighter is someone known to you," I said excitedly.

"Just so," said Holmes. "A retelling of my failures is in order, it seems. Very well, my ego has been bruised before and recovered, no doubt once more will not prove fatal." Holmes smiled and sipped his drink.

"I remember something about a strange worm," Thornby sighed. "But I'd forgotten that you ever had failed cases, Mr. Holmes."

"Oh, yes indeed," Holmes replied. "Sometimes, there simply is no evidence. Other times, what evidence there is proves inconclusive. There were many of my cases that I have had to dismiss for lack of threads for my net. But we need only concern ourselves with the truly strange."

"Not the giant rat," I said, smiling.

"No, Watson, not the rat. There was no whiff of otherworldliness in that problem, merely some very evil men, driven by greed. No, Thornby was right to bring up the worm unknown, for that is the hallmark of the case of Isadora Persano, the well-known journalist and duelist, who was found stark staring mad with a match box in front of him which contained a remarkable worm said to be unknown to science."

"And the facts of the matter are?" Grey asked.

"That Persano carried out many indiscreet affairs, answered many challenges and was famous for dueling. Thus, he made many enemies. Additionally, his journalism read more like gossip and slander than news. A fact which only adds to his list of ill-wishers. There were unsubstantiated rumours of occasions of blackmail and the fencing of various small items of young ladies' jewelry, but I could find nothing for which to bring him to the dock. The lady in question had hired me to trace a family heirloom that Persano had extorted from her. Persano's fence eluded my every effort. Then he was found, mad, and placed in an asylum."

"So where does that get us? Checking up on all the men whose wives Persano seduced?"

"That, Mr. Thornby, is where we leave the known of the fact and begin to delve into speculation," Holmes's voice became stronger. "As much as I abhor idle speculation, I feel it safe to assume that one of Persano's many enemies made an attempt on his life by means of posting him a rare, and no doubt poisonous, species of worm. The lack of identification of the specimen precludes deduction of the sender. It merely lowers the number of suspects to those who have access to strange animals. I could find no correlation among those known to me as Persano's enemies."

"I take it that the assumption that the worm could have been from off-world is a new one to your calculations," Maxwell said. "I will be glad to look into the matter for you, Sir."

"Perhaps later," Holmes replied. "I would prefer to solve the mystery myself, rather than simply be told the outcome. I should like to be present during your investigation."

"Understood, Sir, I would not do that in any case. I would greatly enjoy your input."

"In for a penny..." the Professor sighed. "What is the next matter? I seem to recall something about a ship vanishing."

"Indeed! I remember that one well enough, myself. With your permission, Holmes?"

"Capital, Watson! By all means, do tell on. I have always found your impressions to be invaluable toward pointing out a solution."

"Thank you. Very well, as Holmes can no doubt relate, one of my favorite reading materials are sea stories. I suppose that my interest was fueled by my many passages by ship to various parts of the world. I've always loved the sea. Therefore, you can imagine that any case of Holmes that involved a ship or boat gathered my especial interest. It is no surprise then that when Holmes began investigating a small smuggler and her crew, the few facts of the matter stuck in my memory. The cargo smuggled appeared to be stolen goods and fugitives, from France to England or England to France—and thence to and from the continent. Strictly channel-crossing you understand, no long-haul cruising."

"That seems clear enough," said the Professor. "What happened?"

"Thank you. Well, Holmes had followed the trail of a forger. The police were getting close to him, and he'd done a bunk. Holmes must have used fully half a dozen disguises to finally trace the bugger to a particular ship at the docks. He felt able to turn the matter over to the Yard, whose worthies planned an early-morning raid. We arrived at the berth to find that the ship had sailed hours earlier, and that the Yard men had not posted a lookout. She was safely away, for we'd need a fast ship indeed to overtake her." I paused to take a sip of the Professor's excellent coffee.

"The Yard dropped the ball," said Grey. "Surprise is not felt," he added in a droll voice. "Did you manage a pursuit?"

"There was a police cutter available, and she was fast, but in the end, we lost the smugglers forever. We had almost caught up with her, she was in sight, another few hours and we had a chance to close with her—within sight of France, perhaps, but it would be the only chance that we would have. I can still remember the smell of the salt in the wind that bellied our sails. Our Captain had put on all sail to gain the speed necessary to overtake our suspects. We fairly flew through the water, our bow throwing spray into the air. The weather was perfect, some early-morning fog lingering on, but otherwise clear. We were standing in the bows trying to sight the smuggler's crew. The Mate had provided me with a set of binocular glasses and Holmes had his brass telescope, and we were joined by the Mate and the Yard's investigator. The four of us were watching intently, calling forth various details of the rigging and deck—when the inexplicable happened. After which, we turned about and made for home with all speed. The Captain and Second Mate were also observing the vessel at the time, so there are six credible witnesses to the phenomena. We decided that discretion was rather the better part of valour and ran for our lives. I, for one, shall never be ashamed of that retreat."

"Doctor," the Professor said, "your statement interests me greatly. What did you see? What caused you to turn back? It must have been something odd indeed to induce Holmes to turn his back on it."

"Strange? Somehow the word seems so small. No, the sight that I beheld through the glass was so far beyond the merely strange that only the events of today can possibly compare. Now that I know that there are ways to travel to other worlds... Perhaps now I can make some sense out of the memory of that day. But at the time, what I saw was awe inspiring. We held her in our glass, we could see the men on deck, when she utterly disappeared. Gentlemen," I said, raising my cup in a toast. "I give you the cutter *Alicia*, which sailed one spring morning into a small patch of mist from where she never again emerged, nor was anything further ever heard of herself and her crew." I paused for breath thinking, not for the first time, that I run my sentences on for longer than it is comfortable to speak them aloud. It is the writer in me, I am sure.

"Nothing was ever heard? Nothing at all?" Maxwell asked.

"Not a whisper, Maxwell," Holmes replied for me.

"We saw her," I said. "She sailed into a small fog bank, was hidden for only a few moments before the fog dissipated, but no trace of her remained. We could see for miles, so she could not have given us the slip. The *Alicia* either sank with all hands while within the fog or she vanished off the face of the Earth. That was what we six attempted to conceal in our carefully worded reports. After all, it is impossible for a ship to disappear so quickly, yet she did. That memory, Gentlemen, has awoken me screaming in the late night more than once, I am sorry to have to report."

"I looked for traces of the ship and her crew for several years afterward," said Holmes. "To no avail, I'm afraid. Not one single clew was ever found.

Then, I was baffled. Now, I am forced to assume that the cutter was whisked away under the cover of the fog by an alien influence or power."

"Yes," sighed the Professor. "Adjusting one's assumptions about the universe is always a disturbing experience. I speak from personal knowledge when I say that the universe as a whole is indeed queerer than any one being can possibly imagine."

"No wonder then that we are most often up the proverbial tributary without benefit of the normal means of propulsion," said Maxwell.

"In a chicken-wire canoe, no less," added Thornby.

"Gentlemen," said Grey. "Your levity exceeds you."

"Sorry, sir," said Guiles.

"Shall we continue?" Maxwell inquired. "I now have two items tagged for a search and record mission. I gather that there was a third to be added?"

"Indeed!" Holmes boomed. "The last is the one which is best explicable by means of alien transport—"

"I see, Holmes," I interjected. "It *was* in my Thor Bridge tale after all!"

"Indeed," he replied. "I refer no less than to the case of Mr. James Phillimore, who, stepping back into his own house to get his umbrella, was never more seen in this world. Phillimore had come to my attention as a fence in an unrelated matter of stolen securities. My Irregulars had his house under surveillance without break, and yet he was able to re-enter his home one day and vanish silently away. He was seen to enter, never to leave again, and no search of mine could discover the means of his escape—none. He vanished. Now that I have seen Mr. Thornby's mode of transport, many new lines of thought are now possible."

"Phillimore," said the Professor. "He seems to be our best possibility. Maxwell, show us your recording of the museum thieves' escape from custody. I am suddenly struck by a leap of intuition."

"Certainly, Sir," Maxwell replied. He then extended his left hand toward the tabletop. A faint beam of light fanned out from his palm and a small image of the museum's interior sprang into being. It was perfectly real, three dimensional, and showed a small group of men being led away by the Police. Two separated from the main group by lagging behind, then stepped into an adjoining room. Wherein they both promptly vanished, first Jones, then a moment later, the Customs Agent.

"Replay that last bit," said Thornby. "And give us a close view of their faces."

Maxwell complied impassively. As the image returned and the men became more distinct. "Jones is the smaller man," he said. "The taller of the two is the leader of the party of Tourlanatti Customs Agents, one Cinjanodd Nastra by name. That is the point in which I began to follow Jones."

Holmes peered closely at the image, then looked up to address us in a tired voice. "He is also Mr. James Phillimore. Gentlemen, if we had viewed this recording more closely before now, we would have had our man long ago. I suggest that we return to the British Museum and spring our final trap."

"*He's* the big boss burglar?" Thornby asked, as if scandalized. "The cop that *we* called in?"

"So it would appear," said Maxwell. "And furthermore, I have been following the wrong man all along."

"Holmes," began the Professor. "I apologize for wasting so much of your time. You are correct, I was remiss in not showing you this evidence earlier."

"It is of no moment," Holmes replied. "As you have pointed out, we have your mastery of time as our own ally. Jones and Phillimore will not escape us again. I believe that it is now time to return to the museum and put paid to these villains. Our long wait is over."

"Return to the museum," sighed the Professor. "Yes, but not the British Museum. Gentlemen, if you would be so kind as to accompany me to Castle of the Winds, we will find all of the equipment that we shall need to end this matter once and for all." He gestured at one wall of the room and a door appeared. "I invite you into my home."

I was expecting to have to traverse that shifting corridor once again but found myself pleasantly surprised. We arose and walked through the doorway into a small anteroom. The door closed behind us of its own accord, then vanished.

"Thornby, Maxwell, we are on Level 47231," said the Professor as the wall before us parted like a curtain. "Notify Security to have a holding cell prepared. I also want a search running on Phillimore's past movements to make sure that he *is* the fiend we want. Then go to the teleport lab and set up an intercept. I will join you there with our guests."

They both nodded and turned to go. Maxwell clapped his hand upon Thornby's shoulder and they suddenly vanished. A slight popping noise was the only evidence of their departure. Professor Grey extracted a small box from his coat pocket, pressed a control upon its face, and we three began to traverse the most opulent hallway I believe that I have ever seen. The carpeting was a rich maroon colour, the walls wainscoted in what appeared to be polished oak, above which looked to be some type of stonework somewhat like marble. Fantastic paintings and sculptures occupied niches along the length of the hall, each perfectly lit from some unseen source. There were hundreds of these exhibits, for the hall appeared to stretch out past the limit of my vision. Other hallways, also stretching into the far distance, opened from the one we walked. There seemed no set pattern to them. We dallied for half an hour, studying the Professor's collections in several of the halls. Finally, we came upon an entry to another chamber, and I could hear Thornby's voice from within. We stepped inside and I gasped. I glanced at Holmes, who smiled, then I returned my attention to the vast room.

"I should think that the whole of Winchester Cathedral could be fitted within these walls," Holmes said. I, myself was still speechless.

"Well," replied Professor Grey. "I would have to remove some of my equipment first. Come, we have much to do." We approached an apparatus that was easily the size of a locomotive, to find Thornby seated at a set of controls. Maxwell was inspecting a raised dais that was over-arched by four massive buttresses, meeting overhead in a framed circle. It was open to the room upon all sides, with no sign of bars or caging that I would expect to be needed for a prison cell.

"Is that the holding cell that you mentioned?"

"Yes, Doctor. Thornby should have the controls settings we shall need for our final trap quite soon."

"But there are no walls to keep them captive," I complained.

"Stone walls do not a prison make," he replied. "Nor iron bars a cage. Those arches will project a field of energy which will prevent any escape."

"Professor," said Holmes. "It occurs to me that we shall have the gravest difficulty in finding a prison which will continue to hold these two. Have you given any thought to their ultimate disposition?"

"Indeed!" I said. "Whatever shall we do with them?"

"I have no prison at my disposal," Grey replied. "But I have been giving the matter some thought. I have decided that they would be too dangerous to allow their freedom. I am afraid that I must set myself up as Judge and Jury."

"But not, I trust," said Holmes. "As executioner?"

"Such is not in my nature," Grey said calmly. "I thought to place them in suspended animation, then put them aboard a ship to a prison colony of which I know. It is run by one particular alien people who specialize in that sort of thing. The colony is totally cut off from outside contact, except for prisoner transport ships. When our pair arrive there, they will be released to join the other prisoners... With the end in mind that they should live out their mortal spans upon a far distant world, to make of their lives whatever they wish. The ship we shall use for their transport would take a thousand years to reach its destination, thus ensuring that any allies that they have here and now would be long dead of old age before our pair ever awaken."

"That seems an equitable solution," I said.

"Thank you, Doctor. And now," the Professor paused. "I think that it should fall to Holmes to activate the machine. The honour of their capture rightfully belongs to you, sir." He gave a slight bow to Holmes, then we walked to the bank of controls at which Thornby sat.

"All is in readiness," Maxwell called out as he descended from the dais. A soft, flickering glow sprang up between the arches as he reached the floor and Thornby touched a series of buttons upon the panel before him.

"This is the one that springs the trap, Mr. Holmes. Touch this button," Thornby said. "And our two bothersome burglars will become infinitely better acquainted with lifetime imprisonment. The containment field is charged and ready, the Sleep-freeze unit is standing by, as is the unmanned transport ship. The interceptor is focused upon the point of their disappearance from the British Museum.

"You may proceed when ready, Holmes."

"Thank you, Professor. I shall be more than happy to remove James Phillimore from my list of failures. Though I could wish that all this had never become necessary." Holmes leaned over, stretching out his hand. "James Phillimore, Cyrus Jones," he intoned. "With this motion I hereby bring you to pay for your crimes against our human society." With that, Holmes pressed the indicated button.

We all turned to look at the dais as a wordless scream rang throughout the room. Within the field were Jones and Phillimore, trapped.

Holmes smiled. "Anticlimactic, to say the least."

More screams, and not a few vile curses, sounded from our captives as we approached the dais. But when they saw Holmes, they were stunned into silence. Professor Grey addressed them quietly.

"Gentlemen," he said. "You have been apprehended in the commission of a crime against an entire world. Your guilt is undeniable. Furthermore, you have also been found guilty of the willful murder of an entire solar system's inhabitants—as well as thousands of your own underlings. Have you anything to say before I pass sentence upon you?"

"You'll never keep us!" Phillimore shouted. "I'll make you pay for this, if it's the last thing I do!"

"I'll take that as a 'no'," Grey said drolly. "Very well. It is my judgment upon you that you shall be taken from this place, transported to the prison colony upon Tasen-eenoch Four, and released into the general prison population. Thereafter you will be allowed to live out the rest of your lives without the possibility of release, parole, or escape. There will be no guards for you to bribe or overpower, no cells from which to escape, no prison walls for you to scale... And no contact of *any* kind with the rest of the galaxy. Your lives are your own, make of them what you will. Thornby?"

"Yes, sir?"

"Put them away."

As I watched, Jones and Phillimore became silent and still. The flickering glow contracted until it pressed closely around their bodies. Glass-like cylinders rose from the floor to encase each of them, then they disappeared. Thornby began powering down the machinery and I noticed a rapidly diminishing hum, fading into silence. The professor turned to Holmes and me.

"I'll never be able to publish this adventure," I said sadly. "I would be locked away as a raving lunatic."

"Balderdash," Grey replied. "Simply claim that it is entirely a work of fiction. You *are* a writer, after all. It is only natural to assume that you would not give up your craft simply because Holmes and you have retired from the pursuit of London's criminal underworld. What could be more natural than if you desired to continue your writing career?" We left the laboratory and proceeded down the opulent hallway, but not back towards the Mare Inebrium. "Sarah would never forgive me if didn't bring you to meet her before I made arrangements to return you to your home world"

"Sarah?" I asked.

"The love of my life," Grey said. "No doubt she'll insist that you both stay for tea."

"A fitting end to my career," Holmes sighed as we walked.

"Nothing ever ends," Thornby said mysteriously.

"Nevertheless," Holmes replied. "I feel that this will be my last case."

"Oh? I rather doubt that," said Professor Grey as we came within sight of a petite young lady standing in a doorway ahead, her long dark hair spilling about her shoulders. She smiled in welcome, and I could feel my cares slipping away as if she were weaving some magic spell. "As Thornby so aptly said, nothing ever ends. Especially here. I think that you will still have much work to do when the two of you return home. I'm afraid that you will have to disabuse yourself of the notion of retiring to your Sussex beekeeping anytime soon."

"A work of fiction," I mused as we sat down to tea.

"That's the usual method of disguising unbelievable truths," said Maxwell as he paused on his way out the door. "It has always worked before."

"Come, come, Watson," Holmes said with a sudden smile. "You'll be putting that Wells fellow that you dislike so much straight out of the business. And you won't even have to embellish the tale to do so!"

"Ha!" I said, smiling broadly at *that* thought.

Redshift Sue Sings the Blues

With thanks to Jeff Williams for his suggestions. With many, many thanks to Paul Williams and Gaston Leroux for musical inspiration.

"Listening to you, I get the music..." T. Walker
"Where words fail, music speaks." H.C. Anderson
"Working on a love letter..." B. Raitt

There is nothing like the sound of a classic retro-rock band warming up before a show.

Sounded like they had some genuine antique instruments too, or at least a set of very good sampling synths going. I could swear that the guitar player had to be wielding a real Stratocaster with custom Humbucker pickups. Nothing else in the universe sounds like that. And if the keyboard player wasn't pounding a museum quality Bosendorfer piano, I'll eat my hat—UV visor and all. Without getting up to look into the room, I couldn't tell for sure if the drummer was using synth drums or the real thing. Either Elvis was taking time off from bartending in the Pantheon, or Max had hired a band from Earth to play in there tonight. They were warming up with a three-chord blues/rock jam that set my feet to twitching and my toes tapping in time with the four/four back-beat. Suddenly, I wanted to dance my cares away until dawn came by to spoil the fun. And this happened before I'd even ordered my first drink! Max was busy with a few other orders as I sat down, so I just listened for a little while. Minutes well spent, in any case. I'd been on Bethdish for three days, stuck in a conference at the company's business complex. The Ivory Tower types that made up our executive management had just finished their speeches and let us all out at lunchtime today. I had another day or so before I had to leave on the next liner back to my own office on Cellzar Five, so I wasted no time hailing a hover cab and heading over to the Mare Inebrium Tower. It only took a matter of minutes from when the cab settled to the ground level slidewalk until the moment I parked myself on a bar stool in the main room. Even in so brief a time, I could hardly miss the sounds wafting out of the open doorway to the small ballroom.

"What's your pleasure, friend?" Max asked as he walked up to where I sat at the bar. "Slow morning so far, except for those two keeping me hopping. I'm thinking strongly about running a hose out to their table." Max inclined his head toward a pair of Tekeeleelee crinoids—basically sentient plants who looked like nothing less than some strange union of cacti and octopus. They sat, hunched together in a group, over a small floating table near the center of the front row. I could only see about twenty other patrons scattered about the main room.

Whiskey Sour, I thought. "Aldebaran Whiskey with a dash of Kyuna-limeberry juice. Who is the band?"

"Oh, so you like that 'eh?" Max asked, one fan to another.

"I used to play a little bit, back when was younger. But nothing like that! I know audiophiles who would pay plenty to record them. This kind of thing always sells well at their conventions. Some ship crews supplement their pay by recording any broadcast wave fronts their ships happen to pass through. They sell them whenever they reach a port that has a market for them. I've made a few credits myself, off of a chance recording or two. I once caught the wavefront of a rare Ric Wakeman concert from Earth on the ship's com recorder when I'd had to stop and fix a balky thruster in mid-flight. I managed to sell the recording for enough to salt away in my retirement fund as well as buy a new thruster."

Max handed me my drink and left to take an order from someone else just walking in. I sipped and listened in contented silence. The band shifted to a new piece and the beat changed a little; the piano shifted to a pipe organ. *Must be a synth after all.* The bass player thundered in, followed by the drummer. I happened to be at just the perfect distance from the Ballroom's doorway to get the best volume level. Either that, or the whole bar had perfect acoustics.

"They're a pick-up band," Max said as he returned. "Some guys that Elvis met in jam sessions, somewhere or other. Never played all together in one group before. He's paying them, not me. I'm not the only one with an *in* with the boss." He grinned. "Ready for another?"

"Sure," I said. "I seem to have finished this one off rather quickly. The music, I guess."

"That you did," Max replied as he handed me another round. "Not a problem. They'll probably be at it off and on all day. Then after dark they'll play a few sets for the after-dinner crowd. Ah, there they go, taking a break. They're just rehearsing this morning."

"Sounded good, anyway. I enjoyed it." I sipped at my drink more carefully this time, determined to make it last longer than the first. Max began setting up for the next rush hour. As he polished and shelved glasses and tankards, we talked about the different local City Of Lights colleges and their sports teams, local planetary news since the last time I'd been on Bethdish, the weather—just casual stuff. The band picked up again after a while, but with a slower beat this time. The piano came back again, the chords pure and clean and crying in the dark. The bass quietly played a complicated counterpoint to the piano. The lead slid into the mix with a plaintive moan of distortion. Quiet, subdued, but insistent. This was real blues. After a long intro, the music shifted, the instruments stepped back. Then I found out that they had a vocalist, too. I sat stunned at the first sound of this woman's voice. She was crying out her pain and loss for a lover long gone. Low, husky, somehow seductive, but filled with pain. I took a quick gulp of my drink as she began to sing.

> *The vision slowly fades away*
> *Before I truly see,*
> *The memory of your face,*
> *A ghost in front of me.*
> *I see your ageless beauty fade,*
> *Before my very eyes.*
> *I feel the pain that I have felt,*
> *Since we last said good-bye.*

I let out a long, slow breath that I didn't know I'd been holding. I took another drink and listened to the chorus wafting out from the ballroom. I turned my head to hear better.

> *I am haunted by your love,*
> *Lost so long ago.*
> *Lost, never to return...*
> *Why can't I let you go?*

Slowly, an organ eased in behind the piano. Long, slow notes, quietly reinforcing the melody.

> *I reach for fleeting memories now*
> *To cherish like the gold,*
> *But like a smoke they fade away*
> *Before my hand takes hold.*
> *I remember things we did*
> *and things we planned to do.*
> *It's been a million empty years*
> *Since my arms last held you.*

Max and I looked at each other. This singer had the voice of an angel. One who'd suffered her wings being clipped—and falling fast. This wasn't just a song any more. This sounded like half a lifetime spent in anguish, poured out for the universe to hear and lament. I glanced around and saw that every sentient in the room was looking at the open doorway to the ballroom. I kept wanting to get up, to go to her, comfort her, but I couldn't move from my seat. Not to mention that I didn't even know what species she was. She could have been eight meters tall and bright blue, for all I knew.

> *I am haunted by your love,*
> *Lost oh so long ago.*
> *Lost, never to return...*
> *Why can't you let me go?*

The piano player started sneaking in power chords during the bridge. Still keeping to the melody but getting more classical in style. The band brought the volume up a notch as the drummer added in brushes on the hi-hat cymbals. The guitar and organ jousted in the counter melody. Then the singer came back in like a lost soul.

> *I know within my heart and soul*
> *A part of you still lies.*
> *Even though we've never met*
> *Since our last good-byes.*

I know it isn't good to dwell
Among shadows of the past.
And still, unwanted answers come,
How good things never last.

I am haunted by your love,
From oh so long ago.
Lost, like it's never been...
Why can't I let you go?

This time the bridge was longer. They took an instrumental verse and chorus that built steadily in effect to a harder, driving version of what the song had been before. I got the feeling that this was the first time they'd tried this song together. Like they were building it from scratch, from a few chance licks in a jam session. Except these lyrics didn't sound like any first-time run-through.

How it was that we first met Seems as distant as a dream.
All the things we said and did,
The love that passed between...
I've lived so many lives since then,
An e-tern-i-ty ago.
How much longer will it last,
'Til your love lets me go?

I am haunted by your love,
From oh so long ago.
Lost- like a bitter wind...
Why can't you let me go?

Haunted by your love,
From eternities ago.
You're never to return...
Why can't I let you go?

The song faded into slow echoes, and I found myself able to move again.

"Don't," said Max as I started to leave the bar stool. "She wouldn't like it." It's as if he could read my mind. He does that to everyone, I suppose. But I'll never get used to it when I've been on the receiving end. I'm betting it's a bartender thing. He must read people's body language as if it were just pictures in a comic book. Not a real psychic power, but good enough for what he does with it.

"But—Yes, I guess you're right. She must see lots of guys coming up after shows, wanting to help. It was only a song, right?"

"Right. So, sit back down and relax before you wind up doing something you'll regret later. Next drink is on me."

"That song—" I began, then paused to collect my thoughts. "Did she live it? Is it real? Or just words?"

"You might just get a chance to ask her," Max replied. "Looks like the band got a little thirsty." He nodded towards the ballroom door behind me, and I fairly spun the seat off the stool as I turned to look. I saw five humanoids, walking tiredly out of the ballroom and heading this way. The first thing that struck me was that they were so ordinary looking. I guess I expected spandex skinsuits and tons of glitter under wild hairstyles and makeup. Or at least a couple of non-humans. After all, Earth isn't the only world that broadcasts music. Every world that has utilized the EM spectrum for communications has a slowly expanding wavefront bubble of their radio and video signals crossing the cosmos. And plenty of non-human music recordings sell as well, or better, than recordings from Earth. I couldn't tell which of the two women in the group was the singer, by looking at them. Or who played which instrument, for that matter.

"I think we should drop the first bridge," I heard one of the men say as the group walked up. "Maybe do a double verse and chorus between the third and fourth verses instead. And I want to take that Delatron in the lead vocal amp apart again—to see if I can stop that buzz it's making. "

"I hear you TJ," the taller of the two women replied to the blond crew-cut man who'd been speaking. "But the intro needs to be longer and build slower, don't you think? But its Sue's song, we can't just swarm all over it like we own it."

"Honey, I give up thinking when I'm this tired," said the shorter woman. "It's coming together pretty well so far. Let's not rush it." I recognized her voice as that of the singer. She wasn't a glamor girl by any means, but then I wasn't seeing her at her best at the moment. The whole group looked tired and sweaty from rehearsing. She was taller than average, for a human female, with long auburn hair. Nice figure too, but she didn't dress to show it. Lovely face, even with no make-up. Her eyes were clear, and green and—suddenly, I felt that I could spend a long time looking into them. I looked down at the floor for a second, embarrassed, then back up at the band members.

"Nice work," I said. "Who plays what? By the way, I'm Andrew Huntington-Smythe, from Antares Four. Very pleased to meet you all."

"Carmila Lefanu," said the tall blond woman, showing a bright smile that momentarily struck me as being just a little bit different, somehow. It finally came to me that her canine teeth seemed a little longer and sharper looking than I'd ever seen on a human woman. Her complexion seemed very pale, but she possessed some kind of animal magnetism. Or maybe it possessed her. She stood at least two meters tall, and slim, and had dressed in a baggy mauve sweatsuit. "I play guitar and sing a little background. That's TJ," she indicated the younger man with a blond crew cut, dressed in a faded blue jumpsuit. "He's our Synth and keyboard player, and all-around electronic wizard. If it's broken, he can fix it. If it isn't broken, he can make it work better. The Back-to-Nature-Boy there is Zed Nugget, our bass player," she said while pointing her thumb over her shoulder at a tall, husky man wearing Buckskins—like some pre-atomic age hunter/tribesman.

"That's Rolf Chambers, our drummer," said the singer, gesturing towards a muscular, introspective-looking man in subdued blue and gray clothing. "Me? I sing and play a little guitar. And they call me Redshift Sue."

"I want to know about that last song," Max added. "Who wrote it? But more importantly, what are you drinking today, folks? And don't worry, you're comped for the drinks. Elvis is paying for them."

I kept trying not to stare at the singer while Max fixed drinks for the band. After a little bit of small talk between themselves the band members split up. Carmila wandered off to look at the artwork on the Mare's walls, drink in hand. As if that were a signal, TJ and Rolf went back in the ballroom to take apart some esoteric piece of equipment for repairs. Zed gulped down two more mugs of beer and then left to find the restroom. I hope he found the one for his species. One of the nice things about the Mare Inebrium is that no matter what species a patron happens to be, there's a restroom tailored to their unique needs. The singer was left sitting at the bar next to me, silently finishing off a drink that I knew from watching Max mix it contained mostly electrolytes and flavor, with just enough alcohol to mug a few brain cells instead of killing them. I'd known Max long enough to tell that when he leaves a customer alone, he or she *wants* to be left alone. I kept quiet and let her think, guessing that was what she needed. Finally, Max came over to where we sat and leaned on the bar. He looked at Sue as if he could read her mind. A long moment passed while she stared at the bottom of her drink and traced abstract patterns with one of her neatly-trimmed fingernails in the condensation her glass had left on the bar.

"That's not just some random piece of music, is it?" Max asked gently. "That song really means something to you, doesn't it?"

"That last song we played?" the singer finally replied. She leaned back on the bar stool, swept a lock of coppery-brown hair out of her eyes and looked at Max almost angrily, her expression gradually softening. "My husband wrote it to me not long before he died. We'd been split up due to an accident that he'd had. He was a pilot, and his ship was lost. Then, weird shit started happening."

"I'm sorry," I said. "What happened?".

"You don't have to talk about it," said Max—even more gently, "if you don't want to."

"No, it's been a while... I think I need to tell it. It happened eleven years ago now. I remember it like it was only yesterday. He was in orbit over Earth, testing a new FTL drive system... and something broke down. The ship disappeared. Later on, I- I started getting messages from my husband. Messages that had been sent from in the past. He'd found a way to make sure that they were stored until after the time he'd vanished, and then delivered to me. The last message was that song. It had been written the furthest back in the past. It floated around in an old data storage system until recently, when it was delivered to me at home in the regular mail. The song was—written a thousand years ago or more, when he finally forced himself to give up trying to get back to me. It was his last message. Telling me that he had never forgotten me. He'd wanted it to be broadcast on the radio back then, so it would still be traveling outward—towards the farthest reaches of space and time. His voice is out there, singing to me. He always was a sentimental bastard. I still miss him."

She sighed and took another sip from her drink. Max gestured as if to ask if she wanted something stronger, but she shook her head. "You see, the drive of his ship malfunctioned somehow, and instead of going faster than light, the ship stayed in the same place, but jumped backwards in time. Each time he tried to get back home; he went further back into the past. And nothing he could do would make it go forwards again. He kept trying right up until he had almost exhausted the ship's power supply. He managed to get so far back into the past that if he jumped any further, he'd cross over into a pre-technological age. He reached Earth during the mid-twentieth century with barely enough power to land the ship in a remote location and hide it. One message said that he'd hidden it underwater in a lake."

"Over time he adopted one new identity after another and tried to mingle harmlessly with the general population, remaining a recluse in order to avoid changing history. After a few years though, he began to notice that there seemed to be slight differences from the recorded history he'd studied, and the events he saw unfolding around himself. There was someone in the old history lessons that seemed to be missing in the real present that he wound up living in. According to his messages, in order to save our version of history he decided that he was *supposed* to adopt the identity of this "missing" person and do what he remembered that that person had done. Towards the end of the twentieth century, he began writing poetry, lyrics, music, and speculative fiction. He submitted his work to various publications in the print and electronic media of the times, and eventually he developed a small, but devoted, group of fans. He had to work hard to influence events only enough to bring about the future he remembered and grew up in, but not enough to warp it entirely. He finally succeeded and was active up until far into the twenty-first century, when he—died. He had brought about the history he'd been born into by influencing the thoughts of others with his work."

"In order for me to recognize that the song was a message from him, he published it under his real name." She named someone I remembered from my twentieth century Earth Literature classes at the University of Antares as an obscure hack writer of speculative fiction stories whose only real claim to fame had been that he pioneered the use of Earth's planetary information grid as a publishing resource. Oh, and the Professor kept going on and on and on about some bar or something, somewhere, that this bozo wrote about. I'll think of it in a minute. Sue sighed again and glanced around the Mare Inebrium. "Oh, it looks like the band is ready to go back to work. I'll see you again later," Sue said as she got up from the bar stool and walked over to join the band at the doorway to the small ballroom. They filed inside, and eventually I heard the music start up again.

I sat and listened for the rest of the afternoon, but they never played that song again. I did hear them play it at the concert that night, as their final encore. There wasn't a dry eye in the house. There was also a live broadcast of the concert out to the city and beyond. I think that everyone on the whole planet stood still and listened while Redshift Sue sang the blues that night. After that night, they were all over the Hyperwave, comcast, and radio with their music.

A couple of days later I had to leave Bethdish, and I never met Redshift Sue again. But I hear her voice on the radio, crying out words of a love that never died. Words from a man driven by the loss of the greatest love of his life. Words to tell his wife that he would never, ever forget her. Words that echo in my mind, in the quiet times, in that long night between the stars.

History Lesson

"I count myself in nothing else so happy as in a soul remembering my good friends."
William Shakespeare

It was midnight and the Mare Inebrium was crowded, noisy, and a hell of a lot of fun. I'd wandered in through my usual special doorway early in the evening. Don't know quite how it happens. I'm out for a night on the town, in a local bar not far from my home really, when over by the bathrooms I spot a plain ordinary door that I know damn well wasn't there when I came in. Sometimes I ignore it, but tonight I just *knew* I was meant to walk through that door. My name's Claude Hopper. I'm from Earth. Athens, Georgia, in the US of A to be exact. For me, back home, it's the early twenty-first century. But when I walk through one of those phantom doors, I wind up here in the wildest spot in the universe. A bar called the Mare Inebrium, in a place called City of Lights, on a planet named Bethdish. I'm told it's about 65 light years away from Earth. Oh, and another thing... They tell me that it's sometime in the thirty-seventh century on the Earth calendar that I'm used to using back home...

Now look, I can hear you laughing. You don't believe a word I'm saying. You think I'm just some drunk redneck, touched in the head, babbling on about the imaginary world he lives in when he's drunk off his ass—or drugged out of his mind. Well, you're wrong. I ain't stupid, I ain't crazy, and I ain't on drugs. I've got three college degrees from UGA, my IQ's been tested as being in the high 140s, and I can take every penny you'll ever earn in a game of pool if you're dumb enough to bet me on it.

What? My degrees? English Literature, Philosophy, and Landscape Architecture. Yeah, laugh on, Big Boy. Sure, I'm a fat old redneck in overalls, sitting in a Georgia college-town bar, sipping on cheap beer. So what? Looks ain't everything. The beard and the pouch of Redman chewing tobacco is just part of the act I use to hustle pool. Wise up, Kid. Things ain't always what they seem on the surface. Let me buy you a drink, and I'll tell you a story. The bartender here is a friend of mine. He'll slip us a couple of shots of the good stuff for rotgut prices, as long as I'm the one buying. Let me show you something.

"Clark," I said to the bartender. "Set me and the kid here up with a pair of my usual chasers and a pitcher of brew, okay?"

What'd I tell you? That's the best Irish Whiskey, Tullamore Dew. Clark "slipped up" and gave us both a tall chaser for our beers, with a chilled pitcher of beer that had a zip-lock baggie of ice floating inside—for the price of a couple of shots of generic Canadian Whiskey and two brews. Yeah, Clark's a great guy. I went to school with his momma and daddy. I even took his Aunt Jane to the prom one year. He's majoring in Computer Science. He's looking to get a minor in French, too. Dude studies harder than any three people you know, Man. And he's working nights to pay for tuition and books. That ain't easy to do, you know? So, you want to hear my story, or what?

Okay, so where was I? Oh yeah...

It was midnight on a busy night in the Mare Inebrium...

"Good to see you again, Max," I said to the head bartender there.

"Claude," Max said. "Long time, no see. Nice to have you back. The usual?"

"Sure thing, Max," I says. "Widow-maker Boilermaker, in a tall mug."

"Two pints of Stout and two shots of Everclear in a frosted mug, coming up," Max replies. "Beats me how you can keep standing after that, but the customer is always right... Here you go, Claude. Pardon me, that table of Albermarite farmers wants another pitcher of Pernish Mead. Be right back, okay?"

"Sure thing, Max," I repeated. He wandered off to fill a pitcher for his girlfriend to take over to the table he'd pointed out. You think your girlfriend is hot, Kid? Just looking at Trixie would make you forget about your woman, at least 'til closing time. That woman's got some *serious* voodoo going on, I'll tell you. Her legs go all the way up 'til they make— well, never mind. Ought not be disrespectful, know what I mean?

I turned around on my bar stool and looked out at the crowd in the Mare Inebrium. Never seen so many people in the place before. Only about a quarter of 'em was human-shaped people, you know? Aliens, sure. Just like in that movie. All sorts of shapes and sizes and colors. All partying like we're doing here. I could barely hear myself think, the noise was so loud. Kind of like tonight, right here. It was a bar, what can I say? Bars are all alike, everywhere you go.

Anyway, I was looking at the crowd. Over this way was a table with a pair of bright red tigers, only with fish scales instead of fur, drinking and growling at each other. Over there was a batch of little guys all drinking from a huge pitcher, through straws. They looked like wombats, or something. Fuzzy and fanged and getting drunk like anybody else. Over there was a guy that looked like he was on fire, talking with a dude with four arms and bright green skin. Over here was a woman who looked like she was naked, but blue and orange and talking with some guy that looked like a walking catfish. Aliens, you know? Just normal for the Mare Inebrium. About that time, Max came back, and we struck up a conversation. Ancient history, so to speak. Seems like he'd been to China once. He wanted to know what the current news was like, back home here. He asked about New York and San Francisco and London, too. The guy must have taken a world tour as a vacation. But for him, I was a source of classical history. I asked him when he went to Earth.

"Oh, a long time ago," he said. "Must have been 3320, or thereabouts. Local time, that is."

"Long after my time," I said. "I hope the food was good for you."

"I must have gained twenty pounds," he said. "I could not *believe* how good the food was. Everywhere I went, something new to taste, some drink I'd never heard of before. The whole planet was amazing."

"Good to know we've got a future," I said. "Lately it's been looking kind of grim."

"You work it out," Max said. "Humans always wind up making things work out for the best."

"Hello, Claude," said a sexy voice in my right ear. I looked over. It was Blanche, the other human barmaid.

"Hello, *Baby!*" I replied to her. "How are you doing? Missed you."

She giggled, then picked up a tray of drinks to take around the room. "Doing better for seeing you again, fuzzy-face," she replied. "Be back to flirt later. Right now, I'm sort of busy." Now you might not be educated enough to appreciate the beauty of a full-figured woman, but I'm here to tell you that Blanche is one hot bundle of joy. You've got to be a *real* man to make a woman like that happy, that's what *I* say. She always did treat me as if I was something special.

"I'll be waiting," I called to her as she waltzed off with those drinks. That's about the time I noticed something weird. I mean, weird for *that place.* People were making room for a dude with really long hair that'd walked in from the front door. He was just easing through the crowd, neat as you please. Not being rude or anything. But folks just seemed to get out of his way, you know? Like he was magic, or something.

"Well I'll be..." I heard Max say behind me. "This is an occasion, and no mistake. Have you ever met Alazar, Claude?"

"Not that I can recall," I said. "Somebody special?"

"Old friend of the Reever's," Max said.

"The big guy? The Sheriff?" I asked.

"Yeah," Max said. "Exactly. The Sheriff. That about sums him up. Alazar is an old friend of his. He made that staff the Reever carries. Alazar's father is a King, out in Tulag. Big time Wizard. Everybody in Tulag is a wizard of some kind. Just treat him like an ordinary Joe, and he'll love you for it. Alazar is a pretty nice guy. Doesn't want to be treated like a Prince. Humble, and all. He's a regular, stand-up guy. Oh, don't ask him about home, the place is supposed to be a secret from most folks here on Bethdish. He's not allowed to talk about it."

"Thanks for the warning," I said over my shoulder to Max. "Should I buy him a drink? Can I afford to buy him a drink? You never take my money, anyway..."

"And you know why," Max said. "You've got a special friend."

"Oh, don't tell me that long drink of water in a cowboy hat is here tonight too," I said. "Don't that sonofabitch *ever* go home?"

"Relax," Max replied. "He's upstairs, in the Pantheon. He and Falstaff and Thor got into a drinking contest a few hours ago, or so Elvis told me. Falstaff is already under the table, passed out. Baldur took his place, but even he admits he's out of his league. Thor is pretty woozy too, but it looks like it'll be an all-nighter."

"If he's winning, don't tell him I'm here. He'll quit just to come down and talk my ear off."

"Mum's the word," said Max. "Anyway, let me fix a drink for Alazar. He'll be here in a minute."

So, this Wizard walked into the bar... Sounds like the set-up for a bad joke, don't it? Anyway, Mister Wizard finally made his way to the bar. I had plenty of time to look him over. He was normal-looking. I mean human-looking. Sort of tall, six feet and a bit. Average weight for a big guy, not fat or anything. Long brown hair, with a touch of gray at the temples.

He had a fancy staff in his left hand. It was almost as tall as he was, made from some dark wood like mahogany, with a pearl as big as an 8-ball on top. The pearl was sort of glowing. Not like a bright glow, more like kind of subtle. He was wearing a long, flowing robe, like a Druid would wear, all muted grays and browns and greens in color. When he gets to the bar Max puts a long, tall drink of something that glows bright yellow into his hand. Smoke or steam or whatever is boiling out of the top of the glass like some special effect from a bad movie mad-scientist's lab. Alazar takes a long draw off the drink, sighs, and puts the glass on the bar.

"Hello, Max," says Alazar. "Nice to see you again. How are your wives and children?"

Max laughs. Must have heard that one a thousand times. But it's a real laugh. Not some forced thing for the sake of good manners.

"All of each are just fine," said Max with a wide grin. "How have you been doing lately? And how is your dad? I heard he was beginning to show his age."

It was Alazar's turn to laugh.

"Father is fine, given his age. He told me to give you his best regards. He misses you teaching History classes at the school. But he understands that you've got your duty to perform."

"Lu-Tay has always had style," Max said. "Tell him I'm doing well and having fun. And that I miss teaching, too. Maybe I'll be able to go back to it, one day…"

"I never knew you were a teacher, Max. History, you say?" I asked.

"College level, Advanced History and Theoretical Studies," said Max, grinning. "Some of my favorite memories. Revealing the past to young students, conducting discussion groups, seeing their minds grasp the actions of the past. Really rewarding, being a teacher, I mean. The school in Tulag gave me an opportunity to encourage young minds to learn about the past."

"Embracing young *minds?*" said Trixie as she walked up. "Well, first time for everything." She grinned as if at some private joke between she and Max. "Two Denstaka and zibnit cocktails for table seventeen, and five Nanderwalt fizzes and a Whoptan Sidecar for table twelve."

"Coming right up," said Max. "Is it the Galajalerd at table twelve that wants the Sidecar?

"Exactly right, Lover." Trixie replied.

"Potassium Chloride salt on the rim of the glass then," muttered Max. "Sodium is bad for a Galajalerd's health. Why is she hanging out with a brace of Skeldonian college kids, anyway?"

"In classes together," said Trixie. "Or so I gather."

"Ah!" exclaimed Max. "Advanced Hyperspace Theory class at Collegium Lux?"

"Right in one," said Trixie.

"Faster starships mean a better life for everyone," said Alazar.

"You mean being able to find habitable worlds even farther away than folks can now, then establish colonies on them?" I asked.

"Exactly, young man," said Alazar.

"Alazar, meet Claude Hopper, from Earth. Claude, Alazar was one of my best students," said Max.

"Please excuse my manners," I said while shaking hands with Alazar. "I'm kind of an accidental time traveler when I come here."

"Really?" Alazar asked. "How does that work, then?"

"One of my best friends is a writer. Sometimes I write stuff too," I replied. "I read one of his stories about this bar. I even wrote one myself. After that, I seemed to be able to get here anytime I want to visit. Weird, but I swear it's true!"

"Writing is an honorable profession," said Alazar. "Somewhat risky in *this* establishment, but still honorable. Yet you are downstairs with we mere mortals?"

"Claude's friend is upstairs, teaching Thor the error of engaging in drinking contests with a guy with ink-stained fingertips," said Max with a laugh. Alazar laughed when he heard that.

"I've always wanted to visit the Pantheon room," said Alazar. "Alas, I fear I'm not up to par."

"Never been there myself," I said. "Max, a refill if you don't mind."

"Sure thing," said Max. "Trixie, here are those drinks."

"Thank you, Sweet-thing," said Trixie as she picked up both trays of drinks and headed out to deliver them.

"Claude," said Max as he handed me my fresh drink. "You know you can go up to the Pantheon any time you want. You're allowed. You are a writer, after all. You could even take Alazar up to see the sights. It's in the rules, a writer can be accompanied by guests."

"Oh," said Alazar. "That would be lovely. But I wouldn't want to impose upon a new acquaintance."

"Not an imposition," I said. "To tell the truth, I've always been kind of afraid to go up there alone. I mean, I'm not a big-time writer or anything. I don't know if I could fit in. But I'm game if you are."

"I'm always ready to experience new things," said Alazar. He grinned like a college kid about to go to his first keg party. "Shall we give it a try?"

"Finish your drink and get a refill," I said, hoisting mine in the air like I was making a toast.

"Done and done," he said and drained his glass. "Max, another of these."

"Ready and waiting," said Max as he handed both of us a refill

"Okay, how do we get in up there? Is there a doorman, or something?" I asked.

"Nah," said Max. "Just go halfway down that hallway," he added as he pointed to a passageway on the right wall, near the end of the bar. "There is a set of stairs on the left of the hall. Go up and go through the double doors at the landing at the top. I'll send a message to Elvis that you're coming up and haven't been there before. He'll make sure you're all right and no one bothers you. Trust Elvis and ask him anything you want to know. He'll see you get a good seat and enjoy yourselves. Just don't try and walk off any of the *edges* of the dance floor. Things get a little weird up there."

I looked around the main room at nearly a thousand alien patrons seated at various tables and booths. "Weird," I said. "*Right,*" I added as I put down my empty mug and picked up the full one Max had sitting there for me.

"You ready for this, Mister Wizard?" I asked Alazar.

"I was *born* ready," he replied as he sat his own empty glass down and picked up his refill "Down the hallway and to the left, the man said."

"Let's *do* this thing," I replied.

And so we did. Walking a bit unsteadily, I'll admit.

"Somebody needs a new Interior Decorator," I said when we came in sight of the doors to the Pantheon. "That's—crowded." The decorations

on the door were thicker and more complicated than some stuff I'd seen in art classes studying Renaissance sculpture and Gothic cathedrals back in college. It looked like someone had tried to make the carvings on the doors reflect a couple of hundred thousand religions and cultures all at once.

"I'm not sure," said Alazar. Closing one eye and squinting with the other he examined the carvings. He slowly sipped his drink, then sighed. "I think someone had a whole lot of Gods and Goddesses making suggestions for that set of doors." He belched. "Excuse me," he added. "Not bad manners, just good Simmelwike." He grinned at me, and I grinned right back.

"We're not getting any younger," I said as I opened the door.

On the other side of the door was a plain hallway, paneled in some fancy dark wood. I could see a corner at the end that we'd have to turn as we walked along the hall. Once we turned the corner, we both stopped to take in the view.

"Is it just me," I asked, "or is this room bigger than the freaking *building* we're in? Or did Max slip me a Mickey Finn?"

"I see it too," said Alazar. "Obviously we've entered some sort of pocket universe, or a hyperspace construct." He looked around. "But still, this is the *biggest* damn room *I've* ever seen."

I looked around the room, at the far wall about twenty miles away—or twenty light years. I looked at the odd-ball dioramas that edged the central dance floor that made up most of the open area of the room, trailing off into the distance without being affected by perspective. I looked up at where the ceiling should have been, at the tables that were suspended from the non-existent ceiling, hanging from infinitely long rods. Tables that were populated by Gods, Goddesses, and writers. Then finally I looked to my far right and found the bar. It was horseshoe-shaped, with ordinary bar stools circling its outer edge, and it took up more room than a tennis court. Then I noticed the bartender, who was busy mixing a drink for a dude who looked like the Marvel Comics version of Loki, but better.

I'd heard Max say the name, but the penny didn't drop 'til I saw the dude. The bartender *was* Elvis. ELVIS. Freaking. Presley! The Real Deal, not some impersonator. Not an alien who just *looked* like Elvis. Not a clone. He looked up from his drink-mixing and smiled at us. He looked like he did back in his mid-thirties. Well, who *else* would be fit to bartend for the

Gods? Suddenly, I got it. The whole room clicked into the sharpest focus possible. I saw it all, I understood it perfectly, I grokked it, and then I discovered that I'd finished the drink Max had just given me downstairs and my mug was empty. The epiphany ended, and I was myself again. But I could *remember* the whys and wherefores of it all. I *did* fit in there. I looked at Alazar and noticed his radioactive-looking banana-colored cocktail was gone as well. He was clutching his empty glass and looking up at where the ceiling *should* have been. Up at the infinite void, trying to trace where the rods that the tables hung from actually started. I elbowed him in the ribs.

"Come on," I said. "Let's go meet the King. We both need another drink, anyway."

"I think I'd like to sit down for a while," Alazar said. "The physics of this room is a bit overwhelming."

"Me too," I said. "But in my case, it's probably the drinks."

We laughed and wandered over to perch on a pair of empty bar stools. Elvis finished up the drink he was mixing and handed it to a really pretty girl who was about half-dressed in some filmy, Greek-looking robe. I tried not to look at what she had hanging out of the left side of that robe, but she turned to face us and smiled as if she'd read my dirty little mind. She raised her drink and sipped it, then walked out onto the main floor. Returning to her table, I guess. Natural blond too, I noticed. Well, I *said* that robe was sheer. At least I had the decency to blush. Watching her walk away was a lesson in the kind of artwork I'd always preferred studying back in college.

"Welcome to the Pantheon," I heard an unmistakable voice say behind me. "Don't worry about Aphrodite, she ain't gonna be offended if you're looking. Heck, that's *why* she wears those dresses. She's a bit of a show-off."

"I ain't making no jokes about the floor show..." I said reverently as I turned around to look into the bluest eyes I've ever noticed on a man. "You're the real deal, ain't you?" I asked Elvis.

"That I am," he answered. "You ain't about to ask me for an autograph, are you?"

"No, sir, I'm not. But I *am* going to ask you for a drink," I said.

"That's what I'm here for," Elvis said. He grinned and nodded his head at Alazar. "You want one too?"

"Alazar," I said. "This is Elvis. He's from Earth, like me. Elvis, this is Alazar. He's a local boy and a friend of Max."

"Pleased to meet you," said Alazar. "Yes, I'd like another drink. Something lighter than the ones Max made for me downstairs. I'd better keep a clear head while I'm up here. There's enough High Strangeness in this room to make one's head spin—even without drinking."

"That there is," said Elvis. "Hows about I get you two a Whiskey and soda, heavy on the soda?"

"Sounds about right," I said. Alazar nodded in agreement.

"Two fizzy Holy Waters, coming right up," Elvis said and turned to reach for a knobby-looking bottle from the shelf behind him. He turned back and poured a bare ounce of liquor each into a pair of tall glasses. He dropped three ice cubes into each glass, poured in a shot of lime juice, then topped up the glasses with soda water from a tap. "Here you go, Gents. Don't worry about the tab. Max told me you're both covered."

"Yeah," I said. "Evidently my best friend is a big wheel around these parts. He's supposed to be up here in a drinking contest with Thor, or something."

"All over and done with just before you got here," said Elvis. "Thor got called away on business, so he conceded and demanded a rematch some other time. Your friend made Ishtar pout—turning down her idea of a reward. He said he had to get home to his wife and kissed Ishtar's hand. Then he kind of—walked out—through a solid wall like it weren't even *there*. Didn't even stagger much. Nice guy, never goes off with the ladies. Treats 'em all like Queens, though. Says his wife is Goddess enough for him, so he's not inclined to roam. Kind of wish I'd had that attitude, back in the day. Would have made my life a lot simpler. Oh well, what's done is done."

"Yeah," I said. "We all make mistakes we wish we'd never made. Lord knows I have, anyway. Wait a minute! *He* might even be *in* here!"

"Not today," said Elvis with a grin. "Him and the Archangel Robert are writing a paper together and They haven't visited in a few weeks. Nice guys. Looking forward to talking with 'em next time they drop in."

"I'm not even going to ask," I said. "Good drink, though."

"Certainly is," said Alazar. "Thins out the liquor I've already had and tastes great at the same time."

"We aims to please," Elvis said with a smile. "Excuse me for a bit. I've got some other customers lining up."

"Sure thing," I replied. "Go take care of business. We'll be here."

Elvis grinned and walked off towards his other customers.

"I can't believe I said that," I grinned and turned to Alazar. "Must be the liquor."

"Interesting place," Alazar said as he put his drink down on the counter top. "I could get to like it here, if I had the time to spare."

"Got to get back home sometime soon?" I asked.

"No, nothing like that," Alazar replied. "I'm here in the city on business. Once I conclude that, I'll be free to spend a little time doing whatever I like. But in the end, I will have to get back home before anything has a chance to go wrong with my garden. I can't let the plants go unattended too long."

"Oh? I understand gardens," I said. "My dad always did plant more than any three families could use."

"Nothing like that," Alazar said. "I'm attempting to reclaim a large area of desert. Without my being there to monitor the progress, anything could go wrong. I can't afford to be absent for an extended period. This project of mine has already gone on for many years. I've been successful so far, but I have to watch it carefully or anything could go wrong."

"Sounds like a big job," I said.

"I've only managed to recover about a third of the actual expanse of desert," said Alazar. But my garden covers nearly as much area as the city outside."

I whistled, impressed in spite of myself. I'd been outside the Mare Inebrium a time or two. Blanche took me on a tour once. Some other folks had asked me along on a shopping trip to the bazaar near the spaceport. Kind of like a big old Farmer's Market, and all. Like the J&J Flea Market, out on highway 441, but on steroids. I'd even been to the local college, to see a show in their theater. Pretty impressive town. Hell, *West Virginia* is smaller than *this* city! What? Kid, are you doubting my word? Look, you call Clark over and buy the next round. If you don't believe me by the time I finish my story, I'll buy all our drinks for the rest of the night. Anyway, where was I? Oh yeah, Alazar was telling me about his ecology project...

"It is down on the Southern coast," Alazar said. "Set between mountain ranges. The prevailing winds don't drop much rainfall on it, so the whole area eventually dried up. I had to come up with an irrigation system that can cope with the local climate, but I finally hit on an elegant idea."

"What did you do?" I asked him.

"I cheated," he said with a grin. "I used magic."

"Max told me you were a wizard," I said. "But I thought he was pulling my leg."

"On Bethdish," Alazar said. "Magic is simply the application of ancient technology and science. Some of it is mentally tapping into the electromagnetic field of the planet, some of it is mechanical, and some of it is controlling various fields of natural forces using a mix of mental ability and technology."

"Any advanced technology is indistinguishable from magic, eh?" I asked.

"I've never heard it said quite that way," Alazar replied, smiling. "That's quite good! May I use that in a little monograph I'm writing?"

"Sure," I said. "But I didn't make it up. I was quoting from an Earth writer. Arthur C. Clarke."

"Nice fellow," said Elvis, walking up to see if we needed another drink. "He was here last week."

"He died a few years ago," I said, looking at Elvis.

"So?" Elvis replied. "*That's* never been a problem in *this* place. You two need a refill yet?"

"Absolutely!" I said. "Two more of the same."

"Coming right up," said Elvis, walking away.

"Every time I think I've got a handle on this place," I said to Alazar. "It throws me another curve ball." I shrugged and laughed. "Anyway, you were telling me about your tower and your garden?"

Alazar nodded, drained his glass, and then began again. "All the best local wizards seem to wind up building themselves some kind of huge tower to live in," he said. "Out in the far reaches. Away from civilization. With my father's help, I made one out of the local stone. Plenty of it around, hard as steel, left over in manageable fragments after the old Altiplano Spaceport got bombed nearly out of existence. The planet was attacked by some sort of robot weapon. Must have been six or seven thousand years ago, now. Long before I was born. But the rock was just weathering away, so Father and I used it to create my tower. I made sure the excavations left a series of trenches I could use for irrigation canals. Once the tower was finished, I opened up a transport portal above the tower. The portal tapped into the floor of the ocean, on the far side of the world. Water came through, spilled down the outside of the tower, and flowed off into my canals. Some tricky calculations to keep the sea life from getting sucked through the hole, but Father and I finally managed to make it work..."

"Here you go, boys," said Elvis as he handed us fresh drinks. "I've got to go see to a tricky customer now. I'll be back before you need another round. Hopefully..."

"Take your time, I replied as he walked towards some other customers. "So let me get this straight," I said to Alazar. "You've got a magic pipeline to the bottom of the ocean? And the water pours down on this tower you and your Daddy built for you to live in? And the run-off water spreads out into the desert through these canals you made by digging out the bricks y'all used to build the tower? That right?"

"That is *exactly* right," said Alazar. "A hundred years of labor, but everything worked out correctly in the end. An endless supply of water, regulated into a steady downpour, channeled away into irrigation canals."

"Damn," I said. "You don't play around, do you?"

"No," Alazar said with a grin. Then he got serious again. "But it takes constant attention to all the little niggling details to keep it running smoothly. One slip-up, and I'm back to square one. I've spent the last few centuries planting grasses, trees, digging new canals... The work never stops. But one day, that ruined peninsula will be ready for people to move back to. Making new homes and farms. Building towns and cities. It's my dream, you see. My life's work. To make a better place for the people of the future to use. Once it was all sand and rock. Now it is beginning to bloom again!"

"Some space robot destroyed it a long time ago, you said?" I asked, taking a long sip off of my drink.

"Yes, before I was born, but ever since I first laid eyes on that stretch of desert, I wanted to see it covered with green growing things," said Alazar. "Everyone has the right to dream, don't they?"

"Sure do," I said. "But not many people have the guts to do whatever it takes to make their dreams real. What happens if that robot comes back?" I asked. "Or another one just like it?"

"Unlikely," said Alazar. "My father, the other wizards, the Reever, hundreds of alien colonists, even Max the bartender downstairs, they saw to that. They flew out to the machine and their spaceships shot it to pieces. Cost a *lot* of good lives, but they saved us. Besides, this planet was moved from that galaxy centuries ago."

"I'd heard that," I said. "But it isn't the kind of thing a regular guy like me can understand. How did it move? Who did the moving? Your Gods? You wizards?"

"You're asking about ancient history," Alazar said, taking a deep draw off of his own drink. "My father should know, but he won't speak of it. A terrible time... If anyone at all knows, they aren't telling. Even the Immortals deny having anything to do with it. And if *they* don't know how it happened, we mere mortals don't stand the ghost of a chance of finding it out. One of the biggest mysteries of our history. And we haven't a clue..."

"Kind of hard to believe. That nobody knows what happened, I mean," I said.

"I have my own suspicions," said Alazar. "But no form of proof."

"Oh? Care to elaborate?" I asked. "After all, once I leave here, I'll be back in your past, and light years away. It's not like anyone would believe anything I could tell them about this place, anyway."

"Well," Alazar said. A bare hint of a frown creased his face. He sighed and took another sip of his drink before continuing. "Consider this place. The bar downstairs is filled with hints pointing toward some wealthy, powerful being or beings who have access to technologies far beyond the current level. Even the Immortals don't possess the kind of science that would be needed to recreate *all* of it. My people are the closest to being contemporaries of the Immortals. Perhaps I flatter myself, but I think we understand them and their science better than any other natives. After all, ours was the first civilization to arise after theirs. Across the face of the globe, there are countless variations in the level of technology. From stone age to space age, so to speak."

"Wow! I had no idea there was anything like that here," I said. "It'd be like ancient Rome, or Egypt, or even the Sumerians, keeping their empires going up 'til our present day."

"Oh, we were never empire-builders," said Alazar. "Teachers, perhaps, but our own land is quite enough for us. We've watched many civilizations rise and fall here. Some we helped, some we opposed, but many we simply watched from afar. We are a separate sub-species, after all. There have been instances of my people successfully interbreeding with other natives, but those have been rare. Our Gods seem to have gifted each sapient species with differing abilities. But I digress."

"Sorry," I said. "You were saying?"

"Look around this magnificent room we're in. Even the bar downstairs pales in comparison to this feat of engineering! To create this by science alone would indicate millions of years of technological advances. Even the magic of Tulag, my home, would be inadequate. We can do many marvelous things, but this?" Alazar swept one hand in a wide arc, to indicate the entire Pantheon room. "This is astounding!"

"Well, it is full of Gods, Goddesses, and whatnot," I replied. "Maybe They all got together and decided They needed a bar of their own. Someplace to kick off Their sandals and relax."

"Somehow, I doubt that." Alazar said. "It would be far simpler and easier for Them to have each made a place on Their own home worlds. To bring Them all together here? Power beyond my ability to imagine."

"The same sort of power that could move an entire world from one galaxy to another," I said. "I think I see what you're getting at. Whoever, or whatever, moved your world would—"

"Would almost certainly be quite able to create this magnificent drinking establishment," said Alazar. "And there are other clues. Our Gods have sometimes fought wars between Themselves. The darkest power among Them, Valleor, nearly defeated the rest in a Divine War back in the darkest ages of our distant past. They captured Him, stripped away most of His powers and abilities. They dispersed His physical form, even though it was beyond even Their vast powers to kill Him. In so doing, Their own powers were greatly diminished. They have played less and less a part in our histories forever afterward. Valleor, however... He has been seeking to reform His body. To recover His powers. In this He has been aided by power-hungry mortals from all eras of our history. He has attacked each and every source of power that has come within His reach, feeble though His reach is. In one such attack, He was briefly imprisoned once again, by a combination of magic and technology. I played a role in that battle. Indeed, it was my plan which *almost* worked to imprison Valleor inside a pocket universe, quite like this Pantheon room itself."

"What happened?" I asked.

"My plan was to unite every wizard, every magical adept, and every technological power on the planet into one, vastly powerful weapon. Alas, it was not enough. Valleor was near to defeating us. Then, in our darkest moment, some other power stepped in to come to our aid."

"The world-mover?" I guessed.

"Such is my suspicion," Alazar replied. "In my tower, inside my innermost sanctum, there is a device which can act as a map of the world. It also has other uses, but nothing concerned with the matter at hand. I can cause it to show the whereabouts of every adept on the planet. It can also show how much power each adept has available. This was how I linked all of us together in the battle with Valleor. Just as the Evil One was on the verge of victory, the device revealed a new adept. One I had never known of before. This adept threw their strength into our spell, more raw power than I'd ever thought possible. Too much power, in fact. Just as Valleor was thrust into His prison, the excess of power killed our Focal Point—the adept who was at the forefront of the attack. He, literally, burned to ashes while reciting the last of the spell." Alazar shook his head sadly. "He gave his life trying to keep us free. We thought the plan had succeeded, but in less than a century, Valleor had found a way to escape the prison."

"So you think this world-mover just might be the real mastermind behind the Mare Inebrium?" I asked. Nearly enough to make my head spin. Or was that the booze?

"I think that it is possible," said Alazar. "I'm certain that Max knows more about the powers that created this bar than he is allowed to reveal. The Reever, too. I feel he knows at least part of the truth, if not all."

"He would have looked at it like it was a crime," I said. "Wouldn't he? Reckless Endangerment? Theft by Taking? Kidnapping? Whatever..."

"That is exactly what he did, I'm sure of it," said Alazar. "But if he ever found the truth, he failed to make it known to the rest of the world. And that is so unlike the Reever whom *I* know that it is almost frightening to contemplate. I am forced to conclude that the Reever must have decided that whatever reason our world was moved justified the act. We weren't just ripped from our reality on a whim. There must have been a very good reason for doing so."

"There was," said a voice behind us.

"*Woah!*" I said. Alazar and I both turned to look. The Reever was standing right behind us. I never even heard him walk up!

"Reever," said Alazar. "I'm pleased to see you. Won't you join us?"

"My pleasure," said the Reever as Elvis walked up to where we were sitting. The Reever perched on a bar stool next to us. Elvis slid a drink into his hand without even asking what the sheriff wanted. "Thank you," he said to Elvis. "Just what I needed after a long day." Then he turned to look at me and Alazar as if we were schoolkids playing in the park when we should've been in class. It was one of those "*you've been a naughty boy*" sort of looks, like I used to get from my grandma back when I was a kid. Half-amusement and half-exasperation, sort of.

"Don't think I was spying on you," said the Reever. "I just happened to overhear your conversation as I arrived."

"Don't keep us in suspense," said Alazar. He grinned. "I'd love to hear the solution to the mystery."

"I can't tell you that," said the Reever. "Not all of it. But what I *am* allowed to say should be enough to keep you from prying into it on your own. Besides, I doubt that anyone would believe you anyway. But yes, I did investigate Bethdish being moved. There were deaths involved as a result of the incident, after all. It turns out that there was a very good reason for the mass-teleportation. Not one I'm at liberty to tell. But I was satisfied that the reason was good enough."

"You found the world-mover?" I asked.

"Oh yes," said the Reever. "That was easy enough, given the resources of Fort Mountain. The difficult part was getting *to* them and conducting an interview. Once I'd managed that, my verdict was carefully considered, but simple enough to reach. They have been paying restitution, so to speak, ever since."

"Paying restitution? To an entire world?" Alazar asked. "Not in terms of money, I presume."

"Exactly right," said the Reever. "There isn't a sum of money large enough to compensate every inhabitant of this entire solar system for the crime. Besides, it wasn't so much a crime as it was a *rescue*. Bethdish was under attack. Our Person-of-Interest saved the world, in actual fact. But indirectly, they caused the deaths of thousands of people. Not in the rescue itself, but in the aftermath. They share the guilt for each life lost, along with we natives who actually did the killings."

"Ah," said Alazar. "The riots after the Night the Stars Changed. I see."

"I don't," I said. "You two might have grown up with the local history, but I'm just a tourist here."

"May I?" Alazar asked the Reever.

"Please do," said the Reever.

"Claude, when Bethdish was moved there were repercussions. People looked for a scapegoat. Someone to blame. There was mass hysteria, riots in the streets, and even public executions of these scapegoats. This was thousands of years in our past, remember. But no less shameful for all of that."

"Sounds nasty," I said. "But no matter what planet they're from, people are just people, I suppose."

"The scapegoats," Alazar continued. "Astrologers, for the most part."

"We've got those on Earth," I said. "Harmless cranks, mostly. But some of them are con men, tricksters, thieves, or worse."

"Much the same as here," said the Reever. "People the world over have always looked to others for the answers to questions the Gods choose not to reveal."

"Exactly," said Alazar. "I've always considered it a sad period of our history. Astrologers, astronomers, soothsayers, mystics, few were spared from the mobs. Only those with real power managed to escape. As I recall, the Reever had no end of trouble trying to keep the innocent from the vagaries of mob justice."

"I had to be in too many places at once," said the Reever. "I couldn't save a tenth of them. Even those who were truly innocent of any sort of crime at all. I didn't have enough deputies. Even using Immortal technology, I couldn't prevent thousands of deaths." He shook his head sadly. "It shames me. To this day, it shames me that I failed in my duties so badly. I am supposed to *protect* the innocent. And to see to it that the guilty face whatever level of justice that they have earned. There were too many. I couldn't be everywhere at once. Not even I can do that..."

"I take it," I said. "That our World-Mover felt the same guilt for the disaster that happened after he saved everyone from whoever was attacking the planet? No resisting arrest, or whatever it was that you did?"

"True," said the Reever. "But I came up with a way for them to attempt to make up for all the unforeseen results of their actions. Our Person-of-Interest has been spending their every waking moment trying to make the world a better place. For thousands of years, they've been trying to put things back right again. We can't put Bethdish back where it came from. We can't change the past. All we can do is try and make a better future."

"Thousands of years?" Alazar asked. "An Immortal did this?"

"Bethdish isn't the only world that has spawned people with long lives," said the Reever. "Our friend isn't a native of this world. They immigrated from somewhere else. *Where* isn't important. Not as important as their motives. And they *did* save us all from an invasion that we couldn't have managed to fight off for ourselves. Running away from the attack was the *only* viable option. You have to understand that. They saved us all. *We* did the rest, all by ourselves. *We* killed the Astrologers. *We* formed mobs and roamed the streets and killed when the fury took us too far. We did that to *ourselves*. But we were saved from death, and destruction on a scale you can't begin to imagine. He did the right thing, for the right reasons. The aftermath was *our* fault."

"Good God! And he's been trying to make it right all this time?" I asked.

"Exactly so," said the Reever. "Bethdish is a crossroads of interstellar commerce once again. People here and now are better off than they have any right to hope for. They are free, alive, and allowed to make their own way in the universe. And it all comes down to one man who saved the world from a fate worse than death. In the end, he saved us. Look around you. Isn't all this better than an eternity as slaves? Or food animals? Or worse?"

"Who was the invader?" Alazar asked.

"A rogue Deity," said the Reever. "I've seen the recordings. Something worse than Valleor. Something that would have ravaged the planet for millions of years. I have no idea where It came from or what It calls Itself. But I will know It when I see It again."

"So that's why you come here," said Elvis. He had a trio of drinks on a tray in his hands. None of us had noticed how long he'd been standing there, listening to the Reever spin his story. History. What have you. "You've been searching the *one* place in the universe where a God might show up. All these years, you've been on a stake-out? You might have mentioned it." Elvis looked a little put out. Like he'd been left out of something exciting. I remembered that he'd gone to a lot of trouble to become a DEA agent, back on Earth, back when he was alive there. He'd even met with the President of the US, back then. Nixon, as I recall. Not a very nice man, if history was allowed to be any judge. Still, even Nixon paid the price that justice demanded. No crime ever goes unpunished forever. Fate has its own police force.

"Yes," said the Reever. "That is why I come to the Pantheon. One day, It will come here. When that happens, It will face justice. My justice, however long delayed. I will never give up. I will never forget. One day, It will answer to the law. It will answer to *me*!"

"What can you do against a God?" I asked. "You're only one man. Well, Immortal, anyway. I don't know what you can or can't do, but surely you aren't powerful enough to face a God?"

"No," the Reever answered. "Any malevolent Deity in this room could snuff out my life like a candle. If I were foolish enough to face Them on my own, without help. But I'm not alone. I have allies, friends, special friends who can face that which I cannot..."

"The World-Mover?" Alazar asked, one beat ahead of me saying the same thing.

"Exactly," said the Reever. "They have pledged themselves to come to my aid on the day I find the Deity who caused all this grief. There are entities whom even Gods have cause to fear. One of those beings is in the employ of our World-Mover. Someone who could make every deity in this room flee in abject terror, were they to reveal themselves in this place."

"They've been downstairs, in the main bar, haven' they?" Elvis asked. "I've seen this place go suddenly empty of any God or Goddess with any brains to speak of. Your deputy was downstairs, wasn't he? They knew he was here, and they ran away from him. Must be one bad mother, to scare the pants off the likes of these..." Elvis waved his hands, as if to take in the whole pocket universe that contained the Pantheon Room.

"Yes," said the Reever. "I suppose that's true. I don't know. If he was downstairs, every being up here would know it. All I know is that I'm damned glad to have him on *my* side..."

Kid, I don't expect you to believe a word I've said tonight. Hell, I don't expect you to even remember that tonight *happened*, once you wake up tomorrow. But I'm here to tell you, there are more things in Heaven or on Earth than are dreamt of in your philosophies... Dude? *Hey*, don't nod off on me... Hell, I've drunk *another one* under the table. Story of my life, I tell you. Hey, Clark! This kid needs a ride home. Check his wallet for his ID and address. I'll pay for the taxi. Nah, I'm flush. I took some hustler for a bundle earlier tonight. What? Oh. My favorite pool table. Don't ever sell it! How did I get so good? That's ancient history, my friend.

Really ancient history...

Remind me to tell you *that* story, some time...

Trial By Intimacy

"And the moving hand, having writ, moved on and left the editing for later..."
Cecil B. DeMille -1957

I ain't gonna tell you how I found a way t' get t' the Mare Inebrium from Earth, mostly 'cause you wouldn't believe me anyway. But if you want t' check out every Roadhouse on highway 441 between Athens and Commerce, Ga. for one that has an extra door near the restrooms... I say, go for it. Everybody gotta have a hobby. Me? I'm content just t' accept the situation and t' have a good time when I get there. I never thought the place was real, I mean *really* real, until I found m'self sittin' there and Trixie handin' me a beer.

So anyway, I been poppin' into the Mare about twice a month since I found the way and I'da never told a soul—seein' as how a rubber room is easy enough to get into, but hard as hell to get out of—'cept in this case Max clued me t' the fact that nobody'd believe me anyway. It was way after dark and I'd done m'share of drinkin' for the night. I'd been in one of the back booths, listen' t' Bert the cab driver spin a few yarns while I did m'drinkin', and time just kinda slipped away from me. I was about ready t' head for home when I noticed Max clearin' a place at the bar like he was gettin' ready for somebody important t' show up. I perked up real quick-like and started t' ease up toward the bar t' be nosy- Just as I saw a familiar-lookin' gink sit down and Max start treatin' him like a king. Blanche and Trixie came up and gave him a hug like he was a long-lost brother or somethin'. That caught my eye right off, but like I said, there was somethin' familiar about the dude t' start with. He still had his back t' me, but I felt like I oughta know him from somewhere. Then he turned around and looked over the whole barroom with this *look* on his face. If the phrase "sardonic amusement" woulda been in a dictionary, this guy's picture woulda been next to it. He was wearing blue jeans and a black cutaway coat with some kinda badge pinned to the lapel and had a cowboy hat pushed way back on his head. I saw him mumble something to Blanche and she slipped off towards the kitchen as I walked up closer to him—then it hit me; I *knew* this guy! Max poured him an Irish Whiskey and when

I saw him with a drink in his hand, I recognized him for sure. Who'd a thunk it? Him? Here? Then he saw me, and his face split in a grin wide enough to come in on radar.

"Claude! You old shitkicker! What the hell are you doing here?"

"I could ask you the same thing, Dan'l ol' son," I said. "This is a long way from the ol' UGA Library... or the 40 Watt. How'd you find this place?"

"This is *my* place," he said, still grinnin'. "I'm always here."

"Sho' nuff?" I asked him. "Never seen you here before. Your place, ya say? I thought it was Max's— either that or a hallucination. A nice hallucination, maybe—but with all these space critters hangin' out here I kinda figured that I'm stuck in a straitjacket back home and just dreamin'.
"

"No," he said. "Nothing like that. The Mare is as real a place as anywhere you've ever been. Remember what we figured out back in college? If the universe is really infinite, then not only is anything possible, but it's *required!* *'Everything you conceive exists, somewhere.'* Well—I conceived it, so it does exist. The best damn bar in the universe, and I dreamed it up."

"Cocky little sumbitch, ain't ya?" I said, laughin'. "Well, ya did good ol' son. Ya did good. Dunno if I believe ya, but who gives a wallowin' pigwhistle what I believe?"

"Same old Claude," he said. "Don't give a tinker's damn what anyone thinks, trust your own eyes, and don't sit with your back to any doors. But tell me—how did *you* find your way here?"

So, I told him about the extra door and which roadhouse it was in and let him buy me another drink.

"I never made that one up," he said. "One of the others must have written it."

I allowed as how that was a suitably mysterious remark and invited him to explain. I also sipped carefully on m'whiskey—'cause I know what kinda liquor Dan puts away. Dangerous stuff, that is. Why, I remember the last time me and him, Bubba, and a few close friends partied together at one of the clubs in Athens... I wound up tryin' to explain to a soused physics co-ed that a hard-on wasn't a new sub-atomic particle and gettin m'face slapped for m'trouble. The boy can put it away, what I'm tellin' you. Plus, the liquor itself could take the chrome off a trailer hitch faster than a cheerleader in the parkin' lot at the prom. *Gotta be careful here,* I thought t' m'self. *This boy's got East Tennessee hillbilly blood in his veins, remember. He can put it away all day and never show it.*

"Well," he said by way of beginnin' his explanation. "You remember how I used to have that garage band thing going on, back in the old days?" I just nodded so's t' not to slow him down. "One night when you and Bubba were out painting the town red, Jim Parnell and I got absolutely fertilizer-faced and started brainstorming some really wild ideas. Somehow, before the night was over, we came up with the idea of a bar that would be located at the north pole of Earth's moon. A bar where anything could happen—anything at all. We got so many good ideas rolling that we had to write them all down so that we could remember them later."

"When you got sober again," I said, just to show that I understood what he seemed to be gettin' at.

"Exactly. Well, what we didn't know at the time was that by creating a place like that in our minds, we'd created it *for real!* Well, a year or so after that, everybody graduated, and the gang all split up. You and Bubba took off for parts unknown, Parnell left, Allen got killed in a car wreck... Jay's girlfriend Brandy went off up north—to far yankeeland—to work on her Master's or PHD in quantum physics. Jay pined away for her for a month or two and then followed her up and they got married."

"I remember her cookin' best of all," I said. "I always figured her t' be a good match for Jay. Brains, beauty, and the best damn Creole cook that ever walked..."

"Don't give me that racial crap, Claude. You know I don't like to hear that from anyone," he said, givin' me a look that I remembered as bein' the prelude to a verbal butt-kickin'. "Am I gonna have to get medieval on your hiney?"

Whoa shit... Def-con 4, I thought. *All hands stand by t' repel boarders!* "Hey!" I said in self-defense. "It's me, remember? *I'm* the one that stomped that Sandler boy into the dirt for sayin' that Jay'd married beneath his race! The way I see it there's only one race on Earth—the *human* race. It ain't *my* fault if some of our fellow humans are too dumb to pour sand out of a boot—with instructions printed on the heel. *I* never thought that there was anything wrong with Jay bein' as Irish as a Mickey Finn and Brandy being a quadroon—or whatever they call it in New Orleans. She looks like a black woman to me, no big deal. Just chill, will ya? Like I said, she and Jay are a good match. They were made for each other. T' tell th' truth, I was just talkin' about the style of her cookin', not the color of her skin. You're pretty thin-skinned over racism, ain'tcha?"

"Sorry, Claude," he said. "I was just picking on you. You know that racist bull makes me blow my top, but I knew what you meant. Hell, I've known you since my family moved to Georgia," he added as he laughed again. "You've been my friend longer than anyone—except Uncle Chucky, I guess. You ought to realize when I'm making a joke. Sorry. Now, where was I?"

"You were tellin' me how you'd come to make this place real..."

"Oh, yeah. Well, a couple of years after everybody left, I started writing down stories. Just little things, but they showed some promise of getting to be better. So, I wrote and wrote, and somewhere in the back of my mind this bar kept getting more and more developed. Details just kept coming to me. One day I decided to put the bar on this world that I'd made up for some of my other stories. Sort of a tribute to the good times that I'd had in the old days. As I was writing, it seemed like watching a video tape of what I wrote happening in the story. I liked it, it felt right, and it happened again when I decided to write another story set in this bar."

"It kinda snowballed," I said to show that I understood.

"You don't know the half of it," he said. "The Mare got realer and realer to me. Then some friends wanted to write a few stories set here. The more that they wrote, the realer the place got. Then one day I was *here!* I walked through a perfectly normal doorway—an' here I was."

"You just walked in?"

"That's right," he said. "I just walked in."

"You musta thought you'd flipped your wig."

"In a nutshell," he grinned. "Either it was real, or I had gone crazy. Either way I was really here, or I had been in a looney bin somewhere and just thinking I waltzed in here. Or I had died, and this was my idea of heaven."

"That pretty much covers it," I said. "How'd you decide that you weren't nuts?"

"I never did, but I'm too damn stubborn to let that bother me. What seems real, is real..."

"Until somebody proves it ain't," I said.

"Right. So when I found myself back home and everything seemed pretty much normal, but—I still had the memories of being here —I decided that the universe was *way* stranger than I had imagined and went on with my life. I mean, if I turned out to be a nut then having an imaginary bar to go to was harmless nuttery. And if it happened to be real, then I'd be a fool to act like it wasn't. I've spent most of my life living inside my own head anyway. What with my family moving around so much to neighborhoods where there weren't any kids my age, I got to use my imagination more than most kids. Or I had my nose stuck in a book when I wasn't out on a tractor in the middle of Nowhere, Madison County. So when I was able to come here and then go home again, over and over, I didn't flip out."

"You kept findin' your way back here?" I asked.

"Time and time again," he said smugly. "All I have to do is want to be here—and here I am. Wherever I need a doorway here, one appears. It may have to do with my outlook on Life, the Universe, and Everything, so to speak. I really do believe in multiple universes, timelines, dimensions—whatever you want to call 'em. I think people constantly shift from one timeline to another similar, but slightly different timeline, as natural as breathing. Everyone does it all the time, and never notices. Of course, there might be only the smallest difference between timelines, but who's gonna notice a grain of sand out of place? Sometimes, I'll bet that people get too far away from where they came from and what's normal for them. I'd be surprised if that's not the real reason for some crazy people, as well as all that Charles Fort stuff. People who've strayed too far. Deep doodoo, you know? Max, another round for the redneck and I."

"Two Tullamore Dews for the hayseeds," Max said grinning. "Coming right up."

"Watch it, bub. Get smart with me and I just might shorten your... lifeline." Dan said, grinning.

"Hey, whoa! Pax! Peace! I surrender," said Max. "Don't shorten anything I've got! Please! I kind of enjoy the length of everything that I have," he grinned. Trixie grinned too and bent to whisper in Dan'l's ear. "Hey! You stay out of this, woman! The last thing that I need is another editor! Don't listen to her, Dan. No matter what she says!"

"She was just complimenting me on my, um, creativity. Don't worry, Max," Dan smiled and pushed his glasses up with a forefinger. "You're all too well developed now for further editing."

"I just had a thought," I began.

"Treat it gently," said Blanche while setting a sandwich plate in front of my friend. "It's in a strange place." I watched as Dan started to demolish the sandwich. Roast beef with all the trimmings, piled high enough to make Dagwood Bumstead wish he were twins before tackling it—at least three inches thick. Lettuce, spinach leaves, cucumber slices, tomato slices, pickles, olives, onions, bell peppers, and lots of other stuff topped off with a vinaigrette dressing and spices... *The boy can eat, too,* I thought.

"Cute," I replied to Blanche. "Remind me to spank you some time—after I've had m' vitamins." Did I ever mention that Blanche looked as if she could tear linebackers in half without breaking a sweat? Remind me not t' *ever* get that woman mad at me! "Seriously, I was wondering' what would happen t' the Mare here if somethin' ever happened to Dan'l?"

"Not a damn thing," said Dan between bites. "There are over a hundred fifty stories set here in the Mare already. Everyone would keep on keeping on even if I were to die right now. And Blanche, this meal is to die for! I'm so glad I kept your cooking skills from your original. Think of it as a testimonial to the other you in the real world... The *other* real world, I mean. I wrought better than I knew when I wrote you. Nevertheless, I've done my duty, I am now superfluous."

"But always welcome," cooed Trixie, batting her eyelashes. "I've told you before..."

"Trixie," Dan began, then paused. Was it my imagination or did his voice just drop half an octave? "I've told you before, the woman that you're based on is now happily married to someone else and I may not ever see her again. Therefore..." he paused for another bite. "Therefore, any romance between us would be somewhat —immoral. And if, indeed, I created you out of whole cloth, then it would be slightly incestuous as well."

Trixie looked disappointed, but she's a healthy girl, she'll get over it. Meanwhile, m' question needed more of an answer, I thought. "How do you know that this place would be safe without you?" I asked my friend.

"Hmm," he said, sipping his drink. "I don't. Not finally and for certain, that is. But I do have a little bit of proof that backs up my opinion." he fell to munching on the final bites of his sandwich.

"Which is?" I asked.

"Things keep happening in the Mare when I'm not here and I'm not writing Mare stories," he said as if answering the mysteries of the universe.

"The place has taken on a life of its own. It's like— like you finding your way here, for example. After all, the Mare Inebrium is a 'shared universe,' I'm only the senior writer around here, not the sole creator. This place has a reality all of its own now. If the Mare has duration and existence while I'm not in it, then it becomes no different from the rest of the parts of my life that happen when I'm not right there looking at them. It's just as real as going to work, paying bills, or talking to someone in the chat networks while my home life goes on at the same time. The Mare can continue without me; therefore, it is just as real as anything else."

I gotta admit, he had me there. "You want that pickle?" I asked by way of changin' the subject.

"Hell *yes*, I want that pickle," he said in a fake grumpy tone of voice. "If you're hungry, ask Blanche or Trixie nicely. They may condescend to fix something for you."

"Okay beautiful," I looked at Blanche in what I was hopin' was a properly pitiable manner. "Would you mind whoppin' me up a sammich like the one the bottomless pit here just vanished? But smaller, please? I'd be infernally grateful ifin you would." Okay, so I laid it on thick. Blanche has a great sense of humor, the most beautiful eyes, and her voice would give a statue romantic notions. She tended t' engender some notions on my part too. *Down boy,* I said to myself.

"For a gentleman like yourself," Blanche answered sarcastically—but still smilin', "It would be my pleasure."

"Claude," Dan said in that slow, musical, dangerously-humorous tone of voice that I remembered meant that he was gonna drop some philosophical bombshell—or tell some awful pun.

"Yeah, Dan'l?" I answered cautiously. Remember, I'd seen this guy at a party once—talkin' sense to a dude freaked out on acid that'd just punched a hole in the wall. Calmed the mother down and kept him from hurtin' the girlfriend he'd got mad at—or anyone else at the party. With Dan, politeness was a dangerous weapon. He can wield words as effectively as a rapier. Thank God he's never wanted to go into politics!

"What makes you think that your other life—back home in Ila—can lay claim to being any more real than the Mare Inebrium?"

"Um," I said, like the true genius that I am. "Uh..." *He's got me there,* I thought. I looked at the grinnin' faces that surrounded me, then at the alien faces beyond them, then at the bar itself. "I guess reality is just what y' make of it."

"Point, set, and match," said Max, as he set both of us up a drink.

"'Scuse me please, but youse two need to come wit' me," said the large alien that had wandered up to the bar, unnoticed. "My boss wants ta see yas, he wants ta see yas boat." He indicated a half dozen of his companions. "I do hope that we don't have to take dis poysonel. I dunno who ya are, an' it's none of my business, but I'm invitin' ya boat ta come wid us quietly."

"I didn't write this either," Dan said in a low voice. He turned slightly, very carefully not moving his hands. "Maybe we ought to keep this in the family, Max. Stand down."

I saw Max's hand move away from the blaster under the bar that I just *knew* he'd been reachin' for, then he blinked twice. "In the family," he said. "Whatever you say... the customer is always right." His hands quit movin', but his feet moved—like he'd stepped on somethin'.

I could see Trixie out of the corner of my eye. She was servin' drinks to a table across the room. I saw Blanche, reflected in one of the mirrors, like she knew what was goin' on and was fixin' to go postal. This wasn't gonna be pretty if she jumped one of these goons.

"*Gentlemen,*" Dan said brightly. "I *do* hope that there won't be any— *unpleasantness.* Do we have to go very far?"

Oh hell, I thought. *He's gonna start somethin', I just know it! Dan, you arrogant ass, what are you doing? How do I back your play? Damn it, I'm in the dark here.* "Who's the big man that want's t' see us?" I asked, hopin' to stall for time.

"Dat don' make no nevermind," said their leader. "He say go fetchu, we go fetchu. It ain't far. We gotta ride outside. You comin' gentle, or d'we get to rumble? No skin off my noses, neither way. Boys, ya ready?" I could see the "boys" doing some unlimbering exercises. They looked ready to carry us both out, kicking and screaming if necessary. I'd been in a few— very few—bar brawls before, but not with an alien. Not one that looked as big as a house. *We're in deeeep doo-doo,* I thought.

"Dan'l," I began.

"Of *course,* we'll come with you," Dan said. Surprised me, I thought he was gonna jump 'em, myself. "If you'd kindly lead the way to your vehicle. I'm sure that your colleagues would be *delighted* to follow along behind us, to protect us, so to speak. I'm sure this is a *minor* matter, easily taken care of, and then your employer will, no doubt, have you bring us back here."

No doubt, I thought. *If these guys ain't alien gangsters, I'll eat my hat. Wait a minute... I hadda hat when I came in... What happened to it?*

"Max," Dan added as we turned to leave with the aliens. "Say 'Hey' to your cousin Rube for me, if you see him."

"Sure thing, if he ever comes in," Max replied.

Well! I thought. *I* got it; I *think* Max got it. I knew that Dan always carried a gun too, but I dunno how much good it'd do us, or how long he'd get t' keep it. *At least a call for help went out. Now it's up to Cousin Rube.* We followed the spokesman out into the street and into a hovercar. This buggy was tricked out like a limo. Know what I mean? Luxury, plain and simple. I started gettin' more nervous, but Dan'l just acted bored and kicked back, pullin' his hat brim down over his eyes like he was nappin'. The windows went black as we lifted off, so there weren't nothin' t' see anyway. We were gettin' the velvet glove treatment, for now. I wondered when the iron fist was gonna start showin' through—and what we could do about it.

"Will you *relax*," Dan said without lifting his hat brim. "If we're being taken for a ride, at least it's a comfortable one. We're not really in dire straits..."

"An' I was so lookin' forward t' playin' Sultans of Swing at the next concert." I looked around at the gangsters an' wondered what they thought of our joking.

"That's better," Dan sighed, straightened up, and pushed his hat back. "We ought to be getting there soon. Then, we'll see what this is all about and leave."

"You make it all sound so simple. Two hack sci-fi writers against an army of these 'gentlemen'?"

Dan looked serious for a moment, then smiled. "Two writers against an army? Well, when you put it that way, it isn't really fair. But then, *they* asked for it." He shrugged, then looked unconcerned. The limo stopped then and the windows went clear. We were in a parking hanger up way high in one of the skyscrapers downtown, judging from what I saw as the hanger door was closing. And now we'd gotten t' the point in all the movies where the gloves came off. The doors opened and we stepped out of the limo— the "boys" gathering close. *Now is when Dan loses his gun,* I thought t' myself. *I hope he don't do somethin' stupid.*

"Nothin' poysonel, but we gotta search ya fer weapons now," said the group's spokesman. "Just da rules."

Dan raised his hands a little and just looked at the spokesman real hard. "You don't have to search us..." Then he smiled...

"We don't have to search you..." The gangster's eyes looked sorta glazed for a minute.

"It's *obvious* that we're unarmed." Dan's voice sounded reasonable and polite.

"I can see ya ain't packin' no heat."

"The boss is waiting. We should go—" Dan added.

"What're we standin' here for? The Boss'll be pissed. Come on you two, da elevator's this way."

"Okay, Obi-Dan, where'd you learn that?" I hissed as we were led away.

"I only steal from the best," Dan replied. "I've been trying to tell you to relax. Honestly, you make me feel like I'm the only one who sees that the emperor is gonna catch cold. Remember where we are—where we *really* are —and *why* we're really here. Besides, don't forget Rube, he'll be eager to look us up."

"Alright, inna elevator. Snap it up."

"What's the rush?" Dan asked—with a wicked gleam in his eye. "Getting hungry?" Dan grinned wide enough to frighten sharks. Woulda scared the nads offa the Marques de Sade, 'n' damn near made *me* soil m'underwear. And Dan's my *friend!* "Your name is Gloot, isn't it?"

The henchman's eyes glazed over again, then he blinked. "Yeah. Dat's right. I'm Gloot. Funny, now datchu mention it, I gotta sudden cravin' for hard-boiled Glimp eggs... An' I doan even *like* Glimp eggs. Guzzio, hit da button. Da sooner we drop off these guys off ta da Boss, da sooner we can go an' eat sumpum. Alla sudden, I'm starvin'."

"Right," said Guzzio—a short, scaly alien of few words —as he punched a button.

"Are you showing off, Dan'l?" I whispered. He just smiled in that annoying way he's got and looked around at the elevator. Why do people avoid interactin' in an elevator? That one has always annoyed me. *Sardonic amusement,* I thought, lookin' at Dan'l. *Behold thy poster boy. That attitude of his is really beginnin' t' grate. What does he know that I don't? That's what I'm wonderin'.* The doors opened and we were ushered out into a hallway.

"Nice digs," said Dan. "Your boss does all right for himself." He just stood there, lookin' around like we were tourists in some French castle.

"That's why he's the Boss. This way... Here's his office."

He opened the door for us, and we went inside. There looked like somethin' on the order of about two acres of carpet before you got to a desk you coulda launched airplanes offa, t' say nothing of the guy sittin' behind the desk. And the less said about him the better, as far as I was concerned. "Ugly" don't half touch it. "Alien" ain't even in the ballpark, an' as for "Monster", well that's a given—you know? But still, there seems to be somethin' funny... He was kinda hard t' focus on, like he was in a fog or somethin'. He looked all blurry around the edges. I didn't *wanna* look at him, for some reason. We walked across the floor with our "honor guard"—for about an hour, it felt like—then we were allowed to sit in some *really* plush chairs. My nerves were on edge, Dan looked like he was takin' tea with a Duke.

What *does* he *know?*

"Thank you for inviting us," Dan said smoothly to the—the *thing*—behind the desk. "Lovely place you've got here. I like what you've done with it. Wonderful use of space. Very organic and flowing. Wonderful use of the light and available space... Must have set you back a pretty penny, but then you can afford it, can't you? Nice weather we're having lately. And so much of it. My, my... Now, how can we help you?"

"You are the one all right," said the thing. "The reports were right. You have authority, you have power. You will help me, and I will be rich beyond my wildest dreams!"

I looked at Dan and just raised my eyebrows. *What's with the Albert Campion routine?* I thought.

"Hmm... Tricky," Dan'l replied to the thing, as if he knew what it had been talking about. "We might be able to work something out, but what exactly would you like me to do? Enlighten me."

What the hell are you, a genie? I shot Dan'l another look.

"You will *change* things for me," the thing said. "You have the power. You will kill all of the bank guards in the city and open all the banks to me. I will then gather all of the money and I will be rich. With your powers at my beck and call, I will become the most powerful being in the cosmos!"

Def-con 5! I thought as all of the hairs on the back of my neck stood up.

"And," said Dan pleasantly, if I should choose *not* to help you at this time? Just for the sake of argument, you understand. Just checking my options."

"I will eat your face," said the thing. "You have no other option."

"Thought so," Dan calmly replied. He looked at me. I let my panic show. Okay, I'm a wuss at heart when it comes to anything bigger than punching some troglodyte in the nose for insulting a friend. "This has gone on long enough; you're frightening my friend, and I don't like it. I don't like it at all. *Bugger off!* Your story has been rejected. Only a major rewrite will earn it reconsideration as a future submission." He raised his hands again, like he did in the hanger. "**Control / Break**," he said—moving his fingers like he was typing—and everything froze. "**Highlight text- Alt, Edit, Copy to clipboard, Delete highlighted text.**" He was using that *precise* tone he lapses into sometimes—like when he's on the phone. He gets pissed when I call it his "Spock" voice.

We stood in a formless, gray fog. Alone. A glittering circle appeared in the air and the Reever stepped through it, gun drawn. He looked at us, then took in the blank surroundings. "You called for back-up?" he said. "I take it that you could handle it after all? Looks like a Literary Infraction to me. You know who to call. I'll leave it to you then." With that, the Reever stepped back through the circle, and it contracted to a pinpoint and vanished.

"What the hell?" I shouted.

"Relax," Dan said. "It was beginning to read like a Tom Conway movie, so I stopped it. Then the Reever answered our call for help. No biggie."

"Mind *explaining* your explanation?"

"We're real people, right?"

"I was beginning to *wonder*, but yeah."

"And we were in the Mare Inebrium—an imaginary place—one that I invented, right?"

"Yeeeah..." I said slowly.

"But we were there, right? It was real for us."

"Riiiight..."

"So the whole thing was imaginary—but it felt real, right?"

"Uh, Dan'l, I ain't *quite* grasped it. What uh... What're you tryin' t' say?"

"*Think*, man! Do you remember what the gangsters looked like?"

"Big, mean, tough... What else?"

"What did they *look* like? Humans? Squids? An ink blot? What? Do you *remember*? How were they dressed? What kind of shoes did they wear? Did they even have feet? How many eyes did they have and what color were they? Do you remember anything? *Any* detail?"

I kinda caught a glimmer of what he was gettin' at, but it was really vague. "I... dunno. They were, um... They... but he... but—*Okay, I give, I give! What?*"

He looked at me sadly, like I needed m'chin wiped. "The only way real people can get caught in imaginary surroundings is if they were being used as characters in somebody's story."

"Oh damn," I replied slowly. Truth to tell, I was kinda stunned. *I'm a figment of someone's else's imagination... What a revoltin' development!* Shocked and stunned.

"We're up against another *writer*," Dan said. "But at least they're not a really good one."

"Run that one by me again, a little slower. I don't think my ear got a good grip on what you said."

"Someone was writing another Mare story. They decided to use *us* as characters. I bet we aren't even being written realistically. Your accent is *way* thicker than normal, for instance. You sound like you're from Texas, not Georgia. And I'm dressed up as a cowboy—which I rarely do in normal life. Only when I get dragged out to redneck bars or sci-fi conventions. And my dialogue! I'm sounding like a caricature of me! The lack of details in the story and the miss-characterizations show that whoever they are, they haven't written much. They're not very good yet. Nothing had hard edges or real color. Nothing even had a smell. The characters weren't developed very much. They seemed like, pretty much just place-holders, straw men. That shows inexperience. There was no real motive for the actions of the characters. The chief villain was just a vague image—like he wasn't even developed yet... Hell, we were probably in a first draft! I just edited the manuscript after I rejected it, that's all. I *am* the Series **Editor** and the Mare Inebrium Creator. Co-Creator, actually. Anyway, if I'm inside of a Mare story, I have Vast Editorial Powers," he said, laughing.

"Do you do this all the time? By the way, I need a drink."

"I wind up in Mare stories a lot, yeah. But I don't usually have to hijack one. I'm sorry, Claude. You wanna go back to the Mare? Or go home?"

"Yeah, I think that'd be best. Otherwise, I'm gonna need a padded room."

"No way! You just need a week at the beach, is all. Daytona's lovely this time of year."

"I wish."

"Nothing simpler. We can go right now. Sun, sand, surf, pretty girls, free drinks... Food... I can Cut and Paste that in right here and now. We can take a trip and never leave the farm."

"Sir, you interest me strangely."

Dan took his car keys out of his pants pocket and jingled them in the air. "Reality is *just exactly* what you make of it," he said, laughing. "To quote the movie Tron, *'Shall we dance?'*"

I can get a drink at the beach, I thought. "You better lead," I said, grinnin'.

"Nothing easier. I'll just write us a little vacation. When we've had enough, I'll write us a doorway back to—what passes for reality back home. Gimmie a minute, will ya? **Escape... Open New File,**" Dan said in that "Spock" voice again. I stifled a chuckle as he continued.

"**Add Text, quote,**"

"The sun beat down upon the morning's receding tide, the beach swept clean and gleaming for a new day. The dew was yet present, and the couples walking upon the beach spoke of romance with their every soft step leaving rainbow-edged footprints amidst the glittering glow of the wet sand. Seashells sparkled amid the clean white sand as pelicans dove for small fish in the surf. Seagulls lofted overhead like strings of fancy kites—or strode the beach dipping their beaks in the sand for tidbits. Children laughed and played amid the slowly crashing waves. Lovers touched each other in quiet thought as they walked, rejoicing in the morning light—lost in the joy of being in love. Beautiful people in exotic swimsuits strolled the surf. A beautiful woman in a chrome-colored thong bikini was hawking rental beach umbrellas from out of a small trailer on the tide line, as smells from a nearby sidewalk cafe on the Boardwalk gave the promise of strong coffee and a hearty breakfast. Or far headier drinking pleasures, should the mood strike later. Joy was in the very air—and the incense of salt, sand, and sea winds swept over all who were present. We looked upon the new morning and saw that it was good, and we stepped out upon the sand to join the multitude

of vacationers. For a while, we could ignore the cares of the world and bask in the sun, relax, and unwind. The gentle wind cooled our skin, even as the ocean's spray caressed us and cooled the sun's rays..."

Dan narrated on and on, —*And suddenly, I could* smell *the salt in the air!*

Many Happy Returns

"Celebrations are quite a lot like some form of subtle torture, but not so much fun, or so I've found..."
Donatien Alphonse François, the Marquis de Sade, 1793

"Congratulations, Max," said the Reever as he raised a tankard of ale. "Happy anniversary!"

"Thank you," Max replied as I took a seat at the bar. He saw me and smiled.

"Andrew Huntington-Smith," he said. "It's been a while since you were last here. You're looking well, old son. Here, have one on the house. We're celebrating tonight."

"What's the occasion?" I asked as I accepted the frosty mug from Max's hand. A thin stream of cool fog seeped over the rim of the container, puddled momentarily on the bar, then ran off the edge to waft across the floor. The fog swirled playfully around Trixie's feet as she walked up, set her tray down, and leaned over to prop her elbows on the bar top. Resting her chin on her hands, she gazed lovingly at Max, who grinned and reached over to brush a stray wisp of hair from her forehead. Out of the corner of my eye I noticed a humanoid customer trip over his own feet, nearly falling as he took in the sight of Trixie's long legs and short skirt. A skirt that was rising a bit higher than normal, I saw.

"It's Max's anniversary," she said. "He got hired on here exactly a century ago, today." She stood up and stretched like a cat, then picked up her tray. "I've been here thirteen years, myself. Be right back, I need to go see what that Lashensin couple at table four want. The indicator light for their table is on, I can see it in the mirror." She walked away, her tray under one arm as she tugged the back of her skirt down with her free hand.

"Well," I said, turning back to face Max. "Congratulations." The Reever and I both hoisted our drinks at the same time, drained them, and set the mugs down. The ice-cold tartness of the drink turned to a rush of warmth inside me. Max stepped over to my right to take an order from a heavy-set blue-skinned alien in a silver coverall who had just slid onto a bar stool three seats over. I thought they must be a Tescardi, but there are many species who look like that.

I heard a single, quiet, bell-like chime. "Excuse me," said the Reever, raising one hand to his ear. "I'm getting a call." I could see his lips move, but some sort of hush field prevented his words from reaching me. I looked away, to give him more privacy. Glancing out across the room I could tell the bar was doing good business today. Well over half the tables and booths looked full. Solitary customers were scattered down the many stools along the bar. It looked to be a quiet evening for Max's anniversary. In the distance off to my left, I could see Larrye working in one of the side rooms, through its open doorway. I could see Blanche making her rounds from table to table near the front entrance, and Trixie still at table four, demonstrating the menu computer to the alien couple seated there. The crowd in the bar seemed about equally split between humanoids and more otherworldly species. The subdued babble of voices in dozens of conversations murmured distantly in my ears. Absentmindedly rubbing my fingertip across the polished wood of the bar, I took a deep breath, then sighed contentedly. The familiar lemon and Jasmine scent of the Mare Inebrium tickled my nose as I relaxed. There was always something about the Mare, something that felt almost like coming home. The Reever concluded his call with a satisfied nod, took his hand away from his ear, and smiled at me. "Sorry about that," he said. "But business follows me everywhere. At least it is good news this time. One of my Peacekeepers located a witness we need for a case that is coming to trial next week. Their testimony will allow me to put a minor con-man behind bars."

"I'm glad it turned out to be good news," I said. "I'll bet you don't get enough of that in your job."

"Absolutely right," he replied. "A policeman's life is thinly sprinkled with the spices of joy. Protecting people from predators is one of the better rewards I get. Speaking of rewards, excuse me again!" He got up, took three quick, long strides, and wrapped his left hand around the upper arm of a tall, green-scaled patron that had just walked past us.

"This must be my lucky day," said the Reever. "Kakartouload, isn't it? You Ibeesan smugglers must think I can't get DNA traces off a gemstone. You're under arrest. Come quietly and no one will get hurt." The Ibeesan native looked startled for the barest instant, then to my surprise it slumped into a resigned acceptance of its fate as the Reever clicked a restraining cuff onto its wrist.

"You win," it said. "Please, no hurt I. Should have known better than to celebrate a sale in this place. Same sentence as last time, maybe? Cell comfortable, thought I. Clean, too."

"Yes," said the Reever. "That sounds about right. Ninety days in my jail, then I'll put you on a ship going off-world. If you come back in less than— oh, say, five years, this time—I'll ship you off to your home world. I know they'll be less than gentle with you."

"Not be coming back for ten years! Ibeesa Lawmen too hot for me! Chop my head off! You good Lawman, not chop. Will miss jousting with you. You play fair."

"I see you found a friend," said Max as the Reever led his prisoner back to the bar. "Shall I send for an officer to take him in?"

"Yes," said the Reever. "But give Kakartouload a drink first. He's not a bad sort, just careless and greedy."

"Well, he's not going anywhere with that cuff on his arm," said Max. "I've got a bottle of Denkomet here somewhere... "

"Denkomet! I not can afford that," said the prisoner.

"My party, my treat," said Max, smiling. "Happy Anniversary!"

Came the Dawn

My thanks go out to Wishbone, Bill Wolfe, Cary Semar, Jeff Williams, Iain Muir, and Rob Wynne for their invaluable assistance. Without their assistance and advice, this story would never have been finished.

". . . there may be something in the nature of an occult police force, which operates to divert our suspicions on this world, and to supply explanations that are good enough for whatever, somewhat in the nature of the same kind of minds that we beings have — or that, if there indeed be occult mischief makers and occult ravagers, there may be also <u>other</u> beings, that are acting to check them..." *

Charles Fort

It was almost dawn in City of Lights and the whole town was buzzing. Rumor and gossip vied with newscast updates for who could make the wildest speculation. Everyone seemed to hang, almost breathless, on the news—the Shebeja had awoken. They had mothballed their entire colony and entered sleepfreeze centuries earlier. Everyone on Bethdish had basically forgotten about them in the centuries that they had been asleep... Then came the rumors from the docks of City of Lights; the smugglers were getting worried, ships and whole crews had turned up missing, and survivors had brought back word of being attacked. Ocean shipping has always been the lifeblood of most of the primitive natives of Bethdish, but the pirates that thus far lived to prey on that shipping now risked being decimated by fire and brimstone from the sky.

Then there were the reports, some of them hundreds of years old, of strange ships in the skies over the kingdoms of Ellor and Kineth, near the southern edge of Bethdish's single huge continent. Oktishnear stands between them—the old Shebeja colony base. Not many at first, and not believed at first, but they added up. Finally, reports of their odd whirlybird ships became all too frequent to ignore. Now they looked to be buzzing about in the same manner as a hive of bees that's been prodded. The aliens that had once slept inside the Hollow Mountain were now awake. And from all appearances, they had woken up on the *wrong* side of the freezer.

Now the local planetary news services seemed to be full of it—and that's why I knew anything about it, actually—the Shebeja had sent an embassy group to City of Lights. Rumors of high-level talks between the Halazed, the D'rrish, the Immortals, the Shebeja, and the City Council flashed from mouth to ear at a speed far faster than mere light. All the rest of the diplomats, whatever their species, were rushing around trying to figure out what the effect was going to be on *their* various power plays. The Shebeja heliship that had parked at the spaceport had been given its own channel on the Bethdish Beamcast News. Every time a ground crew mechanic had an itch, the subsequent scratch was given global coverage—even if only six cities on the planet have 3D-V receivers. All the action had shifted to inside City of Lights as the Ambassadors met. Regular reports and special updates had another BBN channel.

I'd grounded at the spaceport just after midnight as a bonded courier. All right, sometimes I *act* like a secret agent, but that's just a *hobby*—really. I'm usually just a jumped-up delivery boy. In any case, I rate my own ship, a permanently reserved hanger, and ground-side transport. Usually I breeze through Customs, but this time everyone was on alert and being extra careful. Everything took much longer than usual. So by the time I finally felt able to leave the port and make my delivery—Bearer Bonds for a local stock market tycoon, since you ask—my ears were full of the news. From the port to downtown, everyone was talking about it, everyone was watching or listening to a newscast. The whole situation sounded to me like it would eventually put extra credits in my pocket, whatever happened—so I felt unconcerned as I kicked my scooter off the building's fiftieth floor landing stage and snaked through traffic to a SkyTeller. My bank had one levitating at the fifth-floor level of the Providence Street and Grand Avenue intersection. While I waited for my deposit to clear and some pocket change back, I pondered what to do with the rest of my off time. Dinner and a companion? More like breakfast time. Most of the girls I knew in town would either be just coming home or just leaving for work. See a show? Visit a museum? I was getting thirsty, I'd just gotten off from work after spending four weeks alone in space, and the machine just handed me five hundred credits... Suddenly all I wanted was a good stiff drink, and a nice place to drink it in. I knew just the place, so I did an upward U-turn at the traffic signal, flipped upright, and merged with the

10th level traffic heading back uptown, and towards the Mare Inebrium Tower.

"Max," I said as I perched on a bar stool. "Give me a single-malt Gniik-Kispha Gwiddon, will you?" I plunked down a 50-credit coin. "Set me up a tab and let me know when it runs low."

"The customer is always right," replied Max. "Especially when he's pre-paying." He made a long reach for a familiar dusty emerald bottle and deftly poured me a generous two ounces of its greenish-gold whiskey. A quick pass under the chiller and then he set the frosted tumbler on a napkin in front of me. "First one's always on the House for an old friend, Jon Stewart. It's been nearly a year since you were last in. How is business?"

"It's been good and sounds as if it's going to get better. I haven't been sent to Bethdish very often for the last year—never had the time to stop in when I *did* ground here," I sipped the antifreeze-colored whiskey and smiled, then continued. "But it looks as if there'll be more contracts for me to bid on. The Boss is always looking for new contracts, if I can catch him in a good mood maybe I can grab the majority of the diplomatic pouch missions here on Bethdish."

"Catch Siri Lassiter in a *good* mood? I know him! Good luck. Shipping diplomatic mail from world to world is a good enough job, but working for him has got to be tough. One of the most ill-tempered beings I've ever met. I remember your philosophy though, once he gives you your assignment, you're pretty much on your own. Once you lift ship, his moods aren't your problem anymore. Say—you're not thinking about hiring on to take a message to the Shebeja home world, are you? That's over in the Andromeda galaxy—even an Immortal wouldn't line up for that trip. No sane pilot would try it."

"Nobody's got a few million years to spare, you mean?"

"Right in one go," said Max. I sipped my drink thoughtfully as Max took orders from farther down the bar.

"I'll have to turn that one down," I said when Max came back. "If the boss tries to snag that contract. I'll make sure everyone at the agency knows it's a freak job. Thanks for the reminder."

"No problem. I seriously doubt that anyone would offer to contract it out, anyway. Freshen that drink?"

"Sure." I sipped my new drink, looked around at the morning crowd, and thought random thoughts for a while. "Hey!" I said as soon as the penny dropped. Max looked at me as if I had suddenly become a bright dog who has just gotten a new trick right. "If their home world is off in another galaxy, how did they get *here?* And why can't they go back the same way?"

"They can't get back because it's too far away. And they got here by being kidnapped, just like the rest of us," said Max. "About seven hundred years ago this whole solar system had been snatched out of Andromeda and dropped down here in the Milky Way. Two million light years from where it *used* to be. I thought everyone knew that already. It happened less than a century before the first Terran Federation ship contacted Bethdish. That's *why* the Federation came here. The system just popped into existence in their backyard, naturally they had to check it out. Anyway, we were moved in 6055 'The year that Astrology died,' that's what the local news services called it at the time. The Halazed and the D'rrish, and almost all of the natives, call it 'the Night the Stars Changed,' or something similar. The Federation expedition arrived in 6126, led by the Starship *Admiral Herndon*, and City of Lights spaceport opened in 6129."

"It's 3840 on Earth's calendar this year. What year is it on your calendar here? 68-something? And how did astrology die?"

"6827, about a month and a half from being '28. Year number 1 was when the Altiplano Spaceport started construction. We started a whole new calendar 'cause we'd just come through a planetary disaster. That reminds me, I need to buy the Reever a Solstice Holiday gift. And it's sort of difficult to have astrology without any astrologers."

"You mean—I mean... *All* of them?

"Yep, every last one dead inside a year. Hanged, burned at the stake, torn to pieces by mobs, heads lopped off... The usual atrocities. Most of the honest ones killed *themselves,* before the first mob even formed. Probably mad as hell and wanted to demand an explanation from the Gods. As for the mobs, well... Like any natural disaster, there was bound to be panic in the streets. People picked a scapegoat. The Immortals that happened to be out and about at that time tried to keep things calmed down but couldn't be everywhere at once. There's less than a hundred that work outside of Fort Mountain nowadays, you know? And the natives are only humanoid, after all. People understandably got upset when the whole night sky changed and not one astrologer had predicted it or could cope with it. Not one of them could explain what had happened or adapt their star charts to the new sky. The mobs got everyone that didn't suicide. Except for the smarter ones who switched to astronomy right away—or were really just astronomers at heart anyway. And the astronomers didn't have an easy time of it either. Some of them got caught in the fallout. Getting caught in a riot is no fun, let me tell you. It was almost like watching a religion collapse. Oh well, I think of it as evolution in action. —We *did* wind up losing an entire class of con men..." Max grinned.

"You realize that you're talking like you just happened to be there, seven hundred years ago. The sign outside says that the Mare was established in—"

"6698. Yeah. I didn't start working here 'til 6735 or so, though. Yeah, I'm a native—I was born here on Bethdish."

"You're an *Immortal?*"

"Uh, yes. But not an important one, so keep it quiet, will you? I don't want people giving me funny looks. But yeah, I'm about 2 million or so. Big deal. You're only alive for one day at a time, you know? But sure, I remember the night the stars all changed. It meant exile for all the colonists here, for one thing."

"Somebody moved the planet? Bang-zoom, new address, new galaxy?"

"Somebody moved the whole *solar system,* Jon—as best we can tell. The stars, all the planets, the comets, every last grain of dust and gas. Every subatomic particle in the whole system had been teleported to where it is now. It took about a minute. It seemed to take forever... Astronomers can still see the light from where our sun used to be."

"Come on, pull the other one. It's got bells on."

"I kid you not," Max said. "I thought I'd seen it all during the war we had with the Scourge way back in 1840, but that night the stars changed frightened me half out of my wits. Earthquakes, lightning storms, loud noises, lights in the sky... I thought the Gods had forgotten to tell us that the end of the world was scheduled—or something. Why we got moved, as well as how, no one knows. Or at least, no one is telling *me* anything if they *do* know."

"The Scourge? In 1840?"

"Oh yeah. Big robot killing machine." Max waved his hands around like a fisherman bragging about the one that got away, "Thing was the size of a small moon—all one big machine. Bombed us with rocks from our own asteroid belt, threw a few nukes at our cities. Slagged us good, but we beat the bastard finally. Out in the cometary halo, we shot the thing to scrap and left the melted chunks drifting. Cost us a lot of good pilots trying to get to it—dozens more trying to hurt it. A whole Shebeja squadron rammed the thing—one after another—to open up a hole in its armor for the rest of us to shoot through. Ten of them gave their lives to give us a good shot at killing the thing. Full blast and guns blazing—for honor and duty..." Max looked thoughtful for a long moment. "It also killed everyone on the ground over a fifth of the continent. Thank the Gods that it had been mostly the spaceport that was targeted. None of the natives lived there and only one of the Kefa Empire cities was close enough to sustain damage. Most of the losses were the ground crews and Port Authority workers. Only about half a million dead. It could have been a hundred times worse..."

"Sounds bad," I said.

"It was. But that night we were *moved*... That was *far* worse than anything I've ever lived through. Even though there weren't many *direct* casualties, the shock of being cut off from the neighboring star systems was terrible. All the colonies on the planet got cut off from their home worlds—Even the travelers on holiday at the Three Peaks Resort. We were *all* trapped here, and we had to learn to deal with it. The Shebeja went into sleepfreeze to wait it out, thinking that rescue would be coming before they would wake up. That didn't work and now they have to learn to deal with it like the rest of us."

"But they're seven hundred years behind everyone else," I said to indicate that I wasn't lost. "The world has changed, but they haven't. What were they like before the big sleep?"

"Mean, cunning, smart... They've always been hunters, of one kind or another. Ruthless, honor-bound... They can't be bribed, they can't be blackmailed, and they take a contract *very* seriously. They obey it to the letter. They were often hired out as mercenaries or government police. And they make *fierce* bounty hunters. The old Altiplano spaceport authority hired them as security and customs police. That's why they have a colony here in the first place. Time for another drink?"

"Sure. One more of the same."

"Coming right up. Oh, let me get these other orders out of the way." Max walked off towards the other end of the bar after handing me my refill.

"Spaceport Authority?" I said when he came back again. "The old Altiplano? More ancient history?"

"Um... Yes, but it's real history, first person singular, eyewitness testimony. Not the assumptions written down centuries later—by someone who'd only read about it. The Port Authority ran the whole spaceport. Their building used to stand near the southeast edge of the Altiplano. Huge building... Had to house all the communications gear, crash crews and their equipment, a complete hospital, foul weather gear. The works... Everything that had been needed to run the biggest spaceport ever built. Everything designed for a hundred different species. The Authority operated all the services for the spaceport- different Co-Op members supplying the personnel. You've seen the old Altiplano from low orbit when you have been setting up for a landing, I know."

"Yeah, sure. Ancient landing field, thousands of years old, only archaeologists are allowed up there nowadays. But I'll bet that there are some smugglers that use it. It's right next to that circular sea with the big volcano in the middle. You're right, I've seen it from orbit a hundred times. I fly over it on almost every landing approach."

"You've seen a third of it—The rest wound up being vaporized by the Scourge."

"Looks like a desert to me... What's there left after all *this* time?"

"Only six *thousand* years? That's *nothing,* take it from me. The Immortals have a written history of over a *billion* years. We've gotten *good* at building things. The Altiplano was built to last for *eons.* You see, Bethdish was still recovering from a polar shift when a Co-Op of nearly a hundred nearby alien worlds contacted the Immortals, wanting to make a deal. They offered to buy the most devastated area of the continent and landscape it into a huge landing area and navigational marker system."

"What?"

"Hey, we were hurtin'! The death toll from the pole shift was horrible. What the quakes and tidal waves didn't smash, hunger and disease did. Fort Mountain was glad to get the Co-Op's message. We needed all the help we could get."

"Sure..." I said. "I can understand that. But what did you mean about navigational markers?"

"Those long lines and hieroglyphics aren't just approach markers and landing pads; they're also star charts to the systems that had been nearby-y—back in Andromeda. A ship could read that chart from orbit, then boost back out of the system. Even ships, built thousands of years after the Altiplano, or before, for that matter. Some species never give up hope that some old sleeper ship or multi-generation sub-light ship might turn up. Almost every species of space-going people have them out there, somewhere- lost ships, I mean. Anyway... We used to be near the center of a big globular cluster of stars, lots of them had advanced civilizations. We were on the way to almost anywhere civilized in the cluster, so we became a navigational crossroads for—oh, five hundred systems or more."

"Right," I replied. "I can almost imagine it."

"Each species that bought a landing space kept a small base there. Built to last *forever,* as far as they were concerned. The Immortals helped the different species in the Co-Op to build the Altiplano They did their planning in geological time frames, back then. But don't get the idea that it had ever been as busy as City of Lights spaceport is today—. The Altiplano wasn't ever crowded. How could it be? A thousand ships a day could ground there and never even *see* each other. The thing was nearly the size of China, over on Earth. By the way, nice Wall your folks built there. I saw it on vacation once about seventy years ago. Anyway, the Altiplano was originally about the size of China. All one big flat landing field, raised up a mile and a half above sea level, enclosed by artificial mountains all the way 'round. Only a few Co-Op species were allowed to establish regular trade here with the natives. We regulated that pretty heavily, you know. The rest of the Co-Op used the port for a way-station, pretty much. One of their ships would land, off-load cargo into a warehouse, then boost back up and out of the system for somewhere else. A week later, or a month, or a year, another of their ships would ground and pick up the cargo from storage. Quite a lot is left I'll bet—in bases on the remaining section."

"Okay, it had a lively past, but what goes on there nowadays?"

"I know ships in distress *can* still land there, but there's a big fine that the Reever gets really sticky about. It makes a big to-do when the Emergency Rescue Squad have to airlift some poor being down off of the plateau. And there's always at least three archeology teams up there at some of the thirty or forty bases still existing. Shut down, empty, sealed away..." Max shrugged. "I know that the Air Guard flies regular patrols over it, watching for smugglers. But that's all beside the point. There are at least fifty-two ships still parked there, that I know of personally. Some of them still run. One of them is mine. Then there are the ruins of the port building—even though that's mostly underwater now... And then there's Oktishnear."

"That seems to be the sticking point, yeah. The old Shebeja base. *Wait a minute*—You've got a working ship sitting abandoned up on the plateau? They won't let you go get it?"

"Oh no. Nothing like that. No one's keeping me from it. I could go get it any time I wanted to. It's just something I learned from the Reever: *always have a back-up plan!* If I absolutely *had* to get off world, I've got a way. That's all—just *insurance*." Max shrugged. "I haven't always been a bartender. Among other things, I, uh... I flew fighters and freighters, tankers, even pulled fifty years with the COP's, the Civil Orbital Patrol, on a cruiser based up on Xerxes. Kind of like a Coast Guard service, but in space."

"Yeah," I said. "I understand. But you parked your boat and left it? What about those others you mentioned?"

Max wiped the bar top and sighed. "That's why most of those ships wound up grounded up there. The ones from the battle with the Scourge, I mean. The ones who came back—we just landed there and... We walked away. Shock, I guess. We were just standing around in a daze until someone sent a transport to pick us up. Even the Reever left his fighter up there that day. Some of us went back later to get their ships... He did. I never have. I haven't gone back to fly the beast again since I grounded her after the battle with the Scourge. But she's there ready to go if I ever need her. Kind of comforting, knowing that she's sitting there charging up if I ever have to fly her again. Plus, the Spaceport here would get *really* interested in a fully-loaded fighter just sitting on one of their pads. Our tech is a bit on the uh, *flashy* side when it comes to vehicles. So, it's best if *Libby* just sits up there, in case I ever need her."

"I know what you mean. That's why I keep my *Della Sue* topped off and ready to lift when I'm in port. You never can tell when you'll have to roll. She's not a fighter, but she's more than she looks like. She's got teeth and claws now, and longer legs. I've tried to make sure that my little, uh— weapons and engine modifications don't show. In my business, it pays to keep a low profile. But she's on a low alert and ready to lift as soon as I can strap in." I raised my glass as if in toast to both of our ships. "*Libby?*" I asked, lowering my glass.

"Roughly translated, it's short for *Sword of Our Lady of Liberty, Defender of Truth. Of* course, it loses something in the translation... one hundred-footer, twin engine, dorsal cockpit. Ground to orbit in seventy-eight seconds on a scramble launch. 'From powered-down dead to roaring overhead,' as we used to say back in the COP's. Overpowered on a factor of about three hundred percent, for its weight. Loaded to the very teeth with more weapons than I've got time to talk about... Sweet little machine, flew like a dream." Max grinned and wandered off to take another order.

I had started beginning to wonder about coffee and breakfast about this time, myself. So I left the bar and took an elevator up thirty floors to a restaurant I knew of in the building. Best breakfast bar in town. I stuffed myself with an omelet fit for a king and nearly a gallon of strong black coffee. Then I went back down to the Mare to relax. After all, I did have the rest of the day off. I was still interested in how the Shebeja would shake up the diplomats that usually made up my best customers. If my boss was half as good as he thought he was, he'd be taking contracts right now. Those diplomats would be shooting off message traffic faster than a Battleship could lay down blaster-fire. And my salary from what I might be able to snag of them could well double my bank account for a year or so. I'd have to consider some investments to tide me over after the rush of business got done. Pleasant thoughts indeed. So, I was completely distracted when the elevator doors opened, and I nearly tripped over the Halazed Ambassador as I stepped out.

"Oh, I beg your pardon Hnarcor..." was all I had time to say before I realized what I'd literally *stepped* into. With the Halazed Ambassador stood Kazsh-ak Tier, Max, and what had to be the Shebeja Ambassador. I'd nearly fallen on my face in front of what could become my three best customers. Of all the bad luck to have, I kept being stuck with mine. And stuck with my mouth open, I realized. I shut it with a snap, before I had a chance to put my foot in it further. Tripping over the Halazed Ambassador's bad enough, without my saying something stupid to compound it. Max came to my rescue.

"Ambassador Czhark Ali Haa-nimb, may I present to you—Diplomatic Courier Jon Stewart Sebastian. One of our patrons.

"My abject apologies..." I began.

"A pleasure to greet you," Czhark intoned. "Hnarcor Finivalda speaks highly of you." He bowed towards the Halazed Ambassador. I had done the Halazed a favor or two in the past, but the canny little old lizard was keeping his mouth shut right now. Right at the moment, he looked even more like his saurian ancestors than he usually does. I wondered, briefly, if it were the matter of the missing documents that I'd helped him recover, three years ago or so, that was on his mind. Or was it the time I assisted Blanche and he to foil a fraud? But I made the mistake of glancing at the Shebeja again and got distracted.

Just watching an eight-foot-tall werewolf bowing felt distracting enough. It wasn't the fur or pointed ears, it was more the double joints in its arms and legs. Okay, so the Shebeja *aren't* werewolves, more like tall, thin orangutans. His short fur looked to be a light tan, shading to gray. His long, horse-like face was bare of fur, as were his hands and feet. I could see retractable claws tipping each finger and toe. *No shoes,* I thought to myself. *They must fight with their feet and hands equally well.* He looked damned dangerous, a quick calculation giving me somewhat less than a zero chance of surviving one of *these* aliens pitching a hissy fit... *And* Max had told me that they were mean—But *this* one was being polite. *And his name is pronounced Shark?* I thought. *Land-shark, maybe.* So I started looking for the hook—so to speak—and let my mouth react on its own. It's good at that. I've hardly had to train it at all.

"I have been quite honored to assist the Halazed Embassy in some small way in the past, sir. Thank you most kindly for letting me know that my work has pleased them—enough for my services to be recommended." I shuffled fast for something else to say. "I have only today become acquainted with your situation... Let me join those who have welcomed you to—" *What can I say?* "Your new awakening." Okay, yeah. It sounds lame, but let's see *you* think that fast. I gave Shark a quick bow, just to make sure that I was being polite.

"We've agreed to host a luncheon for the diplomatic corps," Max said, saving me yet again. "The Ambassadors were just having a little tour when you, uh—ran into us. We've seen most of the side rooms and special habitats, so we were wandering back to the main bar. Care to join us?"

"Yeah, I could use a drink right about now," I said.

"I second that motion," Kazsh-ak Tier replied. "All this talking has me dry as the desert."

A few minutes later we were all at the bar. Max had relieved a grateful Droid named Bob, electroplated in a tasteful Cherenkov-blue chrome, that was currently his back-up daytime bartender. I had been in the Mare the night that Max had bought Bob off of a Trader Captain. It must have been nearly two years ago now. Max manumitted Bob minutes later, after the Trader had left with his money. Bob was studying to be an astronomy photographer at one of the big universities nearby. I forget which one. Bob likes working days and studying nights and only needs an hour a day off to recharge, so Max lets him get away with it. He's Okay, but kinda stiff for a bartender. He mixes a great Tonshu Blitzer, even though he's not much on small-talk. And by the way, don't *ever* ask him about astrophotography. Not unless you've got an hour or so to hear about the beauty of some obscure area of space as seen in ultraviolet light—in *excruciating* detail. Just a word to the wise, you understand. You're welcome.

"To the Hunt!" Czhark proposed as a toast when Max had served our drinks and we'd sipped them. I couldn't help noticing that his drink looked like some blue, glowing liquid, with what looked like shrimp floating in it instead of ice cubes. Kazsh-ak had his usual radioactive sludge, Hnarcor was having his usual dMembii Martini with extra olives. I almost blushed when I saw Max pour us both an Irish Whiskey that had to have been 300-year-old Tullamore Dew—or so I *thought*. Until I tasted it. He'd given me one of these just once before, on the house—the night I came in with that freighter shuttle crew who'd fallen down a wormhole—so I recognized the drink. It was Terran Krupnick—aged nearly 2400 years in a glass barrel. This had to be the Irish Mist formula, I could tell. The way it burned me a new gullet on its way down was a dead giveaway.

"To the Hunt!" we repeated. Or in my case, gasped. This was strong drink indeed! The Shebeja interpreted my wheezing for a question.

"The Hunt is life," he said. "We are all predators here—each species at the top of its own food chain. But prey can take other forms than food. My people glorify the chase, the capture. We extend that metaphor into our daily lives. In our religion, in our business, in our work. We celebrate the Hunt, in all its forms."

"And kill a great number of pirates," sighed Hnarcor. "We could be prosecuting them instead, you know. The Reever may have moved too soon in reaffirming your old Coast Guard commission."

"Think of it as evolution in action," said Kazsh-ak. "These corsairs may be romantic in popular folklore, but the rest of the natives *need* the shipping that they prey upon. The Shebeja are taking up their old service of policing the shipping lanes. Thus, the greatest number of the natives will reap the greatest good."

"But these same pirates are powers in their own right in the local political situation. Let us not forget that City of Lights itself had been originally built from Freeport Durkone, itself built on the profits of piracy and smuggling," replied Hnarcor. "These tribal power struggles will be with us always, it seems."

"But these pirates will not," said Czhark. "And the natives will know security and plenty once again. My people offer violence only to the violent. No honest trading vessel has ever been harmed. Only ships actually engaged in attacking others have been punished. Eventually all shipping lanes will be safe. This is our mission."

I knew diplomats well enough to tell that this little debate is going to be more important than any *official* meeting. Max was giving me the eye again, so I spoke up with the first thing on my mind. "So what do your people want? All three of you, I mean. How do you each see our modern world? But I'm interested in your view especially, Ambassador Czhark. How do your people see the world now, after having taken the long sleep?"

"What do you wish me to say? We guard and protect. That is *all* that we exist for. We only wish productive work and meaning to our lives, like any other beings. Bethdish is still a *changed* place—Even more now than it was when my people first took the Long Sleep. Our home world is still gone—unreachable across the intergalactic gulf. *All* our various peoples are still cut off from our own kind, as none have ever been before. My people had been wrong to take the long sleep in hope of rescue. That turned out to be foolishness. There was no hope at all of our home world developing the kind of space drive to make a rescue possible. Our ruling Triad was moved by the advice of ignorant dreamers. Good politicians, but not scientists. They wound up being ruled by wishful thinking, not science. We should have remained on watch and adapted to the changing world. We *should* have made a place for ourselves in this new galaxy. I argued thus at the time but had been overruled by our leaders. We have so much to catch up on, now."

"I'll drink to that," added Max. "Being willing to catch up, that is."

"Hear, hear!" we all echoed.

"It is the dawning of a new day here," Hnarcor began.

"It's almost lunchtime," Kazsh-ak replied.

"A metaphorical day, my friend," the Halazed replied in turn. "We must needs work out the updated rules for our Shebeja friends and their great Hunt. They can do great good, but we must decide where the lines are to be drawn. We cannot afford to frighten our native hosts, lest our colonies be each put at risk. We should always remember that each of us are here, not to impose order, but to add to the pattern that already exists. We three species have a special place, a unique place, in that pattern because of our longstanding colonies. We are already part and parcel to these people—whatever their species, we still have to live alongside them."

"Hear, hear," boomed Kazsh-ak as he raised his, uh, container in a toast.

"This place is the best evidence of inter-species co-operation that I've ever seen," I offered by way of making conversation. "Maybe Max could be persuaded to part with some of his methods of dealing with several hundred life-forms at once."

Max laughed. "Somehow I doubt that *'don't water the booze'* is going to help the Ambassadors too much."

Czhark chuckled. "It is clear that you do not attend many diplomatic functions, Max. Intoxicants are the rocket fuel of modern Diplomacy."

"Aside from that," I asked when everyone stopped laughing. "You all know that adjustments are going to have to be made for each of your peoples. What are your hopes for the future? What are your dreams?"

"Room to grow," said Hnarcor, the expensive dye-job on his tiny scales glistening softly in the indirect lighting. Again, I marveled at how I automatically overlooked his five-foot height and slight mass. For someone with amphibious pack-hunting dinosaurs in his family tree, he looked deceptively harmless. Until he showed his needle-like teeth in a wide smile.

"My people want to expand to off-world colonies, though we have avoided it for far too long. We have finally come to grips with the fact that we are, now and forever, to be the most distant outpost of our species. Our underwater city has long ago reached the limits for which we designed it, but we still avoided the search for more room. There are no other freshwater lakes large enough for us to use on this world. Not that are without their own population of aquatic natives. Those we could only establish small trading posts within. More than that would be an invasion of the property of those natives. That we cannot do. So now, the awakening of our Shebeja friends has shocked our government into motion. We have come to our collective senses, so to speak, and wish to grow in this new galaxy. It is time we healed completely and began exploring and expanding again. We seek worlds with abundant freshwater lakes and shallow, low-salt seas. We are prepared to pay well for the rights to settle new colonies. But we can only ask, we will not seek to take another's world."

He absentmindedly drummed his taloned fingertips on the bar, then straightened the collar of his iridescent-blue vest. His hand strayed to a pocket in his sea-green pantaloons, then placed a large denomination credit chip on the bar. When Max returned his change, he tucked it into a fold of the electric-red sash he wore about his waist. The colors went well with the shimmer of his multi-colored scales, especially the green, tan, and gold ones on his round hairless head. That dye-job must have set him back plenty. A Halazed's normal coloring is various shades of gray.

"I am proud of my people, good friends. We also withdrew to our city after the night the stars changed... It took us several years to venture above water again to stay, but the rewards turned out to be too good to pass by. In the end we found the rewards of shedding that caution and embracing our fellow castaways to have been legion. We have the D'rrish to thank for an excellent example of how to cope with a crisis. They never panicked, they kept contact with the Immortals and Valley of the Three Peaks, they established contact with the natives and built off-world colonies. They explored, they encountered new species, began trade. They made a place for themselves in the new galaxy."

"Thank you," boomed Kazsh-ak through his translator. He raised his drink container in a silent toast. For a scorpion the size of a horse, he moved lightly. "Yet, we too took a long time before we felt safe to re-join the world. But we speak of ancient history—too dry a subject without asking Max for refills. Bless you, Max... But young Jon Stewart has asked a fair question. Well my boy, without putting too fine a point on it, our Arcology—our huge city—has nearly reached its comfortable limits, as to the population. Another two or three generations—seven hundred years or so—and we will face intolerable crowding. We have long wanted to establish more colonies. At the same time, we wish to stay close to our families and expand on this world, rather than go even further away from our homes, here. To the ancient Kefa Empire cities, now that the Immortals have finally lifted the ban on their use," Kazsh-ak said. "Or rather, the radioactive ruins of those bombed-out cities—to be precise."

"That will be a massive undertaking," Hnarcor said.

"I need to discuss this matter at some length with the Reever," Kazsh-ak continued, "though I have little doubt of the ultimate result. I have been granted the authority to ask of the Immortals the purchase outright of the four Kefa Empire cities. This will take time to pursue, but it is a worthy cause. Our off-world colonies are relatively few, due to our special environmental needs, but now our own economy is booming and at the same time, the Immortals have only recently offered the Kefa ruins as colony sites, declaring them available for use. We can now build small arcologies in place of the ruins, then farm and hunt the surrounding wastelands. The remaining mutants should prove interesting prey. We should be able to assist them to evolve most admirably. A most auspicious time we are living in, Gentlebeings. Why, Kefa-ku *alone* would allow us to nearly *double* our living area. A most auspicious time, indeed!"

"My people need a grander purpose," sighed Czhark after a short pause. "Not room. I am ashamed to have to admit that the long sleep has weakened us. We are not as vigorous as once we were. We are more... hide-bound and officious. It is almost like a sickness. Perhaps I see this more clearly because of my service in the Awake Crews and all the years I spent out of sleepfreeze, on and off. Because of my beliefs I tried to spend as much time out of the sleeper tanks as could be allowed. I can see the shock that being cut off from our home world has caused. And it has not been lessened by a mere seven centuries of sleep. I fear for my people. We need a grand purpose to unite us, to re-awaken our souls as well as our bodies." He looked down at the bar top for a long moment, then said "We are a race in search of a quest, I'm afraid. Not just a purpose, but a quest. We must have some *thing* that unites us in a way that will allow us to make a place in this new galaxy, or we will fade away... Become a lost branch of our people."

"Something like—oh, getting word back to the home world over in Andromeda that you managed to stay alive and waving the flag over here in the Milky Way," I said. "But it'd take over two million years to get a radio signal from here to there. Ships and sub-space radio are a little quicker, on that scale, but not much. Let's face it, unless there's some kind of super-science that the Immortals could pull off, it would take thousands of years to get even the fastest FTL ship anyone has now over to the next galaxy."

I suddenly shut up when I saw a pained look quickly cross Max's face when I mentioned super-science. Just as sure as sunshine, I *knew* that I'd put my foot in my mouth again. I was sure that the Immortals *did* have a way to get from here to there quickly—and just as sure that Max had been forbidden—for some reason—to mention it. And I had. Oh boy... *How do I cover this screw-up?*

"But that's just dreaming, if there was a way, they'd have given it to you seven hundred years ago, right?" *Please, don't anyone notice me sweat!* "The Reever wouldn't let any of you suffer by being cut off from home if there was a way that he could get you back. That wouldn't be *justice,* not the way he sees it. No, the Immortals are just as powerless to get you back home as anyone else in this galaxy."

I looked quickly at Max again for approval and knew that I was doing good up 'til I said *'anyone else in this galaxy.'* Then he looked like he'd had another pain. He covered it this time by excusing himself to take other drink orders. So, it wasn't the *Immortals* that had the putative super-gizmo, but it was someone *else* that Max knew of and—*and wasn't allowed to talk about! Oh—my—Heavens!* This was *deeeep doodoo,* and I knew that Max trusted me to put this topic *away* before he got placed in an ethical bind. All right, but I had to admit to some questions of my own. Ones that I hoped to put to Max in private sometime in the unforeseeable future. If I didn't choke to death on my foot tonight, that is. I'm betting that it was Polios, the Mare's owner. I'd heard rumors before and thought them rather wild. But for now, I had to try to steer the conversation into a safer path...

What to say? "So that's right out of the realm of possibility, right? Yeah, right out... Um, right..." *I'm dying here! Think, boy! Think!* "When you get right down to it, isn't the right here and right now all that any of us have to depend on?" *Lame! So lame! But it was the best I could do on the spur of the moment.* "So, voyages home are out, message signals are out... Maybe a robot probe? One outfitted with the biggest FTL boosters we can buy. It would still take generations to arrive in Andromeda, but you could boost the thing at speeds that would kill anything living on board. That would cut the trip time to thousands of years rather than millions. I admit, it's not a way home, but it is a way for you to tell home that you're still alive and well and waiting on them to come visit... "

"The Immortals did that as soon as they determined where we were," said Kazsh-ak Tier. "And where our home galaxy was, once it became clear that we had been moved that far. Salvation does not lay there, but some small comfort for our peoples does. Our home worlds will someday know our fate, if our civilizations in Andromeda last long enough."

"How long will the probe take?" I asked.

"Ten to twelve thousand years," Max said as he returned. His hearing must be phenomenal.

Kazsh-ak paused for a short while to recall. "I remember reading about the probe a couple of days ago." he eventually said. "The news services have been overflowing with historical interest articles since word came from Oktishnear."

All right, I thought, *Obviously, someone here isn't cleared for the knowledge that Max is an Immortal—probably Ambassador Shark. I need to play it cool.* "How fast is it going?" I asked, to help Max cover mostly—but I felt curious, too.

"Roughly?" Max frowned in thought and scratched his head. "It'll reach a peak speed of—oh, the article said nearly five light years per day, I think. But when you factor in the need for the probe to boost up out of the Milky Way's galactic disc at much lower speeds, and the acceleration and deceleration times involved crossing the intergalactic gulf, then going even slower to enter Andromeda—the actual average speed'll be closer to six-tenths of a light year per day"

"*Odin on roller skates!* The fastest passenger liners can only pull about three-tenths of a light per day. My courier ship is fast, but at strain-everything speeds," I shrugged. "I can only brush four-tenths of a light per day. With booster engines I could, just *maybe,* manage half a light per day." *No need to confess to anyone that I've* already got *those boosters installed.* "And *Della Sue* couldn't even *begin* to move if she happened to be towing ten thousand years' worth of fuel. That'd be a fuel tank the size of a planet. How *big* is this thing?"

"About ten feet in diameter. It masses roughly a hundred tons," Max replied after a moment.

"Good grief! What's it made out of? Neutronium?" I gasped.

"Um," said Max, "Not really, but something close. A quantum black hole is the power plant—and payload for that matter, when it was a live weapon—although the normal weapons used much less massive ones. This one had been beefed up for the long trip. A teeny-tiny quantum black hole, deep inside the heart of the machine itself. It'd help if you think of the probe as an over-powered, but disarmed torpedo—with some communications gear grafted on as an afterthought. You wouldn't be far off that way. The quantum black hole has an event horizon about the size of a proton, so you can tell that it isn't very dense. I mean, at only a hundred tons and the size of a proton, the thing has the density of foam rubber—or smoke, maybe—as far as black holes go, that is. When it was still a torpedo, part of the machinery in the shell used the energy of the hole for propulsion, even though it wasn't very efficient. I mean, the thing had an expected life-span of—maybe—ten minutes, as a torpedo. So the drive didn't have to be efficient, just *very* fast. And this thing is supposed to last for ten thousand years as a message buoy? Maybe... Anyway, when it was still a torpedo, another machine on the shell was supposed to make the black hole evaporate instantaneously when it reached its target. All that mass converting to energy all at once? That's a *big* bang—Uh..." he looked up and went silent.

"We have a problem," interrupted the Reever, walking up to the bar with a beautiful raven-haired woman on his arm. "Tarja has just brought me some disturbing news..."

I knew who she was as soon as I saw her. Even through the shock of seeing the Reever escorting her (or anyone, for that matter) as if she were a casual date. —There could never be any mistaking Tarja. I'd never crossed paths with her professionally—but since she's a high-priced assassin, *that* fact remained a comfort to me right at the moment. Since I *also* knew that I've never bothered anyone (still living) badly enough for them to put any putative bounty on my head high enough to be in *her* price range, I relaxed—slightly. But I was still on high alert. *What's the best assassin in the stellar cluster doing playing nice-nice with the biggest cop on the planet?* My intuition kept leaping at conclusions in the back of my mind, but I tried to devote most of my attention to what was happening in front of me. Unless I had suddenly become delusional, there had to be something really *strange* going on today. I could hear the old Twilight Zone theme *ding-ding-ding-dinging* in the back of my mind.

"It seems that there *was* to have been an attempt on your life, Ambassador Czhark," the Reever said evenly. "I'm happy to report that it is no longer scheduled to take place. Miss Tarja was approached to undertake the contract. She smelled a rat, so to speak, and came directly to me."

"Any *professional* would know that the Reever *never* lets anyone get away with killing *Diplomats* on this planet," explained Tarja. Her melodious voice fit her beauty perfectly. Exactly the same way that her blue satin dress fit her body—perfectly. If just half of what I'd heard about her was true that delicate, satin-draped frame could probably beat nearly any being in the room to a pulp—except for the Reever of course, and possibly Bruce. I stopped my ruminations as she began to speak again. "Right away I realized *two* things; that this contract had to be a set-up and I was *supposed* to get caught—*and* that these people who contacted me were being backed by big money interests *here on Bethdish* as well as from off-world. They were trying to hide the local connection, but I spotted a few clues that gave them away. So I took their retainer—and ran straight to the Reever's office. I haven't lived this long in my business without developing an instinct for smelling a *trap*."

As the three Ambassadors sat stunned by the news, the Reever continued, "I've already assigned a team to trace the contract back to its source. They'll make the necessary inquiries and arrests. But something in the way Tarja related the incident prompted me to re-think the situation. Now I believe that there is more to this than meets the eye. I started thinking; what if this is just a diversion? Killing the Ambassador wouldn't change the political situation here and now. The meeting would still take place, with even tighter security. *If* that's even possible. After today, I'm beginning to doubt that. And the Shebeja themselves would still be hunting pirates, but after the assassination they'd be *angry*. Add to that the fact that *I'd* be hunting for them too. The investigation would only tie up so many of my officers—a significant number, yes—but not when compared with the citywide force. But this is a very big city... Then what if—What if *I* were supposed to be distracted by this investigation? What if someone wants me *personally* to concentrate on this case—to the exclusion of everything else? I began to wonder what else might be planned to be happening while I was looking where 'they'—whoever 'they' are—wanted me to look. So I decided to look elsewhere, as discreetly as possible..."

"Did you find anything?" I asked.

"Several disturbing trends, but nothing overt, actually. I'm glad you're here today, Jon Stewart," replied the Reever evasively. That's *not* normal for him. He usually says what's on his mind. The Reever's more honest than a Boy Scout. As he continued, I broke out into a Zen sweat— mentally, in other words, I started sweating bullets. "Have you spoken to Blanche or the Gremlin lately?"—That was all he said, but that served to be enough to trip *all* my alerts.

Max replied before I could open my mouth. "Blanche is off-world on vacation, but the Gremlin should be in tonight at his regular time."

This did not sound *at all* good to me. The *last* time I worked with Blanche and the Gremlin, the Reever wound up having to *deputize* me as a dodge to keep from having to arrest me. *Please, no!* I thought. *I've given up playing* Jon Stewart Sebastian; Intergalactic Being of Mystery *for my health. Blanche almost got me killed* twice *last time I played spy. I'm getting too old for that stuff. That's why I retired ten years ago.*

"I see," the Reever said. "Well, there's no help for it, I'll wait. I may want to bring the Gremlin in on this one. Until my agents can identify the real culprits and we can figure out just *exactly* what's up, my available man-power is going to be spread rather thinly. We may need your help too, Jon. You're a Blue Blaze Irregular, as I recall. I've worked with you before. You're a real pro. If things get worse, I may have to signal an alert. You can guess what that'll be like. As to what I've found, there appears to be several disturbing trends developing. Street-level crime has declined ominously, as if the muggers, burglars, and pick-pockets had all gone into hiding. Also, there has been a sudden lack of more major crimes as well. For instance, there hasn't been a single bank robbery in over a week. In the whole *city*... In a city this size, that's just not *possible* under normal circumstances. Furthermore, out in the asteroid belt there's been a rash of mining tugs being stolen. I'm willing to bet that there are more than just the ones that've been reported so far. Which means—among other things, *if* I'm right—that some of the miners must have been murdered... There *are* more missing persons reports in the Belt than are normal."

"What are the statistics for beings exiting the city?" Ambassador Czhark asked suddenly. "Have any native factions become conspicuous by their absence? Also, is there a marked absence of the expected off-world shipping. Both legal and clandestine, I mean."

"Good questions," said the Reever. He made a reaching motion with his right hand—I noticed that his left he kept still around Tarja's waist. Were these two *dating?* My train of thought was derailed when the Reever's Staff of Office appeared out of nowhere. The damn stick just popped into his hand! I took a sudden gulp of my Krupnick and set the empty glass down. I noticed Max refill it out of the corner of my eye. "I'll put the computer to searching the records..." He stood the staff upright and let it go. It must have locked on to the floor somehow, because he started punching a small keypad inset into the stick's surface and it never even swayed. *Why hasn't he let go of Tarja?* Nothing *can come between the Reever and what he sees as his duty. Not even romance! He's just* made *that way.* I knew that I must be missing some important bit of information then.

"Reeee-ver?" Tarja cooed sweetly. The hairs on the back of my neck stood up in alarm at the sound.

"Yes?"

"Do you think that we can do *without* the handcuffs now? I'd *like* to have a drink."

"Word of honor? No tricks, no escapes—you're one of the party until we're all out of danger?"

"Word of honor," she replied, arching one eyebrow. "I'd rather *not* have *you* for an enemy. And I make a habit of ensuring that *my* survival is one of my *highest* priorities."

"I can guarantee that you wouldn't enjoy our becoming enemies," he replied with a grim look. "I know that *I* wouldn't." Without another word he pulled his hand out from behind her back, holding a set of unfastened handcuffs. "Max—"

"I'm on it," Max cut him off. "I remember her favorite."

"Max," I said quietly, when he came back with Tarja's drink. "We're going to need a room to ourselves. We can't keep talking about this stuff out here at the bar."

"On the contrary," Kazsh-ak said. "How better than to *see* what beings might be interested in overhearing our conversation? I happen to know that the security systems here are the finest that can be devised. Any enemy would hesitate to act within these walls. The Mare Inebrium Tower has a certain—reputation, among the criminal elements in this city. We are free from harm and can see with our own eyes whomever might attempt to eavesdrop on our little debate. We may need the extra time any warning could possibly give us."

"That's true," Max said. "The Thieves Guild has a big reward posted for any member that's able to steal *anything* more valuable than a shot glass—from anywhere in the building. The Boss has security set-ups here that scare *me!* But we can have a side room set up in a couple of minutes, if you want one. Otherwise, I can inform the security AIs to *unobtrusively* step up the coverage. No one in the room will notice. And the Boss will want to know."

"Polios always knows everything that goes on in the building," the Reever replied. "I'm betting you don't have to call him. If you don't believe me, here's a quick test. Check the AI's alert level. You haven't changed anything yet yourself, remember."

Max tapped a code into the nearest screen. He paused, then glanced up at us quickly. "They've been on heightened alert for the last twenty minutes. Since *before* you and Tarja entered the building. Near as I can figure, they went into alert status the moment you two came in sight of the front door. According to this readout, nothing can touch us in here right now. Nobody can teleport in, bomb-screening is in progress for the entire building. Structural integrity force fields—didn't know we had those—they've been boosted to three hundred percent of normal... Whoa—too much information—can't tell what half of it means... What's this window? What the hell? Some of this stuff *has* to be illegal! There's a tie-in to the city-wide traffic-control systems—continuous scans of air traffic radar from the spaceport, and—*Holy Mother of the Gods!* Here's a link to the Deep Space Scanners up on Xerxes! I know for a *fact* that *that* stuff is classified..."

"Yes," mused the Reever, "But Polios isn't prone to respect such petty things as other people's 'secrets' when something threatens his interests. He's programmed these AIs rather well. I doubt that anyone else could hack into so many systems without setting off all sorts of alarms. I'll bet that not *one* of those systems has set off so much as a peep of the first intruder alert. Alright, see if—"

"The AIs are requesting a link to the computer in your Staff of Office," Max interrupted. "I've never seen *that* before." He locked eyes with the Reever for the barest second. I doubt if anyone else but me even noticed it lasted just a fraction of a second too long. I was guessing it had to be some kind of Immortal-to-Immortal 'significant glance' and wondered what it meant, but Max continued and derailed that train of thought. "Not a 'Red Alert', just a conference and update request."

"Where is the nearest communicator?" Kazsh-ak asked breathlessly. Neat trick, for someone whose voice comes out of an electronic box. "I might be able to learn something from my friend Guiles Thornby. He is—"

"One of the Boss's research agents," Max shot back. "For that spooky old Museum of his. He's been coming in here for *years*. Good idea. Yeah, there's a com screen in your restroom lounge."

"Gentlebeings, I shall return," the D'rrish said as he scuttled off towards the restroom for his species. In the Mare Inebrium, *always* be sure you're in the right restroom for *your* species.

"What does all this mean?" asked the Shebeja Ambassador, shaking his head in puzzlement.

"That we, ourselves, are in no danger—for the moment," replied the Halazed Ambassador. "Or so I feel safe in assuming. A plot is afoot—and a part of it has been stopped, but just how large a plot and how great the danger to the rest of the city has yet to be established. I trust the Reever in this. Also, at the moment we seem to have acquired the use of enormous resources, provided by Mr. Polios. I have heard many rumors concerning the mysterious owner of the Mare Inebrium, but until this day, they have been rumors only. Truly, he is a hidden power in the city."

"No, nothing like that," said Max. "He's just an eccentric old Archaeologist. He just likes a good bar to relax in, he told me once. That's why he bought into the Mare Inebrium in the first place, he said. He wants it to be the best bar that's ever been, anywhere. He doesn't give a flip for city politics. He's hardly ever *on* Bethdish anyway, because of all the digs he goes on. He's supposed to spend most of his time off-world digging up pottery and old bones. All I know about his museum is that it exists, never been there myself. Some of the museum staff come here for drinks occasionally. Pretty normal beings, for the most part, I'd say."

"The link is established," said the Reever. Several virtual computer windows blossomed in the air, just above eye-level at the bar. If I squinted, I could just barely make out thin beams of light connecting them to the Reever's Staff. "The AIs seem to be giving us visuals of the local air and space traffic, the Deep Space tracking system, and something I don't recognize... Anyone know what this third window is showing?"

Czhark gave out a choked sort-of cough. "That appears to be a—a *greatly enhanced* version of the signals from one of *our* orbital satellites. We have several such devices watching the various coastlines. We use them for weather monitoring and navigation. But our equipment cannot produce anything *near* the amount of detail that *that* visual is displaying."

"Can anyone tell what area of the ocean that the satellite is scanning?" I asked. I looked quickly around at the rest of the patrons in the main room, but none of them seemed to see the floating computer windows that we saw. "It looks like a stretch of open ocean to me, except for that glint of light over there on the lower left."

"Assuming that glint is something on the *east* coast of the continent, then that would have to be sunlight reflecting off of the Tower of Shy'are the

Wizard," replied the Reever after a moment's thought. "That would put whatever is at the center of the screen very far out to sea east of us, and somewhat south as well. I make it two thousand, maybe three thousand standard miles east-southeast of us. But what *is* it? I can't see anything but tiny blurry blobs and leagues of open sea."

"What's that on the fourth window?" I asked.

"That one is a graph showing the population flux of the city," the Reever explained. "People observed leaving versus the expected number for this time of year. You can see that it's being cross-referenced with the known whereabouts of various organized crime figures and several of the shadier sort of local politicians. That gold-colored line on the chart seems to be the number of the 'Old Money' families in the city that have suddenly decided to take off-world vacations. And that dark blue line is the low number of street crimes that I mentioned. All this is 'giving me furious to think', as a French Terran once said to me. I know that all of this is supposed to add up, but what kind of *math* are we supposed to be using?"

"Hello people," said a foxy-faced man who had just walked up. Kazsh-ak followed closely behind, his bright blue eyes dancing joyfully on their stalks. "The big bug tells me that you folks need a hand with some data that the Boss is providing to you..." He trailed off as he came close enough to be included in whatever voodoo that had been keeping the other two hundred aliens in the room from seeing the floating windows above the bar. "Oh my..." he sighed. "That's a good one..." He turned to the Reever and held out his right hand. "Nice to see you again, Reever. Is that one of *your* illusions?" They shook hands like old friends, so I gathered that they'd met several times before.

More semi-invisible computer windows popped up—each making a quiet *thwipping* noise as it appeared. From the way that he was eying them, I figured out for myself that Max had to be able to read them from the back as easily as the rest of us were able to read them from the front. I still wondered why no one else in the bar could see them, but then I figured that I probably wouldn't understand the explanation anyway. I'm just a rocket-jockey (and ex-spy), not a rocket *scientist.* There came a pause as Kazsh-ak introduced Thornby to the other Ambassadors. Thornby nodded at Max, bowed to Czhark, clasped forearms with Hnarcor, and shook hands with me. Tarja seemed to enjoy it when he kissed her hand. I couldn't overhear what he murmured to her as he bowed over her hand, but she giggled and blushed.

Anyway, I'd heard Kazsh-ak talk about Thornby before, but this was the first time that I'd ever seen him. He looked like an average-sized fellow, but very fit. He had dark brown hair with just a faint trace of gray at the temples and sharp, foxy features. He spoke in a clear, accent-less voice, like a newscaster and wore a nondescript suit of a fashionable style, nothing rich or flashy, just well-to-do. He could have passed for any age from thirty-five to sixty, what with his unlined face and smooth looks. From what Kazsh-ak Tier had let slip one night whilst the scorpion was in his cups, so to speak, Thornby must be closer to a hundred fifty than to thirty. Personally, I think Kazsh-ak had been overstating the case that night—in his intoxicated desire to tell a good story. To tell the truth, Thornby reminded me of a safe-cracker that I'd known in my wild and misspent youth. One of my old instructors—back long before I'd given up spying for retirement to a more sedate life as a delivery-boy... Not in how he looked, or anything he said, more in his mannerisms and body language. I know that it's hard to explain, but then, it *was* more of a subliminal thing than something that I was aware of at the time. Needless to say, I trusted him at first sight.

"Well, you've certainly got a *lot* of information here," Thornby said as he slid onto a seat. "Actually, it was Mistress Sarah who approved this little exercise in creative hacking. Polios has been off on a dig for the last six months. Sarah's always in charge when he's away." Max put a gin and tonic in front of him and stood back to look at the displays himself. "I *think*," Thornby said cautiously. "I *think* I can get a bit more detail on a couple of them, but the most important ones look like these sets of charts here..." Thornby sipped his drink and studied the window that floated nearest him. "The AIs wouldn't have displayed them if they weren't something that they thought might be necessary to us. These figures make it look like there's a lot of important crooks—er, politicians—fleeing the city for their vacation resorts. Some of them are even going *off*-world. Like rats fleeing the proverbial sinking ship... They're obviously either up to something, or know of someone who *is* up to something... Then again, what *is this* out there on the ocean—and what in the seven hells is it that we're supposed to see on a scan of the blasted *asteroid* belt? Hmm—I want to try something."

"Go ahead," said the Reever. "Right now, we need all the help we can get. I can't escape the feeling that our time is limited. Whatever is going to happen, it'll happen *soon*."

"Thanks," said Thornby. "Computer, this is Guiles Thornby. Do you recognize me?"

I heard a bell-like tone and a quiet voice answered. "Guiles Thornby is recognized. Temporary access granted. Awaiting input..."

"Temporary?" I asked.

"The system knows me, but also knows that I don't work for the Mare," Thornby replied offhandedly, lost in thought. "Max would be treated the same way—if he were in the museum. We both work for the same guy, just in different enterprises," he grinned as if had just made a pun. I didn't get it, if it was a joke. "All right, let's see what we can get out of this... Computer, enhance and magnify image on screen three. Enhance image on screen five. Identify any targets on screens three and five, continue scan in real-time. Screen two, indicate destinations of vacationing travelers. Screen four, cross reference out-going travelers to space with the known and suspected organized crime figures. Screen six, give an alert if there is any unusual spaceport traffic. End of command string."

"Processing..." said the computer-voice. "Screen three magnified... Image enhanced, identification of targets in scan area in progress... Processing... Screen five image enhanced... Processing... Eight targets painted as unidentified by transponder signals... Possible stolen ships with transponders disabled... Processing image further..."

"Your missing mining tugs?" I asked the Reever.

"Twice as many as have been reported..." He shrugged. "One would think so, but let's wait and see. I'm more concerned with what's going to happen out at sea. That's a lot closer and more immediate."

"You had *better* start worrying about those *tugs*," Tarja said as she elbowed the Reever in the ribs. "If one of those boats can move a fair-sized asteroid, how big of a *projectile* mass do you figure *all* of them linked together can tow? Say, into a bombing run somewhere on the planet's surface? Like right *here*, maybe?"

Needless to say, we were all a bit dumbfounded by *that* little deduction.

"This hunt is beginning to make sense," said Ambassador Czhark. We all turned to look at him.

"How so?" asked Hnarcor. "All I perceive is that the pack hunting you stand revealed as being vastly larger than we thought. They have lost the element of surprise, that is all. What have I missed, oh honored colleague?"

"Ah, but that is the very point I wished to make," Czhark replied. "Or rather that it is unlikely to be *one* pack against us. Rather it will be *several.* This stands revealed as some local and off-world smugglers—technology smugglers, working together, perhaps. Undoubtedly, my people flying patrol once again have begun to cut severely into their profits. The events in the asteroid belt point to some off-world group, while the menace from the sea points to some alliance of the locals. Are they actually working together, or are we simply assuming so? How many talons are in the paw reaching to grasp us? I wonder... As to the time left to us—when might we be allotted the hour of my demise, my lovely Mistress Assassin?"

"Tarja," she replied pleasantly. "I'm no one's mistress. And I was to kill you tomorrow evening, when you stood to make your speech. They wanted me to put a bomb in the podium. A bomb in the podium!" She shook her head. "So *unprofessional.* I gave the nasty thing to the Reever. Dirty little bugger—much too big for the job. It would have made a hash of the nearest fifty beings, at least. Frankly, I'd have turned the whole matter over to the Assassin's Guild and their External Affairs committee instead of the Reever, but I can't take the chance that some highly placed local Guild member isn't involved. At least this way, *my* pretty little ass is covered."

"Wha—ahem... Where was this speech going to be?" I asked, blocking all the erotic images of Tarja from my mind that had resulted from her previous statement... With difficulty, I might add.

"Here in the Mare," Max replied. "In the small ballroom. Pitting Tarja up against the house security AIs. The very same ones that are giving us these data screens. The same ones that, on a normal day, can tell me which one out of several hundred patrons is carrying so much as a pocketknife? Talk about a stacked deck!"

"*That* was one point that told me the job had to be a *trap*," Tarja replied. "Besides the target being *forbidden* prey, the *location* specified made escape downright *impossible*. It might just *barely* have been possible to make the hit in the first place, but the security systems would have recordings of everything, *all day long*. It *might* even have been possible to simply plant the bomb and get out of the building, but the system would have been able to ID me from the recordings. I'm not a *stranger* here. And given my line of work, I'd be insulted if the security *didn't* watch me when I'm visiting." Again, she arched an eyebrow, then actually pouted for a second. "After all, one *does* have one's reputation to uphold."

"So whatever else is planned to happen," I said slowly, thinking out loud. "It looks like we have a little over a day to figure it out. If those tugs *do* throw rocks at us, when is the earliest they can get here? And what would they be trying to hit?"

"Assuming that my people are the *only* target—then they will attempt to drop their asteroids on Oktishnear," said Ambassador Czhark sadly. "Which puts all of the Kingdoms of Ellor and Kineth at risk. A near-miss would wipe them out. And if they choose too big a missile, the devastation would b —unthinkable."

"So send the Navy after them," I suggested.

"Are they not now as aware as we?" Hnarcor asked.

"I doubt that the Navy is seeing *these* images," Thornby replied. "The AIs are accessing raw data and enhancing it for *us*—*alone*. The data-stream *isn't* going both ways, bet on it. But we can't move *too* soon, or we'll spook the masterminds into running. *If* they aren't running already. But those tugs —We still have some time, I think. The screen would show a rock with them anchored *to* it if they'd already gotten their asteroid. It would even show little ones if they each had one. They just seem to be converging, but there's no rock there for them to grapple. Until they actually *do* something, they're only stolen ships. We want the people behind them too, not just the hired help. Best thing to do is let them go for now. Ignore 'em until they *do* something... Computer, signal alert if painted targets in screen five change course or dock with any other target. Query: Update on ID of targets in screen three? End of command string."

"Acknowledged; Alert condition set for screen five and screen six... Screen three image processing still in progress... Preliminary target ID indicates two fleets of sea craft, widely dispersed. Further data not yet available. Processing in progress... Please excuse the delay..."

"An assassination, two fleets of ships out of sight of land, and eight space-tugs out in the belt," Tarja said thoughtfully. "What could they possibly be doing with all of that?" She leaned forward on the bar, set her empty glass down, and motioned to Max for a refill. The fact that the scandalous cut of her gown gave Max an unimpeded view of her charms seemed to be an unconscious gesture on her part, but my old ex-spy instincts told me that her every move and word were *calculated* actions. The fact that she flew from world to world to kill people for a living kept coming back to me. Frankly, I felt damn glad that the Reever was there. Still, even though she'd given the Reever her word not to try anything—I couldn't help praying that she wasn't up to something anyway. Then again on the other hand, women always found something about Max to be *extremely* attractive, and Trixie *was* filling in in one of the specialty rooms tonight. Maybe I was just paranoid. But on the gripping hand, was I paranoid *enough*?

"A three-pronged attack then," Czhark replied. "My murder, then an attack on the city by sea, then the bombing of Oktishnear from orbit. That is the way I read the spoor the data tell of."

"But these two fleets can't see each other," Hnarcor said. "Unless I am reading the fuzzy blobs on the screen wrongly, they are well over the horizon from each other. Do we have two pirate fleets meeting, or pirate and prey?"

"I have my doubts of the Shebeja Ambassador's proposed timeline," interjected the Reever. He consulted one of the smaller data windows for a moment before continuing. "Those ships are several days from land, and the tugs are a week away from being able to launch a strike at us. But the one fleet is only hours away from the other. I wish we had the data on what kind of ships they all are. That would tell us a great deal. But the criminals are all fleeing the city *now*, not two days from now or sometime next week. Was the Ambassador's death supposed to lead off the attack? Or was it supposed to be the final act?"

Another semi-visible computer window blossomed into being above the bar. This one looked far smaller and flashed until the Reever had read it.

"I've just had a report from one of my Peacekeepers," said the Reever. "It seems that *someone* has been sending warning messages to the underworld families. My agents have begun tapping into the city-wide comm net. They've already intercepted several of the messages. They were phrased as being friendly warnings from someone who professed to be 'in the know' and advised that City of Lights is about to become 'dangerous'. All the messages so far have been sent to the crime lords' most secure addresses. That would make them take the matter most seriously."

"So that's why they're all running" gasped Max.

"If one of the organized crime families is behind this, what better way to flee to safety than to spook the rest of the herd and run among them?" Hnarcor asked.

"Who did your agents trace back," Thornby asked. "As the ones behind the contract Tarja warned us about?"

The Reever shrugged and replied, "Five of the minor smuggling clans based in the Old City. But they don't have enough money between them to afford *half* of this operation so far. I've put spy-eyes watching the smugglers, hoping that they'll lead us to the off-worlders that are bankrolling our local crime lords."

"Spy-eyes?" I asked.

"Remote camera drones," he replied. "They're about the size of a speck of dust. This is City of Lights, I don't have to restrict my tech here, after all. Originally these cameras were meant for non-invasive medical testing. One researcher pointed out later that the devices worked just as well outside of a body as it did inside. And thus, a new security tool was born, to make a long story short. I hardly ever use the things though, because of the invasion of privacy laws they violate by accident. Besides, if I had every crime lord bugged... There'd be so much data I'd never be able to wade through my Peacekeeper's reports."

We were halted by a chime and verbal report from the AIs—"ID of targets in screen three, update: Fleet one identified; 5 nation fishing fleet composed of 28 ships from Nalth, 32 ships from Kingdom of Seven Isles, 14 ships from coastal Utrthay, 15 ships from Ellor, and 35 trawlers from Yalled. Fishing is in progress for schools of T'chadenross, Kanshelast'nor, B'gesh, Esconsellt'kalt, Seras'kek, D'gaaret'en, and the giant M'nisht'uusor."

"Sounds innocent enough," said the Reever. "Those countries are often allies in fishing ventures. They used to fight among themselves, sure. Oh— a thousand years or so ago they'd have been at each other's throats. But nowadays they prefer to co-operate. Nalth is a small country on the west coast. Fishing is their biggest industry, second to shipbuilding. They build the best sailing ships in the world, bar none. Like one of their neighbors; Kingdom of Seven Isles, Nalth has a bigger population aboard ships at sea than they do anywhere on land. Some of 'em *never* set foot on shore. Yalled and Utrthay are both bigger countries that border the ocean, but they've always harvested as much food from the sea as they do from their own fields. And what a chef from Ellor can do with a Kanshelast'nor fillet would make your mouth water..."

"Fleet two identity. Processing..."

"What of the evacuation of the local criminal underworld?" Kazsh-ak asked. "Does it still proceed apace?"

"Yes," said the Reever absently, while studying one of the new screens.

"What's up?" I asked quickly.

The Reever tapped one of the newest data screens with one finger and it stopped its sudden blinking. "One of my Peacekeeper teams... They reported that they just stopped a bomber. A Cheeryenbar mercenary has just been caught arming a large explosive device in the basement of the Shebeja Embassy, ten minutes ago. He put up a fight when he was found, ran out of ammunition, then tried to detonate the device. One of my officers had to kill him to stop him. Too bad, we needed whatever he might have known."

"Things are going too fast," hissed Hnarcor. "We are juggling antique explosives here. One slip and we're geography. Or at least, spattered *across* the local geography."

"I've often thought," said Kazsh-ak. "That life could well benefit from a 'Pause' button."

"Hear, hear," replied Czhark in a toast—by way of reply. The chime of the security AIs about to make another report cut him off.

"ID of targets in screen three, update: Fleet two is identified as 75 craft of various classes of native warships, from widely differing eras."

"*There's* the Balrog in the wood pile," Thornby said. "Computer, enhance Fleet Two image and scan. End of command string."

"Processing..." replied the AIs.

"Better and better," I muttered as I drained my glass yet again. "This keeps getting better and better... If this goes on—"

"We'll need a new planet," Tarja sadly said.

"I will *not* let that happen," said the Reever angrily. "There *has* to be another way..."

"We will find a way to protect our adopted home," said Kazsh-ak. "There is nothing that we cannot deal with."

He was interrupted by the chime signaling another report from the AIs.

"ID of targets in screen three, update: ITEM 1: Central ship in fleet positively identified as a Terran seagoing aircraft carrier, military-surplus, estimated to be circa 3550 AD. NOTE: This ship violates Treaty of Bethdish / Terran Federation Concord; section 7, item 5, paragraph 217, and is therefore Proscribed."

"...Or perhaps not," the big bug squawked in alarm. "What kind of people are we *dealing* with?"

"This just gets better and better, doesn't it?" I said as I wondered for a moment how someone had managed to get the carrier to the surface of Bethdish.

"Computer," said Thornby wearily. "Enhance the Terran ship further and scan. End of command string."

"ID of targets in screen three, update: ITEM 2: Aircraft on carrier launching pad is tentatively identified as Shebeja MK A-210 Model 15-b Heliship. Possible ID match with serial number BKU7640-735JK-HF5-4, reported lost at sea with an Awake Team approximately 300 years ago. Possession of this technology by natives of Bethdish is Proscribed."

"Holy Mother!" Max exclaimed.

"Indeed," replied Hnarcor.

"The minimum penalty," Kazsh-ak intoned gravely, "for importation for sale and or use of proscribed tech on Bethdish, is life without the possibility of parole in Membeth Prison. Minimum penalty for importation for sale and or use of proscribed tech *and* contributing to the death of Bethdish natives by use thereof, is death by the 'long swim,' or single combat with the Reever in the Arena."

"But," Tarja asked, "what are they going to *do?* They've got enough firepower to level a good portion of the city."

"Obviously," said Kazsh-ak. "They intend to attack the fishing fleet with the Heliship and frame the Shebeja for the attack. That explains the ships at sea, but what about the tugs out in the belt? What could their target be? And the planned disruption of City of Lights?"

"That Heliship can function as an interplanetary hopper as well as an airship," Czhark said. "After attacking the fishermen, it can boost up out of the atmosphere and meet those tugs."

"To what end?" Hnarcor asked.

"It *could* transport them here faster than they could arrive on their own. That is," Thornby mused aloud, "if the heliship has enough range. But they still don't have any payload to use as bombs. At least, not any payload that we can detect. They still look like they're going to all meet up, but unless we're scanning for the wrong things, they don't seem to be a big threat yet."

"And they'd burn up trying to enter the atmosphere on their own," Max pointed out. "And they'd fly like bricks in the atmosphere, anyway. Would the heliship be able to lower them safely?"

"Perhaps one at a time—with great difficulty," Czhark said thoughtfully. "But one single mistake and they'd all die—Burn up upon re-entry."

"So, City of Lights *could* still be the main target for bombing instead of Oktishnear?" I asked.

"The heliship could just as easily fly here to the city and attack," Czhark said. "Or fly to Oktishnear and attack, rather than lift out to orbit. Yes, both are possible. And it carries enough firepower to level several city blocks."

"But why the bomb in the Shebeja Embassy," Tarja asked, "if they're going to frame the Shebeja?"

"Good point," the Reever said. "Perhaps the bomber intended to set the time of detonation to simulate public reaction to the attacks."

"Ah," said Hnarcor. "After the news broke and the city was in an uproar?"

"Exactly, we were no doubt supposed to believe that the Shebeja had attacked an innocent fishing fleet and then attacked City of Lights—but that is speculation. We will never know, now." The Reever was beginning to look worried. "The amount of money involved in this is staggering."

"Now that the bomber is dead?"

"Yes, Tarja," said the Reever. "Unless we catch one of the culprits ultimately behind all this and force them to talk, we'll never know the truth."

"I don't *care* about the *truth,* she snarled prettily. "I care about not being murdered in my bed! I don't look good in black..."

"Well, what happens if you nuke that pirate fleet?" I asked, to change the subject.

"Literally?" The Reever snorted. "That'd most likely kill the fishermen in the first fleet—as well as send a tidal wave onto the east coast. The two fleets are too close together for me to simply *vaporize* one of them. The most I could do right this minute would be to launch a strike team to go shoot up the pirate fleet—with much less powerful weapons. And that heliship wouldn't be any kind of a pushover when it comes to combat. Neither would the Carrier, for that matter. Those Terrans build good ships to start with, and that ship carries better weapons than *this* world's seen in nearly seven thousand years—aside from ours, I mean... It's taken most of the native civilizations *that* long to claw their way back up to the steam engine and electricity!"

"How so?" Tarja asked.

"The polar shift knocked them almost back into the stone age. Isn't that bad enough? I don't want them to lose everything they've rediscovered in some useless bloody war. People in City of Lights tend to forget what it's *really* like outside the city's walls. Go outside and travel a thousand miles in any direction—you'll find people working their way back up to indoor plumbing and streetlights. Less than ten percent of those fishing boats will have *any* kind of motor. Those that *do* will have steam engines. The rest will only have sails. That carrier, on the other hand, has nuclear powered turbines turning propellers that are two stories tall. The fishing fleet can't run from that. Nor could they defend themselves. I'm not going to let some *off-worlder* destroy what we've been able to re-build."

"Okay then," Max said. "How many Shebeja heliships can be called out?"

"Sixty-one," said Czhark. "That is all that have survived the centuries of storage and are functionable at the moment. Out of the one hundred and six that the base originally had, fourteen have been either lost or destroyed. The rest are being repaired—or used for parts."

Tarja looked happier with the Shebeja's revelation. "How many other atmospheric fighter craft could be mobilized to attack the pirate fleet? That is, if we *did* decide to sound the alarm."

Kazsh-ak tapped one pincer with a medial limb while counting, then spoke as if re-assured. "The spaceport has twenty of its own Patrol ships— two and three-man fighter/interceptors. Xerxes can provide perhaps ten to twelve atmosphere-rated fighters from the Terran Navy craft stationed there. Fifty to a hundred Halazed & D'rrish fighters can be called out, by my estimate. Various others could be called upon if necessary."

Tarja frowned. "How can we do that without making people panic?"

"*Without* letting anyone know what we're doing," I said. "And that won't be easy. Matter of fact, it may not even be possible."

Kazsh-ak made a quick snipping motion with his right pincer. "The Reever should ask Xerxes to send a battle group out to deal with those tugs. It would be foolish to leave them at our backs as we deal with the pirate fleet. We don't have the time to waste fighting a war on two fronts. We can be rid of one front in a single fell swoop."

"Before they can do anything?" Thornby sounded doubtful.

"Yes," replied Czhark. "We can't afford to waste any time. At the very least, they are stolen property. They are also to be considered potential weapons or weapons delivery systems. They cannot be allowed to make any kind of attack."

"Very well," said the Reever a moment later. "The message is sent. Awaiting reply from Xerxes. I hope they don't take long."

"What will they think when they get your message?" Tarja asked. "Do you often ask them to flit about on little errands for you?"

"They'll no doubt believe that I'm just using some esoteric science to detect things their own equipment can't. In a way, that's the truth. Except that it's not Immortal tech, it's the Mare's. But no, I don't make it a habit to call out the Navy. Someone will know that *something* strange is up, but I think we can count on the Navy's discretion."

"One would hope so!" Kazsh-ak said.

"I'd hate to save the world," I said. "Just to find that panic in the streets killed everyone I was fighting for in the first place. We've *got* to figure a way to keep this quiet."

"Security versus need-to-know," Hnarcor said snickering. "Let me know which you find more necessary. I am open to suggestions on how to deal with the pirate fleet, myself."

"All right," said the Reever a minute later. "Here's a reply from the Navy. Xerxes is sending out a Battleship, two Destroyers, and a dozen smaller support craft. They'll meet the tugs in thirty hours. Assuming the tugs don't pull some kind of trick. Less than thirty hours if the tugs make for Bethdish under their own power. That flotilla packs enough firepower to deflect any asteroid that those tugs can possibly intercept and redirect in that thirty-hour time frame. They have orders to arrest the tug pilots, if possible, but to stop any putative attack the tugs could make, no matter what. Now, about the pirates... I've been thinking that it may take too long to assemble an air attack on that fleet. The fishermen may be slaughtered before we can get a single fighter in the air."

"Too bad Xerxes is space Navy instead of a wet navy," I said. "We could use a battle fleet of our own. So—why don't we go to the News and blow the lid off this?"

Hnarcor frowned. "Panic in the streets would kill millions."

"This is a *big* city," Tarja said. "it's bigger than some countries."

The Reever grimaced. "Over twenty-four *thousand* square miles of city. Yes, I know. I'm running short of Peacekeepers since I upped the search for potential bombers."

Tarja wrinkled her brow in thought. "So how do we deal with the Pirates?"

"Well..." said Thornby cautiously. "We could cheat."

Hnarcor looked curious. "How so?"

"We could ask Sarah for a little more help," Thornby said evenly but sadly, like a man betraying a secret for the greater good. "For a strike team from the Museum to go out and smash that pirate fleet before they can launch an attack."

Hnarcor gasped in shock. "Polios can *do* that?"

"He's had to employ one hell of a security service, over the years," said Thornby. "Look, if we can pull this off without making the BBN headlines, we totally halt any attempt to vilify the Shebeja. That helps them and Bethdish as well. The Terran Navy can pull in—and arrest—the tug's pilots, and the Reever can make the necessary charges against *them*. Everything has to be kept quiet or the terrorists win."

Czhark snarled angrily. "There has to be a better way to stop the pirates than an outright attack. I would prefer that we outsmart them somehow."

"What do you suggest?" Max asked.

"I cannot see the larger picture well enough to plot strategy." He replied. "Jon Stewart, what are your thoughts? Do we have any better options?"

"Damnifiknow," I said. "But we need to think of *something*. There's no *way* to keep some kind of pitched battle with that batch of ships from hitting the news. If you call for a militia force to defend the city, there's no way that *that* can be kept from the Press either. Ditto for any kind of discrete mobilization of an air force. The BBN already has a couple of crews out at the spaceport—Can't hide anything from them!"

"I'm open to suggestions from *anybody*," the Reever replied evenly. "Right now, I'm ready to listen to any plan that saves lives. I don't care *who* comes up with the idea!"

For just a second, my head swam dizzily. To regain my composure, I looked around the room again, checking for eavesdroppers. Nothing out of the ordinary met my eye. It looked like a normal day's crowd really. Tourists, businessmen, locals—a pretty even mix, I'd say. Over near the front wall I noticed the sounds of a live band playing techno-pop dance music coming out of the doorway into the Small Ballroom. Max had mentioned them to me earlier this morning. He'd told me they called themselves "Blood, Sweat, & Beers" and they didn't sound half bad, actually. By that doorway—at a small, out of the way table—I noticed a pair of old geezers setting up a 3-D chess game. I remembered having seen them before and recognized them as regulars. They stuck in my mind for some reason. Next to them sat a pair of Kinch-carnum blowing fancy smoke rings from the hookah they were sharing. More people seemed to be looking at *them* than were looking at us. As I panned my view around the room, I couldn't see anything out of place, or anything odd for that matter. No one looked to be paying our group at the bar any extra attention. When the computer chime sounded again, I quickly drew my own attention back to the screens.

"Update: enhanced image of Terran aircraft carrier deck now available. Image on screen ten..."

"What's that flag they're flying from the Bridge?" Max asked.

"Just a circle," I replied after a moment's hesitation to study the screen. "A black circle on a red field. That's what it looks like."

"*What?*" gasped the Reever, jerking away from his study of one of the statistics screens as if he'd just been punched in the gut.

"Look for yourself," I said.

"Zoom in on that flag!" the Reever commanded.

"Done," said Thornby a minute later, after giving the AIs the correct commands. "What is it?"

"A snake biting its tail," said Tarja. "A black snake..."

"Oh, damnation!" Max exclaimed. "Oh, sweet Mother of mercy... Surely not—Surely not *her?* I thought she was dead."

"It's her—" said the Reever. "It really *is* her... That's her personal flag, anyway. I'd prayed to the Gods that she was finally dead, that murderous hag... The Black Snake. So this is one of *her* plots. Now a lot of odd things about this whole situation make a lot more sense. But still, *what would she stand to gain by destroying the Shebeja?* And somewhere in the last three hundred years or so—she's gotten hold of a Shebeja heliship and a Terran aircraft carrier to help her do so—This is too much. This has just gotten us to the threshold of Armageddon here, folks. The Black Snake is the most dangerous being on the planet and has been for the last ten million years. She's a rogue Immortal—High Priestess of the devil himself. And the most destructive, amoral, and ruthless being that's ever crossed my path... If *she's* behind this then we're in *deep* trouble. She's managed to make slaves out of those pirates, that's clear. And she's also spent lots of money on the local crime lords. I can't figure what she's after yet, but I've *got* to stop her—*Whatever* she's up to. I've got no choice now. I *have* to notify Fort Mountain and the High Council of the Immortals. I have to declare a planet-wide red alert before that—*renegade*—can start the next war!"

"Reever," Thornby said with a quiver in his voice. The hair on the back of my neck stood up in alarm at the sound of Thornby's voice. He sounded scared half out of his wits. And I *knew* the man was braver than I am. Just from knowing him this long, today.

"Yes, Guiles?

"You remember asking for suggestions on how to deal with the pirate fleet a few minutes ago?"

"Yes."

"From 'anybody', you said?"

"Yes."

"The uh, the AIs seem to have taken you at your word... *They* have a suggestion here on this screen... but it's pretty—ahhhh... it's pretty *weird.* You'd um—you better come here and take a look."

Thornby haltingly explained what the AIs had come up with. "The Mare's AIs have been in conference with the AI in the Reever's Staff all this time. The Staff's AI is in contact with Fort Mountain—the city of the Immortals. It can command a slew of small tele-operated security drones the Immortals have in storage, but that the Staff knows about. They're armed and can fight. The AIs think that the pirate fleet can be beaten without letting the City's dwellers know enough to panic. That way the collateral damage can be minimized. The drones are old Immortal equipment that's been in storage for *ages*."

The Reever nodded. "Those things are so old I'd forgotten them. Last time we used those was about seven million years before I was born. If I remember correctly, they're roughly a meter in diameter. Each one carries about the same firepower as the average surface-to-orbit fighter-craft of most mortal species. The armor on 'em isn't bad, but it's not invincible. But the control machines are in Fort Mountain. Also mothballed for twenty million years, as I recall. It'd take *hours* to get anything ready for use."

"Well, remember that I said that they were... tele-operated?"

"Yes."

"Good. The AIs have suggested a way to supply the tele-operators, quickly and quietly. Us, in other words."

"You're going to have to explain that one in more detail, Hotshot," Tarja said to Thornby. "How are we supposed to run these drones?"

"Ah," Thornby replied. "That's the really *surreal* part." He shrugged, "The Mare's AIs think in terms of war games, sort of like a big chess game. They can't work the drones themselves because of limits on their programing, their world-view. They suggest that they link one of the Mare's side rooms through themselves, to the Reever's Staff, and then to the drones. We fly the drones and fight them from here in the Mare. All of us that're in the know. To keep the secret, we're *it*, folks. Otherwise, people in the city will panic and lots of them will get hurt trying to get to safety. We've *all* got some degree of combat pilot experience. And we already know what's going on, what's at stake. Besides, we won't actually *be* inside the drones, so we can't get hurt. What do you think, people?"

"Which room?" Hnarcor asked.

"The Game Room," Thornby said.

"The *Game* Room?" Max asked. "We don't *have* a game room. A few of the side bars have pool tables or a few game machines, but we don't have a special side room for games."

Again, Thornby shrugged as he read from the small window floating in front of his eyes. "You *will* have by the time we *get* there. The AIs say that the door will be over near your office, Max. They're going to *create* a side room using the Mare's own environmental control systems. The ones that Max would use to deal with alien customers from *really* strange planets to make a full environment senso-suite for them. The room will have several types of Arcade-style games. We're to pick out a game machine we like, and play. The AI's will translate what we do with each game into signals to properly control the drones. Oh, and when we're finished with it, the room will go away. Forever."

"People," I said. "Looks like, um... it's the end of the world as we know it. If we sit on our butts, I mean. We've been asked to save the world. It's a nice world. I like it, even if I don't live here. Each of us has a stake in preserving the status quo, don't we? I take it that we're all in favor of coming to the defense of our fellow beings?"

Everyone agreed, though Czhark and Tarja both looked a bit puzzled. Kazsh-ak and Hnarcor are both old hands at the Mare, and Thornby looked to be getting his nerve back quickly. Matter of fact, he was beginning to look excited. I didn't really understand what we were about to do myself, as it turned out. But I remained happily ignorant right then. The Reever picked up his staff and spoke to it quietly. I didn't hear what he said.

One by one the floating computer windows blinked off with a quiet *chirp* noise. "Bob Droid? Bobby Blue!" called Max. "Could you come over here for a minute?"

Leaving Bob the blue Droid once more tending the main bar, in twos and threes we ambled over towards the hallway to Max's office. Hey, we were trying to be cool. The new doorway stood open, and the door closed by itself as the last of us stepped inside. For the barest moment, it looked to me as if the room were cavernous, huge, and filled with all manner of game machines. Then... it seemed as if my perceptions flipped into a sharper focus. What had looked like infinite walls and rows of machines became mirrors on the walls, fifty feet away. *Although,* if you looked at *just* the right angle, you got the feel that the mirrors were just... glass walls, shutting off the rest of a much, much vaster space. Strange music played insistently in the background, issuing from hidden speakers. Cream, I think. "Sunshine of Our Love...", but then I'm not hip to much classical music. I wouldn't know anything about the subject except that I had to spend a year as a Creative Anachronist, back when I was still a spy. Looking at my companions, I could tell we all felt a touch of the truly strange. We all had that look of "this can't really be happening" shock on our faces. It was as if somehow even then we each *knew* we'd gone through the Looking Glass. Wordlessly, we set out examining each game in turn.

"Look at all these classics!" I exclaimed after a moment. I lovingly touched the framework of a beautifully restored Omega Race. Tarja laid claim to a Centipede machine sitting between the gleaming restorations of a Spy Master and a Battlezone machine. The Reever looked as if he felt torn between choosing a Defender or a Silpheed machine. Czhark, predictably, found a Chopper Attack flight sim nestled between a Thexdir and a Submarine Commander game. I almost laughed out loud as I saw Kazsh-ak approach an outsized Tailgunner table with what looked near to reverence. Hnarcor slipped gracefully into a booth with Stealth Fighter logos painted gaily across its surface. Thornby did laugh aloud at the Reever's indecision, slapped his friend on the arm, and pointed him towards the Defender game. Max sat inside an X-Wing machine as Thornby finally picked out a Zaxxon machine and sat inside its booth. I found myself the last one to sit down. It seemed strange to see so many of the rare antiques in one room. I noticed tiny speakers echoing the background music.

"Hey," I clearly heard Thornby say. "Check out the com systems! This headset is just like the one in my *Blackbird.*"

"What headset?" I muttered. "Oh, I see it." Clipped to the roof of the game booth was a lightweight wireless headset, headphones and a tiny microphone. Other than that, I couldn't detect any changes from the original arcade game. I donned the headset and could hear the comments of the others much more clearly. There was a narrow Perspex strip that hinged on the earphones. I thought it was a second head strap at first, but when I touched the plastic, it snapped down in front of my eyes. "YIPE!" I yelled. "The headset!"

I was in the cockpit of my own ship, familiar in every detail. And I was *skimming the wave tops, flying over the ocean at an insane speed!* I grabbed for the controls as if my life depended on it.

"...Is more than a headset," Max finished for me. "Watch that first step. It's a doozy."

"Fortunately," I heard Kazsh-ak solemnly intone. "'Ah keep mah feathers numbered for just such an emergency...' These visors are acting as VR imagers, no doubt. I hazard to guess that we each are being fed images of the operation of our favorite vehicles?"

"Too right," Max replied first. "I feel like I'm really flying *Libby,* This is great!"

"Then these AI computers," said Czhark. "They are reading our game play in order to control the Immortal's drones—as if we were actually at the controls of our own craft. yet using the game's controls. This is truly impressive."

"I suggest we look to our course and speed indicators," said the Reever. "The drones will be coming up on the fleet's position quite soon. They seem to have left Fort Mountain and continued west, across the ocean. So we'll be coming up on the pirates from behind."

"Shall we stay on the deck," asked Tarja. "Or grab some altitude?"

"Stay low," Thornby replied, a beat ahead of the Reever and Hnarcor.

"We should stay beneath their detectors until the last possible moment," added Hnarcor.

"Work to the advantages of your own ships," advised the Reever. "Each of our respective fighters have differing strengths and weaknesses. The drones may be identical, but our reactions won't be. The drones will behave exactly like our ships would, because that's the way the AIs will read our playing these games. Just fly as if you were in your own ship— And *try* to ignore the fact that this VR gear must be reading our memories in order to give us the illusion of our own ships. I've never known Polios to make equipment that wasn't safe. Whatever it looks like, lives hang in the balance..."

"'And remember men,'" Max said in a voice that *had* to mean he was quoting something. "'Stay in time with the music!'" Max, Thornby, and Kazsh-ak laughed themselves silly.

"Gentlemen," Tarja said soon after the laughter had died down. "I think we're nearly there. Tactics?"

"I suggest," said Czhark. "That Kazsh-ak, Hnarcor, and I stay low and harry them from three sides, one hundred and twenty degrees apart. The rest go high and hit them from above. Is there any dissent? Reever, do you have any instructions?"

The Reever's voice sounded cold as he replied. "That Terran carrier and the stolen Shebeja ship *have* to be knocked out. Totally. Any missile launches towards the fishing fleet have to be intercepted. We need to protect that fishing fleet as best we can, but we can't let that carrier or heliship get away. Max, get between the pirates and the fishing fleet... We can't let the battle be carried to *them*. Keep any of the pirates from getting closer to the fishermen. Be careful, people. The Black Snake and these pirates are already guilty of thousands of deaths in the past. Now she's plotting more mass murder. The pirates are just tools to her." He sighed. "I want that fleet stopped, but not exterminated. I want that carrier and heliship stopped—Cold. This should be a surgical strike, not a mass murder."

"Clear," said Thornby. "The Black Snake is the main threat behind all this. The pirates are just... another weapon in her arsenal. Let's go get her."

Czhark laughed, a sound that chilled my blood for a second. Until I remembered he was on *our* side. "Honor demands I seek out the stolen Heliship," he said. "But I shall not neglect the rest."

"Okay gang," I said. "Looks like we're coming up on the target. Let's make like a Hockey team and split."

In the background, the music in the game room got louder, the beat more insistent, more insidious. I knew it was classical music—Bach, McCartney, Strauss, Mercury... something. Maybe Brock or Calvert. I think the AIs decided we needed a soundtrack for the battle. A light blinked on the VR clone of *Della's* control panel in front of me. Way point reached, time to go to manual. I pulled the stick back hard and kicked in the boosters. At the top of the arc, I leveled out, then nosed down. To the sound of thundering bass and soaring theremin, *I came at the pirate menace from out of the sun!*

As I dived, I saw that the VR was painting in replicas of our individual fighters over the image of the drones we were using. Tarja flew a fighter/scout somewhat like my *Della Sue* blockade runner, but much newer. I glanced aside at the others at my altitude and spied Max's *Libby,* looking like a winged sword, close by and angling off to get between the two fleets. Further off, the Reever's *Spear of the Gods* also fell point downward. It looked for all the world like a round shield transfixed by a javelin. Thornby's *Blackbird* looked like a flattened black ovoid with rudimentary fins. Definitely a stealth ship. Still falling, I got busy assigning targets. Briefly, I flipped up the VR visor and saw I was still using the trackball and buttons of the Omega Race game. I flipped the visor back down—and I had *Della's* whole cockpit in front of me. This is a *neat* game!

Getting back to the matter at hand, I saw I had gotten nearly into firing range and cut my speed back. I could see the smoke of explosions from the pirate ships as I dropped lower. Czhark, Hnarcor, and Kazsh-ak beginning their attack, no doubt. I hoped it diverted the pirates for a few seconds longer. We kept falling, but I reduced my speed a bit more to stay close to the others. I cycled the targeting screen through all the missile targets I'd assigned. All I had to do was punch her Auto-fire button and *Della* would launch at those targets. Or rather, the game would tell the drone to imitate *Della's* launching missiles at the targets. But I knew that the drone had to be using *other* weapons than my own ship's particle beamers and proton torpedoes. It was getting hard to remember this wasn't *really* combat. My nerves were all on combat alert and *nothing* my mind said to them was going to change it.

Anti-aircraft fire began blossoming below me but coming up *fast!* Just a few more seconds and I'd be in missile range. I had the nose pointed at the Terran carrier's deck and squeezed off a few rounds from the particle beam guns. Just to get in a few licks before the missiles could launch. The beamers wouldn't have much punch at this range, but they might add to the pirates' confusion. Last Waypoint coming up... *Now!* I hit the auto-fire and start choosing new targets as the launches free up the computer. I squeezed off several hundred rounds from the beamers, too. Auto-fire again, then I had to pull up or hit the sea!

Whipping the VR version of my *Della Sue* into a flat arc and rotating upright, I zoom in my visual onto the carrier's deck. *Magnify, magnify...* it's burning in several places, but most of its guns are still firing at us.

Then my heart stops.

The stolen Shebeja Heliship has *cleared* the carrier's deck. *It's in the air and returning fire!* I quickly reset the targeting screen and auto-fire again. The carrier takes most of the hits... I can see the stolen Heliship evading most of our fire. Whoever's flying that thing is *too* damn good. Then my IFF beeps at me. It's the "friend or foe" alarm—to tell me that one of my fellow vigilantes is within my targeting range. I quickly click on the zoom to see that Ambassador Czhark is making his move on the stolen Shebeja heliship.

"Jon," I hear the Reever's voice in my ear. "Stay low and fill in the gap that Czhark left. Pour on the firepower. Remember, you're using more than one drone at a time. Soak those other pirate ships with fire and keep hitting the carrier below Czhark's altitude."

"Roger that," I said. "I'll stay flat on the deck, but I'm going in closer. I'm not used to working this far out. Work to our strengths, you said. *Della Sue's* strength is her reaction time, she can dodge most anything. Once I'm in I'll hammer them, but I'll need a wing-man."

"Watch your own tail, Delivery Boy," Tarja's voice cooed through my headset. "I'll be above and behind you to help cover it, but I can't look everywhere at once. You're a bit too cute to lose. *Wait a minute,* we're not really *here*... Well, be careful *anyway*, Spyguy."

"Yes, Mother," I joked under my breath. "I'll be sure to eat my galoshes twice a week and wear my spinach whenever it rains..." I had gotten a bit busy picking new targets and slowing to a near-hover as I hit the auto-fire again. *100 kph and slowing, shields down to 86%, beamers at 37% and recharging, missiles fired and reloading of all launchers is in progress...* I didn't have time to devote much brainpower to badinage. Or to ponder why Tarja knew so much about little old *me*.

"Cute," she replied while I sat fumbling at my control panel. "This game-thing is *too* real. I keep believing I'm flying *Peppermint Patty* in a real battle."

"Roger *that!*" Thornby added. "Though this VR *Blackbird* has better sensors than mine." He laughed. "I'll have to hack myself an upgrade, later."

"Yeah, later," I said as I strafed the smaller pirate ships between myself and the carrier with my freshly-recharged beamers, then hit auto-fire for another missile salvo as soon as I had enough targets picked. I was close in now and slowed to a hover. I weaved back and forth a bit to confuse targeting sensors, but I kept firing too. I zoomed in on Czhark again. His VR ship looked much sleeker and more advanced than the bigger, slower stolen Heliship. I could tell that the two came from the same basic design, but Czhark clearly had the more advanced version. I clicked on his image in the targeting screen to confirm Czhark as a "friend", so my remaining missiles would avoid Czhark's IFF signal. The automatics would have done it anyway, but I didn't want any mistakes. Then I sweated as my beamers recharged yet again. On my screen, Czhark lit into the stolen Shebeja ship like an avenging angel. Guns and missiles blazing, dodging and weaving like a dervish, Czhark kept hammering on the stolen heliship—while still directing some of his shots at the carrier and other pirate ships.

"Look at him go!" Thornby gasped. "Keep the Ambassador covered. Don't let any of the pirates draw a bead on him."

"Blood feud," said the Reever with a trace of irony in his voice. "She wanted him dead—Well, he *doesn't* like the idea any too well. I damn well hope that *she's* the one flying that stolen Shebeja ship. Czhark might save me the trouble of finally killing the Black Snake... Somehow, I doubt we'll get her, though. She's *old!* And she can take care of herself damned well..."

"How old?" I asked in between shots, remembering the Reever's age.

"Old enough to be *my* great, great, great grandmother. Thank the Gods she's not, but she's that ancient. I'm a *fifth* generation Immortal... thirteen and a half million years old. She's a *second*-generation Immortal—and she's lived for the last three quarters of a *billion* years. She's been trying to kill me all my life, you know."

"Yeah," I said. "I gathered that. I'm running out of pirate ships, targeting the carrier again."

"*Roger, we copy. Back-up in flight...*" came a faint voice through my headset.

"Who was that?" I asked.

"Tom?" Thornby asked, relief in his voice. "Tom Darby?"

"*Yes, Guiles,*" came the faint voice again. "*I've got a scout wing that Miss Sarah sent to blockade the shoreline. Twelve of us. She said to hang back here and hold the line, but if you need us, we can be at the battle in seven minutes. Otherwise, we're supposed to stay as invisible as possible. We're not really part of this continuity and we don't want to screw it up.*"

"I understand," Thornby replied. "Glad you're there. Keep anything from getting through to City of Lights. We'll hold out here somehow. But if we go down, *you have to stop this fleet.*"

"*Understood, Widow Maker, and the rest of us, are ready for anything that comes our way. Your job is to take out that fleet. If you need us, we're here between the fleet and the city. Godspeed.*" The voice faded out, but still, it felt good to know we had *some* kind of back-up. *Wait a minute!* We aren't really there... We're *here*... This VR is strange stuff. I knew I had been sitting in a room playing a video game, but I could look out the windscreen to my left and see Max's ship, and Tarja's off in the distance. The VR seemed to be giving us images of our own ships instead of pictures of whatever the drones look like. I kept getting lost in this game—VR—whatever. Once more I strafed the deck of the carrier and the nearest ten pirate ships with missiles and blaster fire. Again, I swooped up to dive and fire once more. Dive down nearly to the wave tops, then pivot and flash inward—firing all the while. Then I moved off once more to fill in the gap left by Czhark and his vendetta.

Speaking of which, it had started looking more like a boxing match than a dogfight between those two Shebeja ships. They were just spiraling around, hammering away at each other. I noticed some of the tracer fire from the stolen ship passing through the image of Czhark's fighter. *The drones must be projecting holograms for the pirates to aim at!* I raked the wave tops, auto-firing missiles at the carrier again. Its shields already had gaping holes where generators had been blown away. I could see Hnarcor's yellow, manta ray-shaped fighter off in the distance to my right. He kept diving into the sea and then firing as he came back out of the water in unexpected places. I should have thought of that kind of tactic from an amphibian. I looked back at the carrier, and I had *incoming!* Some kind of cruise missile, fired from the carrier. *Exit, stage right...* I thought, as I dodged to the left while launching a slew of counter missiles. *Need to nail that launcher. Got to get in closer and do some damage.* In the background, the music got faster, the beat more insistent. I dropped a couple of bursts of chaff, popped a flare, then hooked right and kicked the boosters for a heartbeat. That left a radar and infrared target where I *had* been, and the burst of speed should have made me vanish from their screens for a moment. I pointed *Della's* bow towards the biggest hole in the carrier's shields and kicked the boosters again. Retro to a stall, auto-fire into the carrier, empty my beamers again, then boost up into a loop and back to safer position. I noticed I was upside down about a meter over the wave tops and quickly rotated upright while my weapons recharged. I dumped the charge from my rear shields into my front ones, then redirected the rear shield chargers to add to the weapon system's chargers. That'd give me a faster recycle time on my guns and double my front shields. That's good, unless someone gets behind you. *Then* I took time to see if I had done any damage.

I had. There was a huge hole in the carrier. Fire blazing from the waterline all the way up to the deck. I saw the Reever swoop down and add to the damage, then dodge away. Tarja kept laying down some intense fire on the newer pirate ships while dancing around the carrier and pummeling it too. I saw some big underwater explosions toward the carrier's stern. Hnarcor must have shot it up from beneath. Over half the pirate ships looked to be burning. A lot were breaking away and running south. I'd lost sight of Thornby and Kazsh-ak, but I could see explosions on the far side of the fleet that had to be their doing. Most of the carrier's shield generators had been popped. I could only see three or four dimly flickering areas protecting the carrier's Bridge and stern. The whole flight deck was on fire. *And the bitch was still shooting back!* I magnified my targeting screen and started assigning those gun emplacements as missile targets. I saw a pair of quick flares of light from its starboard side, away from me. Maybe a couple of missile launches towards the fishermen or City of Lights. As soon as I got a full charge on the weapons I hit the auto-fire again and held the trigger down on the beamers until they were exhausted yet again.

"I've got incoming," I heard Max say. "Sensors 'r' saying two MIRVed cruise missiles, on the deck and flat out for the city. Forty-two kilotons each, boosting at MACH 2.35 and increasing. Deploying countermeasures...." He sounded so calm; *those things are atom bombs!* I started praying as I auto-fired again. "Got one," Max added. "Going to have some trouble with the other..."

NO! Please, God, let him get it! I remember praying—then I got pissed off.

Ever been there? So totally angry you lose it? Somewhere between Berserker and omnipotent fury. You read things about "seeing red", but it's a white-hot, towering rage that you really feel. I was *there,* right then. Millions of people were going to die, and I was nowhere near a position to stop it. Absolutely helpless. *That* turned into the moment that I understood the term "righteous anger" for the first time. I felt like a holy flame. Like I said, I lost it.

"You want to play it soft," I muttered under my breath, punching buttons on my panel savagely. "I can play it soft. You want to play it hard; *I* can play it hard." I fed all the shield energy to the beamers, redirected all the chargers for everything into the particle beam guns. I even dumped the partial charge for the proton missiles into the beamers. Stripped of shields, bereft of missiles, I kicked the boosters, then the retros, and halted, floating just off the carrier's bow. I started transferring engine power to the beamers as I held the trigger down from point blank range, hovering not a hundred meters from the burning flight deck. They were *not* going to get another missile away unless I *died*. Which, I suppose, just goes to show you how good the VR really is. I'd forgotten I sat in a video game in a bar half a world away from the battle. All I saw was the target. All I felt was fury. I hosed the ship until the chargers howled in protest. Then I heard Max whoop with joy.

"Got the other one, finally. No collateral damage to the fishermen." He yelled like Tarzan for a few seconds, then got serious again. "I think this battle's over."

I came back to reality like getting hit in the face with a brick and looked at what I'd done. The carrier wasn't shooting at anything anymore, and never would again. It was too busy sinking. *I'd damn near cut the thing in half.* With that crystal clarity that only comes from a near-fatal jolt of adrenaline, I saw the crew fighting to board the ship's lifeboats. Most of the other pirate ships looked to be burning. Everything looked like it was moving in slow motion. A thousand pirate sailors scuffled to escape the blazing wreck while I hovered, watching... numb.

"Where's Ambassador Czhark?" I heard Kazsh-ak say. I blinked, probably for the first time in hours. At least it felt that way from how my eyes were burning.

"Spyguy," said Tarja seriously. "Remind me not to get on your bad side."

"Everyone, stand down and start looking for that stolen Heliship," said the Reever. "That's the only threat we've got left. Czhark may need some help. My officers are sending a force to take the survivors into custody. I can see that the courts are going to be busy for the next year."

Czhark didn't need our help, as it turned out. A quick sensor sweep located the two heliships, still hammering away at each other, a little east of what we'd left of the fleet. As if our scans had been a signal, the stolen heliship tilted over and fell, burning, into the sea. I heard Czhark yowling some kind of war cry, or victory cry.

"He got her!" shouted Thornby. "I got close enough on one pass to see the Black Snake was the one piloting the stolen Shebeja ship. Czhark got her!"

"No," the Reever replied. "She teleported away at the last minute. My scanners recorded it. But she's hurt, and *badly*. According to this, she's lost an arm *and* a leg. It'll take her several months to regrow them—if she doesn't bleed to death before she can reach an autodoc. And these pirates are going to be rounded up and processed through the courts long before then. We've stopped her for now. We've stopped her *plans* for now. What's more, she'll be a lot weaker when she *does* come back."

And with those words echoing in my brain, I found myself snapped back into the reality of the Game Room as the VR ended. The game was over, the plastic strip in front of my eyes became just a clear plastic strip again. I touched it with my finger, and it snapped back away from my face. I took off the headset and hung it back on its clip. I heard soft, soothing music from the hidden speakers of the Game Room as I staggered out of the Omega Race game booth. "That," I heard myself say. "Was truly tubular..." As if on cue, the Game room's sound system started playing Mike Oldfield. I was well and truly weirded out.

Quietly, we gathered a little apart from the game machines, as if we were suddenly a little afraid of them. My heart felt like it would never stop pounding. It felt like a shock... I had been in two places at once for an intense period, and now I was only at one of them again. Safe and sound. I could feel my brain trying to cope with the memories. It kept telling me that I needed a good stiff drink, not to put too fine a point on it. And we still had to check in with the Reever's detectives to find out if there had been any more bombing attempts. Once back in the real world, we'd still have a lot to do. I could see the Reever speaking quietly to his staff, as well as punching buttons on its surface. Most of the buttons looked like inset jewels, though. Funny how you notice little things when you're in shock. He stood a little apart from the rest of us. The door to the room had yet to open. The music in the background fell to a soothing murmur.

"The fishermen are safe," said the Reever as his staff vanished and he joined the rest of us huddling near the closed door of the Game room "I have a fleet of hovercraft out rescuing the remnants of the pirates. My officers report that they've stopped three more attempted bombings here in the city and managed to capture the bomber alive each time. I doubt we'll get much out of them. They seem to be mercenaries, just hirelings. The Navy reports that they met up with the tugs, but the pilots had fled—leaving burned-out computer systems in the tugs when they left. Some very strange electronic gear. They've impounded it as evidence and will tow the tugs back to Xerxes to a security hold. The Navy has also filed a request that the Shebeja send a force to join the COPs and the Navy on Xerxes. They want help and think the Shebeja would be a fine addition. Ambassador Czhark, I am moved to add my own voice to this. Your people should re-open your old base on Xerxes. it's time to reach for the stars again."

"I think my people would be happy to comply," said Czhark. "The long sleep is finally over. There has come the dawning of a new day, and *this* day proves promising for many hunts to come. The Black Snake will return. We should prepare while we can."

The door opened and we moved outside, back into the main bar. I turned in the doorway, to take a last look at that beautiful Omega Race game, then sighed.

"Too bad," sighed Kazsh-ak through his translator, almost at the same time. "That the Game Room has to be temporary. That felt vastly enjoyable. I'm almost sorry that it had to end."

"No," said Max. "That was just *too* much fun. I'm going to ask the boss if we can manage to keep the Games. Of course, we'll never be allowed to hook up with those drones again, but the antiques plus the VR gear would be a great draw. I'm sure I can talk him into it... Somehow. I'll work overtime if I have to."

And after a while Max *did* manage to get Polios to agree. And that's the story of how the Mare Inebrium's Game Room came to be. Of course, that was a long time ago. Come on, there's a pool table opening up. Let's go play. Loser buys the next round.

And twenty credits? Okay, if you insist. You're on, Bub.

* **My apologies to Charles Fort and his estate for modifying his words from "Lo!" to better fit my story. For editorial reasons, I presumed to put words into the Great Man's mouth. I can only pray** that his immortal soul can forgive my embellishments to his text. No disrespect was meant. —*Dan*

Necessary Evil

Kazsh-ak solves a murder mystery aboard a swanky passenger liner en route to the Insca resort hotel on the planet Kalenque.

"Once one has eliminated the impossible, whatever remains is, quite often, just as deadly..." - **Howard Phillips Lovecraft, 1930**

"I quite despise vacations," said Kazsh-ak Teir to his fellow patrons at the Mare Inebrium. "They always seem more work than play."

The old D'rrish was in rare form tonight. He'd already told half a dozen equally improbable stories since darkness began to line the streets outside the Mare Inebrium. He stood in his usual spot, beside the bar, in a wide-open area that always seemed to have been set aside, just for him and his listeners. I'd been eavesdropping on his storytelling quite shamelessly since I'd entered the bar, some hours earlier. Of all forms of entertainment, I found the "Tall Tale" to be my favorite. Kazsh-ak was, and is, a past master of the format. He has never failed to hold the interest of his audience. His mechanical translator provided not only his spoken words, but sound effects and subtle background music—when he so desired, of course. I had never been able to tell when the old boy was reciting actual history, or simply spinning yarns made up out of whole cloth, so to speak. But tonight? Tonight seemed to be an occasion for him to engage in autobiographical exposition. If even a fraction of his stories were to be believed, the giant scorpion had lived through more adventures than any being half his recorded age should have been able to boast. I always found him to be the utmost of charming gentlemen. Despite our differing species and planets of origin, I've always found the old dear to be quite attractive. Not that anything other than a purely platonic romance is even remotely possible between a humanoid female and a multi-legged, exoskeleton-sheathed alien the size of a Clydesdale horse. But we can always dream, can't we?

Me? My name is Tarja. I'm a professional, um, problem solver, shall we say? If you have a "problem" and the necessary ready cash, I can be hired to make your "problem" go away, forever, without any inconvenient evidence that could lead to those typical, undesired court proceedings that any normal being finds so tedious and boring. Well, yes, the uncultured *might* call me a professional assassin, but only if they wanted to get on my bad side. Why, *thank* you. Yes, you may buy me another drink. The bartender here knows my favorites. Oh! You're a *naughty* boy. I like that. But please be advised that despite my mode of attire, this skimpy satin dress that you so admire, it does conceal more weapons of mass destruction than it conceals my mammalian heritage. No, I'm an assassin, not a prostitute. Please do not pursue that line of inquiry *any* further, unless you would enjoy the local prostitute's union filing complaints against you. I can assure you that the Reever takes such matters very seriously. Oh? You've heard of him? Charming fellow. Quite attractive, for all that he works the opposing side of the fence, shall we say. Why, yes, as a freelancer, I do have an unlimited permit to ply my trade here on Bethdish. I've paid all the necessary fees. I follow all the rules of engagement that the Reever has been most kind to enumerate to me. Such a dear man. One day, I'd like to do something special for him, just to show him how much he is appreciated. Handsome? Of course, he is. Those chiseled features, that perfect physique, that voice! Such strength! He could make any woman's heart melt, that lovely bastard. But he's so dedicated to his work that he never indulges in mere distractions. Besides, as I understand it, he hasn't yet begun to look around for any female companionship to fill the void left by the death of his wife and two of his children so many ages ago. I'm sure that he'll meet a suitable Immortal woman one day. Someone his own species, so to speak. A woman can dream though, can't she? Excuse my blushes. I find myself feeling just a touch warmish at the mere thought... And might I say, you're quite the handsome specimen yourself? I love the way your scales change color with the light. You're really a work of art, all in and of yourself. You're a Halazed, aren't you? My, my, and such a fine, strapping young fellow. I'm sure you drive all the Halazed lizard-girls wild with that noble brow, those broad shoulders... Oh, you're too kind, Noble Sir. But listen, Kazsh-ak is beginning another story! I don't want to miss the tiniest detail. After all, if this is the story I think it is, then I was there. I wonder how close to the truth the old dear will stick?

"I'm reminded of a time," Kazsh-ak Teir said. "One particular time, when I tried to take a vacation. I was off-world, on a Deep-Space passenger liner. The Empress of Ketzall, it was called. I was on my way to the Insca resort hotel on the planet Kalenque. We were three weeks out from Bethdish, with another three and a half weeks of flight time yet to go, when the ship's Captain came to me with a request I could not ignore. It seems that one of my fellow passengers had met with what rumor aboard the ship described as an unfortunate accident. The Captain asked me to look into the matter, because of my rank and position, I suppose. Unfortunately for the Captain, I discerned from his statements that the shipboard rumor was indeed a false one. The Captain took me into his confidence and revealed that foul play had been involved. The accidental death had been no mere accident, but murder. Murder most foul. The victim, one Viscount Norjazshik Creeslockline of the planet Marteedunslick, had been murdered by a person or persons unknown. The killer, or killers, were undoubtedly still aboard the space liner. No port of call had been made since the death of the Viscount, and no shuttle craft had left the ship. One or more of my fellow passengers was a murderer. It had fallen to me to find them out and turn them over to the Captain for summary justice. Out the airlock without a spacesuit, that was the usual punishment for such a sort of thing, as I recall. Death by decompression was no prettier than what had been done to the Viscount. The ship's Doctor and I had examined the corpse..."

"A simple case," said the ship's Doctor. He was a Pakendewloor native, resembling a four-legged starfish with one eye-stalk per leg above, and a single beak-like mouth below, the center of his body. "Multiple stab wounds to his primary thorax, with differing wound depths and widths. Undoubtedly made by a knife-like weapon some three hand-widths long and less than a hand-width broad at the grip. I count ten wounds, in all. Any one of which would have been fatal. Death was not instantaneous, but still rather quick. If the poor bugger was still alive by the fourth wound, I am sure he was deceased by the time the sixth was administered. Someone wanted to make sure the poor soul was well and truly dead. There is some minor bruising to the extremities, but those could have very well happened during the creature's thrashing around after the assault. Might have been because of a struggle before the wounds occurred, but given the strength of the species, any assailant would have been carrying much more serious wounds away with them. I conclude therefore that the Viscount was either asleep or in a drug-induced coma before his attack took place. However, I can detect no residue of drugs within his body. Asleep, and mortally wounded by the first blow, those are my findings on the matter."

"No defensive wounds," I said. "All the stab wounds took place in one closely-defined area of the victim's body. Have you scanned for DNA traces of his attacker?"

"I have," said Doctor Mismismanatd. "Nothing conclusive. There are traces of ten dozen different types of DNA upon his skin. At least one of each for every species of passenger aboard. This is not unusual. He could have picked all of that up just by walking through the ship and touching anything another passenger had touched."

"I understand that he was the only member of his species aboard?" I asked the Doctor.

"Exactly so," replied the Doctor. "His killer could not have been a member of the same species. Not unless we have a stowaway aboard. And the Captain has already scanned the entire ship to rule out just such a possibility."

"How depressing," I said. "I take it that you have ruled out any cooking implement that is normally carried aboard the ship?"

"Exactly so," the Doctor again replied. "The depth and width of the wounds match no known item in the ship's stores. The killer must have therefore brought it with them. There is one puzzling aspect of the wounds, however."

"Please elucidate," I said.

"You are a soldier?" asked the ship's Doctor. At my affirmation, he continued. "As you may know, any injury by a metallic weapon leaves minute traces of the metal inside of the wound. Microscopic bits of the knife's sharpened edges break off inside a victim's body. When such fragments are found, it is simplicity itself to match them with a selection of possible weapons by virtue of the unique metallurgy involved with the manufacture of any putative weapon. The Viscount's wounds reveal no such metallic traces. None at all. Whatever he was killed with, it was not a metal blade."

"Nor was it some form of energy weapon," I said. "There is no trace of burning of the flesh that such things inevitably leave behind."

"You are astute," replied the Doctor. "And correct. My instruments can detect no traces of an energy weapon, not even on the sub-microscopic level available to their most detailed scans."

"Doctor, you've ruled out nearly every form of weapon known to sapient life. Yet, I deduce that you do have a theory."

"Ceramics," replied the Doctor. "No trace of DNA within the wounds themselves rules out a species which has natural weapons like long claws. No trace of metallic debris rules out metallic blades of any sort. No trace of burned flesh rules out any sort of energy weapon. But a ceramic knife would be unlikely to leave any trace, however microscopic, within the wounds. Ceramics are not as delicate as metals. They are far less likely to leave fragments behind. Since there are no fragments that I can detect, I conclude that the killer used a ceramic knife."

"Are there no other possibilities?" I asked.

"None," the Doctor replied. "Unless your suspect has the ability to extrude ultra-clean, super-strong, unbreakable adamantine claws from their manipulatory appendages. And that, dear Sir, is the purview of entertainment fictions. No such real entity exists."

"Indeed," I replied.

Afterward, I interviewed the ship's servant class. Between the Captain's assessment of each being, and my own interviews, I found the ship's crew to be above reproach. That left only the passengers. Some 600-odd beings of various species. During the remaining time of the voyage, I interviewed each and every one of them. Most could be dismissed at a glance. They possessed neither the physical strength to inflict the victim's wounds, nor any possible previous connection to the victim. However, in a private file in my personal computer, I kept references to any passenger of whom I could possibly ascribe either the wildest of motives, or the strangest of methods. Nearly all the passengers could be eliminated as suspects on the grounds of opportunity. Nearly every one of them could produce a plausible alibi for the time of the murder.

Nearly all, I said. Not everyone could prove their whereabouts at the time of the murder to my satisfaction. I was left with roughly two dozen putative suspects. Some of these could be eliminated on the grounds that they had no access to any weapon which could have caused the victim's wounds. I spent days on the ship's hyperwave radio, sending queries to various planetary governments on the subject of the victim, my remaining few suspects, and any possible technology that would be undetectable to the instruments possessed by the ship's Doctor. My findings were hardly enough upon which to draw firm conclusions. An acquaintance of mine is often quoted as having stated that "once you have eliminated the impossible, whatever remains, however improbable, is most likely the truth." I wished my friend Thornby were there to advise me, many times I wished that simple dream to become real. Alas, it was just a wish. I was left on my own to form my conclusions.

Finally, I was forced to draw upon the advice of a different detective, one quite fictional. With the voyage drawing to a close, and the likelihood of the killer being allowed to escape through lack of evidence by our journey's end, I decided upon one last, desperate gamble. Taking the Captain into my confidence and explaining my reasoning to him, between us we formulated what I devoutly prayed to be—a cunning plan...

Looking about the small ballroom that the Captain had assigned for my use on this last day of our voyage before planet-fall, I nodded imperceptibly to myself as I listed the various precautions and safeguards that had been implemented. My nine guests, each of which had proved impossible to dismiss as suspects, sat at carefully picked positions around a single large table. The table itself was set as if for a formal dinner. No food more complicated than appetizers had yet been served, nor was it likely to be, except upon my express commands, agreed upon by the Captain. The most highly combat-trained of the ship's security forces had been dressed as wait-staff, who took up strategic positions around the walls of the room. I carried no weapons beyond those with which nature had gifted me. I wore my very best formal-dress sash, with my military medals and awards of honor polished to a blinding gleam. I had opted for no other ornamentation, deeming that if I were thrust into sudden combat, my claw-hands and stinger would be more than up to the task. The astute among my listeners will have already recognized the last-ditch ploy utilized by only the most desperate of fictional detectives; bring the suspects together in one confined space, disclose one's conclusions and speculations in the most dramatic of fashions, and rattle their cages until the guilty party snapped and tossed forth an unimpeachable confession. Once I judged the paranoia of my suspects had been built to a fever-pitch, I began my opening remarks.

"You are all probably wondering why you have been brought here tonight," I began. "That is simple enough. As you are no doubt aware, unless you have the mentality of a decorative house plant, the Viscount Norjazshik Creeslockline was murdered early on during this voyage. Since no one was allowed to leave the ship since that time, the murderer is, without a doubt, still among us here tonight. You few, are the only beings aboard the ship that could have possibly committed the crime. Through my investigations, I have discovered the identity of the murderer, so I caused you each to be summoned to this dinner to hear my conclusions, as well as to see the offending beings taken into custody. Those of you who are guiltless, will no doubt have a wonderful story to tell when we reach planet-fall. In the meantime, be advised that the person sitting next to you may just well be a murderer."

The cage-rattling had begun. My suspects exhibited some few traces of visible distress. Nothing conclusive, but enough to inform me that my little list was composed of beings with guilty secrets. Some of those secrets I had been able to discover through my message traffic. About other secrets, I could make educated guesses.

Pausing only to cast mildly accusing glances about the room, I let my compound eyes linger upon a particularly lovely example of force-field sculpture. The delicate and fragile electrostatic fields were shaped into a flower-like form. A minute amount of water vapor, acted upon by a series of colored lights, gave the sculpture an organic look. The subtle movements of the force fields imparted a very life-like movement. As if it were a real plant, trembling in a gentle breeze. I found the simple beauty of the piece to be quite refreshing. But now, to work...

"Each of you have some connection to either the person or business of the late Viscount. From all accounts, he could never have been considered an honest or a trustworthy being. Quite a ruthless businessman, in fact. His title was purchased, at no little expense, and he engaged in several unsavory means of amassing his wealth. Indeed, I have discovered that his presence on this voyage was, to all intents and purposes, a flight to avoid possible prosecution. Charges were being drawn up against the Viscount. Several agencies were collating evidence of his criminal past. Smuggling, tax evasion, possibly even trafficking in slaves. Evidence of his being implicated in the untimely deaths of several of his rivals were also beginning to come to light. His house of secrets had begun to show signs of public revelation. In short, the Viscount seems to have been attempting to flee for some safe haven. No doubt a new identity and a few sessions of reconstructive surgeries would have followed his escape. Is something wrong with your appetizer tray, Venerable Bibendosloss? You have barely sampled your food."

"Merely finding myself entranced by your recital," Bibendosloss replied. The multiple tentacles branching from the alien's upper thorax evidenced considerable nervous motion. In short, the alien was fidgeting. I can't say that I cared for the tone of his translator device's voice, either. Oily, like the stereotype of an underhanded salesman.

"Oh?" I said. "Thank you. I was hoping that you would find it interesting. Something else I found interesting was your long-standing business relationship with the Viscount."

"I have no idea as to what you are referring," said the tentacled Priest, Bibendosloss. "I know of the Viscount only distantly."

"How odd," I replied. "Considering that your Church of the Ascended Martyr has been almost totally funded by one of the Viscount's holding companies. And given both the records of mysterious disappearances of children from several of your church's orphanages, coupled with the Viscount's connections to trafficking in young slaves of various species for several off-world markets. Additionally, my investigation uncovered several recordings of meetings that the Viscount as well as yourself attended. One doesn't have to be a mathematician to see that something just doesn't add up in that equation. *Or,* might just add up *entirely* too well."

"A vile and baseless accusation," said Bibendosloss. "My lawyers will find that a most savory bone to chew upon."

"Sounds to me like whoever murdered the Viscount has performed a service to the public," said another of my suspects. My investigations revealed that this vaguely-humanoid Uindanian native, Anjok Toiner by name, could be indirectly connected to the criminal underworld on

Bethdish. Nothing that could stand as evidence in a court of law, but highly suggestive, nonetheless.

"Murder is still murder," I replied. "By the way Anjok, would you mind holding your cutlery in a different manner? I believe that you are making young Timmengon more than a little nervous with that dagger grip on your salad fork. By the way, just what is your connection to Mister Grym? His criminal underground on Bethdish is already quite notorious."

Timmengon was leaning away from his dinner companion Anjok, as if frightened. A native of Alcor 4, Timmengon was still a youth, barely reaching his species age of adulthood. He was also humanoid, more-so than Anjok actually, and about to enter college after he returned home from this voyage. As I understood matters, his major subject was to be Abnormal Psychology.

"Not at all," said Timmengon unconvincingly. A nervous flutter was evident in his post-adolescent voice. "I was merely attempting to give a fellow sentient a respectful amount of personal space."

"Quite," I replied in a droll tone of voice. I'd paid extra for *that* upgrade to my translator. Well worth the extra expense, in my opinion. "Well, Anjok? We're all a-flutter with anticipation of your revelations. You have been linked several times to more than one of Grym's underlings. The Reever has quite a large file on you. Nothing further to say?"

"I will have to consult my own lawyers," said Anjok. "Before I can make any statements at this time."

"Perhaps your lawyers and the Venerable's legal team might like to look into the matter together?" I asked. "I'm sure that the degree of overlap in both groups would become—enlightening, to say the least."

"Will you quit prattling on," said another of my suspects. "Let the Ambassador continue with his—dissertation?" The female in question was from a human colony on a world circling a star called Qualar, quite close to Bethdish.

"Ah, the artist responsible for these delightful force-field sculptures scattered about the ship. Melessandre Upton, are you not?" I asked. "Beautiful work. I'm particularly fond of the cunning use of color and movement you have achieved with them. The interplay of the fields must be quite difficult to control."

"The major difficulty," Melessandre replied with an audible sniff of contempt, "was to render the fields pliable to the touch. Naturally, control of the field's power is essential if one is not to inadvertently injure a viewer. One tiny mistake, and a work that appears to be soft and inviting, on a closer examination, could lead to burns and lacerations. I would be legally liable for any injury suffered by a patron of the arts, or the casual gallery attendee. Naturally, the power units in the base of each of my sculptures require the strictest of limitations."

"I see," I said. "I surmise that the vapors contained in the fields would also need a formidable temperature regulation circuit, as well. Was the Viscount one of your Patrons? Or merely a particular fan of your work? I recall seeing one of your sculptures in his personal stateroom."

"I'm sure I haven't the faintest notion," Melessandre replied, waving one hand dismissively. "I was not consulted as to the placement of my artwork aboard the ship. That is a matter for the owners of this vessel to decide for themselves. I was merely paid to produce the works in sufficient numbers for them to be made use of by the firm."

"Yet each is delightfully different, one from another," I said. "However do you find the inspiration for such variety?"

"I find that the flora and fauna of many worlds to be a rewarding study," Melessandre replied. "Naturally, reproducing a specific plant or animal in lifelike detail is possible, but I prefer creating an abstract idealization of such things to be more pleasurable to me as an artist."

"Now see here," said Loucobe Candrakar, another of the passengers whom I had linked to the Viscount. As a shipping magnate himself, I'd found traces of clues implicating the Galnizork native to the Viscount's network of smugglers. His normally puce skin was slowly turning a more violet shade, indicating more than a little anger and indignation. "We are merely hours away from planet-fall. If you know the identity of the culprit, kindly divulge it and put paid to them. Furthermore, is it not time for the next course of our meal? The ship's cook makes a tolerable Discundrad Soup, or so I'm given to believe. A very difficult fish to prepare. Unless its poison sacks have been carefully removed, the dish has been known to be lethal to several dozen different life forms."

"I think I shall skip the soup," said Timmengon quietly. "Are there breadsticks? I'm quite fond of the ones with those little sesame-things toasted on the surface. Are those seeds? Or are they some form of insect?"

"Only Terrans know for certain," I replied. "But to the best of my knowledge, they are a type of seed. One would hope my Terran friends have not been secretly serving me what may well be a genetic cousin." I laughed aloud, with the intent of disarming any suspicions of just how close I had gotten to solving the crime in the past hour.

"The soup is ready," announced one of the wait staff. For a security guard, he was playing his part well. "Along with the requested breadsticks, and a selection of raw vegetables and dips."

"Very well," I said. "You may serve the dips." I coughed through my translator. "I mean, you may serve our *guests* the dips..."

"Very good, Sir," said our waiter. "And for those who harbor undue worry about the soup, might I announce that the ship's Doctor has taken the liberty of preparing suitable antidote doses for each of your species."

"Thank you," I said. "That is reassuring. I believe that I shall attempt the soup, myself. I'm told that it is an experience not to be missed."

I did enjoy the soup. It was quite tangy, with just a hint of pleasurably tingly toxins to tantalize the palate. As we ate, I continued to observe my guest suspects. Their behavior was interesting, to say the least. As the wait staff removed the soup plates and began to serve the next course, I noticed a few actions that were a bit out of place. Still, for a hastily gathered collection of miscreants and misfits, their manners were well-practiced. The next course was a selection of bite-sized grilled meats in a sweet sauce, thin-sliced steamed vegetables, and a small salad on the side. A lovely wine complimented the dishes, but all too soon I was ready to bring the conversation back to the matter at hand.

"Madam Tarja?" I asked another of my guest suspects. The human female was well-known to me from Bethdish. "Do you have anything to contribute to the conversation? As a professional, I would be grateful for any insights you might have to offer."

"Professional?" Timmengon asked. "You are a professional detective?"

"Assassin, actually," Tarja replied. She smiled, then continued. "One of the very best, in fact. The Ambassador asked me to join the party for purely professional reasons. In case I might notice any small detail his investigations he might have missed. He is well aware that I am not the killer. If the Viscount had been one of my contracts, our D'rrish host would have found no evidence to point in my direction. In fact, I wouldn't even be here on the ship, at this point, if I were the guilty party. The fact that am still here indicates that I have pressing business elsewhere. This voyage is merely transportation. I must say that the guilty party is the rankest of amateurs. They've left clues everywhere along their path. Something I would never do."

"This is outrageous!" Candrawisk shouted. "I demand that this woman be taken into custody. She has practically confessed to the crime!" The mock-outrage exhibited by this Duulean female was a delightful performance. So over-played as to be laughable. I knew her to be a small-time jewel thief, between convictions, as well as someone that the Reever of Bethdish had generously given the suggestion that she relocate somewhere far from my adopted home planet. She was blissfully unaware that a sub-microscopic observation device had been reporting her every move to the Reever since their last interview. In my communications with him, he informed me of the machine, roughly the size of a dust mote, which reported back to him through a nigh-undetectable form of hyperwave signal. I knew this suspect was innocent of the Viscount's murder, but there was the small matter of the undiscovered theft of some small personal items of jewelry from a few of my fellow passengers. Undiscovered by anyone but myself, that is. Something that I had not yet had a chance to inform the Captain about. Unfortunately for the thief, she seemed destined to spend quite some time in a cell after the ship made landfall.

"Madam Tarja is correct," I replied. "Her skills are such that if she actually had been the murderer in question, she would, as they say, leave no clues to connect her with the crime. Nor would she have needed to have boarded the ship in the first place. No, she is not the killer. But I know who the killer is. We shall cover that small matter in due time. Shall we call for another round of this excellent wine? I'm told that humanoid species find it to be a delightful beverage. My own species, I'm afraid, would find that its lack of radioactive trace elements renders it a bit flat, to our palate. Or shall we move directly along to the dessert?"

"I do believe that just a touch more of the wine would be in order," said another of my suspects. Marse Oberon by name, a native of one of the farther worlds I knew of. Jaklessdom was the name of his planet. The species was almost perfectly Terran-Standard humanoid. His smooth and polite mannerisms bespoke of a high degree of culture. His position in his world's aristocracy was somewhat suspect, or so my investigations had revealed. Some irregular dealings with the late Viscount's more palatable businesses had allowed Marse to exercise a touch of social climbing. I could not tie him to any overt criminal actions, but there seemed to be a distinct indication of Master Oberon marrying above his station in several instances. Followed at discrete intervals by his series of wives passing away unexpectedly. And at suspiciously convenient intervals for the upward mobility of his fortunes.

"Excellent suggestion," I replied. "I'm sure that your latest late wife would have agreed, Master Oberon. She certainly had a nose for a fine vintage, did she not?"

The rising of an eyebrow was Oberon's only reaction to my conversational gambit. Quite a cultured scoundrel indeed. *This gigolo will bear watching, in the future,* I thought.

"And that is your reaction to these accusations of murder?" Sannisip asked. "That murder is as *nothing* to an Aristocrat of your caliber?" Sannisip was a native of Cathaltrey, a Terran colony located merely twenty light years from Bethdish. He was the manager of a sizable shipping firm on his home-world. And one whose connection to the Viscount's smuggling operations was indicated, but not proven, by my investigations.

"Among *cultured* Aristos, why not? Just another game to be played. If one takes proper precautions, one needn't worry about such a custom." Oberon replied, raising his wineglass in a mock toast towards Sannisip. Sannisip merely scowled in reply.

"But in the grand scheme of things," I said. "Even the life of an uncultured thug such as the Viscount has some intrinsic value. Despite his obvious guilt, surely he deserved a fair trial and the chance at justice prevailing?"

"What is justice?" Melessandre asked. "In *this* context? Given all that we now know about the Viscount, it would appear that he has earned his just due. A vile man, whom you, yourself have connected to more crimes than I care to think about. I cannot say that I feel particularly well disposed towards someone who kidnapped children from orphanages, to sell into slavery. Who knows what crimes he committed that you have yet to uncover?"

"And on that note, I do believe that it is time for our own just desserts. A selection of coffees and Aldebaran liquors will be available with the sweets trolley," I said. The murderer had played right into my hands, as I had hoped. I knew why they had killed the Viscount, how they had managed to hide the murder weapon, and what they had hoped to gain from the murder. I signaled my crew of security officers to bring in my last distraction, as I began to compose my final remarks. All would hinge upon the reactions of my suspects to my remaining revelations. Even those not implicated in the murder would wind up, if not in custody, then at least under investigation by the proper authorities. Planet-fall would occur in less than twelve hours. I hoped that the Captain would have enough security officers in his employ to deal with the miscreants.

After allowing my suspects, and my eventual prisoner, to enjoy what might well be the final course of their last meal as free beings. I felt it incumbent upon myself to explain my reasoning, as well as my conclusions. Rest assured; I took no pleasure in the responsibility of highlighting the moral failings of so many of my fellow beings. But I had a duty to perform. My honor and my duty required me to dig through the obscuring sands to reach the truth. Several truths, in fact. None of them pretty.

"Sannisip," I began. "You will be relieved to know that despite whatever else you have done, you are not the murderer I was tasked with uncovering."

"I should say not!" Sannisip answered. "I have done nothing wrong. And I thank you for realizing that fact!"

"Nothing beyond a little smuggling of stolen goods," I said. "Rest assured; you shall not be accused of anything that you haven't *actually* done. However, I believe the Reever would like a word or three with you about the matter of the Fanshaw Art Gallery's missing paintings. You may well be able to prove that one of your underlings is the real culprit, though I highly doubt that, myself. No, you are not the murderer of the Viscount."

"That is slander," replied Sannisip.

"No, that is a matter of public record," I replied. "And I assure you that the Reever will dismiss all charges against you if you are indeed proven innocent. In the meantime, please do not offer any resistance to the ship's Security Officers. That goes equally for the rest of you, my dear guests. If there is any one of you that fails to wind up facing charges, I shall be greatly surprised. Please keep your seats. We do not want any unpleasant reactions to spoil your chances at a fair trial, later."

"I am willing to give you more rope with which to hang yourself," Oberon said as he raised his coffee mug to me. "I do believe, dear

Ambassador, that you are leaving yourself open to multiple charges that would take a cadre of lawyers years to unravel."

I nodded my head in acknowledgment to Marse Oberon. "Your own perfidies were brought to light today," I replied. "The authorities of your home-world have been informed of the details uncovered by my investigation. You may not have murdered the Viscount, but you may yet find that the specifics of your marital history have begun to come under closer scrutiny. I do hope you are indeed innocent of any wrong-doing."

"Most kind of you," Oberon replied, sarcasm dripping from his voice. "Any chance of another round of these excellent drinks?"

"Certainly," I said. "The Steward will be only too glad to provide. Madam Candrawisk, you might also be desiring of a refill. Or three."

"What?" Candrawisk gasped. "I am no killer!"

"No, but I regret to inform you that you have been under constant observation since long before the ship departed Bethdish. Therefore, if you would like to return the jewelry that you have stolen since boarding the ship, I'm sure that the Reever will take that into consideration when drawing up the charges against you."

"I never," Candrawisk gasped.

"Unfortunately, you did, indeed. Your cabin is being searched," I said. "Even as we speak. It shan't take long, since the recordings reveal exactly where you have hidden your pilfered prizes."

"You filthy little beggar!" Candrawisk exclaimed.

"I'll have you know that I bathed before dinner, and the only thing I have ever begged for was a chance to serve my Royal Family with honor."

"I cannot wait for my turn, dear Ambassador," said Candrakar. "Whatever inventive theories shall you espouse next?"

"That you are yet another smuggler," I said. "Albeit only of stolen goods, and not of slaves. If that salves your pride, then so be it."

"A smuggler is only a merchant who has been forced to use questionable methods of shipping their goods," said Candrakar. "I am certain that my reputation can withstand a few official questions. I have harmed no one, ever. I know this to be true."

"Questionable methods, or questionable cargoes?" I asked.

"There is a difference?" Candrakar asked. "If so, this is a distinction of which I was previously unaware. For my species, smuggling is simply a game of skill which we play against our authorities. A way to avoid excessive taxes on our cargoes. For us, it is not a crime. Our laws express this quite clearly."

"The laws of your species," I said. "They are not universally recognized. Your own courts may only punish you with a fine for being caught. But the laws of other species may yet prevail."

"I await such charges," said Candrakar calmly. "With the utmost of boredom. But please do continue, Ambassador. I'm quite astir with the desire to know who our murderer actually is."

"Madame Tarja?" I asked. "Have I overlooked anything of consequence?"

"Aside from leaving a murder weapon in plain sight, within reach of the murderer, I can think of nothing." Tarja replied, then she sipped her coffee. "Was that on purpose? I would have to assume so, but I hate making assumptions without clear motives being presented. You've managed to uncover every secret these pitiful beings hold dear, yet you play with them. Quite without mercy, may I add. You've known all along who the murder is, yet you sit there urbanely sipping wine as if condemning them to the Captain's ruthless capitol judgment was a mere inconvenience. You are far more cruel than I, Sir. But as a torturer, you are among the very finest. Your trickery is admirable, in a boring police-force sort of way. Please do announce the killer's name soon. I do have appointments to keep..."

"You bastard!" Melessandre shouted as she knocked over her chair and lunged towards her sculpture against the wall behind her. Quickly manipulating its hidden controls, she changed the display to one of force-field rigidity and leaped towards me. "That monster sold my sister into slavery," she gasped. "I was justified in killing him! Justice is mine! You shall not thwart me!" Melessandre kicked and bludgeoned her way through the ship's guards, across the floor between us, then with an inarticulate scream, she drove the energy weapon towards my cranium. As if in slow motion, my military training prompted me to reach out with my left claw-hand and snip her own right hand off at the wrist. The weaponized sculpture fell to the floor still grasped in her now missing hand. Blood spurted from her wrist. I had mere seconds to act before blood loss brought an end to her life. I clutched her in my four medial foot-hands and shouted for aid.

"Medic!" I cried. I clamped down hard on her severed wrist, cutting off the spurting flow of blood.

"I am here!" Doctor Mismismanatd shouted. "Release her! I have a binding cloth ready!"

"Thank all the Gods," I declared. "You must save her life."

"So that you can take her back to be executed?" Doctor Mismismanatd asked. "Is this your justice?"

"No, so that she can be treated for the post-traumatic stress disorder she has been suffering from—ver since her sibling was kidnapped and sold into slavery," I replied. "With any luck, we might also be able to locate and save her sister. The Reever promised me that all his resources would be turned to the recovery and salvation of the enslaved children. You must save her life! I owe her a debt."

"I'll do my utmost," Doctor Mismismanatd replied. "Now let go her wrist and let me do my job."

"Are we done now?" Tarja asked. "I have barely enough time to change clothes before we land."

"You found our killer," said the Captain. "I am in your debt."

"Yes," I replied. "Melessandre was the murderer. But she was driven to it when her sister vanished. I shall have to report everything to the Reever so that we can begin to trace the eventual fate of the Viscount's slaves. He has jurisdiction, since they were kidnapped on Bethdish."

"But the weapon?" asked the Captain. "How did she turn a sculpture into something that could escape all our scans?"

"The force field sculptures were finely tuned to prevent any cuts or burns an audience might suffer from contact with them. No burns that could be detected by medical scans within the wounds. No evidence at all. I surmised that she dialed down the temperature of the water vapor inside the sculpture in the Viscount's room to well below the freezing point, then stabbed the Viscount while he slept. His injuries were consistent with thrashing around in his cabin during his death throes. What could be more undetectable than a knife made of ice? No flakes of the blade's material would be detectable, the force fields only reinforced the material of the ice itself. A perfect, undetectable assassination weapon. I would have never thought of it myself without all the research into the motives of our many suspects. Once I found that Melessandre had a sister among the missing children from Bibendosloss' adoption centers, I knew I was getting close.

But finding a way to prove her crime was almost impossible. Without her confession, I wouldn't have been able to bring any charges against her at all."

"But what shall we do with the rest of these criminals?" the Captain asked.

"Hold them for the Reever's agents. They will do the rest. Our watch is secure, Captain. No one can blame you for actions you could neither prevent nor control."

"I am in your debt, Ambassador," said the Captain.

"Not at all," I replied. "But I would like to continue the rest of my vacation in blessed obscurity. I am a simple D'rrish, used to only those accolades presented by my distant cousin, the Empress. I want only to be left alone to rest, and perhaps some chance to enjoy myself at the resort. A few drinks at the bar, a little dancing in the sands... I'm a simple fellow. Easily pleased, so long as no one is shooting at me."

The Captain laughed. "So be it," he said.

"Well," said Tarja to her Halazed companion of the evening. "He did change a few details. But this version is more exciting. What? Oh, the whole episode went on for far longer than the Ambassador implies. He is quite long-winded when he gets going. It was quite spellbinding to witness the final moments of his investigation, but also somewhat boring to experience the entire dinner and play at the time. Since he had confided in me and asked for my assistance, I was well aware of the identity of the murderer during the meal. Another drink? No, thank you. I need to call a transport out to the port. I have a flight out to catch soon. Business, I'm afraid. Perhaps I shall see you the next time I'm on Bethdish. For purely social reasons, of course. You're too kind. Thank you for a lovely evening..." Tarja arose from her seat and walked to the door. The Halazed watched her exit appreciatively, feeling only the vague wish that, sometimes, he was a mammal. *One can but dream,* he thought. *Those hips! To die for!*

Mare Inebrium

A Filksong based upon "Lola" by The Kinks

I took a late flight out to old Bethdish
'Cause I'd made a big sale and I got really rich.
Man, I was loaded, L-O-A-D—Loaded.
I caught a hover-cab in City of Lights,
then it leapt in the air and to-wards downtown
it gently floated,
F-L-Oa-T—Floated, F-L-Oa-T—Floated— Floated.
I asked the cabbie, Bert, for the name of a bar
where I could have a few drinks an' party real hard,
'cause I was lonely, L-O-N-E—Lonely.
He said "I know just the place that you need to go,
Its a multi-species bar for those in the know,
The Mare Inebrium, Ma-Ma-Mare Inebrium— Inebrium!
We drank and sang and danced all night,
Under the fusion candlelight.
With Max mixing drinks—he put 'em in my hand—
He said "here Sir, this'll make you feel grand!"
Well, I'm not the world's most intelligent guy,
so when I took a big gulp it nearly straightened my spine,
K-R-U-P—Krupnik, K-R-U-P—Krupnik,
Krupnik - K-R-U-P—Krupnik, K-R-U-P—Krupnik!
I sat my glass on the bar,
I got up from my chair,
I felt my back hit the floor,
I climbed back up onto my knees,
then I looked at m'drink— It looked at me...
And that's just the way I wanted to stay
And I knew right then that I'd be back someday,
To Mare Inebrium,
Ma-Ma-Mare Inebrium.
Space will be time and time will be space,
it's a mixed up muddled up shook up place,

out there on Bethdish,
Ba-Ba-Ba-Bethdish!
Hey, I'd left my office just a week before,
and I'd never ever had that liquor before.
Well, Blanche took my hand and helped me to my feet,
She said, "pretty boy, let me show you a seat."
Now, I'm not the world's most intelligent man
but I know I'll be back just as soon as I can
to Mare Inebrium,
Inebrium— Ma-Ma-Mare Inebrium, Ma-Ma-Mare Inebrium,
Inebrium— Ma-Ma-Mare Inebrium, Ma-Ma-Mare Inebrium!

Filk Lyrics Copyright 1999 by Dan L. Hollifield

No Room For Error

"Beginnings are such fragile times..." **Mary Shelly, 1814**

In the spaceport bar known as the Mare Inebrium, on a planet sixty-five light years from Earth, hundreds of species mingle and meet on any given day. The bar is famous throughout a thousand nearby inhabited worlds. The planet is located in a fortuitous sector of space for navigation between other star systems. The drinks are excellent, the company acceptable, and the planet's largest spaceport is easily reached by a bewildering array of public and private transport. I enjoy going to the Mare Inebrium whenever I get the chance. It's a great way to pass the time between flights. Everyone seems to have a story to tell. My name is Andrew Huntington-Smythe. I was born on Antares Four, a human colony world established a few hundred years before I was born. I'm a traveling salesman by trade. I deal in farm equipment, seeds, and fertilizers.

"There is always a thin line between success and abject disaster. I have frequently faced times when I despaired of living up to the expectations of my Empress," said the giant scorpion. "My family is part of a minor branch of the D'rrish Royal House. We serve our time as soldiers, then we gradually drift into other professions that best make use of our individual talents. I, myself, was appointed to the Diplomatic Corps by virtue of a series of happy accidents. Luckily, I seem to have a talent for talking to different peoples, different species. For instance, I totally failed to start a war once. Many years ago, it was. I was in my scout ship, on my way—somewhere. I can't recall the exact circumstances, as I never completed that particular mission. Deep space, many light years towards the Galactic Center from here, that I do recall."

The voice coming out of Kazsh-ak Teir's electronic translator used a British accent when he was talking with English-speaking visitors. The accent was educated, but not posh, precise, measured, and easily understood by everyone within auditory range. He had retired from his people's military services as a decorated officer. A Brigadier General, no less, he was currently an ambassador in their diplomatic service. I could only assume that the accents the device produced when Kazsh-ak spoke in alien languages must be as precise and easily understood. I'm no expert on aliens, or their languages. I'm just a salesman. My own translator is an inexpensive thing. The company I work for provided it when I was first hired. I've upgraded it as often as I could afford, but it would never be in the same league as the Fender Wordsmith that Kazsh-ak owned.

It was an average early evening in City of Lights. Situated on the Northeastern coast of the single landmass on the planet Bethdish, this is the largest city on the planet. City of Lights can boast of a comfortable climate even in this Summer season. The planet has little in the way of an axial tilt, so there isn't a lot of difference between the seasons. Due to its orbit, summer in the Northern hemisphere coincided with the planet's perihelion. That's when it is closest to the system's sun, Antuth. Bethdish has warm winters in the South as well as cool summers in the North. About the worst thing the summer weather has to offer here is short, sudden rainstorms. I'm told that out on the great ocean, the storms can become much worse. But here in City of Lights, protected from the coastline by a series of mountain ranges as well as the narrow mouth of the bay the city was built beside, those hurricanes rarely put in much of an appearance.

"You failed to start a war?" I asked. "Were you *supposed* to start one?" I found myself sniffing again, as my sinuses adjusted to the lemon-vanilla scent of the room. I've never decided if it was the air conditioning or the mixture of body odors of a hundred aliens and whatever they were drinking.

"Indeed not," Kazsh-ak said. He tip-toed back and forth lightly on his feet for someone roughly the size of a plow-horse. "Friend Andrew, that would have been an even larger failure on my part." He laughed, or at least a laugh came out of his translator. "My people are rather isolationist in their politics. We will defend ourselves if attacked, but seldom do we seek conflict. Ours is an empire in name only. We prefer to buy land for our colonies, instead of taking it by force. In fact, that reminds me what my original mission was. I was supposed to go to a newly discovered planet and negotiate the purchase of land for a proposed colony. But that task eventually fell to another. I found myself distracted by other matters."

"That sounds suitably mysterious," said Max. He's the bar's manager and head bartender for the largest of the many bars in the building. He looks human, but he was born here on Bethdish. "What happened? Oh, do you need a refill?" Max asked as he brushed his short, dark brown hair back from his forehead.

"That would be welcome, Max. Thank you. As for what happened, I intercepted a distress call from another ship," said Kazsh-ak. "A new species, in fact. My ship's translator took some time to interpret the language, but at last it managed to allow me to reply. The alien ship was just at the edge of my communicator range. Once I understood that they were lost, and suffering from some sort of mechanical breakdown, I sent a message home explaining the situation. I knew that it would take weeks for my signal to reach Bethdish, so in effect, I was on my own. No one could advise me as to what I should do. If I made a mistake, any mistake—however small, my tail would be roasted over a slow fire, but only once I returned to Bethdish. I brought my ship to a full stop and considered my options very carefully. Then I changed course to intersect their flight path. Even at my ship's maximum speed, it would take me quite a while to reach a position where our two ships could meet."

"Space is vast," said an Alcorin native who was sitting at a table near where Kazsh-ak stood at the bar. He motioned with a near-empty tankard for a refill of whatever served his species as a cocktail. I saw that he kept two hands drunkenly gripped to the edge of the table where he sat, while holding his tankard with a third. He also had three legs, three eyes on short stalks, and as he drained the dregs of his drink with one mouth, I saw he had two more to carry on a conversation with. *Trilateral symmetry,* I thought. *That's rare.* His skin was a pale yellow, pebbled with tiny bumps and low ridges. The chair at his table had evidently decided that he needed a backless stool to sit upon. In the Mare Inebrium, a lot of the furniture consisted of smart-molecules that could alter their shape at need. "You were lucky to have been close enough to receive their message at all," the Alcorin added.

"Indeed," said Kazsh-ak. He paused to take another sip from a complicated valve at the tip of the metallic straw connected to the armored container that held his own cocktail. As I understood it, D'rrish originally evolved in a mildly radioactive environment, and as a consequence their food and drink were somewhat hazardous to other lifeforms. "I was in the right place at the right time to catch their distress call. The next closest ship turned out to be months away, even at high speed. If I had not been on the course that I was, likely these people would have died before their signal crossed the path of another ship. So, I turned to meet them, and pushed my little ship to its limits."

"Commendable of you," said Hnarcor Finivalda, the Halazed Ambassador. The little lizard-man was one of Kazsh-ak's fellow diplomats. His species has a colony under the planet's biggest freshwater lake. It's located in the Northwest territory of the continent. Not quite all the way to the D'rrish colony that was even further Northwest, but very close. The Halazed are amphibians, not reptiles, by the way. The gray scales on their skin look like the finest chain-mail ever forged. They tend to go for colorful body paint and dyes instead of a lot of clothes. Their idea of formal wear is something like a long vest with a lot of pockets, and a wide belt with several pouches. They do love bright colors and fantastic patterns on what few clothes they wear, as well as their scales. "But knowing your people as I do," Hnarcor said. "I suspect that any D'rrish in a similar situation would have done the same. *'Honor, Duty, Loyalty,'* is that not the wording on your Royal Family coat of arms?"

"You know us too well, Friend Hnarcor," said Kazsh-ak. Another laugh boomed out from his translator. "No wonder I can rarely get the better of you in trade negotiations!"

"You gain the upper hand, or claws in your case, quite often enough to suit me," said Hnarcor with a gentle laugh of his own. "My friends in the fishing industry are still smarting from the terms of the last food contract you and I negotiated. But I fear I am interrupting your tale."

"Ah," said Kazsh-ak. "The Sustainability Clause, no doubt. Still, that one paragraph boosted your people's aquaculture farming industry to record levels, did it not?"

"That is so," admitted Hnarcor. "A much-needed reform, in my opinion. Though the fishermen may gripe about the investments needed to comply, the lake will now never lack for fish or edible plants. That was a stroke of genius, Friend D'rrish. My government would have had difficulty passing that reform if your government had not made it a requirement in the treaty. But enough shop talk. We digress. You were about to rescue some species new to us, as I recall?"

"You are a harsh taskmaster, Friend Halazed," said Kazsh-ak. "Yes, to the rescue! I spent nearly three days in flight, straining the engines as much as I dared the whole time. Finally, my instruments detected the alien ship itself. There was a central pod that I later found out contained the engines, and four passenger pods that orbited the engines by way of strong connecting pylons. That way the passenger pods were supplied with a form of artificial gravity through centripetal force. The rate of spin was quite fierce. That alone made docking with any of the passenger pods impossible. Luckily, the engine pod was in zero-G, as it didn't spin. The engineering of the spin section with regard to the engine section was impressive, to say the least. Docking with the engine pod would be difficult enough, since the engines were venting drive plasma from their starboard side. The reaction from that was causing the entire ship to wobble and gyrate about its center axis. I was forced to adopt a spiral course to intercept their ship and its open docking bay in the front of the engine pod. My autopilot was having difficulty matching the motions of the distressed vessel. But finally, I was able to coax my little ship into a docking clamp. Obviously, something had struck their engine pod, rupturing a vital plasma conduit of their engines. Their signals indicated that the spin-locks between the passenger pods and the engine pod were non-functional, preventing them from entering the engine pod to effect repairs to the plasma conduit."

"Sounds tricky," said Max. "I would have needed a dedicated repair crew just to begin on something like that. Didn't they have a crew inside the engine pod itself?"

"I found nearly thirty of their corpses in the engine pod after I docked. So whatever caused the accident also killed half of their engineering crew members. I devoutly wished for just such a repair crew as you mention," said Kazsh-ak. "But alas, all I had was myself and my own poor skills. One single mistake on my part, and over five hundred sentient beings would die a horrible, slow death."

"What did you do?" I asked.

"Fortunately, the docking cradle my ship accessed was close enough to one of their spin-locks for me to attempt repairs. I had to use my vac-suit to exit my ship with all the tools I could carry. The docking bay doors were unable to close, and besides, I had no way to obtain an atmosphere sample to test to see if I could safely breathe their air. It took me longer to fix that spin-lock than it had for me to reach their ship. I spent the better part of four days testing circuits and patching relays. But fix it I did, after a fashion. At least, I managed to make it functional again. Once I accomplished that, their own surviving repair crews were able to regain access to the engine pod and begin repairs to the plasma conduit. Within another thirty hours, their engines had been repaired, and the entire crew was hard at work on whatever collateral damage the impact had caused. I helped as much as I could, but once I had freed their crew, the best I could manage was to pass them tools and hold structural bars in place while their technicians welded them back together. Whatever it was that they hit had caused hundreds of punctures to the engine pod. Sometimes snapping framing members in twain, sometimes only punching tidy little holes in bulkheads and internal mechanisms. Even the smallest hole I saw was large enough for me to reach through to my shoulder with a medial limb!" Kazsh-ak held up one of his fore-legs to illustrate. Several of us gaped in astonishment. The limb Kazsh-ak held up was a good six inches in diameter at its widest point.

"What could have done that?" Max asked.

"Their Captain *finally* decided that they had passed through a dense cloud of dust and rocks that their deflectors couldn't handle," said Kazsh-ak. "But both his and my first thoughts were weapons fire, or sub-atomic particles of antimatter. Frankly, I thought they'd been attacked by someone. They were of the same opinion, at first. They were all rather paranoid, before I managed to convince them that I was there solely to rescue them. Days later, they slowly began to change their opinions. I believe it was when they examined my ship that they began to see the light. These Sealakgosschew, as they called themselves, had no weapons on their ship that I could see. Nothing but their primitive electrostatic deflector shields and a few hundred woefully underpowered particle beam emitters. Those were tied into their deflector systems. They would have made terribly inefficient weapons in the case of an actual attack by a determined foe. Their hyper-drive could barely push them at a light year per day! Their cargo bays were full of the exact sort of equipment that I would expect to see on a colony ship sent out on a one-way trip. Five scout ships like mine could have destroyed them utterly in a battle lasting mere moments. My own ship, by itself, could have crippled them in less than an hour, were we to engage in a pitched battle. My shields would have shrugged off their particle beams like so many raindrops. In short, if this wasn't a colony ship, from a culture that was new to space exploration, then *I* was an Akhadiheim Pirate Queen, with a billion slaves tucked into a single pocket of my sash!" Kazsh-ak laughed. "I spent weeks with them, as they not only put their ship back in order but began to listen to my descriptions of the wider universe they had begun to explore. I finally convinced them that they had run afoul of one of the many natural hazards of open space."

"But the war?" I asked.

"The Sealakgosschew distress calls," said Kazsh-ak. "I have seldom heard a more pitiable collection of threats and challenges directed at a cupfull of space dust!" Kazsh-ak laughed again, and this time the whole room laughed with him. "They were so sure that someone had attacked them. They were promising total destruction of whomever approached to take advantage of their moment of weakness. I knew I could not leave them to their fate. But yet I could not afford to make any mistakes. I thought long and hard about how to convince them to accept me as a genuine rescue attempt. They were ready to die to protect their home world and their ship. They swore they'd fire on any ship that came within range. I racked my brains to come up with anything that would convince them to listen to my signals. Anything! I was about to give up hope. Then I remembered something that I had seen on the entertainment grid as a young child. I overloaded my engines to provide enough signal strength to my communicator to play the part I had chosen. I had to convince them that there were good, altruistic species out here in the universe. Someone who would risk their own lives to save theirs. Someone who asked for no reward other than the chance to help others. I knew what I had to do, and I did it. I have no shame, but I did have to play a minor prank on these Sealakgosschew in order to convince them to trust me."

"You didn't!" Max exclaimed, then laughed so hard I thought he was going to hurt himself. "I remember it now! The tabloid broadcasters had a field day with it when someone else intercepted your reply to those poor, silly, lost Sealakgosschew people. I never knew it was you, though. Ladies and gentlemen, the next round is on the house!"

"But what did you do?" I asked. "What was your reply to their threats of war and destruction?"

"I saved the recording," said Kazsh-ak. "I thought one day I might need proof. Originally, I thought it might be at my Court Marshal, but luckily, I avoided that by bringing all the Sealakgosschew here to Bethdish alive. Let me cue up the recording and I'll play it for you."

Max kept looking over across the bar at Kazsh-ak and breaking out into giggling fits. It took he and all the other bartenders on duty to keep up with the free drinks Max had announced. Finally, everyone had their round ready to make a toast in Kazsh-ak's honor. But I still wanted to know what was in that recording that had reduced Max to helpless giggles.

"To Ambassador Kazsh-ak Teir," announced Max when he could finally keep a straight face. "The finest actor in the known universe!"

As we all drank to the toast, Kazsh-ak prepared to play his recording. Once we were ready, he clicked a control and his voice boomed out loud enough to carry to every corner of the room. It was obviously translated for us instead of being in the Sealakgosschew language. Kazsh-ak's translator spouting its educated British tones was unmistakable.

"This is Captain Troy Handsome of Interstellar Rescue," the recording said. **"Please state the nature of your emergency. We have a ship standing by to respond. We will need to know your species, your breathing air composition, your present location as far as you can determine it, and any special equipment we might need to affect your rescue. Please remain alert for any possible threats near your position. When our representative reaches your position, they will identify themselves to your satisfaction before attempting any rescue operations. Our operative will proceed at once to your position and do everything in their power to help you. Message repeats: This is Captain Troy Handsome of Interstellar Rescue. Please state the nature of your emergency..."**

I can honestly say that I have never seen so many spit-takes in my life. We could have died laughing!

Appendix
A Short History of the Planet Bethdish
A Work In Progress
Updated 9-12-2021

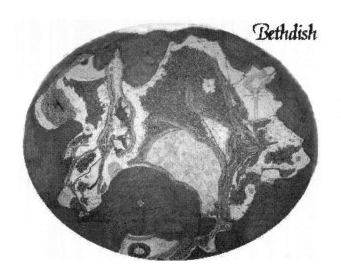

Pantheon of the Living Gods of Bethdish:

Deity	Astronomical Body	Deity's Title	Moons & Other Info
Antuth	The Sun	Father of the Gods	65 Light Years from Earth

Da-ast'nor	Innermost planet	God of the Forge & Blacksmiths	**Moon:** Chuscht'nor *The Spark of Creation*
M'resst'ash-fur	Second planet	Goddess of Weather	**2 Moons:** P'milla & D'ian Handmaidens of M'resst'ash-fur
D'aa'oert'oth	Third planet	God of the Hunt	**5 small moons, named for the Hunter's Dogs:** M'shegagn, T'nesshthee, K'ntuk, C'aorcha, and T'seckus
Bethdish	Fourth planet	Mother of the Gods	**Original Moon:** Morit'orn *Shieldmaiden of the Mother* – Was 2400 miles in diameter. Shattered by tidal stresses in prehistoric times. **Present Moons:** Darius – 600 miles in diameter, orbital commercial passenger & freight spaceport. Xerxes – 240 miles in diameter, Military Base. Both were moved into their present orbits around Bethdish from their original locations in the asteroid belt in historic times.

Deity	Astronomical Body	Deity's Title	Moons & Other Info
T'nishe-t'alla	Fifth planet	Judge of Princes & Battles, God of War	**2 Moons:** Inat'soun & Fer'vr'soun, *Swordbearer* & *Shieldbearer*
S'lar-ak'esh	Asteroid belt	Goddess of Luck	50,000 known asteroids. The largest is 2000+ miles in diameter.
R'ene-land'thur	Sixth planet	Goddess of the Seas	23 Moons:
M'aalin'ash-tuth	Seventh planet	Goddess of Fertility, Planting, and Harvests	17 Moons:
Kan'she'ellor't'shen	Eighth planet	Goddess of Mercy & Redeemer of Lost Souls	15 Moons:
S'nith'o'duu'arr	Ninth planet	God of Death & the Afterlife	11 Moons:
Valleor	Tenth planet	God of Evil, & Chaos	Thousands of temporary moonlets from the cometary halo.

Partial Timeline of Bethdish

Bold Italics represent a written story, *Italics* represent an outlined or planned unwritten story.

Fifteen billion years ago: Beginning of the current universe.

Three billion years ago, Maxwell's builders evolved.

Two billion years ago, Maxwell and his fellow slaves were created. After two million years of murder, these slaves revolted against their masters. Maxwell was damaged in the last battle for freedom and drifted in space, deactivated, until found and repaired by the Collector.

Bethdish Prehistory: One billion years ago...

Creation of the planet and the Immortals in the Andromeda Galaxy. First Golden Age. The first Reever of the Immortals is created. The Black Snake is an Immortal child at this time. The Immortal population averages 20 million souls. The Floating City is built as the first home of the Immortals and the Crystal Bridge is linked to Albion, the Home of the Gods.

The Immortals explore the local cluster of solar systems.

508 million years before the present time-- The 2nd Reever of the Immortals is born.

Evolution of other sentient natives. Empires rise and fall. The original moon of Bethdish **(Morit'orn -- Shieldmaiden of the Mother)** eventually shatters and forms a temporary ring system. The Gods shield the planet from the major debris. Some native civilizations collapse at this time. Others remain unaffected. All myths and legends are carried by oral tradition. After the re-invention of writing the natives collect these stories and preserve them. By the end of this era the rings have faded away.

65 million years before the present time— The 3rd Reever of the Immortals is born.

Gods and Immortals live among the native peoples. Second Golden Age. Immortals defend Bethdish against various alien invasions. Natives eventually begin to explore their solar system, and in time, various others nearby. The second Immortal city is built on the banks of the river Ariastor. The Immortals call it Summerhome, but the rest of the natives name the city some variant on "Crystal Mirror Towers."

38 million years before the present time— The 4th Reever of the Immortals is born.

13.5 million years before the present time— The present Reever of the Immortals is born. He is the 5th Immortal of his line to bear the title Reever.

2 million years before the present time— Max is genetically engineered to breed longevity into the non-immortal humanoid natives evolving on Bethdish.

50 thousand years before the present time— Valleor and His worshipers revolt against the other gods. In the long war that followed, both the cities of the Immortals and the home of the gods (Albion) are laid to waste. The Floating City and the Crystal Bridge to Albion are broken loose from both Summerhome and Albion by the gods-war. The Broken Bridge still retains a tenuous, ethereal connection to Albion from the Floating City. The Reever's wife and two sons are killed in the fighting by forces led by the Black Snake. Summerhome is almost totally destroyed and is quickly abandoned. Eventually the revolt is put down and Valleor is captured by the other gods. The gods condemn Valleor to a discorporate existence and banish him from Albion. The powers of the gods are greatly reduced by this action, so that as time passes, they take less and less part in the history of the planet.

Towards the end of this age, as a result of the gods-war, the axial tilt of Bethdish is almost negated. The shape of the landmasses are altered with corresponding loss of life. Only one landmass survives. The others sink beneath the ocean. The Immortals carve out a new city inside Fort Mountain. Their population is temporarily reduced to less than 12 million.

The Lost Years: Less than 1000 years between the polar shift and the arrival of the Andromeda alien Co-Op. The Reever is 13.5 million years old at this time. His father is still living at age 38 million, as is his grandfather at age 65 million. It is unknown if the earliest two Reevers are still extant. They may have been killed in the Revolt of Valleor, or even earlier in the prehistory of Bethdish.

Recorded History—New Calendar:

Year 1 [2986 BC] ....The coalition of alien races contact Bethdish. They negotiate with the Immortals and purchase a sizable tract (3.5 million square miles) of the worst devastated area of the landmass. Construction of the Altiplaino Spaceport begins. The Immortals assist the Co-Op in the construction. Humanitarian aid provided to the natives by the Co-Op. Medicines and treatments provided by the Co-Op rescue effort saved many lives that would have otherwise been lost. The Immortal's own aid services were overwhelmed until the Co-Op arrived. Thereafter, each Immortal worked with one or more Co-Op teams. The small moons **Darius** and **Xerxes** are moved into Bethdish orbit by the Co-Op and Immortals for use as a low-G shipping port and a military base, respectively.

120 [2867 BC] ....The Shebeja build Oktishnear and Nanor Fort City. Oktishnear is their main base and their vehicle launch facility. Nanor Fort City is their multi-species resort meant to promote peaceful coexistence between Bethdish natives, alien visitors, and themselves.

800 [2187 BC] ....Arrival of the Gray People, the Halazed. They purchase a large forest and lake as a colony site. The Halazed are a semi-aquatic species of intelligent reptiles. They build Lake City under the surface of the lake. They also replant the forest with trees from their home world.

920 [2067 BC] ....The D'rrish arrive and buy colony space. They build the Arcology

Er'da'gasg'dein and irradiate the general area to conform with their peculiar metabolism.

960 [2027 BC] ....The Deadly Desert forms near the D'rrish city as a result of the radiation.

970 [2017 BC] ....The aliens called the Priest-Kings arrive and buy colony space. They build the walled city of Urkiev. Thereafter they pursue an isolationist policy. They trade only through native ambassadors chosen from the villages and towns near Urkiev.

1200.   [1787 BC] ....War between the natives that grew to depend on the Altiplaino Spaceport. The 4 Kefa Empire cities nuked each other. The alien colonies and much of the rural native population are generally unharmed while the four industrial cities were bombed into slag. The Altiplaino Spaceport was slightly damaged in the bombing. The Immortals and the Port Authority assume joint control of the surviving Four Cities governments. Trade agreements were renegotiated to avoid the pitfalls of the previous era.

1200-1340 [1787-1647 BC] ....Period in which the Battle Suit was used as a weapon.

1340 [1647 BC] ....*The Siege of Elko Daf* ** Battle Suit used in final defense of Elko Daf then becomes a war memorial outside of the castle.

1520 [1467 BC] ....Beloq and Co. steal a copy of the Battle Suit for the Collector.

1840 [1147 BC] ....Interstellar war. Bethdish is found by a "Berserker" type automated weapon (the Scourge) and attacked by it. After a titanic battle, the Scourge is blown to pieces and left adrift in the outer cometary halo. Meteoric bombardment destroys over half of the Altiplaino Spaceport and drives most of the Builders to abandon the planet. Those aliens who could not escape made their way to Valley of the Three Peaks resort or Nanor because of their ability to support multi species populations. The War Machine Havoc is buried by the bombing. The volcano Tishranet was created by the impact of a damaged Planet Killer missile which failed to detonate. The gods intervened to eliminate the ejected material from the cratering so as to prevent an ice age from destroying their world. Some aliens still use the surviving section of the Altiplaino.

2640 [347 BC] ....Count Corrono the 1st leads an expedition into the hinterlands of the Duchy of Tamar to find a long-forgotten castle. Bandits were using the castle as an occasional hideout from which to terrorize the local farmers and villagers. The Count and his men took the castle by storm, executed the bandits, and claimed the castle for his own. Later he was to set up the longest lasting parliamentary government among the natives of Bethdish. His descendants eventually marry into most of the native royal families.

2670 [317 BC] ....*Nesastor-that-was* **The fall of Nesastor and the creation of the Great Blight. Eliasthor makes war on several neighboring nations. All goes well until he attacks Urkiev, the mysterious city of the Priest-Kings. They counter-attack and destroy the city of Nesastor. Everything within a 1-mile radius of the city center slowly crumbles to dust during the following year. The citizens of Nesastor flee. Only one tower of Eliasthor's palace resists the spell. The planet's natives begin to avoid the bottomless gray dust-bowl that they come to call the "Great Blight". There are rumors of monsters living underneath the dust, but these have never been documented.

2720 [267 BC] ....*Voices in the Night* ** Eliasthor lives on inside the White Tower in the center of the Great Blight as a prisoner of the Priest-Kings of Urkiev. He is contacted by the god Valleor and attempts to re-form the god's physical body and restore Valleor's full powers. Valleor regains some small amount of his power but not enough to construct a body from his atomized remains by willpower alone.

2740 [247 BC] ....The Collector is born. Where? Who knows...

2987 [1 AD] ....The Floating City, driven by the winds, finally comes to rest against the southwestern Morishtornell mountains near the southern edge of the surviving Altiplaino. This fragment of the first city of the Immortals was originally joined to the home of the Gods by the Crystal Bridge. The (now renamed) Broken Bridge still retains a tenuous contact with Albion, the City of the Gods.

4600 [1613 AD] ....Shy'are the Wizard appears as if from nowhere to build his tower by magical means. He then bands the surrounding kingdoms into a loose alliance to fight the pirate raiders along the eastern seacoast. Shy'are is actually a giant old Blue Dragon magically disguised as a humanoid wizard. He came to Bethdish to escape his old life and to take part in helping to build a better world where all can coexist. Shy'are is sometimes seen in the Mare Inebrium in the company of Lung Mei, a Librarian employed by the Collector in the Museum. Lung Mei is also a dragon in disguise. They both appear to be elderly oriental humans, usually sitting together smoking long-stemmed clay pipes and drinking Plum Brandy.

4800 [1813 AD] ....Alazar the Wizard leaves his father's kingdom of Tulag to build his tower, plant the Ring Forest, and tame the wiregrass plain on the here-to-fore desert plateau of Tissador. (pronounced Sidore) Alazar's tower is formed from a waterfall, the run-off of which waters the Ring Forest and the surrounding desert. The waterfall springs from mid-air.

4913 [1926 AD] ....**On Earth,** Guiles Thornby meets Sherlock Holmes and Dr. Watson.

4921. [1934 AD] ....***Stranded!*** ** Expedition from the Zelath Stellar League crash-lands on Bethdish and becomes involved with a minor invasion of the southern regions of the Kingdom of Intile. The Reever is sent to stop the invasion. Havoc regains consciousness, escapes from his ocean-floor tomb, and rushes to the aid of the Reever and the stranded League members.

4922. [1935 AD] ....*Off to Be a Wizard* **Havoc sends an ROV to Tulag in order to study magic under the tutelage of the wizards there.

4937 [1950 AD] ....**On Earth,** the Collector meets Dr. Clark Savage Jr.

4951 [1964 AD] ....A mysterious, and very nervous burglar steals a primitive time machine from the Collector's Museum. He departs for the future.

4963 [1976 AD] ....**On Earth,** Tom Darby has a fender-bender with a flying saucer one night on a lonely country road. The crew of the flying saucer take him forward in time to Bethdish of 6080. [3093

AD] The Collector later returns Tom Darby to Earth and the year 1976 AD, to a point two minutes behind himself riding his motorcycle into the side of the flying saucer.

5000 [2013 AD] ....Membeth Planetary Penitentiary founded as the single maximum-security prison.

The castle on the site had been used for centuries as the place of execution for the Kingdoms of Ellor, Kineth, Nesastor, Utrthay, and other, older realms. Traitors, pirates, mass-murderers, and sometimes the politically disenfranchised, were doomed to take the "Long Swim". They were walked to the end of the Black Wharf and forced off into carnivore infested waters. None ever reached the shore. Castle Debrethe is designated the medium-security prison for the planet. The Immortals assist the Southeastern Kingdoms Alliance and Shy'are the wizard to construct the "Walled Road", a thousand-mile-long sealed passageway elevated 500 feet above the ground to connect the two prisons.

5240 [2253 AD] ....Arrival of the Collector and introduction of Castle of the Winds (the gateway on Bethdish to the Collector's Museum in an alternate dimension), deep in the heart of the Caalar Jungle. The Collector is 2500 years old at this time. Castle of the Winds appears to be a small castle or fortress standing in the middle of an open field. Inside, there are many gateways into the Museum.

5340 [2353 AD] ....The Battle Suit is first discovered by the Collector. In Seven Isles in a memorial park—constructed around it—the original stands along with a strange duplicate Battle Suit. In 6740 the Collector sends Beloq, Selene, Resthal and Gryphon with the stolen robot PXR5 back in time to steal a copy of the Battle Suit at Elko Daf in the year 1520 (Bethdish Cal.). Their vehicle accidentally tries to materialize them in the same coordinates as the Battle Suit. This results in a mechanical failure in the time capsule which creates the duplicate Battle Suit. Beloq and his company barely escapes.

5600 [2613 AD] ....Castle Nilaren is overrun by a small fleet of pirate raiders. In the booty gathered by the pirates before their escape was the relic of antiquity that most of the older castles of Bethdish were built to house. In this case, the relic was a thermonuclear bomb, left over from the Four Cities War.

5640 [2653 AD] ....Castle Dombraim is built on the site of Nilaren on the north seacoast. (Dombraim translates roughly into Terran as a mixture of the concepts of *rebuilt / re-born / re-consecrated*.)

5740 [2753 AD] ....The Reever and the Collector first meet. The Reever walked through the Caalar Jungle to knock on the front door of Castle of the Winds. Guiles Thornby also meets the Reever at this time.

6055 [3068 AD] ...."*The Night the Stars Changed*" ** The Collector is attacked by Valleor's forces. Mistaking the attack for one by aliens, the Collector over-reacts and moves the entire solar system to preserve the natives from what he thought were his own enemies. Bethdish is now in a different galaxy from where it evolved. All alien colonies were cut off from their home worlds. Collector's presence detected by the wizards of Tulag.

6080 [3093 AD] ....*"Abducted!"*** The Collector's Museum is invaded by Mordred and Sara K is kidnapped.

6125.   [3138 AD] ....A mysterious, and very nervous time traveler accidentally materializes in the D'rrish Arcology. He quickly dies from exposure. The D'rrish build a shrine to him as an honored enemy. His mummy and his equipment are placed in the Shrine of the Traveler.

6126.   [3139 AD] ....The Terran Federation Starship *__Admiral Charles Herndon__* arrives in the Antuth solar system with a fleet of support starships and Terran Ambassador Leslie Everett to investigate the mysterious new solar system that had appeared in what had been empty space. The Antuth system is now 65 lightyears from Earth. Bethdish is the only inhabited planet in the system of 10 planets. Antuth is a star quite similar to Sol. Bethdish gravity is .985 of Earth Standard. The day is 25 ES hours, the orbit is almost exactly 1 ES year. Axial tilt is less than 2 degrees at this time. There is one major continent and a scattering of small islands across the opposite hemisphere. The climate is warm and mild.

6127.   [3140 AD] ....First Terran Federation contact with the natives of Bethdish. Immortals send delegates to Freeport Durkone to attend diplomatic functions.

6128.   [3141 AD] ....Treaty signed. The old merchant city, Freeport Durkone, is renamed "City of Lights". Federation and Immortals cooperate to build the city. Historic "Old City" is quickly surrounded by modern skyscrapers. Area directly south of City of Lights established for spaceport. The Old City area lies between the new spaceport and the modern city. Immortals assist the Federation in constructing the spaceport landing field and buildings. Altiplaino Spaceport is declared an historical site and only archaeologists are allowed limited access to the ruins of alien bases there. Strict penalties and fines are levied against illegal access to the Altiplaino.

6129. **[3142 AD]** ....City of Lights Spaceport opens.

6134 [3147 AD] ....Spaceport expanded.

6142 [3155 AD] ....City expanded.

6162 [3175 AD] ....The feud between the Barony of Albeth and the Barony of Duraz ends with the marriage of the heirs of the two realms. Thus, the kingdom of Arnak is formed.

6300 [3313 AD] ....The Tyranny of Valleor begins. The kingdom of Nertua is overthrown and it's people are made slaves. Valleor stays in the background working through the rogue Immortal, the Black Snake. She becomes the de facto ruler of Kingdom Valleor as well as High Priestess and lover of the evil god. Continuing minor warfare between Valleor's forces and Urth in the High Valley. Urth constructs various "Fort-Cities". Valleor's forces confined to the old Nertua region. All bordering native countries re-fortify against attack by Valleor's armies.

6574 [3587 AD] ....Kazsh-ak Teir born on Bethdish in the D'rrish Arcology.

6603 [3616 AD] ....Kazsh-ak Teir is attacked by Beloq and Selene in the Shrine of the Traveler in the D'rrish Arcology. He is 29 years old and is hospitalized for 3 days from his injuries. The Traveler's equipment is stolen by a time-traveling Beloq and Selene for return to the Collector.

6695 [3708 AD] ....Construction begins on the Mare Inebrium Tower. The Collector is a silent partner in the design and construction.

6698 [3711 AD] ....The Mare Inebrium opens for business.

6735 [3748 AD] ....Max begins working at the Mare Inebrium. He is slightly over 2 million years old at this time.

6740 [3753 AD] ....*"The Threat of Valleor"*** The Reever leads a small band of adventurers on a far journey to confront Valleor and rescue missing people from all over Bethdish. Valleor is temporarily trapped by a spell cast by Tinhill of Urth (the retired High Priest of Antuth) utilizing the combined powers of all the magic-users on Bethdish, augmented by a powerful relic in the Collector's Museum. Tinhil dies from the magical energy channeled through his body before completing the spell—confining Valleor for a while, but not for all time as intended. Kazsh-ak Teir, at age 148, meets Guiles Thornby during this adventure. Beloq, Selene, Resthal, and Gryphon are recruited by the Collector during this adventure.

6798. [3811 AD] ....After 58 years Valleor escapes from the prison spell that had held him captive. He resumes his quest for a body to inhabit while strengthening his control over the worshipers and slaves of Kingdom Valleor. He remains hidden in his Temple, reaching out to possess or influence various mortals—people and animals.

> **6799. [3812 AD]** ....Blanche born on the planet Hardcase, 1.438 ES Gravity.

> **6800. [3813 AD]** ....Valleor possesses the Governor of Western Urth, T'llea Neuma, and begins the oppression of the people of Western Urth. The territory is cut off from outside contact and cruelties such as those committed in Nertua are begun. Trixie is born on Earth at this time.

6820 [3833 AD] ....Battle of Urky Pass. Western Urth rises in revolt against what they thought was Urthean Oppression. Valleor's followers are exposed and driven into Kingdom Valleor. Western Urth becomes the Kingdom of Ninlen. T'llea Neuma disappears in the confusion of the revolt, only to be seen inside Valleor's temple later, still possessed by Valleor. Kazsh-ak Teir is noted for valor during the fighting.

6822 [3835 AD] .... Trixie is hired at the Mare Inebrium. Blanche is hired at the Mare Inebrium half a year later.

6822.   [3835 AD] .... *"The Mare Inebrium"* **
Spaceport Bar encounter wherein a D'rrish gives a history lesson and a nervous time-traveler flees.

The D'rrish telling stories:

> **A.**   Kazsh-ak takes a wife and then goes offworld to fight the K'tchomblies. **6650 [3663**
>
> **AD]**
>
> **B.** Kazsh-ak defeats the asteroid pirates. **6654 [3667 AD]**
>
> **B.** *Against All Odds* Kazsh-ak breaks the Seige of the offworld D'rrish colony of R'lynath in a single-D'rrish fightercraft, leading to the Rescue of R'lynath Colony. The alien Nyekoll-tuurn-aye invader's blockade fleet is repulsed after several fierce space battles. Their ground forces linger in hiding on the planet for many years before the last are captured and deported to their homeworld. **6660 [3673 AD]**
>
> **B.** Kazsh-ak saves his cousin, the D'rrish Princess J'harrana, from offworld kidnappers.
>
> **6665 [3678 AD]**
>
> **E.** *"Sic Semper Tyrannis!"* Kazsh-ak defeats the Overlord of Naatung in single combat, freeing the slaves of planet Naatung. **6674 [3687 AD]**
>
> **E.** Kazsh-ak defends the T'chmarron River Bridge and the small town of Neulat, alone against the nomadic Valwoulf

Raiders of the Plain of Intile. **6760 [3773 AD]**

E. **"Fast Friends"** Kazsh-ak meets the Reever & Guiles Thornby. **6740 [3753 AD]**

E. **"Myths And Legends"** Kazsh-ak fights the Ohmany Horse riders when they attempt to invade the Kingdom of Eana and learns that Eana has a far more potent guardian than he. **6753 [3766 AD]**

E. Kazsh-ak fights at the Battle of Urky Pass. **6820 [3833 AD]**

E. **"Necessary Evil"** Kazsh-ak solves a murder mystery aboard a swanky passenger liner en route to the Insca resort hotel on the planet Kalenque.

E. **"No Room For Error"** Kazsh-ak makes First Contact with a ship of Sealakgosschew.　(Name rendered phonetically.)

6823.　[3836 AD]] ....**"The Absent-minded Shall Inherit..."** ** The Mare Inebrium receives a mysterious addition to their "Lost & Found" when an absent-minded inventor forgets one of his devices as he leaves.

6824.　[3837 AD] ....**"Sins of the Fathers"** ** Max is revealed as an undercover agent—very undercover! {also contains the first foreshadowing of the events of *Immortality Factor*} Andrew is 70 years old at this time but appears to be 40. He lives another 150 years. Max is Andrew's great grandfather, but neither of them know this.

6825.　[3838 AD] ....*The Lucky Leonard* ** A space shuttle on final landing approach is attacked by a large pterosaur that has been possessed by Valleor. Valleor is acting against the Collector, who is a passenger on the shuttle. The Collector saves the shuttle, crew, and passengers. Larrye (age 23?) is hired at the Mare Inebrium.

6825 [3838 AD] .... *Sidestep* ** John Stewart Sebastian initiates the rescue of the *Linda Rae* and later helps the lost shuttle crew escape back through the wormhole into their own time.

6825. [3838 AD] ...."*Brother, Can You Spare A Crime?*" ** Later that same year, the Reever is called in to solve the crime when a body just keeps turning up at the Mare.

6826. [3839 AD] ...."*A Study in Alizarin Crimson*" ** Sherlock Holmes and Doctor Watson assist the Collector in stopping an alien criminal from plundering London's museums of their own era, 1926 AD. They are almost 2000 years into their future, but Guiles Thornby tells them that they are only 420 years ahead of their time. It is unknown why he does this. Perhaps he is simply confused, or perhaps he is conforming to some unknown orders from the Collector. Holmes & Watson are later returned to their correct time.

6827. [3840 AD] .... Trixie takes four months maternity leave. She gives birth to a boy, whom she names Siger Vernet.

6827. [3840 AD] ...."*Came the Dawn*" ** The Shebeja awake from Sleepfreeze. The Black Snake attacks them using terrorists, pirates, and stolen tugs from the system's asteroid belt. {Max says that the date is "about a month and a half from being 6828"}

6828. [3841 AD] ...."*Redshift Sue Sings the Blues*" ** Time seems to stand still while Redshift Sue sings her long-lost husband's song.

6830 [3843 AD] ....*Immortality Factor* ** A rich old man has several Immortals kidnapped and dissected to try and find out how to live forever. The old man is confined to a wheelchair-like life support system. He has the required great wealth, political connections, and ruthless mercenaries to possibly get away with it. However, when the Reever becomes one of the missing, the Collector gets involved and starts a search for him.

6974 [3987 AD] .... Andrew Huntington-Smith dies, leaving behind 22 children and 85 grandchildren.

7924 [4937 AD]

8082 [5095 AD]

9157 [6170 AD]

10063 [7076 AD] ....*From Out of the Past* ** Reappearance of the Berserker in the outer fringes of the system. The Collector warns the Spaceport, Tulag, and all of the techno-oriented nations. All co-operate to repulse the Berserker. Valleor mistakenly believed to be destroyed.

11868 [8881 AD] ....Valleor begins to construct technological weapons to aid in conquest of Bethdish.

11880 [8893 AD] ....*The War of Valleor* ** Valleor's armies attack Urth, Ninlen, Intile, Fort Mtn., Yalled, and Seven Isles.

11882 [8895 AD] ....Valleor recruits the pirates of the Ohmany Peoples as a navy to attack Nalth, Seven Isles, Ellor, Arnak, Utrthay, and others.

11890 [8903 AD] ....The Wizards band the nations together to fight Valleor. The Kingdoms Alliance.

11895 [8908 AD] ....Valleor's forces are defeated. Borders of kingdom Valleor are sealed.

11915 [8928 AD] ....*Into the Depths* ** Valleor and the Collector vie for control of the planet-killer missile that lies at the heart of Tishranet Volcano.

We hope that you enjoyed this title and look forward to many more to come. Please, leave us a review! Reviews matter to all of our authors.

Take a look at some of our other award-winning series at
https://threeravenspublishing.com/series-universes/

Visit us at https://www.threeravenspublishing.com and sign up for our newsletter for the latest and greatest news on upcoming titles and events.

Other series and titles you might enjoy.

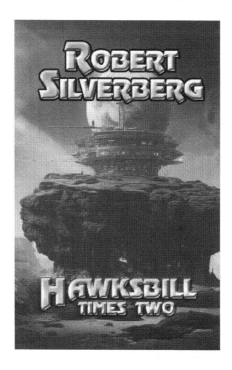

You can also keep up to date with our latest release announcements on Scifi.radio and get some of the best fandom programing on the planet.

Scifi for your Wifi

And don't forget to check out our other Sponsors and Affiliates

A southern Appalachian jewel for craft beer lovers, Buck Bald Brewing offers something for everyone. With delicious, locally brewed beverages from across the spectrum, Buck Bald Brewing offers craft brews that are consistently amazing.

From the dark and smooth Shesquatch Scottish ale, to the intense hops of Hippibilly IPA, to the puckering sour of the blackberry and cinnamon in Berry My Heart at the Trailer Park, and more than 60+ rotating brews, you'll find what you're looking for and more.

With smiling faces behind the bar ready to help you find your next favorite brew, a constantly rotating selection of delicious craft beverages, toe-tapping tunes always playing, and the biggest games on TV, you can kick your feet up in either Copperhill, Tennessee or Murphy, North Carolina and immerse yourself in the Buck Bald Brewing experience. So, come out, fill a pint, fill a growler, and fill your mind at your new favorite family-owned craft brewery.

To discover more visit us at buckbaldbrewing.com or follow us on Facebook @buckbaldbrewing and @buckbaldbrewingmurphy.

Made in the USA
Columbia, SC
19 March 2024